EASTWOOD

A Novel by Dorothy Dunbar

Mary!
Enjoy Dunbar
Dorothy
"The Heart asks..."

This book is dedicated to Janice, for all of her love, encouragement and support over the years we have known each other.

And

For my children, Alexa and Austin
This book is for you!
Follow your dreams - they do come true...

Brewster Family Tree

Colonel George and Amelia Brewster: Patriarch and Matriarch of the Brewster clan.
Son: William (deceased), wife: Rose. Children: Lavinia (Vinnie), Victoria (Torie), and Henry.
Daughter: Matilda Bingham, husband: Captain Jasper, children: twins, Myles and Cooper.
Son: Charles, wife: Alice. Children: Susanna, Edmund, Kitty, twins, Abigail and Sarah.
Son: Christopher (Charles' twin), wife: Emily. Children: twins: Damarus and Dorcas, son Jonathan.
The Colonel's widowed twin sisters: Tabitha and Easter (yes Easter, not Esther!)

PROLOGUE

Boston, May, 1899

Hampshire Street in East Boston was a quiet street filled with slender brick brownstones and small tidy front gardens. Across from the homes stood a park filled with giant chestnut trees and spreading maples. At this time of year a profusion of lilac blooms and daffodils were displayed amongst the shrubs and the short green grass. Iron benches placed invitingly along the tidy paths provided spots for the neighbors to sit and enjoy the peaceful oasis. On this mid May afternoon the park was empty as nannies had taken their small charges home for afternoon naps. Soon the park would fill with school children trudging home from a day of learning, but in the lull, one lone tiny figure could be seen hurrying through the park. The young girl, aged 13, with tears on her cheeks and her dark tumbled curls trailing behind her, dashed through the park.

At 23 Hampshire Street, she stopped and looked up at the tall windows facing the avenue. The afternoon sun glinted off the shining windows and she could not see into the front bay window. She paused breathlessly, changed her course and sprinted down the path beside the house. Rounding the corner to the back she again paused and, catching her breath, peered into the kitchen basement window. The tidy room was empty except for Cook who sat in a chair with her head nodding, a bowl of shelled peas in her lap. Furtively, the young girl tiptoed past the window and dashed for a small play house at the foot of the spacious rear garden.

She slipped inside the playhouse and shut the door quietly behind her. The air inside felt cool and smelled slightly dank. In the corner sat a pile of discarded toys and a small table and chairs, covered in dust. Across the room on a pile of old cushions and rugs, the girl sank down and burst into a torrent of tears.

Soon voices could be heard. The girl raised her head and tried to stifle her sobs, although an occasional sigh slipped out. A slender young lady of 17 and a small bespectacled boy came out of the house accompanied by a middle-aged woman. The woman wore a simple gray dress and a starched white apron. Her hair, pulled tightly back into a bun on the back of her head, had a sprinkling of gray and her round wrinkled face had a look of concern.

"I know Torie," the young lady said, "and I bet she is hiding in the playhouse."

"She would have gone to Edmund's if he were home," the boy added.

The older woman stopped at the door and called, "Torie! Torie Brewster, are you hiding in the playhouse?"

No answer, no stir. From inside, the girl raised her tear-streaked face and held her breath.

The boy, Henry, tried the door but found it bolted from the inside. He rattled the door and leaned over peeking through a knot hole. "I see her Phoebe," he told the older woman.

"Victoria Brewster," Phoebe called out sharply, "come out of that playhouse this instant."

Slowly and reluctantly, the door creaked open. Torie stepped out and faced the three. Silently she looked from one to the other.

Lavinia, the young lady, stepped forward and put her arms around her little sister. "Is it true?" Lavinia asked gently.

Torie nodded, "Miss Mable has expelled me from school." Torie's lower lip trembled, "Where's Mama?"

"Still at her DAR meeting," Lavinia told her. "She won't be home for another hour."

Phoebe, the nanny, took a deep breath and asked, "Miss Torie, what did you do this time?" Her tone of voice was serious, but not condemning.

Torie's eyes filled with tears as she said defiantly, "It was all just stupid. I hate it at Miss Mable's. I am glad I am not going back."

Her little brother studied her with his head cocked to one side, "It had to be awfully serious for Miss Mable to expel one of the Brewster girls. I mean, all the Brewster girls have gone there. Mama, too."

Phoebe said, not ungently, "Miss Torie, I need to know. What happened?"

Torie shook her head and said, "I got in trouble for talking out in class, so Miss Mable assigned me as punishment an essay in French. I was supposed to make up a story and write it in French. So I did."

Phoebe frowned and prodded, "And..."

Torie flushed. "I turned it into Miss Mable and went back to working on my algebra. All of a sudden, Miss Mable got really upset with me and in front of the whole class told me that I was a disrespectful girl and that I had to leave her school and never come back."

A small smile flitted over Lavinia's face. "What did you write about in French?" she asked her little sister, a puzzled frown on her face.

Torie shrugged. "I wrote about one of Henry's stories, the one about the Minotaur and being lost in the maze. I explained how frustrated Theseus was because he couldn't find his way through the maze and so he used a word." Torie reflected on this and added, "It must not mean what I thought it meant."

Phoebe frowned at Torie, choosing how to phrase her next question. "What did you think it meant?"

"I thought he was saying 'Oh, murder', you know, like he was frustrated. But I guess that word doesn't mean that in English. I think it is a bad word in French," Torie said reflecting over Miss Maple's reaction.

Lavinia and Phoebe exchanged puzzled looks. "Where did you hear the word?" Lavinia asked her little sister.

"Oh, when Grandfather was hosting those French officers last winter," Torie explained. "I was listening to them tell war stories and one of them said this word. I liked it."

"What was the word?" Henry asked his sister, curiously.

Phoebe interrupted. "Don't say it," she commanded Torie. Phoebe, shivering in the spring afternoon air, said, "I think we should go inside now. Torie, I don't know what Miss Rose is going to say about this. I imagine she is going to be quite upset with you."

"I don't care," Torie insisted defiantly, although she looked distressed over upsetting her gentle mother.

As they started back towards the house, Lavinia put her arms around her little sister and said, "Yes, but my concern is what will Grandmother say?"

Torie looked stricken and her face blanched as she groaned, "Grandmother!" Henry took her hand and gave it a squeeze.

"Grandmother left this morning with Grandfather for Eastwood," Lavinia told her little sister. "You are going to get a reprieve from Grandmother for a couple of weeks."

CHAPTER 1

The late spring sun sparkled on Eaton Pond in the quiet midday. Small ripples from a beaver cleaved the water and a mother duck encouraged her small yellow ducklings to take their first plunge into the water. Large summer farms and homes dotted the countryside around Eaton Pond. Apple orchards and thick woods crowded homes and fields. Over the trees gleamed the white spire of the village church of Eaton's Grove. The small village consisted of a quaint village square with an octagonal bandstand gracing one corner and a shady park beyond. Tidy homes with picket fences were set back on tree-lined streets while small shops filled the main street. A train station sat empty next to the rail tracks as the townspeople moved quietly about their business.

A medium-sized carriage moved through the town, crossed the red stained bridge and headed along the edge of the lake. The graveled road was lined by a low stone wall, its mossy walls glinting in the spring sunshine. Turning from the view of the town, the carriage travelled up a small hill and meandered through the trees, looking out on estates and farms, with big red barns nestled behind homes. The horses carried on at a good pace and the wheels crunched on the gravel road. Inside the carriage, Colonel George William Henry Brewster and his wife, Amelia, nee Alden, sat side by side. Amelia, blissfully oblivious of the drama that her granddaughter had caused in Boston, took a deep breath of anticipation of arriving at their summer home. The Brewsters had been in the carriage since leaving Boston early that morning and both were thoroughly tired of the rutted road, but as they crossed the bridge Amelia sat up and began to look out the window.

The Colonel laughed and patted his wife's hand. "Trying to get the first glimpse of Eastwood?" he asked her, teasing.

Amelia smiled brightly and sat back. "Do you remember when the children were young?" she asked her husband. "You would pay a penny to the first child to see the house."

"Well," the Colonel conceded with a twinkle in his eyes, "if we had any of the grandchildren in the carriage I would still be offering them a penny. Would you like me to pay you a penny?"

The thrill of anticipation of seeing her summer home ran through Amelia. Amelia and her husband spent every summer of their married life at Eastwood Farm, the Brewster summer home. The Colonel, as he was known to one and all, inherited Eastwood from his parents. The Colonel's great-great grandfather built Eastwood in the early 1700s and every generation enlarged and remodeled the original house several times until it was at its present size. Sprawling and beautiful, the Queen Anne style corner with its round tower and shining white shingled walls caught visitors' attention when it was first visited, but it was the wide shaded porches along three sides of the house that always drew people so invitingly up the steps.

Amelia, tiny and grey haired, was formally dressed with every hair smoothly in place. Her immaculate white shirtwaist with its high lace collar could be glimpsed under her dark gray jacket that matched her plainly cut skirt. The Colonel, older and stooped, wore his own formal jacket with a perfectly knotted tie. A beaver stovepipe hat sat atop his head, covering his balding, wispy white hair.

Eastwood looked imposing from the road, three stories high, plus a dormered attic. The property ran far back towards the woods with a series of green houses, tennis courts and stables on the west side of the house, while the wide green lawn stretched down to the boat landing and small beach on Eaton Pond. The lawn, dotted with spreading chestnut and maple trees and a pretty white gazebo, overlooked Amelia's prized rose garden. Plenty of room remained for croquet or children to romp across the lawns playing tag and other summer games.

Amelia sat with a dreamy smile on her face. She and the Colonel would have Eastwood to themselves for two weeks before the rest of their large family arrived. Their children, spouses and grandchildren would join them, as they did every year, for the long warm summer. Amelia had little concern about the state of her house. Mrs. Musgrave was the best housekeeper and all winter she overlooked the small staff in attendance at Eastwood at all times. Two weeks earlier, the Brewsters dispatched the majority of their Boston servants to Eastwood to help with the spring cleaning. Amelia was excited about spending the summer yet again with her family, but her mind was also on her greenhouses and gardens.

Each year, Amelia added new plants or gardens to her farm. She was famous for her beautiful gardens, separated into what she called rooms. Deep in the shade of the woods was the "White Garden," where all the plants were carefully chosen for their white blooms or white and green variegated foliage.

Over the winter, Mr. Martini, who was Amelia's gardener in residence at Eastwood, cared for her flowers and plants in her greenhouses. During the summer, the two of them worked well together and delighted each other in the amazing gardens they created. Once Amelia returned to Boston for the winter, the fruits and vegetables that Mr. Martini grew in the greenhouses were dispatched to Boston so that Amelia always had fresh fruits and vegetables for her dinner parties. Last summer, Amelia and Mr. Martini put the finishing touches on her latest project, a walled Italian garden. Inside the high walls of the garden were housed lush green plants and flowers, and in quiet shady areas were benches and fountains. Amelia had been in correspondence with Mr. Martini and she looked forward to seeing the newest plants and their growth from the past summer.

As the carriage turned into the long driveway, Amelia craned her head. "Oh George," she exclaimed, "I don't see any roses blooming. I so want them to be in bloom for our 4th of July party."

The Colonel smiled down at her, "I imagine your hands will be dirty before we have been at the house half an hour."

As Amelia laughed in agreement, a small frown crossed her face, "I wish Susanna would have been engaged a little sooner. We could have had the wedding here at Eastwood."

The Brewster's oldest granddaughter, Susanna, expected to receive a proposal from her most ardent beau, Alexander Peabody. Alexander and his parents, Senator and Mrs. Peabody, were expected to visit Eastwood for the large 4th of July party planned. There was a strong expectation that Alexander would ask for Susanna's hand in marriage.

The Colonel turned from looking at the house and smiled fondly down at his wife. They had been married for more than 40 years and while fine lines framed her grey eyes, they were still lively and bright. He knew under her hat there was more silver hair than the brown hair he remembered, but it was still beautiful to watch her brush the long thick curls at night. Amelia remained one of the most correct of Boston mamas due to attention to manners and morals. She was the bane of her granddaughters and daughters-in-law because she was so exacting with her prim and proper decorum and would call them to task if required.

"George," she said excitedly, "Susanna is going to make the most beautiful bride." She sighed happily, "I suppose from now on every summer we will be having weddings and, before you know it, grand babies!"

The Colonel laughed at her as the carriage drew up in front of Eastwood. "You never get tired of babies. It is always interesting to see how many twins the next generation will produce."

Twins and pretty girls were not uncommon in the Brewster family. Every generation produced a fair number of identical twins and remarkably pretty girls. It was Brewster tradition that sons were destined to become great soldiers and, later, enter the family business. Brewsters in the armed forces dated back to the Revolutionary War; the Colonel himself had a distinguished military career in the War Between the States. Daughters were expected to make good matches and to take their place in Boston society. Susanna, the first granddaughter to be married, won the approval of the entire family as she was courted by Alexander Peabody, son of a well known Massachusetts senator.

"Susanna has made us all very proud," the Colonel told Amelia as they prepared to alight from the carriage. "A senator's son. We have not had a senator for a few generations in the family."

Amelia agreed with her husband. "George," she said, "Susanna has done very well for herself and all of us. She is a good example to Lavinia and all of our granddaughters to do just as well."

By custom, no servants lined up to welcome them. George and Amelia had their own special tradition. Robert, the coachman, lowered the steps and helped them alight. Robert then drove around to the back of the house and the barn. Together, the Colonel and Amelia climbed the steps to their summer home, breathing in the soft smells of newly turned fields, the faint marine smell of the lake and the stronger fragrance of the lilac bush that stood at the corner of the verandah. Amelia stopped to take in the view. The afternoon sun began to dip toward the grove of trees to the west of the house, and to the east, the lawn stretched to the gleaming waters of Eaton Pond. Across the pond workers could be seen tilling the fields for spring planting. The sound of birds called from the trees and, in the distance, the faint whistle of a train could be heard.

Amelia turned to George and smiled in anticipation. The Colonel smiled down at his wife and lifted her into his arms as if she were a bride. They tottered a little bit as they crossed the threshold into the hall, but he managed to successfully carry her over the threshold and set her down carefully. Amelia laughed and smoothed her skirts and blouse, and reached up to straighten her hat. George and Amelia had spent the first summer at Eastwood after their honeymoon and the Colonel continued to carry Amelia over the threshold of Eastwood as they arrived every summer of their married lives.

Amelia turned and smoothed the Colonel's jacket and paused, looking around the shining hall. Dark and spacious, the walnut floor under her feet gleamed with polish except where the round Aubusson carpet lay in the center of the room. On the carpet was a highly polished round table, topped with a silver salver and a fresh bouquet of flowers in a crystal vase. Rooms could be glimpsed from the foyer and the large curved staircase in front of them rose directly to a landing, sweeping up to the second floor and the upper hall.

From behind the staircase a small green baize door opened and Pratt, their butler, appeared. The Colonel came forward and shook Pratt's hand. "Good to see you, Pratt," the Colonel said. "How is Mrs. Pratt? I do hope you enjoyed your month off."

Pratt and his wife, Edith, were the butler and cook for the Brewsters in Boston. The working couple moved every summer to Eastwood to take on the extra duties of entertaining there. The Pratts took off every April and visited their grown children who lived in Vermont. From their vacation they went directly to Eastwood to help supervise the spring cleaning. Mrs. Pratt and Mrs. Musgrave, the Eastwood housekeeper, were first cousins.

Pratt welcomed the Brewsters and after a brief conversation, excused himself to oversee the unloading of the carriage and the supervision of the luggage taken to their bedroom. As he disappeared through the green baize door, voices involved in a small dispute could be heard from the kitchen.

As the Colonel and Pratt talked, Amelia wandered around the foyer peering into the immaculate drawing room and the formal dining room glimpsed beyond. Floor to ceiling windows facing Eaton's Pond ran along the wall of both rooms with couches and chairs grouped invitingly. A large walnut grand piano stood in the corner, with a stack of music set upon the bench. The fire place was swept clean of ashes and the brass andirons and fender gleamed.

Alone again, Amelia moved to the table in the middle of the foyer and buried her nose in the fresh spring flowers. She inhaled and as she gently rearranged a half opened bud she looked down and saw a scar in the dark wood of the table. The scar happened two summers before when Victoria, their then ten-year-old granddaughter attempted to throw a ball while standing half way up the stairs to her cousin Edmund who had been standing out on the verandah. The toss went awry shattering one of her grandmother's favorite vases and forever scarring the table.

Amelia reached out and ran her fingers over the scar. "George," she declared, "this summer Victoria is going to become a lady!"

Two weeks later the object of her grandmother's thoughts travelled on a train with her mother, her older sister Lavinia and her younger brother Henry. Victoria had a dejected look on her face and her bottom lip jutted out in a small pout. Torie, as she was known to her family, was receiving a lecture from her mother on how she was expected to behave this summer. "Your grandparents already question my parenting on some of my choices with you children," Rose Brewster was saying in a quiet voice. "I do not need you encouraging them. Victoria, I expect you to mind your manners this summer and not run off with Edmund all of the time."

"But, mama," Torie started to protest, but stopped when she caught an expression in her gentle mother's eyes.

Her mother went on, "I have received a letter from your grandmother and she is horrified over the disgrace of being expelled from Miss Mabel's. This will be a topic of many conversations. I don't know where you will be attending school next fall, but your grandmother is going to express many opinions. Torie, your grandmother wants you to become a lady and honor the Brewster name and she is not incorrect about this. You are almost 13 and it is high time that you remembered that."

Rose shook her head in slight exasperation as she looked at her middle child. They had started out for the train station from their home in Boston in fresh clean clothes. While Lavinia and Henry were still tidy and presentable, Torie had a scuffle at the train station with a newsboy's dog and she now had a rent in her stocking. Although Rose and Nanny Phoebe staunched the bleeding on Torie's knee and retied her hair ribbon, Torie's curls were in a tangle and her dress showed a smudge. "I am sure," her mother said with a sigh, "your grandmother is going to lecture you the minute we get there, and continue on for the rest of the summer."

Torie sat back in disgust, her arms folded. At the train station, she had been in charge of her brother's small terrier, Shep, while her brother Henry purchased a book. Torie had been firmly told to leave Shep in his kennel, which would soon be stowed in the luggage car; he had whined so piteously that Torie let him out for just a minute. She kept a firm hold on his leash while he did his business.

Torie had not noticed the newsboy's grey mongrel lying in the shade of the station until he had jumped up and growled at Shep. Shep only barked one short yip, but the fight was on. The little grey mongrel darted across the platform and Shep, not accepting the challenge, wrapped his leash around Torie in his efforts to flee from his attacker. Torie's screams did little to stop the situation and she tripped from the leash around her legs, at the same time the newsboy cuffed his dog with a newspaper and collared him.

Torie continued to argue with her mother, when her sister Lavinia spoke up, "I think Grandmother is going to be so excited about seeing Susanna that she, hopefully, won't notice one dirty granddaughter among the whole bunch of Brewster grandchildren." Lavinia smiled at her sister.

Torie looked at her older sister gratefully. "Do you think so?" she asked hopefully.

Lavinia tipped her head to the side and surveyed her little sister. Lavinia teased, "Well, I wouldn't stand too close to Kitty. Without a doubt she will be perfectly tidy."

Victoria scowled. Kitty, younger by a year, was known in the family for her fastidiousness. There was never a curl out of place, never a button dangling when Kitty made an appearance. Kitty, a quiet, sweet girl, and Torie had been thrown together since babyhood and Torie could barely tolerate her prissy cousin. Torie preferred Edmund, Kitty's older brother.

Torie and Edmund were fast friends. Over the winters in Boston, they had always played together. Torie was fearless and she and Edmund would swoop down steep snowy hills on his sled or would spend hours ice skating. Summers at Eastwood meant sailing and swimming and rowing and fishing. Sometimes Torie was the leader; other times it was Edmund. The past year had changed as Edmund shipped off to attend his first year at Slater Military Academy. Torie looked forward to learning all about his experiences at military school. What Torie really wanted to be when she grew up was a soldier. Even at her young age she knew girls were not allowed to be soldiers, but she hoped to absorb everything that Edmund was learning.

From the nursery window, Torie loved to watch her grandfather put her boy cousins through their morning military drills and calisthenics. Although Torie begged to participate with her cousins, she was firmly and steadfastly told that she was not allowed to participate. Every summer, her grandfather would make each male at Eastwood over the age of 8 rise at sunrise and do calisthenics and participate in brisk runs around the meadow and morning swims in the lake. Torie longed to join, but had been severely lectured by her grandmother as to what was and was not proper behavior for young ladies.

At Eastwood, one of Torie's favorite spots on a hot humid day was under the hydrangea bush outside her grandfather's study. Torie could relax in the cool shade and overhear the conversation from within. The Colonel often spoke with friends and acquaintances of battles fought long ago and Victoria longed to ride into battle and fight along side of him. Under the open window she would listen intently, barely breathing, her eyes bright as she rode into battle with her grandfather. Edmund was her constant companion during this eavesdropping, drinking in the battle stories. Afterwards, the two discussed the battles further, gathering their little brothers and sisters, cousins and friends to recreate the battles of the Civil War. Torie would be general of one army, Edmund of another. When Torie and Edmund were younger, they would be part of the rank and file of infantry and their twin cousins, Myles and Cooper were the generals. Myles and Cooper were now 16, graduated from Slater that spring and were both headed to West Point in the fall.

Torie's father, William, had been a soldier, just like Edmund's father, Charles. Torie barely remembered her father because he died when she was three years old. Vague reminisces in her baby mind of a tall quiet man who occasionally reached out and rubbed her curls were all the memory she had of her father. Uncle Charles never spoke about his war days. He had spent his military career stationed in Philadelphia escorting pretty girls to balls, which was where he had met Aunt Alice. He never came close to a battle. He always spoke of "the market." Victoria only had a vague idea of what "the market" was and she found it unspeakably boring. Uncle Charles was quite often surrounded by his offspring and Aunt Alice and, while he was kind to his fatherless nieces and nephew, he did not have much time to spare.

To Torie, Eastwood was Edmund. Inseparable, they spent their days fishing, bobbing in the still waters of Eaton Pond and sailing the small sailboat when the afternoon breezes blew. With Torie crewing, they came in a close second at last year's 4th of July race, and hoped to win this year's contest. In their younger years, Torie and Edmund would huddle together in the third floor nursery and whisper ghost tales together, deliciously scaring each other and the smaller children. Soon Edmund departed from the nursery to join the older boys in the dormitory and Torie was relegated to sleeping with her cousin Kitty.

Henry, Torie's little brother, told his own tales in the nursery. Henry was an inveterate reader of books, always ready with a story of Ali Baba or Hercules. Huddled in the dark, with the faint voices of the adults floating up from the open windows of the dining room and verandah, the children listened in fascination to stories of amazing feats of strength and courage, the battling of mythical monsters, and strange lands and countries.

Torie slept with Kitty in the nursery for the summer and Kitty often had nightmares after the whispering of lurid tales. Kitty's nanny, Molly, cranky from having her sleep disturbed, would scold Torie fiercely as she cuddled her little pet, Kitty.

Torie came back from her reminisces realizing that her mother continued the lecture and was waiting for an answer. She had a feeling that a "Yes, Mama," was not the correct answer. Feebly, she tried to think of an appropriate response.

As the silence grew, Henry stepped into the pause, "I will explain to Grandmother that Torie was only trying to save Shep."

Rose turned to her son and said quietly, "Your grandmother will ask why Shep wasn't in his kennel." Rose sighed, "Not a wonderful way to start the summer." Torie and Henry looked guiltily at each other over their mother's distress.

Rose leaned back and looked out the window. In Boston, she had her own small house and the children had a little more freedom. At home, the children were not expected to always be perfectly tidy. Although Rose and Phoebe, her devoted nanny, made sure that everyone was clean for meals and guests, the children had the run of the backyard and the small playhouse at the foot of the garden. The children reveled in the park across the street from her pretty little red brick home and many afternoons were spent at the park running and playing games. Their Brewster cousins often joined them in their games while their mother and Aunt Alice, fast friends, spent many hours together.

In Boston, every Sunday Rose and the children attended family dinner after church at the grandparent's house. At Amelia's home children did not eat with the adults, but sat at smaller side tables. Best manners were expected at all times and quiet, reserved conversation in hushed voices was insisted on by their grandmother.

Rose, married to the Brewster's oldest son, William, had been a widow for over 10 years. Even though Rose was a widow, she was firmly considered a Brewster and spent most of her time deep in the Brewster bosom. During the fall, winter and spring, Rose and her mother-in-law Amelia, attended many events together. Rose's social duties had been heavier this past winter when her oldest daughter, Lavinia, participated in her first social season.

Lavinia, who seemed lost in thought through much of her mother's lecture, turned to her mother, "Mama, I am so excited to see cousin Susanna." Her eyes gleamed with romantic thoughts. "She wrote me the most wonderful letter about Alexander. Susanna is sure that Alexander is going to propose when he comes to Eastwood. It is so very romantic," she sighed. Susanna and Lavinia were less than a year apart in age, but at 16 they had been sent to different schools. Over the last winter, they had come out as debutantes together and both enjoyed a successful season. In the fall, Lavinia would head to Radcliffe and be the first Brewster female to attend college. Susanna, who had spent the last year at finishing school, would stay home and learn housekeeping from her mother.

Rose turned and smiled at her oldest daughter. Lavinia at 17 bloomed with a soft rose color to her cheeks and a translucent look to her pale skin. Lavinia's brown hair, glinting with red highlights in the spring sun, was piled on top of her head in the latest style and her straw hat, artfully decorated with flowers and a delicate pink veil, brought out the color of her green eyes. Lavinia was dressed in a white dimity blouse with huge puff elbow sleeves and a delicate lace collar which rose high on her throat, framing her heart shaped face.

Lavinia and Rose looked at each other, green eyes meeting green. Lavinia resembled her mother very much except that Lavinia was soft and open to all new experiences, while a guarded expression on her mother's face caused her to look slightly forbidding. It was truly rare for anyone to know what Rose Bartlett Brewster was thinking, as she was very adept at keeping her thoughts to herself. Only with her children did she lower her guard.

Rose asked Lavinia with a small smile, "When did you first meet Alexander?"

"At Dartmouth for the Harvest Ball," Lavinia exclaimed to her mother. "Susanna and I went with Elizabeth Tremain and her brother, Frances. You know Frances is studying law at Dartmouth. I was standing there with Susanna when Alexander walked into the room. Oh Mama, he simply had no eyes for anyone but Susanna. He came straight across the room and made the most romantic bow and said, 'Miss Brewster, heaven is missing a couple of bright stars tonight. I think they can be found in your eyes.'" Lavinia let out a sigh, "It was so romantic and that was it. They knew right then they were destined to spend the rest of their lives together."

"And you," her mother teased gently, "anyone special looking for the stars in your eyes?"

"Oh Mama," Lavinia protested. "I don't want to get married yet. I just want to have fun this summer with all the gang." Lavinia's bright eyes smiled at her mother. "Minerva Evans told me all the good times she had at college last year. I am looking forward to meeting college men," she finished with a sigh.

Rose smiled at her beautiful daughter and as her thoughts turned to the coming summer, she again looked out the window at the passing countryside.

In addition to multiple cousins who would spend the summer around Eaton's Pond, there was a large group of neighbors who knew each other from Boston. During the summer, the young ladies and young men spent their days playing tennis and croquet and riding bicycles. Evenings they could be found clustered into one parlor or another singing sentimental songs while they all took turns playing the piano. Inevitably some boy showed up with a banjo. Lavinia and Susanna were popular among the group and flirted with many young men, but Lavinia was more interested in attending college and the opportunity to meet many wonderful men in the college atmosphere. Susanna's expected engagement to Alexander Peabody could change the social structure of the parties.

Rose looked forward to spending time at Eastwood because the quiet calm beauty of the pond and surrounding fields could be quite soothing. In Boston, Rose was very involved in many social and charitable societies. She spent her days going from meeting to meeting and was forever organizing bazaars, writing papers for the literary society or attending a DAR event. Eastwood would be bursting with Brewsters, but there were many shady benches in the garden as well as quiet private little coves to relax. Rose and her children would slip into the slower life style of Eastwood and many of their decisions would be made by Amelia.

Torie watched her mother and examined her bloody knee. Torie knew that Edmund would be interested in her wound and possibly bind it up for her so that they could go sailing. Torie wondered how soon they would be allowed to take out the small skiff.

In a separate private rail car attached to the train, Charles and Alice Brewster and their five children were seated around a table arguing and laughing. As their family had not been together all winter, Charles and Alice preferred to ride in their own spacious rail car due to the size of their family, rather than with their cousins in the public rail car. The car was furnished opulently in deep red velvet cushions and rich mahogany furniture. Sparkling crystal glassware caught the shine of the sun as the train steamed towards northern Massachusetts. Charles and Alice were seated side by side on a settee watching their children spend time together. The couple had 5 living children: 4 girls and the one sole boy, Edmund. Edmund's sisters adored him. At 13 Edmund was beginning to fill out and had the look of the man he would become. His golden curls, the bane of his boyish life, were gone and a very short, very military haircut gave him almost a bald appearance. A year of military boarding school had brought a more concentrated look to his eyes. It was a hard year, but one that he endured. Edmund left Slater Military Academy behind a few days before and was enjoying the attention from his sisters and looked forward to Eaton Pond and Eastwood. His large sheep dog, Major, sat at Edmond's feet gazing up adoringly at his young master.

Seated by Edmund was his oldest sister, Susanna, in love and slightly insufferable. She had taken on airs of maturity and Edmund was tempted to see if he could bring her down a peg. To have a sister soon to be engaged was a peculiar idea to Edmund and he could not decide what he thought about it. Edmund had met Alexander Peabody and found him to be a bit stuffy.

Susanna, as all of Charles and Alice's children, took after her mama with very blonde curls and cornflower blue eyes. Her milky complexion was lightened with a faint rosy tinge to her cheeks and lovely pouting pink lips. As a young pretty girl, Susanna enjoyed her debutante season. Susanna entertained many eligible suitors but knew she had made a good match in Alexander Peabody. She found him very attractive and knew that her parents and grandparents approved of Alexander. Alexander was currently studying law with his Uncle Frank in Boston, so Susanna looked forward to setting up her own little home in Beacon Hill. Alexander's father, the senior senator from Massachusetts, spent a good amount of time in Washington, D.C. and Susanna hoped that she and Alexander could spend part of the year in Washington too.

The idea of becoming engaged thrilled Susanna, but she, too, looked forward to her summer at Eastwood. She and her cousin Lavinia had always been inseparable, and Susanna did not want the fact that she was expected to be engaged to Alexander Peabody to deter her from playing tennis, riding bicycles and singing in the parlors at night with many attractive men. Alexander, busy studying law, would visit only a few times for the summer, but Susanna did not want Alexander's absence to stop her from having a good time. Warner Covington played the banjo and he always sang "Oh, Susanna" to her in such an arch way that it brought gales of giggles from her. Warner had been one of Susanna's biggest admirers, and until Alexander came along Susanna was quite attracted to Warner. All that changed in the fall when she had met Alexander at the Harvest Ball.

On Edmund's other side were the 4-year-old identical twin sisters, Sarah and Abigail. It had been an invigorating day for the two little girls and they were thrilled with the excitement of riding on a train. Both rose at dawn, to the annoyance and frustration of Nanny Molly, and the two little girls had been fairly naughty all day. Blonde and blue eyed like the rest of the family, the two girls pulled each other's hair and tussled over who would sit closest to Edmund.

Seated across from Edmund was 11-year-old Kitty who was always tidy to a fault. Her puffed sleeved pink dress was ironed and fresh and was tied with an enormous bow in the back. A matching pink ribbon was tied in her shining blonde curls.

A quiet contained girl, Kitty watched her bickering twin sisters with a small frown and listened to Edmund and Susanna without comment. Kitty had been very sickly as a toddler and all the coddling had made her rather spoiled. Of all the Brewsters, Kitty was the least excited about going to Eastwood. Fastidious Kitty did not like to swim in the lake or go berrying or fishing. Kitty did enjoy spending time with her grandmother, Amelia, who glowed over Kitty's tidiness and ladylike manners, and Kitty enjoyed most of her cousins. She and her cousin Henry had their own special bond. Close in age, Henry and Kitty shared a quiet nature and Henry never splashed her when they swam or demanded that she climb a tree or teased her for her terror of spiders. Kitty loved to play house on the wide side yard at Eastwood and Henry often sat and read aloud to her as she played.

The number one reason that Kitty was not looking forward to Eastwood was Victoria Brewster. Torie and Kitty were very different from each other. Torie, 14 months older, was very bossy, expecting Kitty to play soldier or tag and calling her a baby when she cried. The two little girls had been thrown together their entire lives and Torie became easily irritated with Kitty's fastidiousness. "Why can't you be more like Kitty?" had rung in Torie's ears her entire life from her grandmother.

Kitty could cause problems for Torie as well. Amelia Brewster never allowed tattling in her house, but Kitty had a way of acting pathetic enough that Torie would still get in trouble.

Unfortunately, this year they would be sharing a bed in the nursery. Kitty privately decided this might be a small blessing since last year, in her solitary bed, she found a snake one night. Kitty brought the entire household to the nursery with her screams, and although Torie denied putting it there, Kitty was fairly certain her cousin hatched the plot.

Alice and Charles, side by side on the settee, watched their children gathered around the table and smiled at each other as they held hands. Looking forward to their summer at Eastwood, they knew it would be a very exciting time with Susanna's possible engagement and wedding following in the fall.

Alice, placid and slightly plump, had been pregnant most of her married life and buried two sets of infant sons. Because of these tragedies Alice and Charles held their only surviving son, Edmund, so dearly in their hearts, although they adored all of their children. In Boston, Charles and Alice lived a full life with the children. Charles, along with his twin brother Christopher, took over the daily running of the family business from their father. The Colonel was still involved in their business, but it was truly Charles and Christopher who made the majority of the decisions. Charles and Christopher would spend the summer in Boston on weekdays and ride the train out on Friday afternoons to spend weekends at Eaton Pond with their families. Christopher stayed at

Harlow Hall also on Eaton Pond. His wife, Emily Harlow Brewster, had her own family home on Eaton Pond and stayed at Harlow Hall for the summer with her parents, although there was much visiting back and forth between the two homes.

Charles and Alice had always been very much in love and were very proud of their brood of pretty girls and handsome son. Sitting on the train, Alice tried not to think about the possibility that she was pregnant. It would be very embarrassing to be a pregnant mother of the bride at her age. Alice loved her children, but at times her frequent pregnancies were embarrassing when facing her family and friends. At the Easter holidays, she explained to Susanna the facts of life that Susanna would need to know as a married woman. It was important that Susanna be prepared for what was expected on her wedding night. By the time she finished, Alice and Susanna were looking anywhere but at each other, their faces very red; no questions were asked.

Alice did her duty and was glad it was over. Because of that conversation with Susanna, Alice did not want to be pregnant again. At 36, she was well into middle age and after Sarah and Abigail were born and survived infancy, Alice felt that she had enough babies. Alice loved Charles very much and loved their intimate time together, but she wished she knew how to stop pregnancies. Alice looked across at her pretty oldest daughter. A shaft of sunlight came through the window and shone directly on Susanna's blond curls creating a halo around her pretty face. Susanna laughed at something Edmund had said and Susanna reached out and smoothed her turned up lace collar. Susanna would make a very pretty bride, Alice thought with pride and before long, Susanna would be giving her mother grandchildren.

In another car down from the Brewsters, the many servants of each Brewster household also traveled to Eaton's Grove. None of the sisters-in-law, not Rose, Alice or Emily, felt they could endure the summer without their nannies. Phoebe, Rose's stalwart nanny and Molly O'Malley, Alice's new nanny, sat side by side in the railroad car. For the last 15 minutes Molly smiled and flirted with Robby Jones, one of the stable men from town. Robby leaned over the seat and engaged Molly in flirtatious conversation. Phoebe, with a stern cold look in her eyes, glared at Robby; Robby ignored Phoebe's stern looks.

Phoebe Sullivan was in her early 40s and serious about her position as Rose's nanny and helper. Phoebe had a solid figure dressed in a dark gray dress and coat. Her soup bowl shaped felt hat sat sternly anchored to her head by a vicious looking hat pin. Phoebe had a plain honest face and was very devoted to all the Brewsters, especially her employer, Rose Brewster. Phoebe came to work for Rose when Rose was pregnant with Lavinia and had been devoted to Mrs. Rose ever since her first day of employment. Phoebe, at the moment, looked at Robby like she wanted to poke him with her hat pin.

In contrast, pretty Molly O'Malley was 16 years old and quite often overwhelmed by her duties with Sarah and Abigail, Alice's youngest twins. Red haired and freckled, Molly was a decent nanny but sometimes a little careless with the Brewster twins. More than once she had been caught talking to strange men at the park while the little girls frolicked close to the streets.

Alice had Nanny Mary for all of her other babies. Nanny Mary had been Alice's very own nanny when she was a baby. Nanny Mary retired after the infant death of Alice's twin boys, too broken hearted and old to continue. Molly came with a good referral, the oldest of 12 children, but Phoebe was not sure that Molly's young heart was into taking care of other people's children. "Oh," Molly said to Phoebe when Robby finally took Phoebe's hint and returned to his seat, "he's a looker! This might turn out to be a mighty fine summer."

Phoebe regarded Molly with a slightly stern countenance. "You listen to me, Molly O'Malley," she said severely. "Mrs. Musgrave will not stand for any shenanigans with the stable hands. At Eastwood, Mrs. Musgrave is in charge of the servants and she will turn you out at once if she catches you dallying with the stable men. You are employed to take care of children, not waste time with stable hands who are nothing but trouble."

"Oh, pooh," Molly said with a shrug, "Mrs. Musgrave doesn't pay me wages. Mrs. Charles could not handle all those children without me."

Phoebe shook her head, looking at Molly.

The argument would have continued if at that moment the conductor had not come through the car calling, "Eaton's Grove, next stop!"

CHAPTER 2

Alighting from their separate rail cars, the many Brewsters greeted each other with much hugging and laughter. Although the families visited often in Boston, they truly enjoyed each other's company and looked forward to their summers under one roof. Amelia sent carriages and a wagon to transfer people and their luggage from the station to Eastwood. The transfer took time to organize.

Torie and Kitty stood side by side on the train station platform. Their greeting was cordial, the look that passed between them was not. Kitty took in Victoria's mussed look, while Torie looked at Kitty's fastidiousness. Torie became more aware of her smudged frock and frowsy hair at that moment. Kitty's nostrils distended as she looked at Torie, not missing a blemish.

Torie turned with a shrug from Kitty's perusal and smiled at her cousin Edmund. "Cousin," she greeted. "Hello! Did you learn a lot of new drills this year at Slater? I can hardly wait to play army with you! I have some ideas for new campaigns."

Edmund laughed at his favorite cousin as he gave her a brief cousinly hug, "Hello to you, cousin!" He looked at her and shook his head. "I am sure Grandmother is going to have you sewing tea towels for hours once she gets a look at you," he teased. Hemming tea towels was their grandmother's favorite form of punishment in the past for untidy little girls. "What have you been doing?" he asked her. "Rolling in the dirt?"

Torie shook her head at Edmund's teasing. "Edmund," she explained, "this awful dog tried to attack Shep and I was only trying to save him and got knocked down. It was so exciting! I wish you had been there to help me."

Edmund laughed, "It does sound exciting, but I doubt Grandmother will agree with you."

Lavinia and Susanna fell into each other's arms. They had spent the previous afternoon discussing what clothes they would bring to Eastwood, but they hugged as if they had not seen each other for months.

Alice and Rose kissed each other on the cheek, and Charles greeted Rose as they all watched their children greet each other.

The two dogs barked and gamboled together on the station platform. Shep, released from his kennel and the baggage car, shook himself briskly and frolicked with Major.

Eventually everyone was sorted out and the pleasant drive to Eastwood went quickly. Amelia and the Colonel waited on the porch for their family. Alighting from the carriage, Torie hastily picked up little Abigail and carried her up the steps hoping that Abigail would hide Torie's smudged skirt.

Abigail did not want to be picked up and let out a wail that brought her grandmother's attention on her. Amelia looked Torie over in one glance, taking in the smudged frock and the raw knee. While Amelia's eyes were warm, there was also the light of battle. With a sigh Torie set Abigail down on her sturdy little legs, and Torie curtsied prettily for her grandmother and greeted her with a kiss.

Before Torie could say anything, Henry spoke up, "Grandmother, it was a big dog and it was trying to attack Shep and Torie was trying to save Shep, so it wasn't her fault that Torie got knocked down."

Amelia looked from Torie to Henry. She simply nodded and reached out and hugged both of her grandchildren. "I am sure it was a big dog," was all she said.

Once inside, people dispersed to their various bedrooms to remove jackets and repair toilets. The luggage wagon drove around to the back of the house and the heavy trunks were carried upstairs to the appropriate bedrooms by the men servants, supervised by Mrs. Musgrave and Pratt, the butler. Mrs. Musgrave dispersed the servants who had arrived with their Brewster employers to various rooms to unpack. Once upstairs, the maids unpacked trunks and valises and as the bags were emptied various men servants hauled the heavy empty trunks to the attic for the summer. Molly stood in Alice and Charles' bedroom shaking the creases out of Alice's frock when Robby Jones appeared. Although hired for the summer as a stableman, Robby had been ordered to help with the heavy trunks.

Molly, finding herself alone with the attractive Robby, stopped and smiled at him invitingly. Robby asked teasingly, "Is this your room, Miss Molly?" Molly giggled and shook her head, Robby came nearer and reaching out he gently touched a finger to

Molly's small snub nose. He smiled at her and suggested in a husky voice, "Maybe later we could take a walk by the pond."

Before Molly could answer, Mrs. Musgrave came bustling in, catching sight of the two standing and smiling at each other. "Molly," she ordered, "let Maria take care of Mrs. Charles' things. The nursery is in a mess and one of the twins has tripped and is crying. Go help Phoebe."

Molly dropped her eyes and obediently answered, "Yes ma'am." As she walked past Robby she allowed him a small secret smile and a wink. Mrs. Musgrave turned to Robby and ordered in a slightly frazzled voice, "Why are you standing there? Get these trunks up to the attic right now." Robby nodded assent to Mrs. Musgrave. Lifting the trunk to his broad shoulders, he moved out of the bedroom.

Molly headed to the back hall and climbed the narrow stairs to the third floor nursery.

As Molly walked into the nursery, she found bedlam. Sarah sat on Phoebe's lap wailing and Abigail held Kitty's doll behind her back while Kitty attempted to wrest it away from her baby sister without destroying the French doll's hair or satin dress. Henry crouched down on his hands and knees and attempted to coax Shep from under the bed where the dog was hiding due to all the noise. Torie knelt on the bed in her petticoat, holding a tidbit out assisting Henry with Shep.

Molly, annoyed with Mrs. Musgrave, immediately walked over and tugged the doll from Abigail causing the fabric to be torn. Kitty wailed as she observed her doll's torn dress and Abigail, so precipitously removed from her prize, joined in the wailing crescendo.

At this moment, Amelia Brewster walked into the nursery. "Just what," she asked in a quiet but stern voice, "is going on in here?"

Instant silence greeted her words, except for a few hiccoughs from Kitty and the babies. Amelia's cold eyes looked over every person in the room. "This is not the way I expect my grandchildren to act at any time in my home or their own," she said in icy tones, taking in the entire situation. "I will not allow bedlam in my home."

"Henry," she turned to him, "I have told you to keep that dog out of the house. Remove him at once." She looked at Victoria and hastily walked past her. She turned to the nannies. "I expect the two of you to keep order in this room at all time. I want it cleaned, the unpacking finished and this room to be kept neat. Those two," she said gesturing to the little girls, "need a nap. Now."

Amelia turned to Kitty, took the doll and examined it. "Kitty, stop crying. It is only a small tear. I expect that you can take a needle and thread and repair it."

Without another word, Amelia swept from the room. The silence remained and Shep slunk out from under the bed with his tail between his legs. Henry slipped his lead on him and drug him down the back stairs.

The nannies coerced the over tired little girls into beds and sent the older girls outside. Kitty placed her doll in her top drawer and left the room, looking for her mother and sympathy. Torie found a clean frock and slipped into it with help from Phoebe, and quietly headed down the servant stairs to the kitchens to greet Mrs. Pratt, the cook. Phoebe and Nancy quickly unpacked and restored order to the large room. Once the room was cleared of trunks and order had been restored, the two women turned their attention to their own small bedroom off the nursery. In the bare room, the two women unpacked their own things in silence. Each had her own small chest of drawers and pegs on the walls to hang her clean frocks. A double bed sat along the wall, a small window stood open, the simple curtains fluttered in the breeze. Their view was of the driveway and sounds of carriage wheels could be heard on the drive.

Down the hall from the nursery was the dormitory for the older grandsons. Austere and simply furnished in military fashion, a double row of army cots were set against the walls. Beside each bed was a small cabinet and at the foot was a trunk. Edmund unpacked and chose a bed by the window. Later he would be joined by his cousins Myles and Cooper when they arrived at Eastwood.

There had been earlier discussion in the spring that Henry would join his cousins in the dormitory, but his mother firmly insisted that he spend one last year in the nursery.

Beyond the boys' dorm room was a sturdy door that was kept shut. This door led to the maids' rooms. Maids were housed two to a room and it was Mrs. Musgrave who chose room assignments each summer. The man servants slept above the stable in rooms designed for them. Austere as the boys' dorms, the man servants had a series of bedrooms. At one end of the stable's second floor was a commodious room set aside for their off time. Meals were eaten in the basement with the maids and house staff. No females, servants or otherwise, were ever allowed upstairs in the stable. If caught, they faced instant dismissal without reference from Mrs. Musgrave.

The Pratts and Mrs. Musgrave had their own apartments in a wing jutting out from the servants' dining hall in the basement. Comfortably furnished as their rank deserved, they could rest and enjoy their free time, although that time was very limited.

The Brewster family bedrooms were up the broad front stairs on the second floor and the wide hall that led off into two separate wings. The Colonel and Amelia had a suite of rooms at the back of the east wing with a beautiful view of Eaton Pond. Amelia's bedroom was large and furnished with pink and green draperies and a pretty quilt. A chaise lounge was situated in front of the small balcony, filled with pretty green plants where Amelia could read on the lounge while admiring her growing plants. She also had an excellent view of the lawn and her gardens stretching to the pond. A bathroom separated her bedroom from the Colonel's smaller bedroom, furnished in strict military style. The Colonel preferred to sleep on a hard mattress with military blankets. His ivory backed brushes and extra cuff links sat with military precision on the top of his bureau.

In the East wing there were three other bedrooms. The first was reserved for Charles and Alice, a pretty bedroom that suited them perfectly. As comfortable as their Boston house, Charles and Alice enjoyed their summer bedroom with a view of the pond and the wide lawn where they could watch their children frolic.

The second bedroom was for the Brewster's daughter Matilda Bingham who would be joining them in a few days. Matilda's husband, Jasper, owned several ships of commerce and spent much of the year sailing on them as he travelled the world trading goods and commodities. Matilda's twins, Myles and

Cooper, recently graduated from Slater and would be attending West Point in the fall. Matilda would be driving out in her own carriage with her sixteen-year-old twins and the Colonel's twin widowed sisters, Tabitha and Easter, later in the week.

The last bedroom in that wing was a guest bedroom always saved for the most important Brewster guests. Susanna Brewster's future in laws, Senator and Mrs. Peabody, would occupy this bedroom when they came for the 4th of July.

Across the wide front landing, the west wing had a different configuration of guest rooms and Brewster bedrooms. The first bedroom was referred to as the "Young Ladies' Room." Here, three sets of double beds were arranged along with spacious wardrobes, bureaus and a dainty dressing table with a gilt mirror over it. Susanna and Lavinia had taken up residence in this room and their trunks had been opened but not unpacked as the maids were still busy in other bedrooms. Filmy, bright colored silk blouses and gowns hung over the lids of the trunk and on the floor were flung several pairs of shoes. Ribbons and brushes had been tossed on to the dressing table and on one of the empty beds the flower bedecked hats worn on the trip from Boston lay in abandon. The young ladies changed their traveling clothes into more comfortable gowns and hurried downstairs to examine the tennis courts and small boat landing.

Beyond the young ladies room was Rose's bedroom, slightly smaller than the rooms in the east wing and beyond that were two other guest rooms. The great aunts' bedroom was the last room on the hall. Tabitha Benson and Easter Campbell were widowed during the Civil War and had lived with their brother, the Colonel, for years. Quiet and sweet, they lived their lives on the fringe of the Brewsters. They delighted in their brother's grandbabies and were always included in every family function, although they tended to sit in corners with their knitting.

By late afternoon order had been restored to the house and the adults gathered on the front veranda, having a light snack and catching up on family gossip. The younger children were on the screened porch having an early dinner, supervised by the nannies.

At Eastwood, the children always dined early on the screened porch. This porch was near the kitchen on the east side of the house, making it handy for the nannies to run back and forth if something was needed from the kitchen. It was a pleasant but plain space. The screened windows looked out towards the lake; the soft spring air wafted through the screens and a little later in the summer the air was always deliciously scented with raspberries as the canes grew directly under the windows. Even on the occasional rainy day, the porch was cozy and rarely too cool to sit out and enjoy.

Gathered around the table along with the nannies, Phoebe and Molly, were the little girls, Edmund, Kitty, Torie and Henry. Joining them for dinner this first evening were their ten-year-old girl cousins Damarus and Dorcas. Their father, Christopher, was Charles Brewster's twin brother. Christopher and his wife Emily had come to join the Brewsters for their first dinner at Eastwood.

The voices of their parents could be heard from the wide verandah that ran across the front porch. The children were lively and excited after their day of train travel. As they settled in for the night their voices were pitched high. Edmund and Torie sat side by side and made plans to go sailing the next day. The small skiff was the perfect size for Eaton Pond and Edmund and Torie worked well together racing the small boat across the pond. Henry, seated on the other side of Edmund, spent the afternoon sitting on the porch swing reading a new book, deep in dreams about riding a ship to the bottom of the ocean. Kitty was seated between the twins Damarus and Dorcas and the three little girls whispered and giggled with occasional glances across the table at Torie. Damarus and Dorcas' little brother Jonathan had stayed at Harlow Home that evening with his nanny as he had an upset tummy.

Molly O'Malley, seated between the twin girls, Abigail and Sarah, alternately tried to encourage them to eat and find time to slip bites into her own mouth. It had been a exciting day for the twins: riding the train and coming to Eastwood with all of their cousins. It was a lot of steps for little legs to the third floor, and Abigail had already almost fallen out of the window of the nursery trying to get a better look at the dogs frolicking on the lawn.

Molly was irritable. She had been up since early morning to finish the packing and the twins had risen early as well. The little girls were very wiggly tonight and when Sarah knocked over her milk into Molly's lap, Molly resisted the urge to slap her small charge. Molly sopped up the mess when Amelia and the Colonel made an appearance on the screened porch. Phoebe and Molly rose and bobbed to them. The children stopped talking and rose to either curtsey or bow and smiled at their grandparents. Molly awkwardly held the dripping napkin in her hand until Amelia Brewster gestured her to continue.

The Colonel was gruff and, as always, a little awkward with the small girls. "So, what's for dinner?" he boomed in a loud voice, leaning over and peering at Kitty's plate. He ran a hand over Dorcas' shiny hair and smiled around the table.

Amelia also smiling observed proudly no elbows on the table, erect backs and napkins properly in laps and, with the exception of the area around Sarah and Abigail, a tidy table. Amelia took in Torie's clean frock and smoothed curls. "Torie," she said with a glimmer in her eyes, "I see that you decided to be a young lady tonight. I am very glad to see a young lady at the table instead of the scruffy little hooligan who appeared on my doorstep earlier today."

Torie murmured a thank you, but turned red and dropped her eyes. She ignored the gleam in Kitty's eyes. She hoped that would be the end of it. Her grandmother addressed both Torie and Kitty. "For the summer, I have engaged Monsieur du Gres," she told them in the tone of voice that sounded like she was gifting them with something special. "He will come three mornings a week and you two will join us in French lessons."

Kitty and Torie for once locked eyes in silent agreement, although neither one of them expressed disagreement with their grandmother's plans. Summer mornings at Eastwood for the ladies and children were always reserved for improving themselves. This included practicing piano and violin, sewing, singing lessons and now, French. In the past, Kitty and Torie had been considered too young for French, but they had obviously graduated to join the rest of the women.

Their grandmother paused and waited for them to murmur polite interest in her plans for them. She then turned to Molly, "I think it is high time the little girls learned to sew. Not," she paused, "in the morning room with the rest of us, but in the nursery. I expect you, Molly," she said with a small iron to her voice, "to oversee their sewing education."

Molly once again stood and bobbed to Amelia. She inwardly seethed. There was no way these little brats were going to sit still with needles and thread. Now she was expected to spend every morning teaching them to sew. She had hoped in the mornings while the girls napped she could slip out and continue her fascinating flirtation with Robby Jones.

The Colonel now turned to Henry and Edmund. "Well, men," he said, his fingers in the lapels of his coat. The Colonel called all of his grandsons "men" from the time they were about six. He spoke to them as if they were young military cadets, which in Edmund's case was true. "I, too, have this summer's plans laid out," he intoned to them. "Men, we will rise at dawn and I expect you to be down on the lawn doing calisthenics at zero dark thirty and a brisk run around the stable before heading to the lake for a good early morning swim. Gets the blood running and your brain working! Then another run back to the house for dressing and breakfast. This is the way real men get ready in the morning."

Edmund and Henry had participated in their grandfather's morning regimen for years, and nodded their heads and answered, "Yes, sir."

The Colonel, sensing a lack of enthusiasm for his plans, focused his eagle glare on each of his grandsons. "Edmund," he barked, a little less jovially, "after a year at Slater I expect you to be running the drills in the mornings."

"And Henry," he paused and looked at his little grandson. Henry's grey eyes glinted back through his spectacles at his grandfather. "You may be going to military school before you know it. You need to be in tip top shape."

"Grandpapa," Torie interrupted this conversation, "may I join you for calisthenics and a run to the lake? I want to be a soldier, too."

Both Amelia and the Colonel turned and looked at this bright eyed granddaughter of theirs. The Colonel started to sputter, but Amelia interrupted him. "Victoria," she said in her iciest tones, "Brewster ladies are not soldiers! We have discussed this in summers' past. I do not want to hear any more of this nonsense."

Brave Torie argued, although a little hesitantly, "But Susanna and Vinnie are spending the summer riding bikes and playing tennis. That is exercise."

Amelia scolded her granddaughter, "Victoria, it is time you learned the difference between lady like exercise and out and out romping. While I admit I have some concern about the bicycles they ride, they are still ladylike in their endeavors and dress. But," she looked Torie up and down, "to romp with the boys! One more word from you young lady and I will not allow you to sail with Edmund." Torie did not say anything but looked at her grandmother. "All summer," Amelia said in a threatening tone.

Torie murmured an apology and sunk back in her seat. "Sit up, Victoria," Amelia ordered. Once her grandmother was irritated she always started nit picking.

After the Colonel and Amelia left the porch, Kitty looked across at Torie and speaking to Damarus she said, "Swimming with the boys. What will she think of next?"

Torie looked across the table and down at the biscuit she held. At that moment Phoebe placed a firm warning hand on Torie's arm. Edmund spoke up for Torie, "Kitty, you know that new doll you were having such a fit about this afternoon? You better keep a good watch on it or she might end up like Maude did last summer."

Kitty gave a small shriek and tears came to her eyes. The summer before, Maude, her favorite doll, had been coaxed away from her and put in a wagon during pioneer play. Unfortunately, the wagon train had been attacked by Indians (led by Torie and Edmund) and Maude lost her hair in a scalping.

A squabble of major proportions might have erupted if little Abigail had not fallen backwards off her chair and pulled the tablecloth half off the table. The resulting mess and crash ended dinner for the younger Brewsters their first night at Eastwood.

CHAPTER 3

Behind the house, the sun slowly dipped in the evening sky touching the top of the woods and leaving dusky shadows across the empty verandah. In the dining room the servants busily set the table and lit the candles. The gas light from the crystal chandelier shone down on the gleaming table, formally set with bone china and sparkling crystal goblets. The silver gleamed and at intervals down the table were placed beautiful elaborately created vases of flowers. The flowers had been grown in the green houses and artfully arranged by Amelia Brewster.

Upstairs, a flurry of activity ensued as the Brewsters dressed for dinner. Bells rang for maids to come and assist with hair or to bring hot water or mend a torn hem. The Colonel's deep voice called to Amelia as he emerged from his steamy bathroom and stated he could not find his cuff links. In the young ladies' room, Susanna and Lavinia sat side by side on the wide bench at the dressing table putting the final touches to their toilettes. Susanna looked pure and demure in a dress that exactly matched the sky on a summer afternoon; Lavinia presented a rosy vision in pink taffeta.

Susanna and Lavinia's hair had been pulled off of their faces and their curls were puffed and heightened at the top, creating almost a nest like appearance in the latest Gibson Girl rage of hair styles. Their slim waists were tightened into spoon bill corsets which caused their bosoms to stand firm and upright under their ruffles and lace, while their full skirts draped and billowed gracefully to the floor.

Susanna and Lavinia discussed plans for a dinner they had been invited to at the end of the week. Both anticipated a summer of playing tennis, boating and riding their new bicycles around Eaton Pond.

Susanna never forgot the possibility that she could become Mrs. Alexander Peabody in the fall. With Alexander finishing up his degree at Dartmouth and Susanna living in Boston, Alexander and Susanna spent hours writing letters back and forth, pouring out their devotion for each other. Susanna did not see why an engagement should stop her from having a good time for the summer. Susanna loved Alexander desperately, but he was away often and she saw no reason why she should not participate in tennis and dancing.

When Susanna lay in bed at night, dreaming of her wedding, she wondered what it would be like to be a married lady. She assisted her mother many times in hosting afternoon teas, dinners and parties. Privately, Susanna thought married ladies led very boring lives. At balls, they sat in clusters whispering and gossiping and occasionally danced with their husbands or some elderly man who stepped on their toes.

When Susanna imagined herself entertaining as Mrs. Alexander Peabody, she saw herself sitting at a table with 200 guests, wearing a stupendous dinner dress, all the while smiling at Alexander from the other end of the long table. In reality, Alexander recently graduated from law school and was newly employed at his Uncle Frank's law practice. While Alexander would expect nightly dinners, he probably would not want to go out every evening or even entertain in such large numbers.

Seated next to her cousin and best friend, Susanna occupied herself with entwining a ribbon around a wayward curl on Lavinia's head. Lavinia talked about how she hoped Adam Brown would drop by Eastwood. Susanna knew that Lavinia had been sweet on Adam earlier in the spring. Her cousin tended to like one boy and then another, so Susanna was surprised that Lavinia was still thinking about Adam.

Filmy curtains floated at the open window in the soft evening breeze and the sound of laughter and shouts from the younger children romping on the lawn floated in through the window. Both girls paused as they heard a shriek followed by laughter. It had not been that long ago that they had spent their summers romping on those same lawns, with some of those same cousins. They dismissed their little brothers and sisters and turned to the fascinating task of attaching lockets around each other's throats and putting earrings in little pink ears.

At the sound of the dinner gong, Susanna and Lavinia stood and blew out the candles. Their grandfather was very particular about dinner hours and they did not want to get a scolding from their grandmother on their first night at Eastwood. Slipping lightly down the wide curved stairs, they continued their conversation about a tennis match the following afternoon. The soft light from the chandelier in the foyer glowed down on their shining heads and rosy cheeks as they passed into the drawing room.

Entering the drawing room, Susanna and Lavinia found parents, aunts, uncles and grandparents already seated, enjoying a drink before dinner. Amelia, admiring her pretty granddaughters who had barely reached womanhood, recalled her Belle de Crecy roses that were just emerging from that magical moment of turning from dewy bud to full blossom. The young ladies eyes sparkled with the excitement of being in their summer home and the anticipation of summer.

The Colonel stood and escorted Amelia into the formal dining room, followed by the rest of the group, with Susanna and Lavinia bringing up the rear. Uncle Christopher and Aunt Emily stayed for dinner and, as the week progressed the large dark mahogany table would be enlarged to accommodate the larger numbers of Brewsters and their friends.

At dinner the talk around the table sounded lively and happy. They discussed the huge 4th of July party that the Brewsters hosted at Eastwood every year. This celebration would include an afternoon picnic served on the wide lawn, boat races on the pond with prizes awarded to the winners, and other games for the children culminating with firework display and a dance. Amelia, already deep into the details, looked to her daughters-in-law to assist her in creating this complicated and spectacular fete.

Talk went from the party to the small village of Eaton's Grove. The preceding winter the old bandstand in the village burned down and a new, much larger bandstand had been built to replace it. The Brewsters looked forward to going into the town for Thursday night concerts and seeing friends and neighbors. The band consisted of retired military bandsmen and other locals who joined together to play the music of Stephen Foster and other fast tempo pieces.

Christopher spoke up, "Emily's father tells me that Summerfield, the old Alden place, has been sold. Bought by some man named Underhill." Amelia, who was distantly related to the Aldens, raised her eyebrow at her son, as all eyes focused on her son. Christopher shrugged, "Westerner, don't know much about him except that he is in discussion to partner with Peregrine Fitch on some business dealings."

Lavinia spoke up, "Oh, I met Collin Underhill at the Browns last winter." As the table looked at her, Lavinia turned to her cousin and said, "You remember, Susanna. He and Adam Brown attended Ashcroft Academy together. He dances divinely." She finished with a small impish grin and a sparkle in her green eyes.

Amid the laughter from her comment, her grandfather said, "Trust you, Vinnie, to find the good dancers. Don't know anything else about this Underhill. If he is going to be doing business with Fitch, we should learn more about him."

Peregrine Fitch was an old family friend whose business often overlapped with that of the Brewsters. Peregrine was known for shrewd business dealings and while it was vulgar to judge a man by how much money he could accumulate, in Boston he was well respected for his business decisions.

Christopher said, "I understand Underhill's father hit big gold in the California Gold Rush. This Underhill, the new owner of Summerfield, made his money in timber or something like that. Lots of new money."

"Oh," Amelia said with raised eyebrows. "We shall see if Mrs. Underhill pays us a visit before we extend an invitation to the 4th of July."

"I understand he is a widower," Christopher said, the source of information.

"Oomph, he is probably looking for a Boston daughter for himself or his son," Amelia said haughtily. She fastened a look on Lavinia, "You had better not encourage his son. Divine dancer, indeed."

Lavinia blushed and said, "Oh, Grandmother, Collin Underhill is a friend of Adam Brown's. I am sure if the Browns welcome him into their home, we should do the same."

Cordelia Brown was considered to be one of the reigning matrons of Boston society. She only allowed the most acceptable people to her dinners and parties.

"I think Alexander met him once, said he was a good fellow," Susanna spoke up, defending her cousin.

The Colonel boomed down the table, "And if Alexander says he is a 'good fellow' that is all you need?" He laughed. "Good start to a marriage if you listen to your husband's words, my dear."

Susanna blushed at her grandfather's words, but she also smiled and nodded at him.

The Colonel turned to Lavinia, "You need to follow your cousin's footsteps, Vinnie. You need to find yourself a husband as excellent as Susanna's match."

"Oh Grandfather," Lavinia giggled, bringing a laugh around the table, "there are just not that many senator's sons out there."

"So, when does the boy come up?" the Colonel asked Susanna, referring to Alexander.

Susanna said, "Not until almost the 4th of July. Alexander's Uncle Frank keeps him busy in the law office and won't let him get away before then."

The open windows caught the happy murmur of the children playing outside. The game of tag had ceased and the children were attempting to catch fireflies. From the side of the house, the nannies called the youngsters to come out of the dark and into bed.

Rose, who had been silent during dinner, was certain that by now Torie would have lost her ribbon and undoubtedly be grubby. Rose sincerely hoped that the children would not come to say good night to the parents and grandparents. Rose was weary and hoped for no lectures this evening from her mother-in-law.

As the laughter and chat eddied around Rose, she looked down the table at Lavinia. Lavinia's face lit up as she chatted across the table with her Aunt Alice. Rose was struck once again by her daughter's beauty. Lavinia's skin shone translucently in the soft shining light and her eyes sparkled with amusement over a comment from Alice. Lavina was an easy daughter to raise. She was a dutiful daughter who listened to her mother whose nature was always sunshiny. Lavinia displayed graceful manners and she rarely received lectures from her grandmother about her decorum.

Rose was interrupted from her reverie by a signal from Amelia. All the ladies rose and retired to the drawing room, leaving the men to their cigars and port.

In the drawing room, Amelia, as well as Rose, Emily and Alice, pulled out delicate needlework. Susanna and Lavinia moved to the grand piano and sorted through the sheet music in the basket. Coming to an agreement, they began to play the piano and sing together. Their voices and musical abilities were passable but not accomplished. Their mothers exchanged smiles as the girls began a romantic ballad.

When the girls finished their song, their grandmother called them over to her little circle and laid out plans for the summer. Amelia outlined a morning routine of French and music lessons and working on social engagements. The 4th of July party always required many details to be successful. Entertaining Senator and Mrs. Peabody would require extra effort.

"Now, young ladies," Amelia said to her granddaughters, "I know there will be socializing this summer, and the Colonel and I always welcome your friends to Eastwood. Please give Mrs. Pratt an idea of how many of your friends will be staying for dinner or when you will be eating out. She would appreciate your thoughtfulness so she can plan meals accordingly."

In summers' past, boys buzzed like bees around the girls as they came to play tennis, sail or row on the lake, ride bicycles or take picnics in the woods. Quite often these young men and ladies stayed for dinner and the Eastwood dinner table would swell with happy young faces. Other nights, Susanna and Lavinia, as well as their cousins Myles and Cooper, would be off to dinner and parties at friend's homes; on those nights the dining room would be a little quieter. The adult Brewsters also often entertained over dinner leading to many lively and enlightening conversations.

The men, finished with Port and cigars, joined the ladies over coffee and tea. The soft spring evening air wafting through the open windows felt slightly chilly and Amelia crossed the room to shut the wide windows. Turning, she looked around the room at faces weary from their day's travels. Charles took Alice's hand and said, "It is a beautiful night, my dear. If I fetch you a shawl, shall we take a stroll down to the lake and see the moon?"

Alice murmured an assent, her eyes lighting up as she looked at her handsome husband. Charles and Alice had been married for almost 20 years and had birthed nine children and buried four, but they were still very much in love.

Rose bade her in laws good night and wearily climbed the stairs to her bedroom. She paused on the landing and looked down at the dear old house. She breathed in the smell of clean rooms, floors freshly waxed with beeswax and the fragrance of the bouquet of lilacs that sat on the table in the center of the foyer. These were all smells and sights that she associated with summer living in Eastwood; it felt like coming home.

Once in her bedroom, Rose changed into her nightdress and wrapper and sitting at her dressing table she pulled the pins from her hair. She began to brush her hair, a darker shade of brown with red highlights that danced in the candlelight. Although she was very tired from her day of traveling, Rose also felt a little restless. Her bedroom faced the woods of Eastwood and in the distance she could see Amelia's pretty little white garden glow in the dusk.

Glimpsed just above the woods on a small knoll sat Summerfield Estate. Summerfield sat empty for 20 years after the death of Mary Alden and her heirs spent years ignoring and wrangling over the small estate. Tonight Rose could see the warm glow of lighted windows just above the tree line. Idly, Rose wondered about the new owners of Summerfield. If Vinnie were friends with the son of the house, inquiries would need to be made. Rose did not pay close attention at the dinner conversation and she could not remember if Christopher mentioned a wife or not. Shrugging and losing interest, Rose continued to brush her hair.

She heard a faint murmur of voices and could see Charles and Alice wandering down the path to the bench placed by the white garden. Charles stopped and caught his wife in his arms and gave her a loving kiss.

Rose turned from the window slightly embarrassed to see such a display of emotion. Rose and Alice were best friends and stood side by side in this Brewster family they had married into. Where Rose was quiet and restrained, Alice was a lively happy little creature whose face was always alight with love and delight in her husband and large brood of children. Alice had the reputation of engaging servants for life. Her various servants worked diligently and cheerfully for her, exhibiting rarely any disorder in her household or family.

Rose thought back to the long hot summer as William, her husband, had lingered near death. Alice had been the rock that

Rose had clung to as she sat broken hearted by her husband's side. Motherly Alice gathered up Lavinia and Victoria and took them to Eastwood, making sure that they received all the sympathy and care they needed. Alice also made trips into town and sat with Rose in the darkened room that long, hot summer, holding her hand as they watched William struggle to live.

The bond the two sisters-in-law had forged that summer never loosened. They never referred to that summer or any aspect of Rose and William's marriage, but supported each other as they raised their children within the demanding Brewster family.

Rose put the summer of William's death firmly out of her mind and, instead, remembered the first year of her marriage when she came to Eastwood as a new bride. Her shy diffident husband would take the brush from her hand and brush her long soft curling hair, delighting in the crackle and silky softness of her loosened tresses. Later, William would spread her silky hair out on her pillow and admire the reddish glow in the soft candlelight.

William had been a sweet husband. Rose and William met in the autumn when he was a new cavalry officer and they married the following spring. Quiet and shy, 24-year-old William wooed 17 year old Rose with a determination accepted by both families. Rose, an orphan, was raised by her aunt and uncle, and would come into an inheritance on her 25th birthday. Rose met William at the beginning of her debutant season. He smiled sweetly as he claimed her for a dance and with delight he escorted her to balls and parties.

As the eldest son of Colonel George Brewster, William had been raised in severe military style. He had been a quiet boy who did not enjoy playing the rougher games that other little boys played. Returning from the Civil War, the Colonel had sent William to military boarding school at a very young age where bookish, delicate William endured a miserable existence. He steeled himself to be a good soldier because there was no other avenue. Not until he joined the cavalry did he excel. Horses became his passion and while riding and serving in the cavalry he garnered most of his awards and honors as a soldier.

As a young husband, William had been sweet with Rose, a shy young bride. Over the breakfast table William would reach out and pat her hand. William would sit with Rose in the evenings and read aloud while she sewed baby clothes once she became pregnant with Lavinia. Rose and William resided in their own little brick home at 23 Hampshire Street across from a green and lush park. They led a quiet life. William was never very forthcoming about his days in the military, and sometimes Rose would look up from her sewing to see William gazing at her with an odd, almost tortured look in his eyes.

Lavinia was a delightful baby from the beginning and William seemed to be thrilled with his baby daughter and ignored the Colonel's disappointed comments over the baby's gender. Rose and William had been married for a year and a half when William was posted to the West to assist in the Indian Wars. Lavinia, six months old, and Rose were left behind for 3 years. Rose, baby Lavinia and Nanny Phoebe closed their little house and moved in with Amelia and the Colonel.

During those years, Rose accompanied her mother-in-law on her various social rounds and volunteer activities, but she was happiest when she was in the nursery watching Lavinia grow from baby to toddler to little girl. Rose and William exchanged letters during his absence. Rose wrote of Lavinia's growth and her social activities with his mother; William wrote short stilted letters that said very little. William never wrote of his involvement in the Indian Wars although he occasionally mentioned how he longed to come home to Boston.

But, William had never really come back to Rose. The man who returned after three years of Indian fighting was silent and strained, not the William Rose knew. Rose looked in vain at the tense colorless man for the sweet boy she had married. With his premature grayness and his tightly pulled facial skin, gentle Rose was shocked and unsure how to communicate with her husband. Rose reached out to touch him gently as she passed and felt a shrinking in William even from that slight contact. Once established in their own home during their quiet dinners, William would not answer her gentle questions about his time in the service. Baffled, Rose did not pressure him to speak.

William returned from the West with nightmares, a fact that was shameful to him. He began sleeping in a narrow bed in their dressing room and only came to Rose in the darkness. He remained a quiet lover, never demanding. Rose performed her wifely duty when he asked, but there was no passion between them. His clumsy fumbling in the dark seemed embarrassing to both, and in daylight no discussions of personal times took place.

When Victoria was born, William was fascinated and slightly repelled by this screaming little mite who was impatient and demanding. Quiet little Lavinia was easier for him and he often took her for walks in the park where they observed the flowers and the birds. As Torie grew, she resembled her grandfather in looks and temperament and William would shrink from her when she threw a tantrum.

Only with his horses did William find true happiness. Rose would see a tightening of his jawline after a bad night of nightmares, but a day in the solitary saddle riding, riding, riding would bring home a more relaxed man.

In the end, William's beloved horse betrayed him. Riding in the country in a solitary effort to outrun his demons, William was thrown from his horse and lay for several hours in a muddy ditch before he was discovered When they finally brought home his broken body, Rose wept. A few weeks later, as William lay unconscious and unresponsive, Rose realized that she was pregnant with Henry. That long summer became a horrifying memory of morning sickness and the close smell of the sick room and the dying man.

The Brewster family took turns to help Rose, giving her the chance to rest as her pregnancy advanced, but she could not tear herself away. The accident finished off the broken man who returned to her five years previously. Rose read to William from his beloved books by Ulysses, Homer and Plato. William never awoke; he never acknowledged the pressure of her hand, he never looked at her.

And that was all. Rose put down her brush and once again went to the window. Charles and Alice had departed their bower and returned to the house. Rose looked out at the evening sky and smelled the newly mown hay. The moon would be late in rising, and Rose's room faced the field and wood so she could not see the lake. A silent quiet lonely night... a night for old women.

Rose shivered and wrapped her arms around her. She was not old. She was 35 and had been a widow for over 10 years. During those years she remained alone at night. Remembering back to that last summer of William' life made her ineffably sad, and tonight Rose became restless. A vague longing rose inside of her. This longing, deeply buried in Rose's heart, pulled on her conscious. Rose gave herself a shake and decided to flee her barren quiet room.

Rising from the window seat, Rose adjusted the belt of her wrapper around her slim waist and stepped out of her room. She paused at the young ladies' room, but could hear much giggling and whispering. Released from being adults during the dinner hour and the time spent in the drawing room, Susanna and Lavinia shared in gossip and chat. Rose knew Lavinia was fine; Lavinia was always fine.

Quietly taking the narrow stairs to the 3rd floor, Rose passed into the nursery. Here a solitary lamp flickered and the quiet sounds of children sleeping peacefully in their beds greeted her. Rose paused at Henry's bed first. Henry had fallen asleep while reading, his steel framed spectacles askew, his book collapsed on his chest. Rose gently removed his spectacles and picked up the book. Glancing at the title, she saw The Tales of the Arabian Nights. Henry displayed amazing intellect and curiosity for foreign things. He was a favorite teller of tales. In the dark on the back porch or out on the boat landing, the children would be enthralled while he related the stories he had read. Henry was also the one who had the best ideas when it came to playing make believe.

Henry had a slender build like his father and he looked bookish. His eyes were often alight with far away dreams and ideas. Henry spoke of traveling to foreign lands and seeing strange animals and faraway cities. Henry wanted to dig for ancient civilizations and discover new old worlds.

Rose gazed lovingly on her only son as she smoothed his hair. Physically, Henry was very much like his father. He had William's light brown hair and gray eyes, although Henry's eyes were always clear, as opposed to the tortured look in William's eyes. Henry had a confidence created by his mother's and sister's acceptance and love for him. Henry had no difficulty in joining in games with the other children, but if he decided it was not something he wanted to do, he would dig his heels in and adamantly refuse, no matter the pressure.

Lavinia and Torie learned early on that they could not easily coerce Henry to play in activities of no interest to him. They adored their small baby brother and always defended him if their grandfather began to lecture Henry on the joys of being a soldier or a more manly man. Henry showed a promise of being an excellent sailor and would play tennis or swim with his cousins, but he also would take himself off to examine the woods and fields around Eastwood. Walking through the meadow with Henry invariably brought out knowledge of butterflies and birds or the small animals that inhabited the under grass and bushes.

Even while Rose reached out a hand and smoothed Henry's soft hair, she frowned slightly. Rose expected a battle with Henry's grandfather this summer over Henry's schooling and she would have to steel herself for an all out battle.

Turning from Henry, Rose looked at her middle daughter's bed that she shared with her cousin Kitty. Even in sleep, Kitty slept with a tidiness and unfussiness. Her neatly braided golden hair lay outside the blankets, her bangs smooth on her forehead. Kitty's hands in sleep seemed artfully posed, one across her chest and the other gracefully curled next to her pink cheek.

Torie sat in the window seat looking out the window. The nursery faced the lawn and lake and Torie watched the water glistening in the starlight while listening to a chorus of crickets and frogs. Rose fondly placed a hand on her middle daughter's dark head and sat down beside her. "Hard day?" she asked gently.

"Oh Mama," Torie turned to her mother, tears on her cheeks. "I got you in trouble with Grandmother and I didn't mean to. Grandmother gave me such a scolding over my expulsion from Miss Mable's. I tried to explain, but she would not listen."

Rose shrugged it off. "If we did not start the summer off with your grandmother exasperated with you and me, it just would not be Eastwood," she said with a small laugh. "I, too, have spoken with your grandmother about Miss Mable's. I think at this point she is disinclined to listen to either of us."

Through her tears, Torie clasped her hands tightly together. "I just want so much in this world. I don't want to be a girl and have to learn to sew and play the piano and arrange parties. I want to get up and exercise with the boys! I already asked Grandfather and he didn't answer; he just shook his head and walked away.

Grandmother had a lot to say about it. She said it was time I remembered I was supposed to grow up to be a lady."

"Torie," her mother answered in firm tones that were not to be brooked, "you will not get up and join the boys in their morning calisthenics. If you think your grandmother was upset about the expulsion, you can imagine what she would have to say about her granddaughter swimming with the boys."

Torie didn't answer, but looked out at the evening sky. Distantly they could see the moon rising over the hill behind the town. "Penny for your thoughts? What is really bothering you?" Rose asked gently.

Torie looked at her mother and shook her head in bafflement, "I don't know what it is, but Edmund has changed. When I suggested we drill tonight, he didn't want to."

Rose smiled and picked up her daughter's hand. "My darling, Edmund is growing up. After a whole year as a military cadet, he may not want to play army with you this summer. Edmund may want to take a break from his winter activities."

"But we have always played war. I want Edmund to grow up to be a brave soldier like my father," Torie said indignantly.

"Shhh," her mother hushed, looking around at the sleeping children. "Torie, Edmund needs to grow up to be Edmund, not what you think he should grow up to be." As Torie started to argue, Rose stopped her, "It is time you were in bed and asleep. The summer will bring what it brings. And now, you need to get to sleep. Your grandmother has you working on your French first thing in the morning."

Rose escorted her daughter to bed, tucked her in and gave her a kiss. She retraced her steps down the back stairs and once again in her room, she drifted to the open window. The young ladies had quieted and only silence came from their room. Somewhere in the house, she heard soft murmurings of masculine and feminine voices.

Rose and William indulged in pillow talk at night their first summer at Eastwood. Under the cover of darkness William admitted to her how much he hated the army and detested the life he lived. Even in the dark, he would not admit to his sweet innocent wife the horrors of military boarding school. The twins, Charles and Christopher, two years William's junior, joined him at

Slater at the appropriate age. Bluff, congenial Charles and athletic Christopher managed life at the military school much better than William. The twins dutifully excelled where they needed to excel and had actually defended William against the more brutal hazing. Accepted and easily liked, Charles became known as a bit of a prankster and took his punishments lightly. Christopher's excellence on the playing field won him respect. William did not take his punishments lightly and felt his lack of acceptance deeply.

One night at Eastwood after he had returned from the Indian Wars, William opened up to Rose. She was pregnant with Torie when William told Rose that he hoped all of his children would be girls. At Rose's startled exclamation, William informed her he was in the process of making his will and that if something happened to him, while his father would always oversee her finances, Rose alone would be the one to decide the education for their children, in particular sons.

William uncharacteristically reached out and gripped Rose's abdomen feverishly. "I don't want my sons to grow up to be in the military," he told her with vehemence. "I want them to grow up to be what they want to be. When the time comes, I am going to stand up to my father on this, Rose. But, if something happens to me before then, promise me that you will stand up for our boys. Promise me!"

Rose, pregnant and saddened by this stranger who had returned to her, acknowledged with little thought to what that would mean. Why should something happen to William? Rose always had a man to take care of her, first her uncle and then William. Rose readily consented.

William remade his will exactly as he had stated. The Colonel managed Rose's finances and she received a generous monthly allowance out of her estate. The Colonel paid most of her monthly expenses for her brownstone in Boston but she paid the wages of her staff. When each of the children came of age, trusts were set aside. But, an unexpected surprise awaited Rose.

Pregnant and distraught over William's lingering death, Rose sat barely listening as the will was read. Her father-in-law's exclamations over the paragraph of educating children, she bore with equanimity. William, always in awe of his father, had not discussed his desires with his father before his death. Although there was a letter left to his father to read in private, William hoped to outlive his father.

Rose had not expected the other surprise in the will: for William had thrown his father a boon. Rose had to stay unmarried. William stated that as long as Rose remained a widow, all monies and governance of the children were her option. All sons would be educated as she saw fit. If she chose to marry, the money and all choices for the children would revert to their grandfather.

Colonel Brewster became incensed over the will. While laws for women were slowly changing, it was an accepted fact in the tight knit Brewster family that the oldest male would oversee widows or any orphaned children. Rose realized the shock to her father-in-law when those words were read. Colonel Brewster never listened to William and had always dispatched him where he felt would be best for his first born. The Colonel was quite befuddled over William's words. Over the last ten years, the Colonel argued long and loud with Rose over her decisions and she became adroit at avoiding him when she could feel a lecture about to occur. Rose did not feel a military education would enhance Henry's life or future career.

Rose was unsure of her small son's future. Possibly, he would join Brewster and Sons and become a merchant, but more likely with his fascination with all things old, he would be off to explore the world. Rose's old friend, Peregrine Fitch, often took Henry to lectures on explorations of Egypt and the Nile and Henry would return home, his eyes shining. After a lecture, Henry would spend days out in the back garden pretending he was navigating Africa and shooting big game.

So, Rose stayed a widow. She did not look for or long for a husband. Following William's death, Rose, along with the help of Nanny Phoebe, raised the children. Rose took her proper role in Boston society as a widow of a Brewster. Often, Rose sat at her mother-in-law's side during parties and at the symphony. She attended DAR meetings and volunteered with the Ladies' Aid Society. She turned her talents to assisting the organization of various fund raisers.

Rose accompanied Lavinia as she came out in society, and she held an open house every winter just after the new year for family and friends. Alice and Rose were frequent visitors to each other's home. Alice would drop by on a quiet afternoon and the two women would sit in front of the fire mending children's clothes and talking light Boston gossip or sharing Brewster family news.

Rose's sister-in-law Alice quietly applauded William's will when it came to Henry. Her own son, Edmund, dutifully enrolled in Slater Military Academy the prior year. While Edmund had completed his first year admirably, he did not seem as engrossed as had been hoped. Since returning, Edmund had not spoken to his mother about his school year. That silence was worrisome to both of his parents.

On the train from Boston, Alice watched Edmund's expression as he sat at the table with his sisters clustered around him. He created a mixture of manliness and boyishness with his longer jaw and his stretched out limbs. Something deeper, Alice was sure, troubled Edmund.

Back in her bedroom at Eastwood, Rose watched the moon rise, turned down the lamp, and climbed into her lonely bed. Not often did she feel this way, but next fall Henry would enroll in Ashcroft Academy for boys and Torie would be the only child at home. Torie would be attending day school, somewhere, and Lavinia would start at Radcliffe Women's College. Radcliffe was across the river from home, but Vinnie would live in the women's dormitories.

In the east wing, in Amelia's bedroom, the Colonel and Amelia were having their own quiet conversation about their children and grandchildren. Amelia sat on her chaise lounge looking out at the moon shining on the pond; the Colonel sat at her side holding her hand.

Amelia breathed in the clean country air, very content. "It is so wonderful to have most of the family under one roof again, George," she said, squeezing the Colonel's hand.

The Colonel laughed softly, "You are never happier than when you can keep an eye on all of the Brewster brood."

"They are all growing up so fast," she told him with a sigh. "The littlest twins are leaving babyhood behind. Susanna almost married and Matilda's boys are leaving for West Point in the fall."

"I am anxious to see Myles and Cooper," the Colonel said. "They are going to make exceptional soldiers." He paused and said with a note of irritation, "In September Henry should be joining Edmund at Slater."

Amelia silently agreed with him, but said, "Rose will fight you to the death, George. Maybe you should leave it alone until next year."

The Colonel spoke irritably, "Why set him apart from the other boys? He's always got his nose in a book. He needs his mother and sisters to stop mollycoddling him and let him grow up to be manly. The only way that is going to happen is if he becomes a soldier. Soldiers make respectable men, disciplined and hardworking. That is what we want in our Brewster men."

Amelia was thinking about Henry. "Henry is growing up," she agreed. "He startled me today with how similar he looks to William."

At the mention of his deceased eldest son, the Colonel made an involuntary movement. "He did not want to go to military school, either. In the end, it made a man out of him."

Amelia thought painfully even after all these years about her oldest son. She would not admit to the Colonel that she sometimes awoke in the night from nightmares remembering William's tortured eyes. Not even to herself would she admit how helpless she had felt as she watched her oldest son grow into a tortured man.

William had been sent away to school at a very early age. The Colonel had been off fighting the War Between the States and when he returned, he had not been happy with the small delicate boy he found. William dutifully went to military school and never complained during his time at home, although he had gone from a quiet cheerful little boy to someone strained and withdrawn.

Amelia's motherly instinct sensed William's unhappiness even as she fully supported her husband in all decisions regarding their offspring. Amelia softly sighed; it was a man's world, and boys needed to learn how to grow up and be responsible in this man's world.

"What if Slater," she asked softly, "is not the right choice for Henry? There are other military academies out there. I sometimes wonder if, after all these years..." her voice trailed away.

The Colonel's voice rose, "Amelia, Slater is an excellent military academy. Our other boys did fine there. Myles and Cooper sailed through without any harmful gossip coming to their ears. Slater made our oldest son an excellent soldier," he said with emphasis. "He was a brave soldier."

Amelia nodded quietly. "Yes, George, I suppose you are right." Amelia looked at her husband with pain in her eyes. The Colonel never referred to their oldest son by his Christian name. It was always 'the boy' or 'our son,' but never William.

The Colonel turned to her and gave her a kiss. "Don't worry, my dear." he told her. "I shall work on Rose and Henry, but I won't make anyone miserable this summer."

Amelia, knowing her daughter-in-law's steel core, wondered if the person who would be most miserable in the end would be the Colonel, but decided to say nothing.

CHAPTER 4

Dawn at Eastwood created a soft pink in the Eastern sky as the sun peeped over the hill and a pearly sheen enveloped the old house. Bird song in the woods started with the first light, and the earthy smell of the pond rose on the fresh morning air. The Colonel, rising at the first bird call, soon had corralled the males on the estate on the wide lawn. All male servants with the exception of Pratt, due to his advanced age and lumbago, were present as well as all Brewster men from Uncle Charles to the youngest, Henry.

The Colonel led them through a rotation of calisthenics and stretching, followed by a brisk run around the pasture and a quick dash down to the pond. Brewster boys, old and young alike, dressed in their red long sleeved, long legged flannel swim wear. Servants dressed in a variety of clothes, and some began to pant from the exertion. The water was icy at that hour as the Colonel lead the pack into the pond with a jack knife dive off the boat landing. He insisted that everyone plunge in the water, swim to the far end of the boat landing and back again. The swim itself took less than 5 minutes, but as they emerged from the lake shivering, the early morning sun suddenly felt warmer on cold heads and wet backs.

The dripping men, led by the Colonel, took a rapid trot back to the house and around to the kitchen stairs. The Colonel called out a brisk "Hup, two, three, four" as they dashed for the house. The men servants hurried, shivering, around the house towards the stables and fresh clothes and breakfast. Servants who had been in Brewster households for years were familiar with this morning ritual, although newly hired servants were slightly in shock at the experience.

The Colonel entered the kitchen followed by his sons and grandsons, leaving dirty, wet footprints across the kitchen floor and trailing drips of water from their clothing. The Colonel greeted Mrs. Pratt cordially and led his shivering, dripping pack of sons and grandsons towards the back stairs. Tilly, the scullery maid, sighed. Her first task of the morning at Eastwood always was to sweep and clean the tracks left behind by the men. Mrs. Pratt, with her long affiliation with the Brewsters, was accustomed to this practice. She would not cook in a dirty kitchen, so Tilly spent time every morning mopping the kitchen floor.

Charles entered his bedroom and found his wife at the window brushing her hair. The morning air smelled sweet and a chorus of bird song floated through the open window. Charles gave Alice a light morning kiss before he reached for a towel and began briskly rubbing himself. "The old man never slows down," he told his wife with a small laugh. "The amazing thing is that he keeps right up there with all the boys."

Alice smiled up at her husband. She awoke that morning to find that her pregnancy fears were unfounded, and she felt relieved. In response to her husband's comment she said, "Well, wait until Myles and Cooper show up this week. We shall see if the Colonel can keep up with them."

Charles agreed with a small laugh and disappeared into his dressing room.

He came out dressed for the day and picked up Alice's hand as she continued to sit and stare out the window. "Are you feeling well, my darling?" Charles asked her.

Alice nodded and said, "I am just a little weary from the move down here. I am thinking about keeping to my room today. I am sure by tomorrow I will be feeling fine."

Charles, understanding, said, "I shall have a breakfast tray ordered up for you."

He kissed her again and left the room.

At the breakfast table, the Colonel entered and greeted his wife and various relatives engaged in breakfast. He went first to Amelia and kissed her on the head. He picked up one of her hands and examined a scratch on it. "Been at your roses already this morning?" he asked her with a smile.

Amelia nodded and smiled back at him and asked in return, "Did you enjoy your swim?"

"Best way to start a day," the Colonel intoned. "Exercise, it gets your whole body going. The blood flows to the brain and you can think better."

Torie finished her breakfast and made her way to the morning room for French lessons. She paused outside the Colonel's study. Torie was drawn into the room by the large painting hanging over the fireplace of her grandfather as a young soldier. Dressed in the Union Army officer's uniform, the Colonel cut a dashing figure.

Torie gazed at the painting when her grandfather strode into the study. "Good morning, Victoria," he greeted her cordially.

Torie lost in thought, asked, "Grandpapa, what do you think about Mr. Roosevelt?"

The Colonel looked at her fondly. While her grandmother had little sympathy for Torie's interests in military and politics, he appreciated the fine mind that it represented. The times were changing and an intellectual woman would be an asset to a future husband. They discussed politics and Cuba for a while.

The Colonel seated himself at his desk. Torie came over to his chair and put her hand on his arm. "Do you know what I really want to be when I grow up, Grandpapa?" she asked, looking him directly in the eye.

The Colonel waited, a small smile on his lips. "A Rough Rider," she pronounced. "I would have loved to charge up San Juan Hill and take out the Spaniards. It must have been terribly brave and exciting. I know my Papa would have ridden alongside Mr. Roosevelt."

The Colonel looked at her in astonishment and a little pain. Patting her arm, he said, with a small grimace of sympathy, "Your grandmother would die of mortification if any granddaughter of hers ever suggested that she would not want to pursue lady-like accomplishments and entertained an idea of becoming a soldier so I suggest you keep that idea to yourself."

Then he added, giving her a quick kiss on the cheek, "Your papa would have led the charge on San Juan, Victoria." The Colonel agreed softly with a nod, "Your papa was a brave soldier."

Torie saw a look pass over her grandfather's face that looked something like pain. Just then her grandmother called her to come to the morning room. She leaned over and gave her grandfather a return kiss on the cheek and hurried out of the room.

After she left, the Colonel sat and stared out the window for sometime. He thought of William, his son. The Colonel assured himself that he had done right by William. Slater had turned William into a man. A brave soldier.

The Colonel sat in his study, his shoulders slightly hunched. From birth, William had been his pride and joy, the son that was to excel and rise through the ranks of military. The son who would make a great career out of the military. He expected all of his sons would have illustrious military careers, especially William as his first born.

During the Colonel's brief visits in the midst of the war years he found a quiet, shy little boy. William would look at his gruff father with awe and a little shyness. After the war, the Colonel attempted to pull William into the more rough and rugged pursuits a boy should wish to follow. William, ever dutiful, obeyed his father but not with any enthusiasm. William had always been destined for Slater, but the Colonel, concerned over William's lack of interest, moved up William's entry at a younger age.

Upon graduation from Slater, William attended West Point and graduated as an officer. William served his time in the military, but had not distinguished himself. Conversations between William and his father, always respectful, became even more distant as William grew into a young man. A dutiful son, William had courted and married 17 year old Rose at his parents' suggestion. After Lavinia's birth, William accepted his deployment to the West without a word of dissent. From the time William came back from the Indian Wars, he would hardly speak or look at his father. All questions about the campaign went unanswered. The Colonel wrote letters to William's commanding officer and received back satisfactory reports, as he had throughout his son's military career. The reports said: William always was correct in military etiquette, William went on every raid requested, William saved his fellow soldiers from an attack, William earned medals for his valor. Nothing seemed to explain this diffidence, this constraint.

At family gatherings, the Colonel saw a strained look in Rose's eyes as well. William needed time to adjust to civilian life and to married life, the Colonel told himself and Amelia in their private conversations. A good business awaited William, children and a regular routine. That was all that was needed. Not every military man could stand to be away from the army. If in a year or two William still seemed at a loss, the Colonel thought he might suggest another military campaign. But, the Colonel wanted to wait until after a son was born to William and Rose.

The Colonel loved to watch his son with his horses. The Colonel took great pride in William's understanding and care of his horses, in his ability to understand horses better than humans. Only when in the saddle or in the stable did William look totally relaxed. He became one with the horse and was fearless when it came to jumping fences or riding full tilt across fields.

The damn will! What had William been thinking? The Colonel received a private letter from William at the reading of the will that he never shared with anyone, not even Amelia. Even now every word was seared into his brain. It was a shameful letter and the Colonel would never share it with anyone. Shy, diffident William found his voice in written words that he would never have been able to state to his father face to face.

The Colonel made a noise of dismissal and turned to his newspaper.

In the morning room, three generations of Brewster ladies were seated on various chairs listening to Monsieur du Gres explain his schedule for the summer. Kitty and Torie, seated side by side on a hassock, watched with longing as Edmund and Henry walked by the open window with a small toy sailboat in their hands.

Torie sighed, the boys must have finished practicing their music lessons quickly and were now on to the fun. She had at least two hours of French, sewing and music lessons yet to be completed before she was free to join the boys. By then, they would be on to some other pursuit.

Monsieur du Gres asked her and Kitty a question in French, testing their abilities. Torie answered with admirable ease. French came easy to her. Kitty stuttered and stammered and blushed over her mistakes.

Amelia praised Torie for her French knowledge and the room seemed to smile down on her. For once the center of positive attention, Torie curtsied to her grandmother and thanked her in French.

Kitty, rankled, said in a soto voice, "The only reason you are better at French is because of all the times you were in trouble."

This was true. At Miss Mabel's school, one of Miss Mabel's favorite punishments was assigning a page of French to translate. Due to Torie's wayward behavior, she had often been assigned French.

Torie turned to her cousin. Nothing was said, but her dark brown eyes promised revenge.

After lunch, the carriage containing the Brewster daughter, Matilda Bingham, arrived along with her twin 16-year-old sons, Myles and Cooper, and the Colonel's widowed sisters, Tabitha Benson and Easter Graham. The entire house turned out to welcome and greet them joyfully.

Matilda kissed her mother's cheek and nodded to her sisters-in-law. Matilda was a tall thin woman with sharp features and not given to outward displays of emotion. Her husband, Captain Jasper Bingham, was a merchant and owned several ships and sailed the world looking for trade. Jasper owned warehouses in many far flung outposts that needed his attention. Jasper was away on business for months at a time and Matilda ran her house in his absence with military precision. Matilda missed Jasper at times with a great longing, but lighthearted Jasper also wore on his wife if they spent too much time together.

Kitty and Torie stood side by side to greet Myles and Cooper, both jumping up and down slightly at the sight of their tall handsome cousins. The girls were something of a contrast as Kitty, with her blonde curls, was dressed in a floral pink dress, lacy ruffles on her high necked collar. Torie, dressed in her navy blue sailing suit, a small sailor hat bedecked with a crimson ribbon cocked on her dark ringlets, was ready to leave with Edmund and go for a sail on the pond.

Absently, Cooper and Myles greeted their young cousins. Cooper reached out and gave Torie's ringlet a tug as he and Myles brushed by to say hello to Susanna and Lavinia. Torie and Kitty looked at each other, exchanged shrugs and turned to greet their great aunts, Easter and Tabitha. These little old ladies, the Colonel's sisters, were delighted to see their great nieces and nephews and gave each of the girls a hug and kiss. They wrapped their ancient arms around Edmund, too, and gave him kisses that smelled slightly musty. Edmund, not so excited about his great aunts' embrace, was impatient to get out on the pond. He called to Torie and she left the group and followed him across the lawn.

After the new arrivals settled in and lunched, the adults congregated on the porch for the afternoon, to gossip and make plans. Matilda looked around at the green lawn, the shady trees and the sparkling pond and breathed a deep sigh of contentment. Matilda rarely sat still for long. A born organizer, she preferred the role of being in charge of the Ladies' Aid Society. Even as she sat enjoying the country quiet and listening to her mother's plans for the 4th of July, her mind was busy with the duties she wanted to take over to help with the 4th of July party.

In the deepest shade of the verandah, on the edge of the group, sat Tabitha and Easter, the Colonel's twin sisters. Born on Easter Sunday, their grandmother had feared such two tiny scraps of life would not survive the night. As the first light of dawn alighted on one baby's face, she had opened her eyes and looked around. Her grandmother had instantly named her "Easter." They had grown to be beautiful women who had each married a Union Army officer. Unfortunately, they had both been widowed during the War Between the States and had resided with the Colonel and Amelia ever since. The two sweet old ladies lived quietly, but delighted in all the Brewster grandchildren. Good natured and grey haired, the elderly twins always were willing to teach a little girl to tat lace or read a book or listen to dreams expressed by one of the many grandchildren. For Henry, they gathered stamps from friends who travelled the world and saved them for him for his collection. Loved and revered by all, the aunts spent their summers at Eastwood collecting blossoms and making potpourri and culling the shore for small stones, empty birds nests and other small natural items. Then the two spent the winter painting their found treasures or creating dioramas and gifting them to their relatives for Christmas.

As the conversation went on, Susanna, Lavinia, Myles and Cooper appeared. The young ladies were dressed in darker colored skirts and jackets, with glimpses of white lace collars peeping out, their straw hats firmly anchored to their pouffed hair styles with strong hat pins.

At Amelia's questioning look, Susanna explained as she pulled on blue gloves, "We are going to take the pony cart to town and Cooper and Myles are going to ride their bicycles. The twins want to see the new bandstand and Vinnie needs some hair ribbons to match her new ball dress."

Waved off, the adults watched the boys and girls disappear around the house towards the stables where their bicycles were kept. A short time later, the fat pony trotted by with the girls sitting in the small straw cart. As Susanna held the reins, she waved her small whip as they passed by. The twins also waved as they headed down the graveled avenue on their bicycles. Out on the lake, in the distance, the sail boat with Edmund and Torie swept by.

Matilda smiled and drew a deep sigh of contentment. "I think summer at Eastwood has arrived," she said congenially.

"Myles and Cooper are looking very good," Alice said to Matilda. "Are they excited about West Point?"

Matilda nodded, "We received letters from General Grigsby. He is looking forward to having Brewsters at West Point again."

The Colonel, delighted, said, "Grigsby is a good man. He will make excellent officers out of those two. They had a good start at Slater and I am looking forward to hearing reports as they progress."

"Any news of Jasper?" Charles asked his sister.

Matilda replied that she had received notice that he was on his way home from the Orient and hoped to be at Eastwood before the end of the summer. "He certainly wants to be home when the twins head off to West Point," she added.

The talk turned to other family matters and gossip. A maid arrived with tea and small snacks and the laughter grew.

"What neighbors have arrived?" Tabitha asked, her gentle eyes sparkling.

"The Browns, the Sparrows, the Harlows," Amelia told her. "I also understand that Peregrine Fitch is spending July at Briar Hill with the Browns." Amelia smiled briefly at Rose.

Peregrine Fitch had been William Brewster's best friend since childhood. In the years since William's death, Peregrine stayed close to Rose and quite often escorted her to social gatherings. Although he never expressed improper interest in Rose, he was a constant acquaintance. Peregrine had always taken interest in William and Rose's children and they felt as close to him as they did to their own uncles.

Alice spoke up, "I also understand Samuel Gardner and his children have taken on Maplewood for the summer." She turned to Rose, and said teasingly, "I hear Sam is very anxious to find a new wife and mother for those horrible children of his."

Here she was interrupted by her mother-in-law. "Alice Brewster," Amelia scolded, "I will not have you being vulgar. Roxanne Gardner only passed right after Christmas. Mr. Gardner is not even out of mourning yet."

Alice apologized to her mother-in-law, but quietly she hissed to Rose, "You still need to be aware. Gossip has it that he is looking for a new wife and that you are at the top of the list."

Rose looked at her sister-in-law with a small frown of annoyance and shook her head. "Don't be silly," she whispered back to Alice. "You know I am not looking for a husband. Samuel Gardner also knows that."

Alice's eyes were alight with teasing, "Sam Gardner told Jonathan Harlow that he had always thought you were the prettiest widow he had ever laid his eyes on. And you know he can't handle those children on his own."

Samuel Gardner had three children who were considered by most of Boston society as rather wild and slightly ill mannered. Giles Gardner, the oldest boy, went to school with Edmund at Slater.

Rose, catching Alice's infectious spirit, laughed. She said, "Thank you for warning me; I shall be aware."

A little later the bicycle riders and cart returned and soon the thwack of tennis balls could be heard along with shouts of laughter and shrieks from the girls as they played a match with their cousins.

Torie and Edmund, out on the lake, came about and the boom swung across the boat and the sail gave a loud crack as it filled with air. Afternoons on Eaton's Pond brought about a fresh breeze making it perfect weather for sailing. Torie loved crewing for Edmund, and as she securely set the sail, she sat with her chin on her arms and looked across the lake at Eastwood. White and majestic, the old house sat amongst the tall leafy trees that spread shade over its many verandas. Its wide lawns were inviting and the sweeping driveway was hidden from view. The upper story windows were open and filmy curtains could be seen fluttering. Beyond the house, men worked in the fields cutting the hay.

Torie squinted at the cluster of relatives sitting on the porch. She could make out her grandmother sitting in the shade next to the tall person who could only be Matilda. Even at this distant Amelia looked regal by the way she held her body and head upright.

"Edmund," Torie said, "do you ever not want to do what Grandmother wants you to do, just because she wants you to do something?"

Edmund, who was intent upon steering the boat, glanced at his first mate. "Torie," he said with a small smile, "you bring trouble down on yourself all the time."

"No I don't," she protested. "I just want..." she struggled with her thoughts. "Oh, I don't know. Do you think," she continued, "that Grandmother ever did not do the proper thing? I mean, what kind of little girl was she?"

Edmund started laughing, "I imagine Grandmother was a whole lot like Kitty."

At the mention of her cousin, Torie scowled as she remembered Kitty's words from the morning French lesson.

Edmund interrupted her thoughts and said, "It is time we came about. You need to get ready to release the sail."

Torie agreeably left her thoughts and moved to release the lines.

Edmund and Torie returned from boating and joined their other cousins in playing games on the side lawn. The badminton net had been strung up between two trees and Torie and Edmund spent a warm hour chasing the small feathered birdie back and forth. Under the shade of a huge maple tree, Kitty created an area to play house with her doll, forming different rooms by using the roots of the tree. Henry sat close by absorbed in a book.

Torie, chasing after an errant birdie, collapsed next to Henry to catch her breath. He acknowledged her with a brief nod and watching him, Torie asked, "What are you reading?"

He showed her, "The Iliad."

Torie's eyes lit up, "The story of Helen of Troy and Paris and Troy and all that?"

At Henry's nod, Torie said, "I have an incredible idea. Let's play Troy."

Henry's eyes also lit up. Henry enjoyed Torie's enthusiasm for his books and she loved to act out the stories he absorbed.

Torie turned to all the smaller children. "Come on," she called them to her. "Let's play Troy." Abigail, Sarah and Edmund came over to see what she had in mind. Kitty continued serving her doll tea. Torie called, somewhat imperiously, "Come on, Kitty."

Kitty looked up from her absorption in her play and shook her head at her cousin. Torie came over to her cousin and observed the little house that Kitty had created.

"Come on Kit," Torie wheedled, "We want to play the battle of Troy and only you could be Helen."

Kitty looked at her and frowned, "I don't want to play at war, Torie. And you can't tell me what to do. Besides, who is Helen?"

Torie took a deep breath and her eyes were agleam with mischief, "Helen of Troy was the most beautiful woman in the world. She was stolen from her father by Paris, who loved her. He kidnapped her and took her to Troy and they had a big battle and everything. Come on, Kitty. It will be most exciting."

Kitty, intrigued, asked cautiously, "Did Helen battle?"

Torie shook her head, "Oh no, she was shut up safe and sound waiting for her brother-in-law, Agammemnon, to rescue her." Torie hunkered down and watched Kitty place her small tea set on her pretend table. "Listen, Kitty, it was written about Helen that 'this was a face that launched a thousand ships'. She was the most beautiful woman on earth." Impressed that her cousin thought her pretty, Kitty reluctantly left her tea party and joined the group.

As the afternoon started to wane, Amelia looked up from her knitting as she sat on the front porch. She had been telling Tabitha and Easter her plans for adding an orchid house to her green houses, explaining to them about the many varieties of orchids and how they were cultivated.

Rose, sitting at the far end of the group, glimpsed Alice's nanny and one of the stable men walking along the water's edge in deep conversation. Rose knew she needed to alert Alice to the possibility that Sarah and Abigail were not properly supervised. At that moment shrieks and screams erupted as all of the children came racing around the house. Kitty rode in the wheel barrow steered by Edmund. The rough ground caused Kitty to wail as she bounced and bumped around. Henry ran along side the wheel barrow brandishing a stick like a sword. Torie, Sarah and Abigail trailed behind, screaming. Henry's dog, Shep, and Edmund's dog, Major, barked excitedly as they ran and jumped on the children.

Their grandmother bounded down the steps, her hand held up to stop them. "What is going on here?" she demanded.

Kitty tumbled out of the wheel barrow, wailing. The children stopped making noises and the dogs immediately slunk under the bushes. Amelia's eyes took in the general dishevelment and Kitty's tears.

Henry spoke up, "We were playing Helen of Troy, Grandmother." He explained, "Helen was the most beautiful woman in the world and Paris kidnapped her."

Kitty hiccoughed, "I don't want to be Helen any more. I don't like being kidnapped. Torie promised me that Helen would be locked up safe and sound."

Her grandmother looked them over, a glimmer of amusement showed in her eyes although she kept a stern countenance. "Play time is over. Go upstairs and get ready for your dinner. Kitty," she put a hand on her shoulders, "stop crying. You are not hurt. Go get cleaned up."

Amelia fastened her eye on Torie. "Victoria," she said attempting to be severe, but having a hard time keeping a straight face, "I know it was your idea to do this to Kitty. You should be ashamed of yourself. And you need to apologize to your cousin."

Torie started to argue, but realized the entire group of adults were staring at her. Hastily, she dropped a curtsey and murmured, "Sorry, Kitty." Then Torie beat a hasty retreat around the house in the footsteps of the rest of the Trojans.

Amelia came back up the stairs and looked at Rose and Alice. "I am glad we are starting the summer off with the classics," she said, smiling at them.

Matilda asked Rose and Alice, "Where are the children's nannies? They should be watching their charges."

Rose and Alice looked at each other, put away their mending and stood up. Phoebe woke that morning with a headache and Rose told her to take a nap, but Molly should have been in the garden overseeing the children.

Life settled down at Eastwood into something of a routine. Charles and Christopher from neighboring Harlow Hall departed on Monday morning for the city leaving the Colonel and Amelia with the house full of women and children. They returned late Friday afternoon as the sun was setting to join their family in the quiet nest of Eastwood.

In the mornings the ladies followed their routine, which involved their work on the 4th of July party. RSVPs were pouring in and plans were falling into place to help cover every detail.

One afternoon, Rose wandered from the house with a book in her hands. That morning had been busy as duties related to the 4th of July party heated up. The Colonel kept glaring at her. Rose knew that he was looking for a time to speak to her about Henry's schooling and she was avoiding him. She also felt the need to spend a little time alone, away from so many Brewsters. A group of young men and ladies played on the tennis courts while the other children frolicked on the side lawn. Amelia accompanied Mr. Martini as he tended her rose garden and the great aunts napped in their rooms. Alice and Matilda continued to sort through the RSVPs and created ribbon rosettes for decorations. At this point Rose slipped out of the house quietly.

Rose skirted the greenhouses and followed the narrow path that ran along the edge of the pond. With bushes on one side and the pond on the other, Eastwood was hidden from view and the sound coming from the tennis courts was dampened. At this distance from the house, a quiet afternoon peace lay over Eaton Pond except for the soft sound of bees in the blossoms. Even the men stopped working in the fields and had gone in for their midday dinner.

Rose parted the bushes, found a favorite shaded cove on the water's edge and settled herself into a comfortable nook. The day was warm for June and she unbuttoned the top buttons of her high necked blouse and pulled up her skirt and petticoats to allow for the slight breeze to cool her. Rose was deep into Shakespeare's Romeo and Juliet. A lock came undone from her hairdo, she absently pulled on it and wrapped it around her fingers while she read. As the play came to its dramatic conclusion, tears ran down her cheeks. Rose shut the book, clasping it to her breast and allowed the tears to flow.

To love with such abandon! Rose knew that she had never felt the emotions that these two young lovers had felt. Once again, that disquieting feeling that she had harbored in her heart all summer stirred. There had to be something more to her life, Rose thought. Something or was it someone?

Her tears abated and she wiped her eyes and blew her nose with her lace handkerchief. Rose stood and walked to the water's edge to dampen her handkerchief in the lake so she could wash off her tear stained face. The cool water felt delicious on her hot cheeks and she reached to rewet her handkerchief and lathe her neck and decollete as well. Rose hunkered down, her skirts pulled clear of the muck on the water's edge when she heard a ripple in the water. Startled, Rose looked up to see a small row boat rocking in the ripples of the small cove, fairly close to shore. A man sat in the boat, resting his arms on his shipped oars, a look of concern was on his face. Rose had the feeling that he had been watching her for some time. His broad shoulders were powerfully built and he wore a leather vest without a coat and his white shirt was open at the neck. Around his bare neck he had knotted a red kerchief, and a straw hat shaded his face from the sun. His skin was deeply tanned and a lock of his dark brown hair fell on his forehead.

Rose became aware that her skirts were hiked up and her blouse was open. Hastily she stood up and gave her skirts a shake. Flustered she looked around to flee, but his boat did not come any closer. Frozen, they stared at each other for a full minute. The man gave her a small wave and a nod, and then pulling powerfully on the oars, continued beyond the cove and on up the pond. Long after he left, Rose continued to stare after him with a small frown.

Rose returned to the house and slipped into the kitchen. She nodded to Tilly who was washing dishes and went up the back stairs to her room to repair her hair and change into a clean dress before joining the family on the front verandah. Once in her bedroom, she paused and looked out her window at the tennis courts. She saw a cluster of young people and a rather intense tennis match taking place involving mixed doubles.

Going down the wide front stairs, her hair and dress neat and tidy, Rose passed through the open double front doors onto the verandah. Amelia had a small table set up and was creating a flower arrangement from the roses chosen earlier and the great aunts, awake from their afternoon nap, worked on their interminable tatting. Rose poured herself a restoring glass of tea and sat down to watch Amelia work magic with the beautiful blooms.

The tennis match finished and the group came up on the side porch for a light refreshment. Rose and Amelia watched their bright eager faces and listened to their laughter and conversation. Amelia looked over the group recognizing the grandchildren of many of her friends, but she became aware of Lavinia talking earnestly with a young man who she did not recognize. Lavinia's eyes shone brightly and she talked animatedly as she rested her hand on his arm. He was an attractive young man with sweat glistening on his brow. He looked to be the age of Warner Covington and Adam Brown, but Amelia was sure that she did not know him. As the group finished their refreshments, they moved off the porch and back towards the tennis courts.

"Rose," Amelia asked quietly watching Lavinia and the young man walk side by side out of view, "who is that young man?"

Mystified, Rose shook her head. "I don't think I have ever met him in Boston before," she told her mother-in-law. "He must be staying with someone here at Eaton Pond."

Both Rose and Amelia had a second look at this mysterious young man later in the evening as the tennis party joined them for dinner. Lavinia very prettily introduced him to her grandparents and mother as Collin Underhill. Amelia looked Collin over rather carefully with a small frown. So, this was the young man whose family purchased Summerfield.

Collin easily answered the Colonel's questions regarding the remodeling of Summerfield and his schooling. He had a deep quiet voice that was pleasant to the ears and he presented deferential manners to Amelia's conversation.

Amelia tried to remember what had been said, something about him being at Ashcroft Academy with Adam Brown. Looking at him Amelia nodded her approval of his manners and felt he was as acceptable as any of the other men, but there was something more wide awake about him than the other boys. Amelia's sharp eyes watched Lavinia's wide-eyed smile and attention to this young man, although she certainly smiled just as invitingly at Adam Brown when he suggested they play a duet on the piano after dinner.

After dinner the young ladies and men retired to the drawing room and soon the tinkling of the piano and the sound of singing could be heard. The latest music craze was for a brighter, lighter kind of music. Sentimental ballads sung by young men in harmony to bright eyed girls brought gales of laughter and talk in the parlor. Matilda and Alice sat in the smaller morning room with Rose and Amelia listening to the sound of the chatter, music and laughter across the hall. The Colonel retired to his study, his door open and the smell of pipe smoke drifted from his room.

Warner Covington, Adam Brown and Collin Underhill stood on the driveway in the moon light. Singing "I Dream of Jeannie With the Light Brown Hair," in three part harmony they serenaded Susanna and Lavinia as they drove away with Liddy Maxwell and Jenny Snow, two young ladies who were staying for the summer at Eaton's Pond. The buggy wheels crunched on the driveway and Susanna and Lavinia entered the house, turned down the gaslights and retired for the night.

Up in their bedroom, dressed in high necked, long sleeved white batiste nightdresses, Susanna and Lavinia lay side by side in their bed whispering and giggling. "Vinnie," Susanna asked her cousin, "are you sweet on Collin Underhill?"

Lavinia lay on her back staring at the ceiling. Her fingers played with her loosened brown hair. "No," Vinnie said finally, 'I mean Collin is the most exciting man I have ever met. There is something about him, but," she paused and was honest, "I don't think he is, you know, the one. Besides," she yawned, "Grandmother would have a fit if I did not follow in your footsteps and find someone to marry who was impeccably suitable."

"Alexander has not proposed yet," Susanna reminded her cousin.

"But he will," Lavinia assured her cousin. "You know he is just waiting for the right time. And when Alexander is here at Eastwood with his parents... oh Susanna, I just can't see how he won't ask you!" Lavinia reached over and squeezed her cousin in the dark.

Susanna, her eyes bright in the moonlight, said, "I wonder how he will do it. I mean, there are so many romantic places here at Eastwood that would be perfect for a proposal."

Lavinia agreed and said, "I think Grandmother's Italian Walled Garden would be so romantic in the moonlight. Of course, out on the pond in a canoe. And then you are going to become Mrs. Alexander Peabody."

Susanna sighed a delicious gasp of anticipation and was quiet with her thoughts.

Lavinia, still wide awake, turned to her side and spoke to her cousin, "Susanna, Liddy Maxwell told me that when you go to college there are three men for every girl. College men are so sophisticated." Lavinia finished with a sigh, "College men like Brooks Carter."

Susanna, who would never attend college, instead choosing to do her parent's bidding and attended Madam Lavalie's Young Ladies Finishing School for one year, shrugged, "Alexander says it doesn't do for a lady to have too much schooling." Susanna turned the subject back to Lavinia's last statement, "Are you sweet on Brooks?"

In the dark, Lavinia rolled her eyes. "Oh, well," she said, slightly nettled, "I am sure I shall find a man at college who wants a woman to be educated. Brooks is just so sophisticated, and I like his blue eyes. His papa has promised him one of those new horseless carriages when he graduates."

The talk swirled around Brooks and the newfangled horseless carriages then drowsily started to pause as Susanna drifted off.

Her thoughts on something else, Lavinia turned on her side and said softly, "Susanna?"

"Um mmm," Susanna answered, her thoughts on Alexander and dreams.

"Do you," in the dark Vinnie blushed, "do you think when you and Alexander get married you are going to do what your mama talked about last winter?" They had both had the talk with their mothers, and had a few vague discussions about it.

"Vinnie!" Susanna exclaimed, blushing and suddenly wide awake, "I will be a married woman and mama says it is a wife's duty. You know that is how babies are made, so I guess we will have to do it to make a baby." She felt so embarrassed. "But Vinnie," she assured her cousin, "Alexander respects me. He won't make me do it too often."

Under the cover of darkness, Vinnie became a little more bold, "Susanna, I mean, you might see his, his, um, you know!" She was red hot with embarrassment, but struggled on, "And he might see you, you know, without your clothes."

"Vinnie!" Susanna turned her back on Lavinia and pulled her covers up over her hunched shoulders. "That is why we have night dresses. You are being vulgar. I don't want to talk about this any more," she said shortly.

Lavinia subsided, but Susanna lay there in bed, now fully awake. She did not understand how it all worked; it sounded horribly embarrassing and awkward. Susanna thought about Alexander's kisses; they were wonderfully warm and his moustache tickled her a little when they kissed. One night last winter, as they sat alone in front of the fire in her parent's parlor, his kiss became a little deeper and Susanna returned his kiss happily. She felt a funny sensation deep inside of her and when he reached up and touched her breast, she had jumped at the warm sensation but had not broken the kiss.

The amazing tingle Susanna felt when his warm hand gently squeezed her breast through her blouse had brought a small gasp to her lips and when her pink rosebud mouth had opened, Alexander had flicked his tongue inside her mouth. This motion had the effect of pouring cold water on her and she broke off the kiss and looked at him as if he were deranged.

Since then there had been other evenings and other kisses. Alexander slowly warmed Susanna to the idea of his tongue in her mouth, but Susanna did not enjoy it as much. She did enjoy Alexander's nibbles on her ears and neck, which caused shivers to race down her spine and gasps from her lips. Susanna loved Alexander's long deep kisses, and some wanton part of her had come to enjoy the feel of his hand on her breast.

But, from there? Susanna had some concerns about her wedding night and how they were going to move from kisses to other things. Susanna idly thought about Warner Covington. She had known Warner since they were babies and when she was 13 they had shared their very first kiss on the back steps of Eastwood on a dare. They both found it rather icky and it only lasted for a brief second. The elder Brewsters had always thought Warner would make an acceptable husband for one of their granddaughters, and only the sublime perfection of Alexander Peabody (due to birth and position) had mollified them.

Tonight Warner looked at her with a warm smile and, without thinking, Susanna threw back a flirtatious smile. Susanna sternly reminded herself she was a woman about to be engaged to Alexander Peabody, the Senator's son, but she felt her heart beat a little faster at Warner's attention. Alexander and his parents would arrive soon and she must not think about Warner's smiles.

With a deep sigh, Susanna joined the slumbering Vinnie in sleep.

CHAPTER 5

Thursday night the entire Brewster clan drove into Eaton's Grove for a band concert in the park. Everyone attended except Charles and Christopher who were still in town working. Emily Harlow Brewster and her children joined the group, along with her parents.

The band stand, painted pristine white, was a pretty affair in the shape of an octagon. Each of its eight sides contained gleaming white arched fretwork and in the center of each arch hung a basket of brightly colored flowers. The band was a collection of local farmers who enjoyed playing music. The space around the band stand opened to green lawns on three sides, with the fourth side backed by a wooded area of the park. The shady park was filled with many paths to meander and benches were placed invitingly in quiet corners. Young lovers often found their way to a bench and to enjoy their solitude until discovered by parents or chaperones.

Wooden folding chairs and blankets were set up on three sides of the band stand and families and couples brought picnic dinners to eat while listening to the music. After finishing dinner, a group of old soldiers gathered their chairs around the Colonel's and, while tapping their toes to the marching music of John Phillips Soussa, they relived the battles of the War Between the States and discussed Mr. Roosevelt's escapades on San Juan Hill.

Torie and Edmund sat side by side on a red plaid blanket, not far from the Colonel, listening to the reminisces of the old soldiers' glorious past, and of battles fought and won. Torie had a far away light in her eyes as she listened, enthralled with her grandfather's words. Myles and Cooper, Matilda's twins, sat in chairs on either side of their grandfather and occasionally asked a pertinent question, answered with enthusiasm. Edmund, growing restive, tried to coax Torie to come away and join some other children in play; she refused to budge. Eventually, Edmund left Torie to the blanket and wandered off to join some friends playing baseball.

This evening Lavinia Brewster felt in fine form. The music caused her little foot to beat to the music. She wore a moss green gingham checked skirt that had arrived that afternoon from her mother's dress maker and her new white blouse had tucks and puffed elbow sleeves and a high lace collar. Lavinia's 3/4 bell sleeved jacket matched the exact shade of the green in her skirt and when Collin Underhill told her that she looked like a wood sprite, Lavinia smiled at him with an inviting light in her eyes. Collin did a double take and smiled broadly back at Lavinia.

Brooks Carter, sharing the blanket with Lavinia, was deep in conversation with Becky Parker. Lavinia looked from Brooks' inattentive face into Collin's appreciative eyes and asked, "Are you going to the Campbell's hay ride next week? A bunch of us are thinking about organizing a party and we will all ride over together."

"I will be there, Miss Lavinia," Collin promised her with a warm smile. "Especially knowing that you will be there, I wouldn't miss it."

Vinnie reached down and picked up a red ripe strawberry out of her picnic basket. "Hay rides are always fun," she assured him. "You just sink down in the warm hay and Warner will bring his banjo and we sing and there is always moonlight and the stars." As she spoke, she bit into the strawberry. A small red drop of juice clung to her full bottom lip.

"Riding under the moon light and the stars with you, Miss Lavinia, would give me great pleasure," Collin told her, as he reached out with his thumb and wiped away the juice from her lips, his warm hand lingered against her jaw line. He continued, "I hope I can be your partner for the evening."

Under Collin's hand, Lavinia's pulse beat fast against his finger. Mesmerized, Vinnie stopped chewing and looked up breathlessly into Collin's deep brown eyes. "Would you care for a stroll?" Collin asked her quietly, standing up and offering her his hand. Vinnie, sitting on the blanket, looked up from his hand to his eyes. After a quick darting look to see if her mother was paying attention, Lavinia smiled and placed her small hand in Collin's and allowed him to pull her to her feet and escort her towards the woodsy shadows of the park.

Collin and Lavinia chatted and laughed as they strolled along the leafy walkway, catching glimpses of other couples and small children dashing down the trails playing hide and seek.

Around a corner, poorly concealed from all eyes, Lavinia saw Molly O'Malley, Aunt Alice's nanny, laughing with Robby Jones, the stable man. Robby had his hands around Molly's waist as she smiled up at him. Molly wrapped her own hands around his neck.

Lavinia turned hastily away from Molly's display and looked at Collin. Lavnia felt all atremble and she returned Collin's reassuring smile as they headed deeper into the wooded park.

Rose sat with her relatives, enjoying the music and watching her various children and nieces and nephews at play. Some of the young adults danced on one side of the bandstand and she and Alice watched with some interest as Susanna danced with Warner Covington. Susanna was filled with laughter as she looked up into Warner's smiling face. Kitty danced with Henry as they carried on a deep conversation. Damarus and Dorcas, Christopher and Emily's 10 year old twins, spun around and around and laughed. Little Abigail and Sarah watched the dancers and hopping up and down, crumbled cookies grasped in their grubby little hands. Jonathan, Christopher's youngest, sat in the dust with some other children trying to catch doodle bugs.

Rose turned to Aunt Easter to answer a question, when she heard her name called. Looking up, Rose saw Samuel Gardner. Sam was a portly gentleman with a balding head and a tendency to perspire. His tailored garments always looked a little snug on him and, since his wife died the previous winter, occasionally in need of some mending.

Rose went to school with Roxanne Gardner and always secretly wondered what the lovely Roxanne found of interest in Samuel Gardner. Bluff, loud Sam always seemed to be looking over Roxanne's shoulder at other women when they were together. Roxanne died shortly after the new year from complications of a miscarriage. The Gardners had produced three very lively boys who had a reputation among the younger children for being overly aggressive at games. Giles, the oldest son, was Edmund's age and attended Slater, too. At Slater Giles had a reputation for a certain degree of brutality.

Rose greeted Sam cordially, but she did not linger over their conversation. Rose, aware of the gossip that Sam sought a new wife and mother, did not want to become part of the gossip. As chairs on either side of Rose were occupied, Sam stood awkwardly over the ladies as he attempted to engage Rose in active conversation. Rose, feeling slightly trapped, turned as Abigail came wailing to her mother with a small trickle of blood oozing down her leg. Abigail climbed into her mother's lap and sat sobbing, while Alice staunched the small flow with her handkerchief. Rose, sitting next to Alice, gave Sam Gardner a nod of dismissal as she helped tend to the sad little girl.

Sam Gardner wandered away but continued to watch Rose help Alice with the little girl. Sam sighed in frustration. The Gardner name was every bit as old as the Brewster's. Both families could be traced back to the Mayflower and each set up their own commerce in Boston in the 1600s. Certainly, Gardners had been as prosperous until Sam's father, Fuller, took over the family business and married Belinda Davies from Savannah, Georgia, in 1850. When the War Between the States broke out, Belinda encouraged Fuller Gardner to invest in her Southern relatives' business dealings which practically bankrupted the family. Sam, marrying Roxanne Snow, helped refill the family coffers, but Samuel and Fuller had an unfortunate predilection for gambling and Sam horrifyingly ran through much of Roxanne's fortune. Sam was not on good terms with his wife's family and could not look that direction for loans, so Sam desperately sought fresh funds. Rose Brewster filled his need, due to the fortune she had inherited from her parents, plus William's trust. Sam also found Rose beautiful, with her smooth white skin, shining hair and her quiet contained looks. Sam could never be quite sure what Rose thought when he observed her. Rose had always been cordial to Sam, but never encouraging. Even when Sam married Roxanne he always found himself looking at Rose, with her regal bearing and slim waist.

Sam had known William since they were boys and had always found William to be soft, even as a soldier. William and Sam were at Slater together, along with Peregrine Fitch, and Sam had loathed William. Sam, along with most of the men he knew, squired Rose to dances and other social pursuits and had been quite surprised when the engagement of William and Rose had been announced. At the end of the day Sam offered for Roxanne instead.

The evening sky darkened and Alice and Amelia made the decision to round up their party and head home. Alice's nanny, Molly, was no where in sight, so Rose offered to look for Molly and to gather the Brewsters. Rose stood and shook out her skirts, then moved to the side of the bandstand to the dancing couples. As she walked she called to Edmund and Torie to finish up their game of tag and to Susanna who now danced with Brooks Carter.

Rose headed down the path into the wooded park looking for Molly. She walked along in the growing dusk and peered into dark corners at couples and other children. She came around a particularly dark corner and two things happened at the same time. She bumped into a hard masculine body and almost lost her balance and at the very same moment, she saw her daughter, Lavinia, locked in an embrace with a boy, Collin Underhill.

Confused and startled, Rose felt strong arms come around her to steady her balance. Rose pulled herself away from the man with a jerk and stared at her daughter, horrified. Rose said in shocked tones, "Lavinia!" at the same time the man said, "Collin!" Lavinia and Collin swiftly stepped away from each other and stared aghast at the adults. A swear word slipped from Collin's mouth as he realized who discovered them and Lavinia hung her head, wringing her hands together.

"Collin!" the man said again. "Apologize at once for your language." He then turned to Rose. "I assume," he said speaking to her, "this is your daughter?"

Collin murmured an apology to the general air with a strange look on his face. It was obvious that he had never been in this situation before.

Rose did not answer the man, but stared at her daughter with a shocked face. Nothing in all of her 35 years prepared Rose Brewster for this embarrassing situation. Rose attempted to pull her ragged dignity around her. "Lavinia," the first thing she could think to say, "what would your grandmother say?"

Lavinia raised her head and gave her mother a small look, half defiant, half embarrassed. Lavinia raised her hands in a small flutter and a ghost of a shrug raised her shoulders.

Angry, Rose turned to Collin, "What were you thinking, young man?" She scolded, "Kissing my daughter!"

"Excuse me, Mrs. Brewster," the man beside her spoke, "but I think your daughter was kissing my son."

Astonished, Rose turned to look at him for the first time, surprised he knew her name. She was momentarily silenced as she recognized him as the man who had watched her from the row boat the afternoon she had been reading in the cove.

Rose recovered from her shock and said, emphatically, "My daughter would never kiss a boy in such a public place. You are mistaken; your son was kissing my daughter."

"Well," he said, with a glimmer of a grin, "shall we just say they were kissing each other?"

Rose glared at him as she turned back to Lavinia and Collin. "I have no words for the impropriety of this, this, this situation. This is not the proper behavior of young ladies or gentlemen. What were you thinking?" she asked, pinning Collin with a piercing look.

Beside her Collin's father made a movement and she looked up at him and saw the small grin had turned into a broader smile. "I think," he said, with laughter in his voice. "that you are making too much of an innocent kiss."

"Innocent?" Rose repudiated. "You are condoning this behavior? You find this situation amusing?" She opened her mouth to say more and stopped. Her mouth opened and closed as she looked from him to the young man and her daughter; words failed her.

Collin's father said quietly, but with a smothered laugh in his voice, "I am not condoning this behavior, but when a pretty girl smiles so invitingly at a boy, about what else are they both thinking? And they weren't doing anything all that improper."

Rose said, furiously, "I will decide what is proper or improper for my daughter, thank you. My daughter was not encouraging your son. She was brought up with higher moral standards." Rose was flustered and thoroughly uncomfortable. She turned to Lavinia and ordered, "To the carriage, young lady." Lavinia opened her mouth and her mother said, "Now," in tones that brooked no argument. Rose turned to the two men, and in a very cold tone she said, "Good night." Turning, she swept down the path with a chastened Lavinia following.

The two men stood and watched Rose and Lavinia sweep down the path, both slender and pretty, Rose's head held very erect, Lavinia's sunk between her shoulders.

Just before they reached the entrance to the square, Rose turned and laid her hand on her daughter's arm. Rose's face was very stern as she spoke to Lavinia in quiet undertones, "We will not discuss this at this time, young lady. Not one word in the carriage on the way home, unless you want the lecture of a lifetime from your grandmother. And I am in no mood to listen to your grandmother tonight going on and on about impropriety of young ladies or my lack of chaperonage."

Lavinia readily agreed, nodding her head up and down rapidly, relieved her grandmother would not be told. Rose and Lavinia entered one of the waiting carriages that Amelia was not riding in and sat side by side silently in the carriage. Tabitha, sitting on the other side of Vinnie, gently patted her arm. Torie, sitting across from her mother and sister, darted a funny look at her mother and sister but did not say anything.

Charles poked his head in the carriage and asked Rose, "Did you find Molly?"

Rose, having forgotten all about the missing Molly, silently shook her head. In the search for Molly, Lavinia and Rose's silence was overlooked by the rest of the party. Eventually, the Brewsters gave up on the missing nanny and returned to Eastwood without her.

Once home, the family wearily scattered to their bedrooms. The children climbed to the third floor, excited but tiredly chattering about their evening. Alice went upstairs to help Phoebe get the little twins in bed and explain about the missing Molly; Rose went immediately to her room after saying a quiet good night to Amelia and the Colonel. Amelia's sharp eyes noticed Rose's set face, but she did not say anything. In her bedroom, Rose changed into her night clothes and angrily pulled pins from her hair when there was a tap on the door.

Lavinia poked her head around the door, and entered at Rose's short command. Lavinia closed the door carefully, leaned against it and turned to her mother. "Mama," she said, with a defiant tilt to her chin, "it was just a kiss."

Rose turned from her dressing table and flung her hair pins down, and exclaimed, "Just a kiss!" She looked at her daughter, her voice lower, "Lavinia Brewster, you were brought up to be a proper young lady and proper young ladies do not go off to dark corners in parks with young hooligans. What if your grandmother would have caught you?"

Lavinia blanched at the thought of her grandmother and then shook her head and said in a calm voice, "First of all, Collin Underhill is not a hooligan. Second of all, do you really think he is the first boy I have kissed?"

With this announcement, Rose's mouth dropped open and she looked at her daughter like she had never seen her before.

At Rose's continued silence, Lavinia went on determinedly, "Mama, in a few months we are going to be in a whole new century. Times are changing and most girls my age have kissed a few boys. It isn't like the olden days when you were young."

Rose looked at her daughter in amazement. "A few boys?" she echoed, her voice rising.

Lavinia shrugged. "You know, at parties and things. It's just fun, and the boys expect it." A small smile crossed Lavinia's face as she admitted to her mother with a twinkle in her eye, "I like it."

Rose looked at her daughter, thoroughly shocked. "Whether it is the olden days or new," she said slowly, in an even voice, "kissing a boy in the park or 'in fun' is a good way to ruin your reputation. And, Lavinia, you do not want to be known as a wanton girl."

"Wanton?" Lavinia exclaimed. "Oh Mama! No boy is going to think I am a bad girl because I share a few kisses. Susanna and Alexander kiss all the time."

"That is different. Susanna and Alexander will soon be engaged," Rose quietly said, trying to choose the right words. Rose looked at her beautiful daughter, and realized how innocent Lavinia was, regardless of her words. Rose crossed the room and took her daughter by the shoulders and pulled her down beside her onto the bed. "Lavinia, listen to me. Young men will say one thing, but they will always be after taking liberties." Lavinia started to interrupt, but Rose went on, "An innocent kiss is one thing. But, you don't know if that Underhill boy won't tell his friends, and, er, elaborate what went on with you."

"Collin wouldn't..." Lavinia started and then a confused look on her face caused her to say, "I don't know what you mean."

Rose struggled with her explanation, and shook her head, "Boys who kiss girls in dark corners sometimes say that girls do other things. Then other boys don't want to marry those girls."

Lavinia looked thoroughly confused. Rose finished with a firm note to her voice, "I need you to remember that you are a Brewster and Brewsters have a certain reputation to uphold. I do not want your name linked with gossip. And," Rose said with strong determination, "I do not want your grandmother to hear about any of this."

Rose took a breath, then said, "I would like to consider this matter closed. I will not speak to your grandmother about this unseemly behavior, but I do not want you to have anything more to do with that Underhill boy." The threat was implied.

"Mama," Lavinia argued, rolling her green eyes. "I see Collin almost every day. How can I not be polite and say hello? Besides, grandmother invited the Underhills to the 4th of July party." Again she insisted, "I think you are being ridiculous and making too much of this. It was just a kiss."

A small frown on her face, Rose asked, "Do you like this boy?"

Lavinia shrugged, "Collin is a lot of fun. I think he is really cute and he is my favorite tennis partner. Back in Boston his father has bought him one of those horseless carriages. Collin has promised me this fall that he will give me a ride in it."

"If his father is of good breeding," and Rose said it in a tone as if she doubted it, "he will keep his son away from you after tonight. He will realize that the Brewsters do not want Collin Underhill at their house uninvited. You may be polite and greet him, but Lavinia, no singling him out. And absolutely no riding in anyone's horseless carriages without my permission," Rose said firmly.

The argument would have continued, if a knock at the door had not interrupted them. Alice came in, a frown on her usually complacent face. "What on earth could have happened to Molly?" She was obviously eager to discuss her missing nanny.

Lavinia, annoyed with her mother's attitude, turned to her Aunt Alice. "Have you checked to see if the stable man is missing?" Both women stared at her. "I saw them in the park," Lavinia said and flung at her mother, "kissing." With that she flounced from her mother's bedroom.

Alice listened to the slam of Lavinia's bedroom door and then turned to look at her sister-in-law, her eye brows raised in question.

Rose shook her head and crossed the room and shut the door. "Alice," she said wearily, "there is a lot to be said to marrying Susanna off at her age. It closes the door on being lectured by your daughter on the new times."

Alice laughed. "What is that supposed to mean?" she asked.

Rose and Alice had few secrets when it came to raising their children. Both devoted mothers, they often consulted each other on child raising issues. Rose knew that Alice would not run off and tell tales to Amelia. "I caught Lavinia and Collin Underhill kissing in the park," she told Alice, a horrified look on her face.

Alice, a little more complacent than Rose, laughed. "Oh, they think that is the new thing that all the young ladies and men are doing these days. Of course, young men and women have always sparked." She sighed with a soft expression on her face. "I remember when Charles and I..." her voice trailed away as she looked at her sister-in-law's slightly embarrassed face. "Well," she finished, "maybe that is one memory I need to keep to myself."

Rose looked at her sister-in-law. "That wasn't the worst part," she said to Alice. Alice raised her eyebrows in question, and Rose continued, "I was looking for Molly and I discovered Lavinia and that young scamp at the same time that I collided with Collin's father. It was most embarrassing."

Alice could not contain herself. She burst out laughing. "Oh, Rose," she gasped, "our children can put us in situations we never dreamed. What did Mr. Underwood say?"

"Well," Rose said, no smile on her face, "he had the audacity to blame Lavinia for kissing his son. He and I had a few choice words, then he began to find it amusing. I have never been so humiliated in my life." Rose looked at her sister-in-law's face as a small smile formed, "Oh Alice, and then I returned home to lecture my daughter and she informed me that this is not the first boy she has kissed and that everyone is doing it."

Alice settled herself next to Rose on the window seat. Rose shook her head and said, "Some days I feel so weary and old and out of date."

Alice agreed sympathetically, "I know. Susanna and Alexander don't think we know what is going on in the parlor in the evenings. That her father and I, well, you know," she said, "ever couldn't keep our hands off of each other. And Susanna has such ideas about how she is going to set up house keeping," Alice said, slightly veering off the subject. "She keeps telling me how she is going to do things versus how I do my housekeeping now. I think she is in for a sad surprise." Alice's eyes twinkled at Rose.

A worried frown crossed Alice's face as she admitted to Rose, "Susanna is young and she seems to be enjoying herself with other young men this summer. I am going to need to have a talk with her about flirting with young men once she is engaged. Of course, Alexander will be here next week and, I certainly hope that he proposes. That should put a stop to all this flirting."

Rose agreed with her, and the two sisters-in-law looked at each other. Rose admitted, "I really do not want to encounter Mr. Underhill at any social functions. I do not know if the man is a gentleman or not, and I don't know what I would say if he brought up this humiliating incident."

Alice said, thinking aloud, "I have met him on a few occasions last spring when he first came to town and I think he will not go around gossiping about this. He is anxious for his son to fit into Boston society and college and I don't think bandying around such behavior would help with the Boston Mamas. And," Alice said pragmatically, "he and Peregrine have gone into business together and they are cobbling some deal together with Charles and Christopher. I would think Mr. Underhill would want to be on his best behavior with all of us."

Rose silently disagreed but she decided to let it pass for now. Alice changed the subject, "What am I going to do about Molly?"

The more comfortable discussion about domestic affairs and speculating over the scandalous behavior of Alice's missing nanny led the women to a good gossip.

Late that night, Molly returned, sneaking up the back stairs only to be met by Mrs. Musgrave, the housekeeper. Molly was slightly inebriated, her hair and clothes mussed. Mrs. Musgrave, knowing when to choose her battles, led tipsy Molly to the maid's dormitory and put her in an empty bed to sleep off her excesses.

The following morning, young Molly stood in Mrs. Musgrave's small sitting room with her head hung low, tears seeping out of her blood-shot eyes; occasionally she sniffled. Molly's head ached dreadfully and her stomach was queasy; she was very afraid of the housekeeper. Mrs. Musgrave sternly faced Molly, while Amelia, Alice and Matilda sat in a semi circle of chairs listening.

"Shameful," Mrs. Musgrave was lecturing. "You left those poor babies alone and Miss Abigail hurt herself. What if she had gotten lost or seriously hurt? And you, I have watched you flirting with that young Mr. Jones ever since you got here. You were not hired to flirt with stable men, Molly O'Malley. You are here to take care of Mrs. Alice's precious babies."

Molly murmured, "Yes'm." Molly's head ached abominably and her stomach was very queasy. Tears oozed out of her eyes.

Mrs. Musgrave was only getting in stride. "A wicked girl, that is what you are," she spit out.

At this Molly raised her head. "I am not a wicked girl!" she exclaimed defiantly. "Robby was a perfect gentleman."

"Perfect gentlemen," intoned Mrs. Musgrave, "do not give ladies drink and make them intoxicated. Molly O'Malley, you are being given one chance. If it were up to me I would dismiss you at once, without references. But," she nodded towards Alice, "Mrs. Brewster needs help with her babies, and she wishes to keep you in her employ."

A small ripple of relief passed over Molly's face, but Mrs. Musgrave's next words caused her to turn red. "But if it turns out you are carrying his brat, you can consider yourself off the property immediately."

Molly raised her head and, hung over or not, she was incensed. Molly took a step closer, her fists clenched at her sides and looked Mrs. Musgrave directly in the eye. "I quit," she spat out. "My cousin, Mary Kathleen, works in one of those shirtwaist factories in New York and she has been after me to come work with her. There a decent girl can work and keep her wages and see men after work without being scolded for being natural. Mary

Kathleen says I can live with her in the city and help with the rent. It must be better than stuck here in the country with all of those children."

Before Mrs. Musgrave could reply, Molly turned to Alice, "I am sorry, Mrs. Brewster. You have been good to me, but those twins wear me out. Up all hours day and night. And nobody talks to me the way she just did," nodding towards Mrs. Musgrave. "Besides," she flung at the group, "maybe you should tell Miss Lavinia about what happens when you kiss men in the park." With that she flounced out of the room, tears pouring down her cheeks.

Mrs. Musgrave, exchanged a look with Amelia, and silently followed Molly from the room to oversee and escort her from the property. The Brewster ladies looked at each other. Amelia saw Alice's face and asked in a very serious tone, "What is she talking about?"

Alice shrugged and admitted, "A small kiss. Rose caught Lavinia with a boy in the park and has lectured her and dealt with it. Not a large matter. I think you should leave the matter alone," she advised her mother-in-law.

Rose and Lavinia, along with Susanna, Torie and Kitty, were already in the morning room working with M. du Gres when Amelia, Alice and Matilda swept in. Amelia apologized to M. du Gres for their tardiness and picked up her book to begin the French. Rose, puzzled by something in Amelia's face, caught Alice's warning glance.

The French lesson ended and M. du Gres exited. Amelia said in a cold voice, "I wish for Rose and Lavinia to stay for a moment." Matilda, ever at her mother's side, stayed in her chair. Alice, with a sympathetic glance at Rose, escorted the other girls from the room and quietly shut the door.

Rose and Lavinia exchanged a guilty look. Amelia launched into an interview with Lavinia over the details. Rose, aghast, wondered how Amelia knew. Rose was certain that Alice had not broken her confidence.

Fifteen minutes later, a chastened Lavinia left the room with tears streaming down her face. Her grandmother had sternly lectured her and Lavinia had not had the temerity to express to her grandmother about a new century, a new generation and her ideas on kissing. Rose remained seated, silent during her mother-in-law's entire lecture. Rose was angry with Amelia over her words and wanted to defend her daughter. Before she could speak, Matilda spoke, "Rose Brewster." Matilda rounded on her sister-in-law. "You are all together too soft with those children. You let them get away with too much. If William were alive..."

As Rose had endured a difficult sleepless night the previous evening reliving the scene in the park, she snapped at Matilda, "If William were alive, what, Matilda? Lavinia would not take a walk with a boy in the park? We are all making mountains out of this. It was a small indiscretion. I dealt with my daughter last night and the matter is closed."

Rose so rarely lost her temper that the two women stared at her.

Matilda drew herself up rigidly and argued, "Torie is constantly in trouble because you allow her too much freedom. She has been expelled from one of the finest schools in Boston. Now Lavinia is acting up. We have all watched her chasing one boy after another. If you don't provide Henry with a military education, who knows where he will end up."

"It was one small kiss," Rose emphasized quietly and struggled with keeping her anger in check. "Matilda, until you have daughters to raise, I suggest you cease with your censorship and allow me to do what is best for William's children. They are my children, too. Matilda, you do not know how many girls your own sons have taken for walks in the park and kissed," Rose pointed out.

Matilda turned red. She opened her mouth to argue when Amelia stepped in. "Matilda and Rose! Enough! At this time I will leave Rose to monitor Lavinia and make sure that she behaves herself properly. Until then, we have a rather large party to see to and Alice is short a nanny."

Rose retreated to the sewing room to work on a pinafore for Torie. Her face burned over Matilda's words. Rose was shocked over her own vehement protest. What was coming over her? Rose always passively allowed Amelia and Matilda to dictate their thoughts about her children without comment. Often she ignored what they had to say. Rose felt a little fire begin to burn deep inside of her. It felt good to stand up to Matilda. Too often her sister-in-law involved herself in Rose's life and Rose was tired of politely accepting Brewster criticism.

The Friday afternoon wore on and the women gathered on the porch with sewing. Alice read aloud to the group. For once, the tennis courts stood empty and no neighbors visited. Eaton's Pond was filled with small sailboats, the full sails catching the wind while laughter could be heard drifting over the water. Myles and Cooper were out with the Brewster sailing boat, and occasionally they skimmed past the landing, their sail full to catch the breeze. Susanna expected Alexander and his parents the following week. She sat in a dreamy reverie, her thoughts circling around her expected engagement and her intended. Lavinia, chastened from her grandmother's lecture, remained quiet that afternoon. She sat at the far end of the verandah, next to the great aunts, reading a novel.

The Colonel came out of his study and joined the ladies on the verandah, Emily came over from Harlow Hall and her children played croquet with their cousins on the wide green lawn. The children came up on the porch for a light snack of lemonade and cookies. The sun was behind the house, leaving the verandah shaded and cool. A contented peaceful feeling permeated the entire group. Torie told her grandfather about the battle that she and Edmund had organized that afternoon when the sound of carriage wheels on the avenue drew everyone's attention.

Charles and Christopher alighted from the carriage after their week in the city. Pandemonium broke out as children, young and old, tumbled down the steps and swarmed across the lawn to their father's waiting arms. Wives followed close behind the children.

As the porch cleared, Rose's three children drew closer to her, the same look of longing on all of their faces. Henry leaned his small body against Rose's leg and Lavinia abandoned her book and crossed the porch to take her mother's hand. It was a Friday afternoon ritual at Eastwood that was always painful to Rose. Her children had no father to greet. Never did her children feel so acutely the lack of a father as the afternoons when their uncles returned from the city.

Amelia and the Colonel also took in the situation. Amelia turned to Lavinia and asked her a question about her ball gown for the 4th of July, while she slipped her arm around the girl's slender waist and gave her a squeeze. The Colonel reached out and pulled Torie to him and said, "Now tell me, Torie," he said, "more about this battle of yours and Edmund's. Do you have the rear flank covered?"

Torie gave one last longing look at the scene on the lawn and turned to her grandfather and answered his question. As she explained, Torie's eyes returned to the families on the lawn. "Don't you think it's a good plan, Grandpapa?" Torie asked, her eyes full of longing, with a small quiver in her voice. "Don't you think it is as good a battle plan as one my father would have organized?"

Torie turned and looked at her grandfather. The two faces close together shared an amazing resemblance. Their dark brown eyes met each other, hers with a pleading look. Her grandfather patted her hand and agreed, "Every bit as good as one of your father's military campaigns."

Great Aunt Easter came out of the darker shadows of the verandah and, sitting beside Henry told him she had a letter from her friend that afternoon and the stamps had come all the way from Egypt. Easter promised Henry that she would give the stamps to him after dinner. Across Henry's head Rose and Easter exchanged warm sympathetic glances.

Charles came up on the porch, Sarah in his arms and Abigail hanging on his leg. Kitty and Edmund were on either side of him and Susanna and Alice, their arms around each other's waists, followed closely behind. Setting Sarah down, Charles kissed his own mother and greeted his father. He also reached out and gently tugged one of Torie's dark curls and let his strong hand rest on Henry's shoulder for a minute as he talked.

Christopher, with Jonathan in his arms, and Damarus and Dorcas holding onto their mother, Emily, also greeted his parents and relatives on the verandah.

Room was made for the men, and new pitchers of lemonade and small nibbles were brought out as they talked of the city gossip and their week at work. The children were dismissed to get ready for their dinner. The small hoard disappeared into the house. Their chatter and footsteps died out as they climbed to the third floor. Christopher assured his wife that he had picked up some important boxes from the dress makers.

Charles turned to Rose and told her, "We rode out on the train with Peregrine Fitch. He will be staying at Briar Hill for the month of July with the Browns. I am sure he will be by at some point to pay his respects and catch up on how you all are doing."

Peregrine Fitch had been one of William Brewster's oldest friends. William and Peregrine had known each other since early childhood and attended Slater together. After Slater, Peregrine had not pursued a military career, but went to Harvard and into business with his father upon graduation. William and Peregrine stayed friends all the years until William's death.

After William's death, Peregrine had been a strong support for Rose. Peregrine, as not many in Boston did, knew the details of William's will and had never overstepped the bounds of propriety with Rose. In Boston, Peregrine often escorted Rose to various social events. At balls, he always danced properly two dances with her, and he would also drop by for an evening to talk with her and the children when they were at home.

Rose and William's children looked upon Peregrine as a very special uncle and he doted upon them. On the night of Lavinia's debutante ball it was his honor to partner Lavinia for the father-daughter dance. Peregrine was never too busy to stop and listen to the details of Henry's latest novel he was reading. Torie, because he had known her father, would talk to him for hours about her father's military honors. To Torie, he listened politely, but never with much enthusiasm for her zest for all things military. Peregrine had a fond tolerance for Torie's other escapades and would sympathetically listen to her as she poured out her troubles into his ear.

Rose found Peregrine a comfortable friend and confidante. As she sat across the hearth from him on a cool winter evening, the fire crackling and mending in her lap, she had a very contented, domestic feeling. Peregrine listened to Rose's small challenges over her daily domestic issues and laughed with her over the pursuits of her children. Rose appreciated that Peregrine, who had loved William, tried to fill the role of William in some small way with William's children.

Sometimes, when dancing with Peregrine, Rose would look up into his handsome face and wonder why she had never fallen in love with him, or he with her. Tall, dark haired and slender, Peregrine Fitch was the object of much interest from Boston Mamas who would like to marry their daughters to the Fitch fortune. Handsome Peregrine was the eternal bachelor, always willing to squire one young lady or another. He filled that most appreciated role of the extra man at dinner parties, but Peregrine had gracefully side stepped marriage or entanglements with over eager young ladies.

In Rose, Peregrine found the perfect companion. Peregrine could always count on Rose to be at his side, but never demand love or marriage. Boston closely watched for years their friendship but never found any reason to gossip or censure. Rose always found Peregrine to be a comfortable escort, and it was to him that she spoke of her children and her determination to follow William's wishes to have Henry educated away from the military. Peregrine, who had not enjoyed Slater any more than William, fervently supported Rose in her skirmishes with the Brewsters. Peregrine, aware of Henry's interest in ancient civilizations, would bring the boy new books or would take him for an afternoon to the museum to see new exhibits.

Back on the verandah at Eastwood, the afternoon light had fled. Christopher and Emily scooped up their children and headed back to Harlow Hall for dinner. From the back of the house, the sounds of fine china and silver being set out on the table could be heard and the delicious smells of roast chicken and other dinner delights wafted through the house.

The adults lingered on the porch, enjoying the cooler evening air and comfortable chairs. Charles continued to tell his father about some business deal when Rose heard the name Marcus Underhill.

Rose displayed her usual contained self as the conversation dipped and wheeled around her, but at Charles' remark Rose turned to him and asked, "Marcus Underhill? The man who took on Summerfield?"

Charles nodded, "Yes, and Underhill is shopping for a home in Boston as well. He has sold his company in the West and has set up a partnership with Peregrine. A very shrewd business man. I am looking forward to working on a business venture with him that we are setting up. Have you met him?"

Rose gave a small shrug, and said shortly, "The other night at the band concert. Briefly, in the park." Her eyes darted to Lavinia, who had missed the entire conversation as she was in deep discussion with Cooper about a planned outing. "His son has been here quite a bit with the cousins," she finished.

Rose took in this information silently, her head turned to the pond and the gathering gloom. Inside, she was agitated. Quite often, men who had business dealings with the Brewsters would stay for supper, which meant she could find herself with Marcus Underhill sitting at the same dining table. Rose truly hoped to never see the man again.

CHAPTER 6

As the 4th of July got closer, Eastwood became a hive of activity. The many plans were finalized, checked and rechecked. Guest bedrooms were aired, windows washed and the last of the RSVPs were received. In the stuffy sewing room on the third floor the little peddle machine clacked on for hours as finishing touches were made to tablecloths and new dresses. Downstairs, furniture was rearranged and rustic tables and benches were set up on the wide lawns under the shade of trees. In the basement, the ballroom floors shone with fresh polish on the parquet wood floors and the crystal chandeliers sparkled with freshly cleaned brilliance. The crystal and brass wall sconces were washed, polished and fitted with creamy white beeswax candles. Heavy potted plants and a small gold fish pond were wrestled in by sweaty workmen and placed exactly where Amelia felt they would create the most inviting and refreshing corners. Delicate gold and white chaperone chairs were placed along the walls and a small windowless room on one side of the ballroom was set up with card tables and a bar for the gentlemen. The French doors leading out to the lower terrace were opened and fresh air filled the spacious room, as stray breezes caused the great chandelier to tinkle gently. In the garden, Amelia's roses were in full bloom; every shrub and brightly flowering plant in her gardens were trimmed and cut to the peak of perfection. Hanging baskets with trailing flowers in red, white and blue were hung in the arches on the verandah.

On the second of July, Alexander Peabody arrived from Boston along with his parents, Senator and Mrs. Peabody. The entire family and household staff turned out to formally welcome such an august personage as the senator and his family. Susanna greeted Alexander with a gentle embrace and a kiss on the cheek. Alexander was tall, blonde and good looking in a slightly chinless way and, he too kissed Susanna gently on the cheek before turning to greet her parents and grandparents.

Amelia took great pains to ensure that the Peabodys were impressed with the Brewster summer home and she, Mrs. Musgrave and Mrs. Pratt had spent hours going over the details of the guest bedroom and every dish for every meal. The Peabodys, for all of their grandeur, were pleasant and appreciative. They were most anxious for Alexander to make Susanna his wife and showed nothing but warmth to the Brewsters.

The first night of their visit, Mrs. Pratt the cook outdid herself at dinner with a variety of dishes and fresh produce from the Eastwood gardens. Conversation was lively and the talk centered around the current president and his policies. Dinner ended and as the ladies started to leave the gentlemen to their port and cigars, Alexander pulled Susanna's chair away from the table and asked if she would like to accompany him on a canoe ride. Susanna's blue eyes shone brightly, but her mouth went suddenly dry and her hands grew cold as she stared up at Alexander. Conversation in the room dwindled as every eye in the room focused on the young couple. Alice broke the spell by gently suggesting that her daughter take a shawl as the air coming off the lake could be cool. Alexander helped Susanna drape the shawl over her shoulders and taking her by the hand they left to make their way to the boat landing and the canoe. All eyes watched them leave the dining room and Lavinia suddenly felt warm moisture in her eyes as she watched her cousin leave. Lavinia was seated next to her Aunt Alice and Lavinia reached out to clutch her aunt's hand and smiled warmly at her. Alice returned the smile and Lavinia saw that her aunt had tears in her eyes as well.

Silently, the young couple crossed the lawn. Alexander seated Susanna carefully in the canoe. They slid away from the landing as the grand old house dwindled away in the dusk. Susanna settled herself in the canoe and faced Alexander as they made their way out into the lake; Alexander smiled reassuringly at Susanna, but she ducked her head, suddenly shy. Susanna raised her head and looked around the countryside they passed, breathing in the warm night air scented with the earthy smell of the pond as well as the scent of fresh cut hay coming from the fields. A full moon rose and the silver light trailed across the pond, shimmering on small ripples. Dotted around the lake were large spacious homes, their windows alight with a warm glow, and from lawns and porches voices floated faintly over the water. The sounds of children's laughter could be heard and from inside some house the faint tinkling of a piano wafted its way over the pond. Susanna cocked her head and smiled at Alexander. She hummed along, trying to catch the tune and then broke out into the words. "Just a song at twilight, when the lights are low, And the flick'ring shadows softly," Susanna's voice trailed into humming as she tried to remember the words. She tilted her head to the side and laughed at Alexander and then haltingly finished the refrain, "Still to us at twilight comes Love's old song, comes Love's old sweet song."

Alexander stopped rowing and looked at Susanna in the twilight. In the deepening dusk, her blond curls shimmered in the moonlight and Alexander could see her lustrous eyes sparkling. Susanna turned her head from his intent gaze and reached out to trail her fingers in the water. In the stillness, Alexander leaned forward and captured Susanna's hand. "You are so beautiful," Alexander said very softly, kissing her hand. "Susanna, would you be my bride?"

Susanna looked at Alexander for a brief moment and then burst into tears, almost upsetting the boat as she flung her arms around him. The two young lovers spent another hour floating around Eaton's Pond, cuddling and discussing their future and their love. Eighteen-year-old Susanna, looking into Alexander's handsome face, knew she was doing exactly what she had been trained her whole life to do. Susanna felt that she had been put on the earth for this exact moment, to marry the perfect man. Susanna knew that in her family's eyes, Alexander Peabody was the perfect match. He came from a respectable family; he had fortune and ambition.

The entire clan of Brewsters and Peabodys sat on the verandah waiting in expectation, enjoying the cool evening air when Susanna and Alexander came up from the boat landing hand in hand and announced their news. Alexander had privately asked Charles for permission for Susanna's hand the week before when they had lunched together in Boston, so the expected event came as no surprise. The lack of anticipation created no lesser excitement from the ladies as Susanna passed from mother to grandmother to aunt to cousin. Alexander's hand was shaken by all and his mother kissed him with tears on her cheeks. Susanna ended up seated between her future mother-in-law and her grandmother. Mrs. Caroline Peabody patted Susanna's small hand and beamed at her, telling her that she was looking forward to having such a pretty daughter-in-law to host in Washington.

The 4th of July dawned clear and bright. Colonel Brewster, along with his sons and grandsons, resplendent in their military and cadet uniforms, left for Eaton's Grove to participate in the annual 4th of July Parade. A large contingent of local farmers and land owners, veterans of one war or another, came together for this special day in their various military uniforms to march behind the rousing band. Senator and Mrs. Peabody, as guests of honor, sat next to the mayor on the viewing stand. Torie, Henry and Kitty, along with Damarus and Dorcas stood on the side of the road and whooped and cheered proudly as their male relatives marched by.

At Eastwood, the women had been up early to help with the final preparations. After a hasty lunch, guests began to arrive. Games for the children were organized: potato sack races and three legged races for the youngest children, badminton and croquet for others. At the little station in Eaton's Grove, the noon train arrived and disgorged families coming from Boston to celebrate the birth of the nation and to enjoy the Brewster hospitality at Eastwood. The Brewsters had carriages awaiting to bring their guests to Eastwood but some of the younger visitors chose to cross the bridge and walk the short distance from the village. The carriages and buggies drew up to the front of the house as people disembarked, carrying specially made dishes to add to the meal, and called greetings to friends. The drivers were then directed around the house to the field to settle horses for the day. The carriage drivers and nannies were then free to join in the merriment.

The old grand house stood majestic in fresh whitewash. Red, white and blue bunting was festooned around the railing on the verandah, held up on the posts by enormous rosettes. American flags proudly waved from several flag posts and the flag for the state of Massachusetts hung below the national one on the flag pole in the garden. The wide lawn was dotted with people as friends and family came together and there was much laughter and chatter as old friends and new greeted each other. Blankets and chairs spread across the lawn as groups settled down to enjoy their holiday. Smells from the back of the house and the barbeque area filled the air with delicious cooking meats; broad tables on the verandah were set with salads and side dishes. Back by the kitchen steps, ice cream was slowly churned by the strong arms of the stablemen as they took turns at the long task. Everywhere could be heard a crescendo of laughter and conversation, accentuated by the occasional pop of fire crackers.

Colonel Brewster, fresh from the parade, was in his element as he stood by Amelia and cordially greeted his guests. Today the Colonel was dressed crisply in his military uniform and his medals shone brightly on his proud chest. To the Colonel, the 4th of July represented all that was wonderful and magnificent about his country and all that he stood for as a man of consequence. Here in America, a man could stand up for what he believed in by fighting the enemy and also by having success in commerce, and raising a family he could take pride in. Colonel Brewster stood on the lawn at Eastwood next to his wife and greeted his guests with congenial hospitality. Amelia, at the Colonel's side, was dressed today in a navy blue skirt and a crisp white blouse with a small red bow tied at her neck. Amelia greeted each of her guests with warmth and with a flick of her hand she directed a servant to relieve the guests of their tasty dishes and to set them out on the verandah tables. Amelia would invite her guests to enjoy the food and beverages, to enter the interior of the house if they needed to refresh themselves after their journey or to join in the fun and games on the lawn. For her guests' servants, clutching boxes with ball gowns and evening clothes in their arms, one of Amelia's servants directed them to the back of the house where they would climb the servants' stairs to the bedrooms and hang up the evening clothes for the ball. Once relieved of their burdens, the servants were free to join in the festivities and spend the day gossiping with their friends behind the house, closer to the stables where an area had been set up for their own party.

Susanna, a vision in Madonna blue, with a matching small straw hat perched on blond curls artfully arranged above her face, floated down the verandah steps with her arm securely in the crook of Alexander Peabody's arm. Alexander from time to time covered the small hand resting on his arm with his own hand and gave it a tender pat. Susanna, her cornflower blue eyes filled with excitement and blooming under Alexander's adoring gaze, turned from him to greet friends arriving at Eastwood and to make introductions. It had been decided that their engagement would be formally announced that evening at dinner, so Susanna was not sharing her secret, but old friends who arrived could not mistake the golden glow that enveloped Susanna and Alexander.

Charles and Alice attached themselves to Alexander's parents and made sure such honored guests as the senator and his wife were not left out of introductions or any of the excitement. The Brewsters were acquainted with the Peabodys from years of socializing in Boston. Charles and Alice, along with Susanna's grandparents, had hosted Alexander and his parents for dinner in Boston that spring. Alexander and Susanna strolled hand and hand across the lawn and down to the boat landing to have a small private moment. Several pairs of approving eyes followed them as they made their way through the crowd, greeting friends as they passed. From under the shady chestnut tree Lavinia watched her cousin with her new fiance stroll through the crowd, and Lavinia felt sudden moisture in her eyes. Lavinia turned to her mother, who was standing at her elbow, and sighed, "Oh, Mama, they are so romantic." Lavinia and Susanna had been awake most of the night after Alexander's proposal. The two girls laid in bed happily talking and crying for hours over the excitement of the wedding and Susanna's new life.

Rose watched the young couple and then smiled at her own pretty daughter. Lavinia looked very crisp and cool dressed in a navy blue and white striped dress, her blue sailor collar was trimmed in gleaming white lace. The sun shone on Lavinia's dark hair bringing out red highlights and Lavinia's green eyes smiled back at her mother in warm communication. A look of dismay crossed Lavinia's face as she spied Collin Underhill beyond her mother's shoulder. Since the night at the park, Lavinia had kept her distance from Collin. This was not only because of her mother's and grandmother's scoldings, but also because Lavinia was slightly embarrassed over her own wayward behavior. With a small guilty look at her mother, Lavinia turned and disappeared into the crowd. Rose, frowning, turned to see what had caused the expression on her daughter's face, and came face to face with Collin Underhill and his father, Marcus.

Marcus Underhill was dressed in a light colored linen suit, a dark brown vest showed underneath his open jacket, with his dark silk tie in place under his chin. Rose felt herself flush as she remembered the last time she met Mr. Underhill. Rose looked at

Marcus without meeting his eyes directly and realized that Marcus Underhill was older than she had first thought. Marcus had a boyish look about him, but there were fine lines around his eyes and a small dusting of gray at his temples. Rose judged his age to be mid forties.

"Mrs. Brewster," Collin's father greeted her formally, but with a small twinkle in his amber brown eyes, "I don't believe that we have been formally introduced." There was just the slightest emphasis on the word 'formal'. "My name is Marcus Underhill and I understand you know my son, Collin."

Rose realized that Marcus Underhill knew exactly how uncomfortable she was with the situation and was slightly annoyed. Stung, Rose attempted to pull a mantle of refinement over her discomposure and returned his greeting formally, yet coolly. Rose looked around to find other Brewsters and saw Matilda standing not far away. Her sister-in-law was not necessarily the Brewster Rose would have chosen, but was an ally none the less.

Rose called to Matilda and made the introductions. Matilda, a very formal smile on her lips, welcomed the Underhills in cool tones while her piercing eyes sized up Collin Underhill. Collin, squirming under Matilda's sharp censorious gaze, shook her hand formally, saying the proper words of introduction. Marcus Underhill returned Matilda's gaze affably, a small smile on his lips, unaffected by Matilda's starchiness and slight superiority. Rose silently watched Marcus Underhill speak with Matilda in polite tones as they made small talk. Rose was impressed that Marcus Underhill did not appear discomfited by her sister-in-law's reserve and he spoke knowledgeably about Summerfield in answer to Matilda's questions.

Adam Brown called to Collin to join him on the south lawn for croquet. Collin, shifting from foot to foot under the two Brewster women's unappreciative gaze, happily made his excuses and fled in Adam's wake. Matilda, too, was called away and Rose was left alone with Marcus Underhill.

Rose, casting around for something to say, plastered a rather fake smile upon her face. Bringing out her best company manners, Rose asked Marcus, "So, who do you know here? Let me introduce you to some of the families that stay here on Eaton's Pond for the summer and are here for the party."

"Actually, Mrs. Brewster," Marcus Underhill said, his voice deep and soft, with a trace of Western twang, "through the auspices of Cordelia Brown and Peregrine Fitch I have met quite a few of the families residing around the lake, as well as those who have come from Boston today. I also spent a large part of last winter attending to business in Boston and have had introductions there as well. I have met your brothers-in-law, Christopher and Charles, in the course of doing business, and I expect to soon meet your father-in-law. It is just all the pretty Brewster brides that I have not been introduced to."

At Marcus' words, Rose darted a look at him to see if he was flirting with her. His warm brown eyes twinkled, but his smile was sincere. A lock of dark brown hair fell across Marcus' forehead and something in Rose longed to reach up and smooth it off of his face. Rose, shocked at her thoughts, stayed silent. Rose realized that Marcus Underhill was a very attractive man with his dark good looks and when he smiled, his white teeth flashed. Rose was sure that Marcus Underhill knew exactly how uncomfortable she was feeling, and as she was at a loss for words, she nodded a dismissal to Marcus, turned and walked towards the side lawn. Without asking, Marcus fell into step beside Rose and silently accompanied her until they drew up to watch the croquet game.

Lavinia and Collin partnered up on the croquet lawn and joined a group of young ladies and men with mallets and bright colored balls. Marcus Underhill turned to Rose and said, "Shall we keep an eye on those two? Make sure they don't go wandering off into the bushes?"

Rose, still embarrassed over the scene at the park and uncomfortable with Marcus' continued presence, did not see the humor in his remark and turned to Marcus. She said with some asperity, "Mr. Underhill, despite what you might think, my daughter is not in the habit of wandering off in the bushes with young men. I assure you," she finished with a bite to her voice, "Lavinia is a very well brought up young lady."

Marcus raised his hands and dropping his voice said, "Mrs. Brewster, I apologize. Miss Lavinia has impressed me with her very good manners. I realize in the park that night it was simply a young man and a young woman desiring each other. Perfectly normal."

Rose blushed and turned to stare at Marcus, shocked over his choice of words. Marcus' brown eyes were alight with teasing, but staring up into them, Rose could see no maliciousness. Rose dropped her eyes, struggling to find words to express her embarrassment over his choice of words. Normally poised and cool, Rose felt the desire to reprimand him over his words, but also deep inside her was a small tinge of laughter.

Marcus Underhill looked at the range of emotions crossing her face and understood exactly what Rose felt. Marcus broke the tension by laughing, "Mrs. Brewster, I apologize for my use of language. I was truly trying to put the park incident in a lighter context to make you more comfortable with what happened. Maybe I should have used the word "attracted" to each other. I think you and I both realize it was only an innocent kiss between two young people who are very naturally curious."

At Rose's continued silence, Marcus continued, "I assure you that Collin and I had a very serious discussion about his behavior and what I expect of him in the future with young ladies of good breeding. As parents, we are often confronted with scenes that we never expect to have to deal with. And," he smiled at her, "I think Lavinia and Collin were even more mortified to be discovered by two different parents at the same time. Can you imagine anything worse than being caught in such a situation by your parents?"

Rose looked at him and she could not suppress a smile. "Mr. Underhill, I must agree with you. Vinnie was thoroughly horrified in the park to find her mother suddenly appearing before her," Rose confided, a little more soberly. "Worse for Vinnie was that her grandmother heard of it and Vinnie truly was scolded by her grandmother. After that little interview, Lavinia barely left the verandah for a week."

"That's better," Marcus stated with a broad smile. At her questioning look, Marcus said, "You light up when you smile. It makes you look like Miss Lavinia's sister, rather than her mother."

Rose realized that Marcus Underhill was flirting with her as her green eyes met his warm brown eyes and the smile slid from her face as she saw a sparkle of desire in Marcus Underhill's eyes.

Rose felt a flush creep up her cheeks and was saved by Henry and Torie as they ran up to her. "Mama, come quick," Henry cried, grabbing her hand. His spectacles balanced on the end of his small snub nose and his white socks sagged a bit around his knees. "The boat races are going to start soon and Myles and Cooper promised to let me crew for them and Torie is sailing with Edmund. You must see! Uncle Peregrine is going to take the winners for ice cream in his horseless carriage when we are next in Boston!"

Torie, her little round hat firmly attached under her chin and bright red ribbons streaming down over her fat braid, grabbed her mother's hand and attempted to pull her in the direction of the boat landing. "Oh, Mama, Edmund and I have been practicing coming about for the last month. I just know we are going to beat the big boys!" Torie's eyes were bright with excitement and she jumped up and down as she tugged on her mother's hand.

Rose, relieved at the interruption, turned to her children and scolded them gently, "You are interrupting my conversation. Please say hello to Mr. Underhill. Mr. Underhill, these are my other children, Henry and Victoria."

Impatiently the children made their bows and curtsies, then turned back to their mother. They pulled on her hands and implored her to hurry. As Rose allowed herself to be led away by her children, she looked over her shoulder at Marcus Underhill. Rose shrugged and called a hasty good bye with a small laugh.

Marcus Underhill watched Rose walk towards the landing escorted by her two children. Rose slipped an arm around Torie's shoulder as they walked, and Henry hung on her other hand, his short legs scampering. "Good looking woman," said a voice at Marcus' shoulder. Marcus turned in surprise and found Sam Gardner standing beside him. Marcus and Sam Gardner met over a business deal the past winter along with Peregrine Fitch, and Marcus had sized up Sam Gardner as a desperate man in financial trouble.

Marcus turned from watching Rose walk across the lawn and looked at Sam Gardner. Sam's forehead glistened with sweat and the buttons on his vest gaped between each button hole as his paunch protruded. Sam pulled out a handkerchief and mopped his forehead as he continued to stare after Rose. "Good looking woman," he repeated. Confidentially, he tapped Marcus on the arm, "Mean to make her my wife."

"Oh?" Marcus Underhill said, his face impassive. "Won't her husband have something to say about that?"

"Widow," Sam said succinctly. "I went to school with her husband, William. Queer fellow. Been dead a long time. Time she had a real husband. Plus, William left her well off."

Marcus looked at Sam with some distaste. Marcus did not reply but moved away to greet Christopher Brewster.

The gala afternoon wore on. Torie and Edmund triumphantly swept past their cousins by a nose to win the sailing regatta in their age group. Myles and Cooper allowed Henry to assist and his older cousins praised Henry for his help in coming about, although in his excitement over the race he jerked the rigging a bit and caused them to lose precious time. Collin Underhill and Adam Brown handily beat Brooks Carter and Warner Covington in the two man scull competition. The young ladies stood on the shore and shrieked and cheered the young men as they swept past the landing. Alexander Peabody did not participate in the race but stood by Susanna's side as she waved her kerchief and jumped up and down and called to Warner and Brooks as they pulled strongly on their oars. Alexander looked in surprise at Susanna's enthusiasm. Under a spreading maple tree the Senator and Mrs. Peabody sat at a place of importance next to the Colonel and Amelia. Charles and Alice were seated close by but all eyes were on Susanna and Alexander as the young couple moved through the crowd coming from the beach. Susanna, aglow in Alexander's presence, often reached out and touched his arm. Each time she did, Alexander would turn and smile at her. The parents nodded approvingly at each other, looking forward to their children's marriage.

Rose stepped onto the verandah and out of the hot sun. The littlest twins had crawled under a table and were eating scraps of food that had fallen on the verandah floor. Sarah and Abigail tussled with each other. They had absconded with a mostly empty pie plate and busily stuffed blueberries and crumbs into their little mouths. With the abdication of Nanny Molly, the assumption was that Rose's nanny, Phoebe, could handle the little ones until a new nanny could be found. Rose knew that Phoebe was overtaxed with the charge of so many children, and their mother Alice was busy today hosting the Peabodys. Rose crouched down and coaxed the little girls to come out from under the table.

Sarah and Abigail were dirty and their blonde curls rioted in little halos around their flushed and stained faces. Dressed identically in pink flower sprigged dresses, the twin's white stockings were tinged grey with dirt. Both had crumbs and blueberry stains down the front of the dresses. They had consumed a large quantity of food and sweets and were overdue for a nap. Rose bent down and picked up a wailing Sarah. Rose took Abigail by the hand and started down the steps intending to go to the kitchen entrance at the back of the house. She would take the servants' stairs to the third floor nursery and take care of the little girls herself.

Rose paused and turned when she heard her name called. "Mrs. Brewster." Marcus Underwood once again was in front of her. "Are these also your children?" he asked, a small smile on his face.

Rose turned towards him and said shortly, "Mr. Underwood, these are my nieces, Abigail and Sarah, and they need my attention at the moment. Their mother is short a nanny, and my own nanny is busy, so I am helping out. Excuse me."

Abigail began to whine. "Auntie Rose," she fussed, "pick me up, too."

Distracted, Rose tried to get a better grip on Abigail's hand and reason with the little girl. Marcus Underwood went down on his haunches until he was eye to eye with Abigail. "Hey little Miss," Marcus smiled at Abigail, "it looks like your," he paused, "Auntie Rose has her hands full with your sister. May I carry you?"

Bashfully, Abigail hid her grubby face in her aunt's skirts. Rose, flustered, tried to pry Abigail's grubby fingers from her clean skirt. With a little more coaxing, Marcus convinced Abigail to allow him to pick her up. Marcus swung Abigail high up into his arms and gestured for Rose to precede him.

Momentarily at a loss, Rose looked at Marcus. As Sarah squirmed in her arms, Rose turned down the verandah steps to the back of the house and the kitchen. Rose entered the hot steamy kitchen, a bustling busy place where Mrs. Pratt and her army of helpers were busy cooking, chopping and peeling in preparation for the dinner that evening. Rose wove her way across the kitchen and headed for the servants' stairs, glancing back at Marcus. Several of the servants paused from their chores to look at Rose and Marcus. Rose briefly requested that one of the staff find Phoebe and send her to the nursery.

Rose climbed to the third story, very aware of Marcus Underwood following behind her. Entering the nursery, Rose set Sarah down and went to the washstand. Rose wet a cloth and began to wipe Sarah's grimy face. Sarah, thoroughly tired, resisted the wash cloth. Rose, embarrassed that a strange man was in the nursery with her, gently scolded the little girl. Finished with Sarah, Rose rewet the cloth and turned her attention to Abigail's equally grubby face. Rose untied the ribbon from around Abigail's bounding curls and attempted to pull a brush through the tangled hair.

The sounds of the party on the lawn floated up in the air, but there was also a disconnect between the party and the third floor nursery. The room felt very private, very far away from the excitement down on the lawn and pond.

Rose, still unable to gain her composure, said without looking at Marcus, "Thank you for your assistance, Mr. Underhill. I will stay here with the girls until the nanny arrives."

Marcus strolled to the window and looked out. The main party took place on the west side of the house and the nursery faced east to the woods and the white garden. Over the tops of the trees Marcus had a spectacular view of Summerfield, his own summer home, perched on its knoll and looking down on the lake.

"Mrs. Brewster," Marcus began, twirling his hat in his hands. There was a hesitant tone to his voice. Rose looked up. Marcus had an almost boyish appeal in his eyes as he gazed down into her wary green eyes.

Marcus smiled as he began again, "Mrs. Brewster, can we put aside the transgressions of our children and just get to know each other, as adults?"

Rose frowned but did not answer. Marcus went on, doggedly, "Your daughter is a very well brought up young lady. My son just got carried away being in the company of such a pretty girl. I over reacted when I came across the two of them and in my shock spoke to you harshly." Marcus took off his hat and ran his fingers through his hair, then said, "What I am trying to say is that both Collin and I acted abominably and I would like to put that to right."

Rose silently looked at Marcus Underhill for a long moment. Tentatively she held out her hand. "Mr. Underwood," she said simply, "welcome to Eastwood." Then Rose smiled with relief that he was just as ready as she to put the matter of Lavinia and Collin behind her.

Marcus looked down at her hand and up at her face. He smiled slowly as he took her small hand in his, and said, "How do you do, Mrs. Brewster?"

Rose smiled at him in return and said, "You will find here at Eastwood there are many 'Mrs. Brewsters.' If you want my attention you will need to call me Rose."

"Rose," Marcus said, trying the name out on his tongue. With his slight Western twang, her name sounded differently than in the usual Bostonian tone, but not unpleasant.

Marcus and Rose stared at each other, her hand still resting in his when Nanny Phoebe bustled into the nursery, looking slightly distracted. Phoebe was followed by Kitty, who had torn the hem of her gown and wanted Phoebe to repair it. Kitty, stopped just inside the doorway, took in her grubby little sisters jumping on a bed, her aunt and a strange man, all in the nursery. While only a little girl, Kitty's face was reminiscent of her grandmother's as she shot a shocked and reproving look at her aunt.

Rose turned at the interruption, hastily pulling her hand from Marcus Underhill's. "Kitty," her Aunt Rose said formally and evenly, "this is Mr. Underhill." Kitty greeted him with her pretty manners, but continued to look surprised.

Marcus shook Kitty's hand and explained, "Your little sisters needed attention and I helped your Auntie Rose carry Miss Sarah upstairs."

From the bed, Abigail stopped jumping for a moment and contradicted, "No you didn't. You carried me."

The discussion might have continued if, at that moment, Sarah had not landed on her sister, and fresh wails erupted from both little girls. Phoebe moved to corral the sobbing twins, but did not say a word. Phoebe gave a second intense look at her mistress's face and nodded pleasantly to Marcus. Kitty continued to look slightly censorious. Rose, nodding to Phoebe and Kitty, escaped the room escorted by Marcus. Marcus and Rose descended the narrow servants' stairs to the second floor and paused, undecided whether to take the stairs to the kitchen or the wider stairs to the front hall. Many eyes would watch them descend from upstairs together. Rose hesitated as the sounds of women's voices came from the direction of the front stairs.

Marcus took in Rose's reticence and touched her on the arm. Rose looked at him and he suggested, "Why don't you go down the front stairs and I shall descend back through the kitchen, causing less chance of gossip."

Rose realized that Marcus understood her hesitation. She deliberated whether she should politely argue with him and then gave him a grateful look. "Thank you, Mr. Underhill," Rose said simply and quietly and moved away from him. Marcus watched her slender form disappear from sight and turned to make his own way down the back stairs.

Once in the foyer, Rose spoke to several friends, retrieved her sewing basket from the morning room and joined a group of ladies in the shade of a tree. Rose settled down on a chair, pulled out some delicate embroidery and began to have a conversation with Cordelia Brown about Cordelia's son, Adam, and his plans for the fall.

Later, Peregrine Fitch came by. Finding the seat next to Rose unaccompanied, he sat down and gratefully accepted a glass of lemonade. Peregrine had been playing horseshoes beyond the grape arbor and was warm from his exertions. Very old friends, Rose handed Peregrine his glass and took up her sampler.

"So," Peregrine turned to Rose with a laugh, "Torie and Edmund beat the cousins in the sailing regatta! You are going to have a hard time convincing Torie that she can't join the navy now!"

Rose joined Peregrine in his laughter and agreed, "Torie is going to be quite insufferable for some time, and lord it over Myles and Cooper. Of course, Edmund was skippering and his skill had something to do with them winning."

Peregrine drank deeply and their conversation drifted into talk about Rose's children, Peregrine's plans for his month at Eaton Pond and other light gossip.

Rose looked out across the wide lawn and saw Marcus Underhill standing with a group of men. Marcus was deep in conversation with Steven Brown. "Peregrine," Rose asked, nodding towards Marcus, "I understand Mr. Underhill is your new business partner?"

Following her nod, Peregrine looked across the lawn. "Oh, yes," he told her, "Marcus Underhill. He has sold his lumber mill in the Pacific Northwest and has moved the center of his operations to Boston. We are now business partners and are in discussion over a joint venture in town. I have found Mr. Underhill to be a shrewd businessman and a gentleman." Peregrine eyed Rose's face rather sharply, "Why do you ask?"

Rose shrugged, "Oh, his son has been here at Eastwood a fair amount with the girls." All at once, Rose felt a great need to confide in Peregrine. Lowering her voice, Rose placed a confiding hand on Peregrine's arm and said, "Perry, it was most embarrassing. The other night at the band concert Mr. Underhill and I discovered his son, Collin, kissing Lavinia in the park."

Peregrine looked at her stricken face and burst out laughing. "Rose Brewster, if you could only see your face," he spoke in a voice low enough for only her to hear. "You know how much I care for your darling daughter, but I also know Vinnie. I bet you she was doing just as much kissing as Collin Underhill."

"Lavinia wouldn't," Rose started and then she looked at Peregrine in the face, laughing a little herself. "You do know Lavinia," she conceded. "But, oh Perry! It was so mortifying to come around the corner and see such a sight at the same moment as that man."

"From doing business with Marcus Underhill," Peregrine said, "I imagine he was not too happy with the situation. Marcus is anxious that both he and his son are accepted into Boston society. Based on the time I have spent with him, I would assume he will be most discreet and take it in his stride." Peregrine looked at Rose's face, "Maybe even better than you."

Rose reluctantly nodded, "It was not an easy situation to find myself in. I was furious with Lavinia and embarrassed having such a personal discussion with someone I had never met, and a Westerner to boot." Rose finished her words in a tone that suggested you could not trust anyone from west of Massachusetts.

Peregrine laughed again, his lean attractive face smiling broadly. Reluctantly, Rose joined in his laughter. "Let's just say," Rose finished, "it isn't a situation I would like repeated. And Mr. Underhill has been very polite to me today. I believe he wishes to make amends."

"I think," Peregrine told Rose, his face serious, "Westerner or not, you will find Marcus Underhill has perfect manners and will have dealt severely with his son and will not gossip about Lavinia with the neighbors."

Feeling relieved at Peregrine's words, Rose moved on to other topics. Later, as she drifted through the crowds she saw Peregrine and Marcus Underhill talking and laughing. Looking at them together, Rose was struck how different the two handsome men were. Both dressed similarly in afternoon wear, their white shirts tucked into buff colored trousers, their neck ties neatly knotted. But where Peregrine was slender and had a refined quality to him with his sharper jaw line and chiseled cheek bones, Marcus Underhill was more broadly built and had a wide awake look to him, as if he had spent time in broad open spaces and was on the alert for possible danger. Rose realized that Marcus Underhill was tall, almost as tall as Peregrine. Marcus Underhill's shoulders were broader than Peregrine's and whereas Peregrine tapered to narrow hips and long legs, Marcus Underhill was built more solidly. Marcus Underhill's jaw was wider and his dark brows were slashes over his amber brown eyes. The two men surveyed the crowd as they talked and Marcus caught Rose looking at him. He smiled and nodded to her; embarrassed, Rose turned to her sister-in-law, Emily, and began a conversation.

The hot day peaked and the sun began its descent. Families with small children gathered them and went home or caught the 4:15 train back to Boston. Later, more of the party would catch the last train of the night, the 11:30.

At Eastwood, a formal dinner was scheduled, followed by fireworks and a ball. Ladies ascended to the second floor laughing and calling to friends as they began to dress for the evening festivities. Corsets were tightened, fresh silk stockings were donned and flowers were placed delicately on fresh bosoms or into intricately entwined hair styles. Shoes that were better suited for picnics and boating were exchanged for dainty high heeled dancing slippers. Scent swirled through the air from lightly applied talcum powder and from behind pink ears.

On the third floor, the boys' dormitory burst with young men as they changed into formal evening wear and jostled for position in front of the one small mirror. Servants stood by to help tie cravats and assist with stiff collars and cuff links.

In the nursery, Sarah and Abigail, refreshed from an afternoon nap, were allowed to stay up and watch the fireworks. They were very excited to be part of the fun. The nursery bustled with children as their nannies rushed to clean up their charges for dinner. The children's dinner was to be served at the long tables and benches on the wide lawn.

At the Brewster's annual 4th of July fete everyone joined in the dancing. Old and young alike would attend the ball. When it became truly dark, the party would move down to the rocky beach or to blankets spread out on the lawn. Others chose to sit on chairs on the wide verandah and watch the fireworks that would be set off from a barge anchored some 100 yards off the dock.

The barge stood momentarily empty. The fireworks were mostly in place and the men who would set them off had abandoned the barge to have their dinner. The sun had not disappeared behind the woods, but was slowly sinking, leaving the sky an intense orange and red as if in celebration of the great day.

All the upstairs bedrooms on the second floor, with the exception of Amelia and the Colonel's and the guest bedroom for the Peabodys, had been opened for ladies to refresh and change into ball gowns. The young ladies' room was crowded with young women laughing and helping each other dress. Ribbons, pieces of jewelry and odds and ends of dress were shared and exchanged while much serious discussion was put into hair styles. Susanna changed from her afternoon dress of sky blue dimity to a silky frothy white dress. Around her slender waist, Susanna wore a satin ribbon of blue and attached to her bosom was a small nosegay that Alexander sent composed of white roses and blue forget me nots. In Susanna's blonde curls nestled a single white rose against a dark green leaf. Susanna's cornflower blue eyes shone with excitement as she repeated to Lavinia a conversation she had had with her future mother-in-law that afternoon. Mrs. Peabody confided in Susanna that she hoped Susanna would be able to spend part of the winter in Washington to help her with hostess duties. Mrs. Peabody was fairly certain that the vice president and his wife would attend the wedding.

Lavinia, as excited as her cousin about Susanna's engagement, dressed for the evening in a wild rose taffeta dress with a skirt consisting of layers of shimmering tulle and a black velvet belt snug around her tiny waist. The tulle was held up in festoons with fresh pink roses and around Lavinia's slender neck she attached a black velvet ribbon choker with a cameo center. Lavinia's ball gown had appliqued pink tulle roses around the low cut neckline and in the center of each rose was a bead of black jet. Lavinia's shining chestnut hair was intricately entwined with pink ribbons and a black feather waved airily every time she tossed her head. Lavinia's green eyes sparkled with excitement as she applied a light perfume behind her ears and between her bosom.

Even with Susanna's engagement to be announced, Lavinia felt very much like the belle of the ball on this warm summer night. Earlier that afternoon both Adam Brown and Warner Covington told Lavinia that they wanted to have the honor of the first dance with her. Lavinia had not yet decided on which boy to bestow that privilege. She was excited over each boy's insistence that he be her chosen partner. On top of the bureau sat four different corsages from four different men, all addressed to Miss Lavinia Brewster, and Vinnie was in a dither over whose flowers she should wear for the evening.

Down the hall, Rose's bedroom was also full as Rose and three other women tried to peer into the mirror and attend to their hair. Laughter and talk filled this room and the other rooms up and down the hall. Cordelia Brown caught Rose's eye in the mirror. Rose was dressed in a lavender silk ball dress that had a high lace collar and huge puffed sleeves that ended at the elbows. Lying on the vanity table were white elbow gloves to put on before Rose went downstairs to dinner.

Cordelia ran a critical eye over Rose's outfit as she smoothed her gray silk dress over her plump waistline. "You look very pretty tonight, Rose," Cordelia complimented Rose with a warm smile. "I wish I had your slender waist and glowing skin. It makes you look as young as Vinnie."

Rose smiled back at her friend and thanked her. She reached up to attend to a curl and said with a small tinge of sadness, "I am dressed well enough for a chaperone tonight."

Cordelia and Rose came out the same year and, during their deb year, had spent many an hour primping together in bedrooms like this. Seventeen-year-old Rose's engagement to William Brewster had only been announced a week before Cordelia Winthrop's own engagement to Stephen Brown. They attended each other's weddings and, in their early years of marriage, socialized together as young wives. In town they served on the same committees, attended DAR meetings, and chaperoned their children at various festivities.

Cordelia turned to her friend without a bit of sympathy. "There will be eligible bachelors down in that ballroom that always like to dance with the "Widow Brewster." It is time you thought about the rest of your life, Rose. Henry is almost grown and will be off to school next year. Which military academy will he be attending?" Cordelia asked the question casually, without any malice.

A set expression settled on Rose's face, but before Rose could answer, Mary Sparrow chimed in, "I am surprised that Peregrine Finch has never proposed. He is your most ardent admirer. Do, Rose, accept Perry and take him out of his bachelorhood and off of every most eligible list in town. You will break a lot of mothers' hearts."

Amid the general laughter, Rose shrugged and did not answer. With a teasing gleam in her eye, Cordelia said, "Of course, I hear that Samuel Gardner is looking for a wife. You better watch out, Rose, or you will be Mrs. Gardner before Christmas."

"That," Rose said firmly, and with a last pat to her hair she turned from the mirror and picked up her gloves, "is not going to happen."

Cordelia was known among her circle for being a matchmaker, and Rose could see the gleam of anticipation in Cordelia's eyes as they looked at each other. "I am going to have to give this some thought," Cordelia told Rose as they turned and moved out of the bedroom. The ladies passed Vinnie and

Susanna's room and peeked in and saw total chaos as young ladies changed into filmy ball dresses and hair ribbons and flowers were scattered everywhere. The room was redolent with scent and excited chatter filled the air.

Downstairs, the men were formally dressed and restlessly meandered around the drawing room and the verandah. They waited impatiently for the ladies to appear, be claimed and escorted into dinner. Myles and Cooper looked resplendent in full military dress whites. Their mother entered the drawing room and beamed at her very handsome sons as they each gave her a kiss on the cheek.

Like a cloud of beautiful butterflies, a crowd of young ladies suddenly burst into the drawing room. The gas lights shimmered down on their glossy heads of blonde, brunette and auburn, their white bosoms and their vibrant ball gowns. Soft high voices called out to partners as they paired up and greeted each other. The moment she appeared, Lavinia was set upon by Adam, Warner and Collin Underhill. Collin smiled his appreciation as he saw his flowers attached to Lavinia's slender waist. Lavinia smiled at Collin warmly, but she placed her hand in Adam Brown's to give him the honor of escorting her to dinner. Lavinia paused long enough to allow Warner to see that she had written his name on her dance card for the first dance.

Susanna laughed as she watched her cousin, but she spied Alexander and moved purposefully towards him. Rose and the other matrons entered the drawing room ahead of the girls. Rose conversed with Mrs. Peabody and heard all about the Peabody's wedding plans. Rose wondered what Amelia would have to say about some of Mrs. Peabody's plans, but decided not to comment. Mrs. Peabody told Rose that it had been decided that the Peabodys would stay at Eastwood for a week while the December wedding plans were discussed. At the end of the week, Susanna, Alice and Amelia would travel to Washington for a round of bridal parties and some time would be spent with a seamstress in New York. Mrs. Peabody invited Rose and Lavinia to join the party. Rose thanked her on behalf of Lavinia, but very prettily declined for herself and explained that she planned to stay and help oversee Susanna's younger brother and sisters, so their mother could attend and not worry.

Out on the verandah were the younger children. Finished with their dinner they impatiently waited for the adults to have dinner so the ball and fireworks could commence. Torie, her long dark curls tidy and smooth and pulled back with a satin crimson bow over her right ear that matched her sash on her pristine white dress, busily chatted in Edmund's ear. Edmund, also dressed in his military school uniform, looked a little warm from the heat, but he laughed as Torie suggested that they try and sail back to Boston at the end of the summer. Kitty and Dorcas stood in the doorway and watched, enchanted, as the young ladies and men flirted and chatted while waiting for the dinner bell. Kitty longed for the day when she could wear her skirts long and her hair up and have men like Alexander Peabody look at her adoringly, as Alexander was doing that moment with her sister.

Henry stood out on the lawn and watched the men on the small barge put the finishing touches on the firework charges to be lit later when the sky turned dark. Tonight Henry was dressed in a navy blue suit of short pants and a jacket with a wide buster brown collar. His tie was dark blue and his knee high stockings gleamed white. Earlier Henry begged to be allowed on the barge when the fireworks would be set off, and he nearly drove the workers to distraction while they set up the charges by telling them all about the history of fireworks in ancient China. Finally his mother became stern with him and told him to leave the men alone.

In the dining room, the long table was set to a maximum number of places and small tables were set up in the drawing room to hold more dinner guests. The young ladies and men settled into the smaller tables and the high girlish laughter joined with the deeper masculine tones in the room. Mrs. Pratt's skill as a cook was praised as she served a very traditional summer dinner of lobster tails with homemade mayonnaise, cold poached chicken with cream sauce, veal cutlets, small potatoes and green beans. Many side dishes and salads were also served and the entire dinner was followed by a sumptuous dessert of strawberry shortcake and fresh whipped cream.

As the diners finished their dessert, the Colonel rose and announced the impending wedding of his granddaughter Susanna to Alexander Peabody. The entire room clapped and toasted the young couple. Susanna blushed and smiled as she and Alexander stood. He kissed her and they received many felicitations.

From the ballroom in the basement sounds floated up of the small orchestra tuning the instruments. Guests and Brewsters alike rose and descended to the lower regions of the Eastwood ballroom. As the young couple descended the stairs there were many hugs for Susanna and handshakes for Alexander. In the ballroom, the great crystal chandelier's lights sparkled and danced on the shining floor; wall sconces flickered with soft candlelight. In one corner a refreshment table was placed next to a small goldfish pond surrounded by leafy palms and ferns. Potted plants filled dark corners and small chairs lined the walls for chaperones.

Rose sat between Alice and Cordelia and they chattered about their children as they watched them glide around the ballroom. Rose and Alice watched as their mother-in-law and father-in-law swept by during a waltz. The Colonel's military background made him a rather stiff dancer as he tended to dance precisely to the beat, but tiny Amelia looked relaxed and elegant in his arms. Tonight Amelia was dressed in regal black lace and diamonds shimmered at her throat and ears. Amelia looked up at the Colonel as he laughed at something she said. Alice and Rose exchanged glances with something close to awe. Amelia worked very hard for days to ensure this party went off perfectly, yet tonight she looked as fresh and as young as their own daughters.

From time to time, Charles Brewster and Steven Brown would claim their wives for a dance, and they always followed partnering a dance with Rose. Peregrine who had been busy dancing with every lady in the room, had also claimed a dance with Rose. Rose always enjoyed dancing with Peregrine. His palms were never sweaty in his gloves and he was an excellent dancer.

After their dance concluded, Peregrine and Rose enjoyed a glass of punch and conversation, when Peregrine excused himself to dance with Torie. Torie danced a rousing polka with Edmund and the twins Myles and Cooper, had each claimed her for country dances, but Torie and Kitty had exchanged words and Torie looked daggers at her cousin. Peregrine and Rose both saw Torie's jaw begin to jut out, and with a quick nod to Rose, Peregrine stepped in front of Torie and bowed. Torie gave one last glare at Kitty and then curtsied very prettily to Peregrine before he swept her off for a Redowa.

Rose, a smile hovering over her lips, stood by the punch bowl with a glass in her hand, watching Peregrine and Torie swirl around the dance floor. Rose was so appreciative of Peregrine; he always seemed to know when Rose needed that added man's touch with her children and stepped in effortlessly to help her.

Rose thought about the teasing conversation upstairs before dinner. More than one question had been leveled at her over the years with regard to Peregrine. Peregrine was her most ardent supporter, but never crossed the line into making Rose feel that he wanted more from her. Peregrine would make an excellent father, but Rose had never understood why Peregrine never married. Rose was fairly certain it was not because all these years Peregrine had been wearing his heart on his sleeve where she was concerned.

As her eyes casually passed over the dance floor, Rose saw Samuel Gardner advancing on her with determination in his eyes. Rose was backed into a corner between a large potted palm and the goldfish pool and she could not escape. Sam's forehead glistened with sweat and he looked like he had been imbibing heavily in the Colonel's fine wines. Sam swayed a bit as he walked, but he focused on Rose with a purposeful look in his eyes. Rose glanced around for Charles or Christopher, but help came from an unexpected corner.

"Mrs. Brewster," a deep voice intoned, "I believe this is our dance." Stepping directly in front of Samuel, Marcus Underwood held out his hand with a bow. "I apologize for being late," he said rather loudly, a twinkle in his eyes. "I was detained in the study." Placing his hand on her waist, Marcus whisked Rose off before she could utter a word. Samuel Gardner stood there with his hands on his hips and watched Rose fly away in the arms of Marcus.

Feeling his hand on her waist, her one hand resting on his broad shoulder, the other swallowed up in his large hand, Rose felt tongue tied. The dance was quick enough that there was no time for conversation, and it was almost over before they began. As the band moved smoothly into a waltz, Marcus did not let go of Rose but stepped right into the tempo.

As a widow and society matron, Rose often danced with older widowers and other older single men in society. Quite often these men were unskilled dancers and sometimes Rose felt like she was a well water pump that was pumped vigorously or her toes would be trod upon. But, Marcus Underwood was an excellent dancer. A powerfully built man, he was amazingly light on his feet. Rose knew eyebrows would be raised after dancing two consecutive dances with Marcus. Suddenly Rose realized she was thoroughly enjoying herself. Surprising even herself, Rose lifted her head and smiled brightly into Marcus' face.

Marcus, slightly taken aback by Rose's bright smile, returned her smile with a raise of his eyebrows. "Thank you for rescuing me from Mr. Gardner," Rose admitted to Marcus. "I was looking for a way out of the corner and my brothers-in-law were otherwise engaged."

Marcus smiled back at Rose, a sparkle in his warm brown eyes. "I did not realize I was rescuing you," he lied smoothly. Then he added, "I am sure Mr. Gardner would give you a twirl around the room that you would not forget."

Rose joined Marcus in his laughter and felt a sincere enjoyment for partnering with such an attractive man. Rose tried to remember when she had relished a waltz so much, but could not remember. As the dance ended, Marcus and Rose continued their conversation as they stepped out of the wide double doors for a fresh breath of air. They talked of Summerfield and the renovating Marcus was doing on the venerable old house. Rose and Marcus' talk drifted to literature and he asked if she had read Longfellow's poem, "Evangeline." Rose told him she had not, but that she had enjoyed reading "Paul Revere." Her face aglow in the fading light, Rose shyly recited a few lines.

"So," Marcus teased, "under that proper Boston Mama veneer there lies a heart that beats for poetry."

Rose thought about this, and shook her head and said, "No, I do enjoy fine literature and poetry. I am just a simple woman and mother."

Inside the ballroom, the music ended as the band took a break. The Colonel announced it was time to go outside and see the firework display. Amid the general evacuation of the ballroom, Marcus turned and offered his arm to Rose. Rose hesitated only briefly before she smiled up at him and accepted his escort out onto the lawn.

Rose gracefully sank down on a blanket on the lawn and Marcus joined her. The fireworks had not started. The men on the barge waited for the last lingering light to leave the summer sky. Rose was very aware of the man seated beside her. Rather than meet Marcus' eyes, Rose looked through the throng for her children. Lavinia was properly attended to by Adam Brown, her arm firmly tucked into his elbow as they stood on the shore line. A cluster of children stood on the lawn and Rose could see Torie, as always with Edmund and Henry and Kitty gathered together. Along with Christopher's children and a large contingent of neighborhood children, they called and encouraged the barge men to start. Nearby, Alice and Charles sat on a blanket with their twins and pointed out where the brightest explosions would be. Sarah and Abigail's eyes were bright and shiny as they watched in awe.

After the first firework exploded over the sky, amid laughter and clapping, Marcus turned to Rose. "Mrs. Brewster," he said in a deep voice, "thank you again for including my son and me in your festivities. It does look like the whole lake is gathered here."

Rose looked from the sky where the first bright sparkles faded and into Marcus' warm brown eyes. "Rose," she corrected with a small raise of the eyebrow. "Remember this afternoon? Please call me Rose."

Marcus smiled at Rose and tested the name. Before they could continue their conversation, Peregrine came and sank down beside Rose on the blanket and with the two men flanking her, they fell into conversation over her head as the firework display continued. The fireworks finally ended, and Peregrine stood and offered his arm to Rose. She looked at it momentarily and then turned to Marcus Underhill, who had also stood up. "Thank you for the conversation about 'Evangeline' and Mr. Longfellow, Mr. Underhill," Rose said formally. "I will look forward to reading it. Good night."

With a bow and pleasantries exchanged with both Rose and Peregrine, Marcus moved off into the crowd. Rose watched Marcus' tall figure walk away and then turned to Peregrine, who watched her intently, but he said nothing. Rose put a bright smile on her face and with a lift of her brows, moved with Peregrine and the general throng up the lawn and back into the ballroom.

CHAPTER 7

A quiet hung over Eastwood on the fifth of July. The revelers stayed up late into the night enjoying the party and the house was crowded with extra guests. The Colonel gave the boys a reprieve from their early morning calisthenics. They were grateful to sleep off their carousing.

Due to the unusually large number of overnight guests, breakfast had been set up in the larger dining room for everyone to partake.

Rose slept fitfully. Although it had been past 2:00 a.m. and she had been very tired when she climbed the stairs to her bed, once in the dark, sleep eluded her. In her mind she thought over her conversations with Marcus Underhill. It had been a long time since a man had looked at her the way he had at the ball, and Rose felt a shiver in her tummy. Rose tried to remember William. Had he ever looked at her like that? The memories of William dimmed, and Rose could barely remember their courting days. Tossing, Rose felt a smile creep on her lips as she reached up and twined a curl around her slender finger. When they danced, Rose felt Marcus' warm hand against her waist and his hand felt strong and masterful. Her conversation with Marcus had surprised Rose, as she had not realized how educated he was. Seated between the two men on the blanket Rose could tell that Peregrine enjoyed Marcus' friendship and business acumen. On that interesting thought Rose finally dozed.

As the sun peeked over the woods, Rose woke from a restless sleep, abandoned her bed and dressed in a simple white blouse and skirt. Downstairs, the morning smells of bacon and coffee and the conversation from the dining room did not hold her interest so Rose stepped out of the house and followed the path for the back gardens.

Busy workmen removed the lanterns from trees and carried the heavy trestle tables and benches to the barn. The bunting that had so proudly framed the house the day before was hanging in sad swags as the rosettes had already been removed and placed in a box on the front steps.

Rose skirted the house and found the children in the raspberry bushes picking the juicy red berries and popping them in their mouths. Rose waved at the children and Phoebe, who sat in the shade, mending. The children greeted Rose as she walked past in the direction of the cove. Rose took deep breaths into her aching head when she encountered Amelia coming out of a greenhouse with a basket of flowers over her arm. Amelia, tired but satisfied with the 4th of July party proceedings, greeted Rose cordially. Amelia had something on her mind. "Rose, you enjoyed your conversation last night with Mr. Underhill?"

Rose felt her color rising, but answered evenly, "Mr. Underhill? Yes, we discussed Lavinia and Collin."

"I was happy to see Lavinia behaving herself last night," Amelia told Rose with approval. "Lavinia was not overly attentive to any young man and I did not see her leave the ball room once. She had many partners and was not overly flirtatious. Vinnie behaved beautifully."

Rose, slightly annoyed with her mother-in-law's approval of her own daughter, made a non committal answer and started to move on. Amelia, fingering a blossom in her basket, had something on her mind. She said, "You danced two dances in a row with Mr. Underhill." Amelia raised her eyes to Rose, looking intently, her eyebrow slightly raised.

Rose momentarily closed her eyes and said with a patient sigh, "Amelia, Marcus Underhill stepped in and asked me to dance as Samuel Gardner was bearing down on me. To be truthful, I did not want to dance with Mr. Gardner and was happy that Mr. Underhill asked me to dance when he did. We only danced half a dance and as Samuel was still watching, we started the next one. That is all there was to it."

Amelia looked searchingly at Rose. "My dear," Amelia said, not unkindly, "you have been a widow for a very long time. It would not be unusual for you to long to have a man by your side." She looked down at her gardening gloves, smoothing them along the backs of her hands. "George and I have talked. William never expected to die so young, or leave you such a young widow. We would not be against you marrying the appropriate man."

Rose stared in surprise at her mother-in-law. "And Henry's education?" she asked incredulously, but to the point.

Amelia smiled wryly at Rose. "We have all tried to step in and help you with parenting. The Colonel and I feel it would not be amiss for your children to have a father in their lives."

Rose mulled over the statement, not quite sure of what to make of those words. Cautiously, she said, "You aren't suggesting Samuel Gardner..."

Amelia laughed, breaking the tension. "Heaven forbid!" she exclaimed. "I went to school with Samuel's mother and she was a wonderful woman. Something has not gone well with Sam and I would hate to have you saddled with those children."

Amelia went on, rather confidentially, "George has told me that Samuel's business is not doing well and his finances are not sound. Among the many reasons why you are so interesting to him could be that he needs his coffers refilled. Beware, my dear."

Rose nodded in agreement with Amelia. Amelia said lightly, "Just something for you to think about, my dear." Then Amelia turned and Rose, puzzled, watched her mother-in-law's trim little figure move towards Eastwood.

The following week was filled with dinner party invitations, as all of Eaton Pond wished to host such an important personage as Senator Peabody. Susanna and Alexander spent time together rowing on the pond, swimming with their friends and partnering on the tennis court. In the evenings, they could be found in parlors with friends singing and dancing. Susanna, under the spell of Alexander, lit up every room she entered. At the end of the week, the Peabody party left for Washington, DC, for a round of engagement parties. Accompanying them were Amelia, Alice, Susanna and Lavinia. Lavinia, excited to be included in the invitation, chattered away to her mother as she packed her trunk and departed with her cousin Susanna.

Eastwood was quieter with so many people gone. Matilda received word that her husband, Jasper, was coming into port so she packed and departed with her twin sons. Once Jasper settled his ships, they would return to Eastwood. Rose, watching Matilda's face alight with anticipation at seeing her husband, glimpsed the beauty hidden under Matilda's normal stern look. Rose remembered Matilda's debutante season and how popular Matilda had been, but it was handsome laughing Jasper Bingham, always dressed smartly in naval garb, who stole Matilda's heart and hand. Having a husband gone for months at a time over the years took a toll on Matilda's happy heart and caused her to hide her lonesomeness under a stern countenance and a need to manage others. Still she excitedly packed Myles and Cooper and headed home to Boston.

With only the Colonel and the great aunts for company, Rose spent much time with the younger children. Without the older children to host friends, not as many young people dropped by to play tennis or sail. Kitty and Torie called a truce and joined forces in entertaining the littlest girls, who were woeful over the departure of their mother.

One quiet evening, the house felt warm and humid. The Colonel sat in his study reading and Rose, hot and sticky, did not join the aunts on the verandah where not even a stray breeze blew. The children were given permission to have their cousins and some of the neighborhood children sleep over and a large group had gathered on the screened porch for dinner. Later they would sleep on the screened porch, bundled up in blankets and feather mattresses carried downstairs for the occasion. Phoebe took Sarah and Abigail upstairs to bed, as the two little girls missed their mother, and they were too young to join in the fun and games of the older children. The rest of the children played games and caught fireflies and finally settled down on the boat landing to tell ghost stories.

Rose abandoned the quiet verandah and sauntered across the wide lawn to the boat landing. The children did not really need supervision, but Rose hoped to catch the faint breeze that often blew across the lake in the evenings. The boats were tied up and sails neatly stored away; the occasional stray current caused lines to gently knock against their sides. Overhead, the thick clustered stars created bright pin points of light and a large moon rose and bathed the lake in soft shining light.

Rose, unbearably sticky from the hot humid air, sat down on the small dock a little distance from the children and removed her shoes and stockings. Under the cover of darkness, Rose hiked up her skirts and slid her bare feet into the water, the welcoming coolness was a relief from the heat. By the light of the moon and one small lantern, Henry told a lurid tale about a mummy in Egypt, bringing moans from some of the children. Rose wondered if she would be up half the night dealing with nightmares and if she should put a stop to such a lurid tale. Kitty sidled up to Rose and held her aunt's hand very tightly.

Rose's attention wandered, and looking across the lake, she saw a few lights in the small village and in the distance she heard the faint whistle of a train. Rose thought about her children and her life, half listening to Henry's story. Rose mulled over Amelia's surprising words earlier in the week, when she was startled to hear the sound of footsteps crunching on the gravel along the shore line. Several of the children also heard the same noise and some of the smaller girls clustered closer to Rose and screamed as a man dressed in light colored clothes moved across the grass towards them. Rose, herself slightly unsettled over the tale of the mummy, swallowed a small shriek and was quite surprised to see Marcus Underhill strolling onto the dock.

Kitty buried her head in Rose's lap and moaned, "It's the mummy!"

Rose, her own heart racing, was unable to rise encumbered as she was by the clinging Kitty. "Don't be silly, Kitty," Rose hissed as she attempted to pull the little girl off of her and make her sit up. "Mr. Underhill," she said slightly breathlessly, aware of her bare feet dangling in the water, and her hiked up skirt. "What on earth are you doing here?"

In the dark Marcus smiled at Rose, his white teeth gleaming in the moonlight. He bowed to her and explained. "I dropped by with a book for you, and Miss Easter told me that you and the children were down here on the dock. I decided I would see if I could find you in the moonlight."

Rose realized all of the children watched their exchange intently. "Won't you sit down?" she asked cordially. "Children, do you all know Mr. Underhill?"

The children murmured a greeting to him and scooted around to give him room to sit down in their circle.

Marcus settled down cross legged on the dock and asked the group in general, "What kind of stories are you telling?"

"Henry has been telling us stories about mummies," Edmund spoke up.

"They are dead people come to life," Torie added, her eyes gleaming in the moonlight, "only they are wrapped in strips of sheets. It is most exciting."

Rose, cuddling Kitty, watched Marcus in the moonlight with the children. She was surprised at his appearance and his comfortable ease with the children.

"Mummies?" Marcus said, then asked, "Have any of you heard of Sasquatch?"

Each one of the children shook heads in negation. Henry's glasses glinted in the moonlight as he listened to Marcus intently. Marcus proceeded to tell them about the strange monster that roamed the Northwest. The creature was purported to be 10 feet tall and left foot tracks that were more than 24 inches long. The beast, covered in dark hair, was known to cause murder and mayhem in the Pacific Northwest woods. By the time Marcus finished, even Edmund and Torie glanced towards the dark woods.

"Fascinating," Henry murmured, clearly intrigued. "Sort of like the Yetti in the Alps. Mr. Underhill, I must learn more about this beast."

"When my books come," Marcus promised Henry, "I shall loan you a book I have about stories from the Pacific Northwest."

All eyes focused on Marcus and his story when Phoebe, appearing out of the darkness, caused several children to give small screams. "Now, come on," Phoebe called, in a scolding voice. "Time for bed. I have a small treat on the back verandah waiting for you." Phoebe pulled Kitty off of Rose's lap and guided the children toward the house. Reluctantly, the children said their good nights and thanked Marcus, and Henry and Torie gave their mother a good night kiss as they passed. Their voices drifted back across the lawn as they regaled Phoebe with the stories that had been told.

"Do you think anyone will suffer from nightmares?" Marcus asked Rose.

Rose shrugged. "Possibly. Kitty probably," she admitted. "Phoebe and I could be in for a rough night. But I think the mummy story was more scary. My son is fascinated by all things Eastern."

Marcus asked, "Has he always been interested in the East?"

Rose nodded, "Henry loves to read about adventure. He wants to travel some day and see the ancient pyramids and find Aladdin's cave for himself."

"Quite a boy," Marcus murmured.

As they had talked, Marcus maneuvered himself so that he was sitting next to Rose. He rolled up his pant legs, and took off his own shoes and socks and joined her with his feet in the lake.

Rose was a little embarrassed over this rather intimate gesture and started to remove her bare feet from the water.

"Don't," Marcus stopped her with a hand on her arm. His warm hand, even through her sleeve caused a shiver to run up her arm. She looked down at it, glanced at him and looked out across the quiet lake toward the moon.

Aware of his nearness and her bare feet, Rose felt at a disadvantage, and at a loss for words. An owl skimmed past them, its wings beating the warm air. In the faint distance, the sound of a train whistle could be heard. Faint ripples along the shore line hissed gently as some current stirred the water. It was a lonely sound on a quiet night.

Casting around for something to say, Rose asked, "What book did you bring me?"

"A book with the poem 'Evangeline,'" Marcus told her. "The sad love story of an Acadian maiden and her lost love Gabriel, but it also talks about the beauties of the West. I thought you would enjoy it."

Rose thanked him as she took the book and said, "I have, of course, read 'Paul Revere' and found Mr. Longfellow to be somewhat of a romantic. He depicted the Old North Church and Concord beautifully."

"Quite a few poets hailed from Boston," Marcus noted. "It is the place for academia, one of the reasons my wife and I were anxious to have Collin educated here."

Rose did not comment on his words, but said shyly, "One of my favorite Boston poets is Emily Dickinson. Have you read her?"

Marcus shook his head, and Rose promised to loan him her book of Dickinson poems.

Marcus asked her, "Was it Dickinson you were reading that day I first saw you by the pond?"

Rose thought back to that day when Marcus spied her as she stood in the small cove crying. Rose paused, trying to remember, then shook her head, "That was <u>Romeo and Juliet</u> by Shakespeare. So tragic."

Marcus quoted:

"Go hence, to have more talk of these sad things;
Some shall be pardon'd, and some punished:
For never was a story of more woe
Than this of Juliet and her Romeo."

"You know Shakespeare," Rose said in surprise. Then realizing she was rude, she apologized and said, "I am sorry, I did not mean to imply that you were uneducated."

Marcus cut her off with a laugh, "Yes, we are still educated in the West. Perhaps our schools are not as extensive as they are in Boston, but I was educated. I can almost count to ten."

Rose blushed and said, "I did not mean to be offensive."

"No offense taken," he told her. "My favorite quote from Romeo and Juliet is:

"But soft, what light through yonder window breaks?
It is the east, and Juliet is the sun.
Arise, fair sun, and kill the envious moon,
Who is already sick and pale with grief
That thou, her maid, art far more fair than she."

Rose laughed, not quite sure how to reply to that.

Quietly Marcus and Rose sat side by side for a few minutes. Rose, slightly uncomfortable with the silence, cast around for a topic and asked, "How is Collin faring with the Brewster girls out of town?"

"Collin has been over at the Brown's a fair amount and tonight went in to Eaton's Grove for a concert in the park," Marcus told her. He then added, amusement in his voice, "I hope he doesn't have some girl in a corner kissing her where her mother would discover her. I am not there to save him from her wrath."

"I wasn't that bad," Rose protested and then laughed. "All right, maybe I was a little furious with both of them. And, I remember," she finished, "so were you."

"I want my son to behave himself, even with pretty girls," Marcus said with a small chuckle. "Young men these days have ideas and it seems like every argument any more begins with an allusion to the new century and new attitudes."

Rose looked at him in amazement and said, "Do you get that argument too? Vinnie is adept at bringing that argument into any discussion we have regarding what is proper for a young lady and what is not." The moon shone down causing a pearly sheen on her pale cheeks, her lustrous eyes glittered in the moonlight. "It makes me feel old," Rose admitted to Marcus. "Hidebound in the old ways."

Marcus leaned closer to Rose and whispered in her ear, his breath tickling her. "In the moonlight you look as young as your daughter. What do you think is proper and what is not with this new century coming?"

Rose looked at the moonlight shining on the pond, and ignoring Marcus' first comment, asked with a laugh, "For young ladies and young men?"

"For grownups," Marcus said, teasing. "You see, Rose, when a man is in the moonlight with a pretty girl, his thoughts turn towards interesting things."

"But I am not a girl," Rose protested with a startled look in her eyes. She turned her head to look at him and found herself lost in his dark eyes. Her mouth was open and she could not speak. For a brief moment they stared at each other and then Marcus leaned just a little closer and gave her a small soft kiss. Unbidden, Rose returned the pressure of his lips briefly before she pulled away. Once again, she stared up into his eyes and then as his head lowered a second time, she shut her eyes.

The second kiss lasted a little longer, but was still on the lighter side. A stray breeze caused the lines to slap against the hull of the boat and Rose jumped as if caught. Rose was aware of what she was doing and where she was and, flustered, pulled her feet from the water and barely drying them on the hem of her skirt began to shove her still damp feet into her shoes. Rose bundled her stockings into small balls and shoved them into her pocket. In her haste she dropped Marcus' book, missing the water's edge by inches.

Marcus stood and looked down at Rose. A range of emotions washed over her. Rose, breathless, was horrified that she had sat there in the moonlight kissing Marcus Underhill. She wanted to throw her arms around Marcus and kiss him again. With a glance to the house, she worried that the Colonel might have spied them in their intimate position.

Wordlessly, Marcus reached down and retrieved the book and handed it to her. Rose clutched it to her breast and would not look at Marcus. He gently lifted Rose's chin with his warm fingers so he could look down into her eyes.

Facing each other, Rose looked up into his face, blurred and indistinct in the moonlight. Rose felt his fingers on her chin, his warm nearness. Rose opened her mouth to say something and he put a finger on her lips. "Shhh," he gently scolded, "don't you dare begin to tell me how we were inappropriate. We are two adults. And I for one, find you very attractive."

At his words, Rose pulled away from Marcus, embarrassed. Rose was a tangle of emotions as she could still feel the warm pressure of his lips on hers. Her stomach fluttered and her heart raced. Rose suddenly remembered that she had been out here on the dock for some time, alone with Marcus Underhill. Rose worried that she had been missed. She did not want the Colonel to come looking for her.

In the silence, the sound of a night bird could be heard in the woods behind Eastwood. In her confusion, Rose turned and looked in the direction of the dark woods. Marcus attempting to lighten the situation, quoted:

> *"It was the nightingale, and not the lark,*
> *That pierced the fearful hollow of thine ear;*
> *Nightly she sings on yon pomengranate-tree:*
> *Believe me, love, it was the nightingale."*

Rose managed to laugh and Marcus said briskly, "I am going to escort you back to the house and bid you adieu as a gentleman. But I would like to see you again, tomorrow."

A moment of silence passed and as Rose Brewster looked up into Marcus Underhill's eyes, something deep inside her moved. The vague longing Rose felt all summer suddenly swelled and fractured into a million tiny little pieces. Rose realized that she was as excited as a young girl over the kiss. The careful lonely barrier that she had built around her emotions over the years cracked. Looking at Marcus, Rose knew she wanted to be held by Marcus Underhill, to feel his hands and lips upon her, to feel... To feel what? Rose wasn't sure.

Rose was silent for so long that Marcus thought that she was going to refuse. He marshaled his arguments when she spoke, breathlessly, "Tomorrow afternoon. The cove where you first saw me." Swiftly Rose kissed his cheek, gathered up her skirts, and fled up the lawn towards the house. Marcus reached up and touched his cheek where her warm lips had been and listened to her swift footsteps scamper into the darkness.

Rose crossed the lawn and at the front steps paused. She changed direction and followed the path to the back of the house to avoid an encounter with the Colonel. Rose was fairly certain that her face was a dead give away to her emotions and she did not want to face anyone tonight. She wanted to be alone with her emotions.

Rose could hear faint laughter from the servants in the direction of the stables, and nearer, the children were still on the back verandah. Rose swiftly ran up the steps to the screened porch and entered the empty darkened kitchen where all was clean and spotless. The smell of something yeasty and rising touched her nose and the faint smell of spices and delicious cooked dinners hung in the evening air. Rose quickly climbed the servants' stairs and made it to her room without encountering anyone.

Once in her room, Rose shut the door quietly and leaned against it, still clutching Marcus' book. Rose's mind was a flurry of emotions. Elated, horrified and near tears, Rose felt as giddy as a young girl. She moved to her dressing table and pulled her pins from her hair and picking up her hair brush began to brush her thick dark hair briskly. As she brushed, a song came to her lips and she hummed as her beautiful hair crackled with electricity. Rose realized that she was humming the waltz from the ball that she and Marcus danced to the other night.

A light in the distance over the dark woods drew Rose's attention. Rose moved to the window seat at the open window and stared at that light. It came from Summerfield, Marcus Underhill's home. Thoughtfully, Rose leant her chin upon her hand. Her hand idly rubbed her chin and a slender finger reached up and outlined her lips, reliving Marcus' kisses. Marcus Underhill kissed her. Unbelievable, but true. She, Rose Brewster, widow of William and a proper Boston matron, sat in the moonlight and allowed Marcus Underhill to kiss her. Being brutally honest, Rose admitted to herself that she had returned Marcus Underhill's kiss. She liked it. A large slap of reason suddenly smacked her. What was she doing? What could she possibly be thinking making secret appointments with Marcus Underhill? What explanation could she offer if they were caught sneaking off together?

Rose thought back to Marcus' kiss and felt chills run over her body. Rose's heart gave another delicious thrill. Rose looked around her lonely bedroom and then thoughtfully back at the distant light. Regretfully, she couldn't meet Marcus tomorrow. Rose told herself strictly that she had simply allowed herself to be caught up in the moonlight and poetry. But, what was wrong with meeting a man, she argued with herself. Because there would be no end to the Brewster's disapproval. Rose shivered at the thought of Amelia's lectures, the recriminations, the accusations. But, Amelia wasn't here at Eastwood; Amelia was at the Capital with the Peabodys.

Wasn't it just a meeting to discuss poetry? Trying to justify her actions, Rose argued with the mythical Amelia that she and Mr. Underhill simply found a common interest in poetry and shared an interest in authors. How could Emily Dickinson be an improper threat to the Brewsters? But, Rose knew that she did not want to meet Marcus to discuss poetry. Lonely Rose Brewster wanted to feel a man's hands on her. This sobering thought caused Rose to rest her chin onto the windowsill. Rose stared across the treetops at the light when it suddenly went out. Long after it disappeared she continued to stare at it.

Rose went to her bed with the decision that she would not go anywhere close to the cove and Marcus Underhill. Rose decided that she would return his book by courier in the morning and thank him formally with a note. Lying there in the darkness she relived the kiss. For the first time in more than ten years a man kissed her on the lips; it was quite a shattering experience. What if they met and did just discuss poetry? What could it hurt? Rose slept very little that night, but was jarred awake at dawn by the calls of the Colonel and the morning calisthenic routine. Rose abandoned her tossed bed with relief, a slight ache behind her unrested eyes, determined to send the book back to Marcus immediately after breakfast. A short formal note would thank him but explain that her duties would keep her elsewhere.

In the light of day, Rose slipped off her nightgown, and caught a glimpse of her nearly naked body in the mirror. Rose paused. Rarely did Rose look at her body without clothes, but now she critically looked at her slender waist and slight tummy pooch from birthing three children. Her round white breasts gleamed in the soft morning light. Embarrassed, Rose turned and slipped on her underthings and petticoat and turned attention to her white lacy blouse. Rose thought about her decision to meet Marcus in the cove and scolded herself for having such silly ideas, sure she would not be doing any such foolishness. Determined and with her mind made up, Rose went down to breakfast with the plan that she would work with the little girls on their sewing and then after lunch she would pay a call on Cordelia Brown. She and Cordelia could spend the afternoon in discussion about the Ladies' Guild Society fall meetings. For someone who had very little sleep, Rose looked very wide awake and alert as she entered the smaller dining room.

The Colonel was reading the paper and drinking his coffee as Rose entered the dining room. Her hair was tidy, her clothes were neat and pressed, but something about Rose's face caused the Colonel to put down his cup and look at her for a minute intently. Colonel, in charge of ranks of men for years, glared at Rose suspiciously. Rose seemed more blooming this morning. Rose, already in a rumpled state of mind, greeted the Colonel cordially and turned her back on him as she helped herself to a slice of toast and a small bowl of strawberries.

The children had eaten and were about their daily routines; their friends and cousins had left for home. From upstairs could be heard the faint tinkling of the piano and the discordant sound of the violin as the children finished their morning music practice. From the kitchen could be heard some small disagreement and through the open windows drifted the sounds of the men working in the fields.

The great aunts entered and greeted Rose and the Colonel. They sat and quietly talked together about plans for making potpourri from petals they had collected. Tabitha made a comment to the Colonel and he answered his sister rather shortly, as he hated to be interrupted when reading his morning paper. Rose toyed with her toast, but did not eat. These two sweet women had been widows for almost 40 years. They had lived under their brother's roof and had quietly spent their lives sewing, tatting lace and sitting in the shade of the verandah and watching their brother's children grow and live lives. Was that what she was destined for, Rose wondered? Rose thought back to Marcus...

Early afternoon and the house was warm and drowsy. The Colonel was in his study with his handkerchief over his face, faintly snoring. Aunt Easter and Tabitha nodded in the deep shade on the far end of the front porch. Upstairs, Phoebe sang lullabies to the little girls for their afternoon naps. Edmund and Torie took the boat out and lazily sailed back and forth across the pond. Henry and Kitty spent the afternoon with their cousins at Harlow Hall. All was still and peaceful.

Rose, shaking, sat on the front verandah, her sewing limp in her lap. She watched a sail boat skim by and then with shaking hands pulled a small book from her sewing basket. Rose glanced at the napping aunts and with a small furtive look at the open front doors, she quietly slipped down the front steps. Casually, Rose walked around the path to the back of the house and then with one last furtive glance at the many windows, she skirted the green houses and hurried towards the cove.

Parting the bushes, Rose stepped into the small private cove and found Marcus waiting for her. A blanket was spread out and an open book lay on his lap, next to a small picnic hamper. Marcus' row boat was pulled onto shore against the muddy sand. Today he was dressed informally in his white shirt and vest. Once again his red kerchief was knotted around his neck inside his open collar, where just a glimpse of tanned smooth skin could be glimpsed.

Shyly, Rose looked at Marcus as he scrambled to his feet when he spied her. "Good afternoon," Rose greeted Marcus faintly but formally with a deep breath. Marcus greeted Rose in return. Rose stood at the edge of the clearing, poised to turn and flee.

Marcus seeing the indecision in her face, gestured toward the blanket. "I brought a picnic," he told her, his voice deep and quiet. "Would you sit down and share some food with me?" Rose hesitated and then reluctantly perched on the edge of the blanket. Rose's heart pounded as she realized how thoroughly the shrubs sheltered her from Eastwood and her family. Looking up at Marcus, Rose realized how tall and strong he looked. She swallowed nervously.

Marcus knelt down on the blanket and as he reached for the picnic basket, Rose flinched. Marcus sat back on his haunches and a small grin crossed his face as he asked lightly, "May I ask you something?" A small bottle of lemonade was produced from the basket and Marcus poured out two small glasses, offering one to Rose

Rose accepted the glass and cautiously nodded her head.

"Last night was quite a wonderful surprise," Marcus told Rose as he set out a plate of chicken and red ripe strawberries. "I actually did not think you would come today."

Rose looked from the food to Marcus and delicately raised an eyebrow. "That wasn't a question," she pointed out to him.

Marcus smiled at her and answered, "I hoped you would come. But, why did you come today?"

Rose took a sip of the lemonade and shrugged her shoulders. She accepted a plate from Marcus and looked across the pond towards the farms and stately homes across the blue grey water. Rose remained silent for a long time. Marcus wondered it she would ever answer when she suddenly started to speak. "I don't know," she answered. Then looking up at him, she shook her head. "That isn't true." she went on, "I wasn't going to come. I tossed and turned all night," she admitted. "And I woke up this morning and was going to send your book back and tell you that I could not come.'

"It was the aunts," Rose said, as if that explained everything. At Marcus' mystified look, Rose shrugged and put down her plate. "Mr. Underhill, Colonel Brewster's sisters were widowed in the Civil War and they have lived with him and Amelia since they were young women. They are included in every family function; they are well taken care of, but they," Rose paused, struggling with her thoughts, "but they have never lived."

Rose waved her hands in the air and looked at Marcus' amber
brown eyes intently. "They sit in the corners and tat lace and as I
looked across the breakfast table this morning I suddenly saw me,
becoming them," Rose explained, her voice trailing off.

Marcus looked at Rose puzzled. "Let me get this straight,"
he said with a frown. "You are afraid you will spend the rest of
your life in a corner? You who have three lively children and are
beautiful? Rose, that is the most ridiculous thing I have ever
heard."

Rose blushed under the compliment and struggled to get
her point across. "I have been a widow for ten years, Mr.
Underhill," she explained. "I did my mourning period and I have
devoted myself to my children and my various social and
charitable functions. In Boston, I am accepted as William
Brewster's widow, but," Rose struggled. "at the 4th of July party
you did not look at me like the Widow Brewster, but like I am me,
Rose," she finished lamely. Her green eyes shyly met Marcus'
amber eyes, then her long dark lashes hid her eyes from him.

Marcus took in what Rose said silently, puzzled over her
words, not exactly sure what to say. Seated on the blanket, Rose
munched a chicken leg quietly, uncomfortable with his silence.
Abruptly changing the subject, she said, "I know so little about you
or where you came from. Tell me about the West."

"The West is big," Marcus laughed. He took a breath, as if
to clear his thoughts. "I was born in San Francisco, a beautiful little
town on the bay." He told Rose about the excitement of growing
up in San Francisco, a jewel of a town.

Relaxing a little, Rose told Marcus that her husband,
William, had been stationed at the Presidio for a time. The letters
he had written to her told of the modern and beautiful San
Francisco.

Marcus also explained that as a young man he left San
Francisco and moved to the Puget Sound area in the Pacific
Northwest to open a timber mill. The beauty of Seattle was vastly
different from the beauty of San Francisco, much wilder and more
simple.

"It all sounds so beautiful," Rose said quietly. "Are you
really leaving it all behind?"

"My wife," Marcus explained to Rose, "was born in Maryland. Maggie wanted our son to be schooled in the East and I have honored her wishes. It was hard to do. Collin came East to school at age 10 and Maggie died the following summer from typhoid fever." Marcus reached down and picked up a round smooth stone. He turned it over and over as he spoke, "Maggie has been gone for a long time and my brother and partner, Paul, died last winter. I am fairly certain that Collin will be settling here in New England. He is the only family I have left and I want to be near him."

Rose, who knew heartache and grief, looked at his bent head in sympathy. Rose, her green eyes warm with emotion, told Marcus, "I, too, have had loss in my life. But, the Brewster family has made me and my children part of their family. They are always there to help me with my children, good or bad. I can not imagine life without them."

Marcus and Rose smiled at each other in understanding. Marcus took the stone in his hand and skipped it across the surface of the still lake. Then Marcus turned and he and Rose stared at each other. That same electrical current Rose felt at the dance seemed to jolt each of them. Rose's breath caught in her throat, and she could barely breathe.

"What will you do with yourself in Boston?" Rose asked, uncomfortable with Marcus looking at her.

"Lumber brokering, among other things," Marcus answered. "I have always had an agent in Boston, and will now handle the operations here personally. I sold my holdings in the West and Peregrine Fitch and I are in the process of our first joint venture. We will invest in a variety of businesses, but I will continue to sell lumber from Boston."

Rose lifted a pebble from the beach, and tossed it at the lake. She said with a smile, "I imagine that whatever you turn your hand to, you will be very skilled." They both watched as a small barge floated by on the lake, the skipper sipping a cup of coffee. The barge disappeared from sight and they exchanged a look; Rose's heart began to pound.

Marcus began to pack away the lunch remains. Rose handed him her empty glass. "Thank you for telling me about your life," Rose said softly, smiling shyly at Marcus. Rose dropped her eyes and stared at the knot of his red neckerchief. Her breath caught in her throat and Rose felt fluttering deep inside. Rose tore her eyes away from Marcus' strong throat and looked at the low hanging bushes as if she were about to flee.

Marcus, reading her thoughts, took her fingers in his hand and kissed them softly. "Enough about our families. You liked that I looked at you as a woman?" Marcus asked softly.

Rose tried to speak as Marcus turned her hand over and with his hot open mouth kissed the palm of her hand. Rose sighed, "Oh," and she tightly closed her hand into a fist, but she did not pull away from him.

Marcus raised his head and looked intently at Rose, then he gently tugged her onto his lap. Rose hesitated only a minute, and then allowed him to settle her onto his legs. They stared at each other for a long moment and then he lowered his mouth to hers. It was a sweet kiss. He smelled of leather and tobacco, and he tasted faintly of strawberries. Marcus' hands felt firm and warm as they rested on Rose's slender waist. Rose clung to Marcus, and returned his kiss with an innocent abandon.

The kiss broken, Marcus held Rose and asked gently, "Better today?"

Rose, shyly, nodded in reply. Her hands trailed across his broad shoulders and she looked up into his gold brown eyes. Rose's green eyes held a sparkle of invitation and she leaned into Marcus. It was all the invitation Marcus needed. Gathering her close, Marcus' mouth grew warmer as he intensified the kiss. Rose, her heart beating wildly, clung to him and returned the kiss with all the pent up passion and feelings of a lifetime of loneliness. The kiss grew deeper and Marcus' mouth trailed across her cheek as he tugged gently at her ear with his lips and nibbled at her neck.

"You smell so good," Marcus murmured against her throat. He inhaled deeply, "Lavender?"

Rose, murmured an assent and clung to Marcus. His warm mouth on her neck caused shivers to run down her spine; her legs felt like jelly. She found herself lost in a maelstrom of feelings and emotions, and discovered she was lying on the blanket with Marcus on top of her. Rose ran her fingers through Marcus' soft curls and clung to him as his kiss deepened.

Rose opened her eyes and looked into Marcus' amber eyes and saw warmth and desire. She hesitated for a long moment and reached up to caress his rough cheek. Marcus was overwhelmed with Rose's surrender, and surprised at her eager kisses. He found her soft female body entrancing as she formed herself against his long hard body. Marcus longed for more, but he slowly became aware of their surroundings and he broke their kiss and sat up breathing hard. Rose, lying on the blanket, opened her eyes and also slowly sat up. She turned her back on him, as she silently began to adjust her clothes and run her fingers through her hair. Marcus reached out and trailed his fingers down her back. Rose glanced over her shoulder, a shamed expression in her eyes.

Marcus looked at her long and hard and said, "Rose, you are not some young inexperienced miss. You have been a wife and you have children. You have been a widow for a long time and what you are feeling is not wrong."

Rose blushed at his words.

Marcus could not bear the look of shame in Rose's eyes. "My darling girl," he said softly, his voice trailing away.

Rose continued to stare at Marcus. She fought an internal battle with her feelings. Part of Rose wanted nothing more than to continue kissing Marcus Underhill. The other part of her was filled with shame at her wanton behavior. Green eyes met brown and Rose saw the contrition in Marcus' eyes. Rose realized that he was not a man taking liberties with a woman, but someone who was attracted to her, Rose Brewster. Deep in Rose's heart she knew that she could trust this man, that Marcus would never do anything to hurt her

Rose looked up and realized the afternoon was fading. With a sigh, Rose began to tidy her hair. Standing, she shook out her skirts and reached down to retrieve the blanket. As Rose tidily folded the blanket, she smiled quietly at Marcus. This time it was Rose who moved into Marcus' arms.

Marcus was surprised at her boldness. With his lips against hers, Marcus whispered, "You should be heading home. When can I see you again?"

Rose thought it over, "While Amelia is away, I can probably escape most afternoons, if I don't have callers. But we need to be careful, Marcus," Rose added with a warning. Rose thought about it. "I need to be on hand tomorrow afternoon as a group of ladies are coming over to play tennis. I think I shall be in the small walled Italian garden tomorrow morning after breakfast inspecting Amelia's blooms in her absence. You might want to inspect them yourself. The gate is never locked." Rose smiled up at Marcus, a small invitation in her eyes.

Marcus smiled back at her and gave her one last lingering kiss. "Adieu, my lady." He stored the basket and blanket in the boat, then pushed the boat into the lake. Marcus swung over the side and pulling at the oars strongly he blew her one last kiss before turning toward Summerfield.

Rose watched him row away with a dreamy expression on her face. After he disappeared, Rose sat down on a boulder and thought over the afternoon and Marcus Underhill. From the moment of their dance the other night, Rose had been awakened to feelings that she thought had long disappeared from her heart. Rose felt like a school girl with her first crush. Rose told herself that she was playing with fire, but she was helpless to resist Marcus. Had she ever felt this way before in her life?

Rose thought about other men she had met and socialized with in Boston, and in particular, Peregrine. Peregrine had held her hands, escorted her to many events and had never done more than kiss her hand. The feel of his warm mouth on her hand had never raised a spark in Rose's heart. To be truthful, she could barely remember feeling anything when William had kissed her. Vague memories of her husband were all that she remembered: his brushing her hair and spreading her shining hair on the pillow in their first year of marriage, followed by him blowing out the candle and fumbling in the dark.

Rose blushed to the roots of her hair over the memory of William. What was wrong with her? It was not decent to think of such things, and she and Marcus were not... She could not even voice the thought to herself.

Rose realized the afternoon shadows were growing long. She pulled herself from the rock and with a happy sigh headed back to Eastwood.

CHAPTER 8

Rose awoke to another beautiful July day on Eaton Pond. The Colonel and the boys splashed around in the pond longer than normal and returned to the house feeling refreshed. The night had been sticky and hot and the men's morning dip felt good on sweaty bodies.

From her bedroom window, Rose heard the men and boys rounding the house and returned to look in the mirror. Her gaze reflected the same Rose, but somehow differently. Sleep eluded her once again and Rose felt she should be heavy eyed; instead she looked awake and alert. Rose tossed and turned much of the night, her sheets feeling damp and cloying in the heat, her thoughts on the cove yesterday and Marcus Underhill. Over and over Rose relived her time in Marcus' arms. His warm kisses built an excitement and breathlessness in her that she did not understand. Rose felt vague longings deep inside for what she knew not.

With her thoughts so tumultuous, Rose was reluctant to face the Colonel over breakfast. Last night at dinner, Emily came from Harlow Hall and Cordelia and Stephen Brown also joined them at dinner. Lively conversation ensued and Rose, seated far down the table from the Colonel, had not interacted with him.

This morning, with only the quiet great aunts at the table, Rose was afraid the Colonel's sharp eyes would notice something different in her. Rose felt like a private who had shirked guard duty and gone AWOL. Rose feared that under the Colonel's eagle eye he would discover something amiss and question her until the truth was ferreted out. Rose knew her absence from the breakfast table would be noticed. With a sigh, She abandoned her room and descended to the lower floor.

Something in her entrance did momentarily catch the Colonel's eye. The Colonel, an eagle eye for indiscretions from subordinates, was unsure of the expression on Rose's face. She looked guilty of something, yet at the same time, there was a glow from within, a sparkle in her eyes. Rose greeted the Colonel quietly and then turned her back on him while she poured herself a cup of tea. She shuddered as she looked over the crisp bacon, the fluffy eggs, buttered toast, and fresh melon from the garden. Rose seated herself at the table and began to sip her tea. She was glad when the Colonel returned to his paper.

Rose's thoughts drifted back to the past afternoon. She was lost in a reverie when the Colonel folded his paper and turning to Rose informed her that he would like a word with her in his study.

Rose jumped and then agreed. Once again the Colonel was puzzled at the guilty look on her face. Rose was sure he knew about her indiscretion from the afternoon before and wondered how on earth he could have found out. She spilled her tea and, abandoning the clean up to Pratt, meekly followed the Colonel from the room.

The Colonel's study was cool and the leather chairs were slightly clammy. Rose, her hands gripped tightly in her lap, watched as the Colonel settled himself at his desk and rearranged a few papers. Rose raised her eyes to look at the painting of the Colonel that hung over the empty fireplace. Looking at the same deep set eyes, Rose marveled that the Colonel already had a commanding presence as a young man. Thinking back to William, she wondered why her husband never inherited his father's steel.

The Colonel made a noise in his throat, which made her jump, and then he began. "Rose," he said slightly sternly, "we need to have a talk about the boy."

"The, the boy?" Rose asked, at a loss, her thoughts on Marcus.

"Yes, Henry, your son," he said as if she needed to be reminded she had a son.

Rose looked at the expression on the Colonel's face and knew by the light of his eyes that he had marshaled his arguments and was ready to battle.

"Has Henry done something wrong?" Rose asked lightly, hoping to put him off.

"No," the Colonel told her. "Watching him with the other fellows, he is just as strong as they are. He can do more sit ups than Edmund."

"I did not know you were concerned about Henry's health," Rose tried once again to make light of the conversation. "Dr. Edwards looked in on him this spring and marveled at how healthy Henry is. We can have Henry checked for anything you are concerned about."

The Colonel glared at her. "You know damn well that I am not concerned about the boy's health," the Colonel barked at Rose as if he were talking to a slow private on the drill field.

At the swear word, Rose raised a delicate eyebrow, but said nothing.

The Colonel apologized for the slip, but went on in a slightly lower tone, "Rose, Henry would make an excellent soldier. Rose, I know it is your decision, but I want you to think about this. There is good breeding there and you don't want to make Henry different from the rest of the Brewsters."

Rose stayed silent, listening. She pulled her lower lip between her teeth. She knew that anything she would say would fall on deaf ears, so she decided to wait until he was finished.

"You are a woman and you don't understand these things," the Colonel went on. "Some day Henry is going to be in business with his cousins and they won't be able to work together. Soldiering makes a man tough, makes him good in business; a soldier must be good at issuing orders and obeying orders. Henry needs to learn all of these things. A good military education would prepare him for life."

During his conversation, Rose had turned her head slightly and she looked out the window. She had heard all of this before.

The Colonel continued, "You and I both know the details of the will. Amelia and I have been talking. Henry needs a father."

At this, Rose turned her head and looked at the Colonel, a surprised look on her face. The Colonel continued, "Henry needs a father, one who is well versed in the military. Teach the boy discipline."

Rose's irritation with this conversation pricked. "I was not aware my son was out of control and needed discipline. As for a husband, did you have anyone in mind?" she asked quietly.

The Colonel missed the irony in her voice. "Henry's problem is that his nose is always buried in a book. A sound education is one thing, but he carries it too far." The Colonel moved a few more papers and cleared his throat. "I have had a letter from my old friend, Colonel Denby," Colonel Brewster told her. "His son mustered out of the army and moved to Boston. Could be a good match for the boy and you."

Rose saw it clearly. If they could not convince her to send Henry to school, the Brewsters would marry her off to someone who would.

"Amelia alluded to the fact that you and she would consider the idea of my marriage," Rose said quietly. "But, I thought she was suggesting Peregrine."

"Fitch?" the Colonel spat. "No."

At the surprised look on her face, the Colonel continued, "Fitch is a good businessman. Couldn't be better, but you know he didn't care for the military all that much."

Rose looked out the window again and then back at the Colonel. Possibly due to her lack of sleep or whatever had ruptured in her soul this summer, the rebellion in Rose grew. She heaved a large sigh and said in a still even tone, "So you would marry me off to a man who would force me to send my son to military school?"

"Now it isn't like that," the Colonel protested. "I am sure Denby's son is a good man. You need a husband too, Rose. I won't always be here to oversee your finances. And you need to do your duty as a member of the Brewster family." The Colonel missed Amelia. He was not in a very good mood. He needed Amelia by his side for these arguments with these damn daughters-in-law. It was the absence of his wife that made the Colonel speak a little more abruptly.

As Rose stood up, her hands formed fists at her sides. She advanced to the Colonel's desk and leaned on it, looking him in the eye. "Henry will not be going to military school," she said quietly, but firmly. Her anger soared and her voice rose, "I am not some piece of property that you can just sell off so that it can be developed properly. I am a woman and I will not allow you to force me to marry who you think is an appropriate father for my son." Rose went on, "This argument ends now! Henry Brewster will not attend Slater this year, not next year, not ever. As long as I have breath in my body I will honor William's wishes and I shall not send my son to Slater. William," she repeated, "my husband, your son."

"That damn will!" the Colonel repeated. "There was nothing wrong with the education or experience that my sons received at Slater. What was he thinking? He was a fine soldier and an excellent officer. I was right to send every one of my sons to Slater and my grandsons should attend as well."

Rose, pushed beyond endurance, pounded her small fists on his desk and demanded, slightly hysterical, "William. Why do you never say William's name?"

There was a moment of silence and then the Colonel, with pain in his eyes, demanded, "What are you talking about?"

Rose pushed herself away from the desk. She breathed heavily and there was the threat of tears in her eyes. She said angrily, "William. You never say his name. It is always 'my son,' 'him' or 'Henry's father.' You never call William by his name."

There was a brief silence and then the Colonel expostulated, "I don't know what you are talking about." He waved his hand at her as if shooing a fly. Annoyed, he shouted at Rose, "Besides, we are not discussing my son at this time. We are discussing my grandson. We are discussing Henry's future. You are ruining him."

The color drained from Rose's face as she stared at the Colonel. Before Rose could say anything the Colonel went on, in a quieter tone, but still harshly, "I know what my son was like after he came back. Maybe if you had tried a little harder as a wife he would have been a different man, happier."

Shocked at his attack, Rose gasped, "Me?" All of sudden, she had had enough. "Maybe," she said, her patience at an end, "you should have tried a little harder to be a better father."

The Colonel, shocked at such insubordination, barked, "What are you saying?"

Rose said with the threat of tears in her voice, "William was your son. William was my husband. You may have chosen me for him but I was the best wife I knew how. I know how you went to my aunt and uncle and persuaded them to allow me to marry William." Rose's breath caught in her throat, her hands gripped fiercely together. "I will honor William by respecting his wishes." Rose looked at the Colonel, her eyes sparkling with tears and wrath. "You never say his name," she said with emphasis. "Why do you never say his name?" With the last word her voice raised.

The Colonel stood and came around the desk, towering over Rose. "I will not discuss my son with you," he spat. "Rose Brewster, mark my words, you are ruining your children, especially Henry. You are making him different from all the other boys and I don't want him growing up to be like, to grow to be...," the Colonel could not finish his sentence. His face grew very red. He threw down his pen and stomped from the room.

Rose stood in front of the desk, alone, her shoulders bowed, tears running down her cheeks. She was furious at the Colonel, hurt at his words.

Rose slowly walked out of the study. She felt crushed and desolate. Great Aunt Easter stood at the foot of the stairs, a shocked look on her face. She had obviously heard every word of the argument. She took a step towards Rose and murmured, "Oh my dear."

But, Rose, awash with tears, shook her head and rushed from the house.

Marcus let himself into Amelia's walled garden. The garden was a pleasant space, with unexpected hidden bowers, gleaming statues and a tinkling fountain. Tall shrubs created enticing shady groves and underfoot Shasta daisies and clover clustered together. It was an unstructured garden, looking very natural at first glance. Upon deeper inspection, the riot of plantings were definitely under control, with vines clipped back and small shrubs carefully shaped. The soft tinkling of the fountain added to the music of the birds in the trees. As Marcus stepped deeper into the garden he glimpsed a small brown rabbit as it hopped out of sight.

Marcus moved around the garden, exploring, but his mind was elsewhere. Marcus spent a sleepless night thinking about Rose. From the first meeting, Rose Brewster intrigued Marcus. Rose did not know that Marcus had watched her in the crowd the night of the band concert. Rose sat among a group of women and Marcus had been attracted to her sparkling eyes and laugh as she replied to the woman sitting next to her. Her acute embarrassment when she came upon Collin and Lavinia amused Marcus. She was out of her element and horrified at the discovery. Rose's eyes snapped fire as she scolded the two young people and yet it was interesting to watch her draw a cover over her emotions.

Since the death of his wife, Maggie, Marcus had not felt such a strong interest in any woman. Certainly he had dalliances and he never suffered for feminine companionship. But, Rose Brewster with her clear green eyes, her crown of shining hair atop her proudly held head, her slender waist and her bright smile... Marcus tossed and turned half the night haunted by Rose's green eyes and her soft eager kisses.

Marcus had been surprised that Rose agreed to meet him in the cove yesterday. Rose surprised him with her kiss in the moonlight that first evening and her even warmer embrace yesterday. Marcus knew she was not the type of woman to meet men clandestinely. Yet, Rose allowed him one small indiscretion after another.

Aside from the sexual attraction that Marcus felt for Rose, some quality in her made him want to shelter and protect her. Rose could stand amongst a large group of Brewsters and yet seemed to be a solitary figure. He glimpsed a thirst and longing in her eyes, even as she tended to her children.

Rose startled Marcus as she burst through the gate into the garden, slamming it shut behind her. She looked as if she were pursued by all the hounds from hell. He had never seen this Rose. Rose's eyes were brightly shining, her cheeks were very red and stained with tears, her hair had little wisps hanging down from its usual tidiness and she gripped her hands to her chest. Rose gulped deep breaths as if she had been running and she looked around wildly. Rose surprised Marcus by rushing at him and throwing herself into his arms.

The kiss was eager, if a little unskilled, and Marcus was surprised at her boldness. The kiss broken, Rose lingered with her arms still on his shoulders, looking up at him with a challenging gaze. Marcus put his hands on her arms, holding her slightly away from him. He could see a mixture of emotions in her eyes, not all identifiable. He saw her longing, but her eyes were also bright with shyness and even deeper, if he were not mistaken, a glimpse of anger and hurt. Rebellion, too.

"That was quite a welcome," Marcus said drily.

Rose looked at Marcus and then dropped her eyes, but she said nothing.

Marcus, puzzled, waited. When the silence grew he asked gently, "Do you want to tell me about it?"

Rose dropped her hands from his shoulders. "I am sorry. I do not know what came over me," she murmured. As quickly as she had charged into the garden, Rose wrenched herself away from him and ran to the gate. In Rose's haste, she struggled with the catch and finally pulled it open, but Marcus had followed her and leaning over, he slammed the gate shut. Marcus turned Rose around, gripping her shoulders, but she would not meet his eyes.

"Let me go," she pleaded. As Marcus released her, Rose slumped against the gate, then she dropped her face into her hands and began to weep.

Marcus pulled Rose into his arms and let her cry on his shoulder. Finally, the tears and hiccoughs slowed and Marcus handed her his handkerchief and said gently, "Do you want to tell me about it?"

Rose dried her eyes and blew her nose. She shook her head while Marcus continued to gently rub her arms and back. Rose felt cold and Marcus' warm hands on her arms felt life saving. Marcus reached up and took Rose's face in his hands. He lifted her face and kissed her lips gently. Marcus said, "You know, Rose, I would like to help you. You can tell me anything. Maybe I can fix it."

The silence grew as Rose looked into Marcus' understanding eyes. Finally, she said bitterly, "I was informed this morning that I am a bad mother, I was a bad wife and I am a bad Brewster. I have decided to prove them correct." Rose raised her head and looked at him with hurt, unshed tears in her eyes. "And that is why I am here." She looked at him and said, "I might as well prove them correct by meeting you clandestinely. So, here I am!" She waved her hands in the air.

Marcus looked at Rose confused and, ignoring her second statement, asked, "Who said you were bad? The Colonel? Did he find out about us?"

Rose realized that he had come to the same conclusion that she had at the beginning of her argument with the Colonel. She shook her head. "No, he knows nothing about our meetings," she said. "The Colonel decided today was the day to tackle me and force me to send Henry to Slater Military Academy."

"Force you?" Marcus could not understand what she was talking about. "How could he force you to do anything concerning your son?"

Rose put a hand on his arm. "Oh Marcus, there is so much about my life that you don't know. But the Colonel," she stopped, at a loss for words, the threat of tears once more in her voice.

Marcus, sensing something was not right, gently prodded, "The Colonel..."

Rose turned to Marcus and said wearily, "The Colonel tackled me today about Henry's schooling." She paused, "It got nasty. This is not our first argument, nor will it be the last," Rose said as she once again dissolved into tears, her fists clenched. "It just never stops. They keep hammering and hammering at me. Some days I just don't feel like I can take it any more."

Marcus, utterly confused, looked at this wild looking woman in front of him. "Come," Marcus said and led Rose unresisting deeper into the garden to a concrete bench under a shady arbor. He took her icy hands in his. They sat silently side by side for some time, her threatened tears abated; Rose felt exhausted. The garden was quiet. The droning of bees gathering pollen from a nearby patch of blossoms could be heard, as well as the faint rustling of some small animal in the bushes. A warm midday drowsiness blanketed the entire garden; even the birds were silenced.

Marcus gently squeezed her hand and said, "Rose, when you are ready to talk about the argument I will listen. If you don't want to talk about it today, I won't press you. Just know that I would like to help." Marcus paused as she straightened her shoulders and slightly shook her head.

Rose looked at Marcus sideways and took a deep breath. She tried to explain, "Mr. Underhill, I am a widow. I am a widow of a Brewster." Pulling her hand out from under his, she reached up and smoothed her hair. With a small sob she said, "I will always be a widow, Marcus. And because of that I have not, naturally, gone around involving myself with men. I really do not know what has come over me the last few days. I am not being respectable."

Marcus let her last comment pass, but asked incredulously, "Do the Brewsters truly expect you to never marry again?"

Rose was silent as she tried to find the words to explain. "It is and it is not really the Brewsters," she said slowly. "I will never marry because of William, my husband." There was a small pause and then to emphasize Rose reached out and thumped Marcus' arm. "I can not marry because of William," she insisted.

"Cannot?" Marcus asked with a frown. "Do you mean to tell me that you loved your husband so much that you never want to," he paused searching for the words, "be with a man again?"

Rose allowed a shaky laugh to escape her lips and said, "Not quite." She shook her head. "Marcus, I can not explain." Rose looked at his warm strong hands grasping hers and pulled away from him, crossing her arms and tucking her hands against her sides.

Frowning, Marcus urged, "Try to explain, please."

At his confused tone, Rose took a deep breath and smoothed her skirts. She shrugged and said, slightly crisply, "I am simply a widow raising her children with the help of her deceased husband's family." Rose shook her head. "We all make choices in this world, and these are the choices that I have made. I will never remarry."

Silence fell over them again, and Rose slowly said, "William." She paused, feeling the need to be honest, "I think I need to explain to you about William. And the will."

Marcus, silent, sat beside Rose and forcibly pulled her hand away from her body and began to chafe it. Rose said, "I was just 17 when I married William. My husband was a dashing military officer. My parents died when I was very young and I had been raised by my aunt and uncle. My parents left me with a substantial inheritance and my aunt and uncle and the Brewsters felt that William and I made an excellent match. So, we married." She paused and then continued, "William was a lieutenant in the Cavalry and we had not been married long. Soon after Lavinia was born William was dispatched to the West. William spent three years fighting the Indians. After he returned, it was obvious William had lived unimaginable horrors that he could not share with anyone, not even me." Rose stared unseeing and then continued, "The only respite William could seem to find from his demons was with his horses. In the end, it was his horse that caused his death."

"Where in the West did he serve?" Marcus asked.

Rose told Marcus and he said, "Ah," understanding.

"It was his own private hell. He returned and everyone thought he was a war hero. His father was so proud," Rose said with bitterness. She reached down as she spoke and pulled a daisy from beside the bench. Slowly she pulled each petal off. "William could not let me in and he could not get out." Rose moved a little on the bench, then said, "I think it started earlier with William. From birth, his father insisted that he be a soldier, as generations of Brewster fathers have done with success. The Colonel came back from the Civil War and did not like the little boy he found. The Colonel thought William was a soft little mother's boy and he felt he needed to be toughened up. So, the Brewsters sent him off to Slater at age eight.

There was a long pause; Marcus waited. The pause went on so long that he started to say something, when Rose said, "It was because of Slater and his time out West that William wrote his will." She spoke in a tone that made it seem self explanatory.

Marcus prodded, mystified, "The will?"

Rose said dully, "His last Will and Testament. William did not want any of his sons to face the horrors that he had. So, in his will he stipulated that as long as I stay unmarried, all of our children, especially sons, will be educated as I choose. No one else, certainly not the children's grandfather, shall dictate the education choices except for me." She said this last with firmness, remembering her argument from earlier in the day. "By law, as a single mother, all care and keeping of the children should by rights go to a male relative. The Colonel oversees all of our finances, and the children's and my trusts, but he has no say over the children's education. That stipulation rescinds if I choose to marry."

Marcus stared at Rose, mulling over her words. Finally he said, "You are sacrificing yourself for your children."

Rose looked at Marcus and shook her head. "I am not sacrificing anything for my children. I am a very happy mother, most of the time," she amended with a wry laugh. "I have been able to give my children secure childhoods amongst a very tight knit loving family." Rose shook her head, for the first time a small sparkle returned to her eyes. "My daughters are forever reminding me that a new century is just around the corner and Torie tells me that women will have new stronger roles. I just want all of my children to be able to embrace their dreams."

Rose took a breath and continued, "Henry is an amazing little boy, and he has never shown any interest in the military. He worships his older cousins, but he has never expressed an interest in following in their footsteps. Henry is intellectual and drawn to older civilizations. It wouldn't be hard to see Henry living in Egypt someday digging for pyramids." Rose finished with a rueful laugh, "Now, if the Colonel was hellbent on sending one of my children to follow in their father's footsteps, it should be Torie. She idolizes the soldier her father was and longs to be a part of the military."

Marcus looked at this beautiful woman and thought about the decisions that had been thrust upon her. The silence deepened as he went over in his mind all that she had told him. Slowly he said, "Your husband was a coward."

Rose turned and looked at Marcus in astonishment. Rose shook her head, "William was an army hero."

Marcus shook his head, and restated, "Your husband was a coward. Do you mean to tell me that your husband did not have the courage to stand up to his father, but he made it so that you would fight his battles for him?"

"William never knew that he was going to die so young," Rose protested. "I did not even know I was pregnant with Henry until after William's accident, William never knew he had a son."

"So you are going to sacrifice your entire life for this?" Marcus asked her, unbelieving.

"I am not sacrificing my life," Rose disagreed. "I have everything I need. My children are my life. I lead a life that I enjoy. In town, I am a vital part of the literary society. I also help out the widows and the orphans, routinely accompany my mother-in-law on her social rounds and I attend the symphony with my sister-in-law." Rose said ruefully, "I accompany and chaperone Lavinia on her pursuits in society. Until recently, I thought I was a very good chaperone. What more from life could I want?"

Marcus pondered Rose's words as he looked at her. Her eyes were swollen from her tears, and her nose and cheeks were red. Even in her disheveled state Marcus still found Rose to be a very attractive woman. Marcus thought about Rose standing up to Colonel Brewster. Having had business dealings with the man, Marcus knew the Colonel to be hard headed and stubborn. Marcus wondered at her brief marriage, especially marrying so very young.

Marcus looked at Rose, and saw her innocence, but also her strength.

"You must think me a fool," Rose said, tears in her voice again.

"No," Marcus said sincerely. "I am honored that you felt comfortable enough with me to allow me into your heart. That you came to me for comfort and solace."

Rose leaned back against the stone bench as if she could no longer support herself; she felt exhausted. "Marcus, I need to be honest with you." Rose looked at Marcus, her eyes swollen, and said, "I don't know what has happened to me this summer. What I do know is that you do attract me, as no man has before, and that I trust you." Marcus reached to gather her in his arms, but she held out her hands to stop him.

"I may be very attracted to you, but that doesn't matter," she said as she raised her swollen eyes and looked at him. "I have said it before; I can not marry."

Marcus could not help himself, and blurted out, "You can still be involved with me without marriage."

Rose looked at Marcus in slight shock and answered, "I cannot carry on a scandalous affair in public. I cannot be anything to the world but the Widow Brewster, prim and proper. We must think of the children."

Marcus looked at her set face. "All right," he finally said with a nod. "I understand the rules. What I am going to propose is this: in public, you are the Widow Brewster, but just for the next few weeks, while we are living at Eastwood, we manage to bump into each other and get to know each other a little better. At the end of the summer, when you go back to Boston, we shall see."

"It will not be any different," she told him sadly. Rose thought over his words. What if she took a chance, and just explored this man a little more. What could it hurt to have a mild summer flirtation? Rose knew in the back of her mind that she would be playing with fire, that this was not a mild summer flirtation. The Colonel's words rang through her head: "bad Brewster." Why not prove him right?

Marcus stood and took her in his arms. It was a gentle kiss, a soft sweet kiss. At the touch of his lips, Rose felt the tears rising again. Rose shook her head at Marcus and the tears receded.

"Thank you," she said softly. "Thank you for listening to me today."

"Shall we meet again, tomorrow?" Marcus asked her. "How about back at the cove?"

Rose looked up at him and nodded her agreement. The light was returning to her eyes and she was so irresistible that he gathered her to him. Slowly the kiss ended and, standing, he pulled her to her feet and escorted her to the gate. Marcus stood silently for a long time after listening to her footsteps die away.

The ten days that followed were among the happiest of Rose Brewster's life. Always the proper lady, she was on hand to act as the Colonel's hostess when guests called. In the mornings, she met with Mrs. Musgrave and dealt with housekeeping concerns. French lessons with M. du Gres had been suspended while Amelia was away, but Rose still practiced French with Kitty and Torie every day and oversaw the children in their music lessons. She found time to cuddle Sarah and Abigail and read them stories.

Every day Rose found odd moments to slip away. She and Marcus never met in the same location; it could be the walled garden, the cove or deep in the woods. Rose and Marcus slipped away several times and sat on the blanket in the quiet cove. Marcus would read sonnets to her as she dreamily listened, her eyes unfocused on the lake. Other times, Rose would read to Marcus and he would lie, propped on one elbow watching her face.

At times they would just talk. Talk about their childhoods. Marcus told her about living in the Pacific Northwest and he told her about Maggie, Collin's mother. Maggie had been a strong woman who had abandoned her family in the East and had made a home with her husband in the raw woods. No matter how rough the living situation, Maggie was always able to make a place feel like home.

Rose told him what it had been like to lose her parents at a very young age and to be brought up by her elderly aunt and uncle. They were childless and had been unsure about raising a young heiress.

Always they would turn to kisses and words of affection. Rose refused to discuss their own future and Marcus did not press her. Privately, he had written to an attorney friend in New York and broadly questioned about the validity of the will without explaining why he was interested.

Marcus, due to his business dealings with the male Brewsters, began to hold a good understanding of the family dynamics. Although Christopher and Charles were strong business men, they allowed their father to dictate their business and personal lives. The Brewster family created a strong net of family dynamics and, while supporting each other, also held each other in strong check.

Peregrine Fitch became a very good friend of Marcus' and an excellent business partner. Marcus puzzled over Peregrine's attitude toward Rose. Peregrine was protective of her, but at the same time, a little reticent. Peregrine's attitude toward Rose was almost that of a doting uncle. Marcus knew that Peregrine had been William Brewster's best friend, and assumed he felt a devotion to Rose due to his friendship. But, there was something else that Marcus could not put his finger on.

Peregrine became a strong business ally with Marcus and together they worked to take over Sam Gardner's business in Boston. Sam's financial state proved incredibly shaky due to several poor business choices. Peregrine and Marcus had several deep discussions and attempted to go about this quietly, mostly for the Gardner's sake. The two men did not want Sam Gardner or his children to lose social standing in Boston society. It would not be the first time that a family faced financial ruin due to poor business decisions and still managed to maintain their standing in society.

Marcus and Peregrine also explored other business ventures and Marcus could not always step away easily. Usually he found an excuse to break away for an hour or two. As both he and Peregrine spent their days on Eaton Pond, most of their business could be conducted from Marcus' study, although they made a few trips into Boston.

One afternoon, the brilliant morning sky turned cloudy with a yellow cast, promising a thunder and lightening storm. After lunch, Phoebe took the little girls upstairs for their naps and the children settled in the screened porch. Henry and Edmund worked side by side on the model of a ship. The tiny little parts were fiddly and Kitty and Torie sat across the table watching the boys work.

When the small cannon that Edmund tried to attach slipped from his fingers for the third time, Kitty came around the table and with her smaller fingers held the piece in place while her brother applied the glue.

Edmund thanked his little sister and looked up to see Torie scowl at the praise. "Crab cake," he teased her.

Torie was indignant. "Pooh, that isn't so special," she said, with a shrug.

Kitty had been focused on the ship, raised her head and looked across the table at Torie. Kitty let a small satisfied smile cross her lips, but she did not say anything.

Torie scowled again, and looked away. "Kitty," Torie asked, slightly goading, "what do you want to be when you grow up?"

Kitty looked at her cousin with a puzzled look. "I want to grow up to be a lady," Kitty told her cousin. "I want to be like Susanna and have beaux and dance and marry someone like Alexander." Kitty sighed as she thought about Alexander. Kitty found her sister's fiance to be the epitome of her dreams: Alexander, with his golden hair and his fair good looks. Kitty had spied on Alexander kissing Susanna one evening; it had been a most romantic sight.

In turn, Kitty asked her cousin Torie, "What do you want to be when you grow up?"

"Not a lady," Torie said with assurance. "Back home, all our mothers do is attend meetings and drink tea, day after day. And they never read papers and..."

Edmund spoke up, interrupting Torie, a frown on his face, "Torie, nobody works harder than our mothers. And they are not just sitting around drinking tea. They raise lots of money to help feed widows and orphans. They do lots of good things."

Torie looked at Edmund surprised. Edmund always supported her ideas. It was not often that Edmund disagreed with her.

Stung, Torie shrugged and walked over to the window. She looked out at the darkening sky and sighed. "What I mean," Torie tried to explain, "is that I think there are better ways to help people. Besides raising money to help widows and orphans, maybe we need to work in an orphanage. When I grow up, I just want to know that I am making a difference."

"Well," Henry said, always the peace maker, "Kitty can raise the money and you can spend it."

A sudden gust of air shivered through the porch and the distant sound of thunder rolled over the afternoon sky, interrupting the conversation. The sky turned from grey to yellow and out on the pond small white capped waves splashed up on the dock. Edmund joined Torie at the window to gaze out at the weather. As they watched the storm approach, they saw Rose come from the direction of the walled garden. She hurried as large drops of rain began to fall and the wind caught her hair and pulled it from its usual tidy topknot. Without looking at the children, Rose walked past the screened porch to the front of the house.

Rose shook droplets of rain off of her clothes and put her hands up to tidy her hair. Sighing, she settled on the verandah with the great aunts. The two older ladies smiled at Rose and Easter waved the shawl she was knitting. The two elderly ladies reminisced about storms that they experienced on Eaton Pond when they were little girls. Rose listened, but her mind was back on the walled garden. She and Marcus had just settled on the bench when the storm broke. Rose pleaded with Marcus to leave the canoe in the cove and walk home through the woods.

Rose smiled as she remembered Marcus' warm greeting as she stepped into the walled garden. The wind swirled through the closed garden and the slight smell of sulfur filled the air. Rose nestled her head against Marcus' broad chest, protected against the gusts. She could hear his heart beating strongly.

Marcus kissed the top of Rose's head as she wrapped her arms around his waist tightly. Rose raised her head and looked at Marcus. He was surprised to see tears in her eyes.

She dropped her head and shook it. "It is just that Amelia and the rest of the family return on Friday," she told him. "Marcus, this has been a stolen season, and it is about to come to an end."

Marcus cupped her face in his warm hands. "It doesn't have to end," he told Rose, his deep voice soft.

"You don't know how hard it will be to slip away," Rose protested. "The house will be filled with people and Amelia loves to garden. She spends every second she can out here working on the plants and..." Rose stopped to gulp and Marcus ran his hands up and down her shoulders, soothing her.

Marcus looked at her hunched shoulders, her arms clutching his waist. "Do you know," Marcus slowly told Rose, "at night, I know which bedroom is yours. I look at the light and long to be beside you."

Rose blushed. "Marcus," she began, then stopped. "I don't know what to say." She then admitted softly, "I, too, look across at your light at night. I don't know what we can do."

"Rose," Marcus gathered her up into his arms again, "don't fret. You mean more and more to me every day. This is not just a summer fling. I want to tell the Brewsters how much I care." Marcus looked down at Rose with a warm boyish light in his amber brown eyes.

Rose looked up at Marcus with a glow in her eyes. Then the light dimmed, and she shook her head, "You can not tell them."

The light in Marcus' own eyes dimmed a bit. "No?" was all Marcus said. As Rose started to protest, Marcus said, "I want you to at least think about it. What is going to happen when we go back to Boston?"

The argument might have continued if lightning had not spiked across the sky. They kissed briefly and parted for shelter.

On the porch Rose still dwelled over the fact that the rest of the house party would return the following Friday. Rose knew her time with Marcus would be limited. The house would once again be bursting with people, and it would not be as easy to slip away; her absence would be noted.

Men's voices from the Colonel's study floated out of the open window and the voices grew louder as the men stepped out of the house. To Rose's surprise, Peregrine and Charles came out onto the veranda, accompanied by the Colonel. Charles had stayed in Boston while Alice was gone, and had come to Eastwood to discuss some business with his father.

Peregrine and Charles greeted Rose and the great aunts cordially. They looked out at the storm. Peregrine excused himself and started to move down the front steps. At Tabitha's protest to wait out the storm, Peregrine looked out at the wild weather and shrugged. "I am only going as far as Summerfield," Peregrine explained. "I need to talk with Marcus Underhill over our discussion with the Colonel."

The group on the porch watched Peregrine drive off and the great aunts, shivering at the ferocity of the storm, moved into the house. Charles settled himself next to Rose and accepted a cup of tea. Together, they watched the vivid forks of lightening and the crashing of thunder.

Charles told Rose he received a letter from Alice. The group was having a delightful time in Washington. Rose, who had not received any word from Lavinia, smiled as she told Charles she was sure Lavinia would be excited to tell her mother every detail when she returned.

Charles and Rose paused as a particularly loud boom rattled the front porch. Immediately after that, the storm began moving away down the pond. Charles looked at Rose intently and she smiled back at him. "There is something different about you this summer, Rose," Charles told his sister-in-law. "Has something happened?"

Rose jumped guiltily and then shrugged and smiled slightly. "No," Rose disagreed, "I am just the same old Rose."

Charles darted a look into the house to make sure no one was about, then he leaned over and took Rose's hand and gave it a small squeeze. "My darling Rose," he said to her, "I don't know if I have ever seen you looking so happy. I think I know the reason, and I just want to say that I am not going to repeat anything. Rose, I know you tried very hard to make my brother happy. And I think it is time for you to be happy."

Rose colored and laughed shakily at Charles. "I don't know what you are talking about," Rose said weakly.

The sound of the children floated around to the side of the house. With the storm's passing, the children left the screened porch to look at the blown leaves and debris littering the lawn. Charles gave Rose's hand one last reassuring squeeze. "I am here if you ever need a confidante," he promised her. "And I won't say a word to my wife. Alice would be so excited to see you happy and in a relationship that she would start planning your wedding." Rose stared at Charles as he turned his attention to the children.

Chapter 9

The imminent arrival of Amelia and the rest of the party weighed heavily on Rose's mind as she accompanied the family into Eaton's Grove for a Thursday night band concert. Rose gave Phoebe a well deserved night off and Sarah and Abigail were handed over into the special care of Torie and Kitty. The two older girls were specifically told to keep an eye on the little twins. Rose settled down on a chair next to Great Aunt Easter. The Colonel, as usual, gathered with a bunch of cronies, once again reliving the glory days of war.

Rose listened to the band and hummed softly as Emily sank down next to her with a sigh of relief. "I swear, Rose," she said quietly, "if Christopher invites those wretched Gardners over for dinner one more time, I am going to scream."

Rose looked at Emily with some understanding. "Who is worse," she asked, with a smile, "Sam or those children of his?"

"It is a toss up," Emily assured her. "Without a mother around, those boys run wild and Sam just ignores them. I have to keep an eye on them around my children constantly. And every possible chance Sam Gardner gets, he reminds me that you are alone and need protection." Emily laughed, "You need protection from him!"

"I don't give him an iota of encouragement," Rose assured her. "In fact, I try to excuse myself as politely and quickly as possible when he is around."

"I have heard," Emily said with feeling. "He complained to me the other day that you were always going off for walks by yourself. You would think there were murderers around every bush, the way he talked." She looked at Rose with a frown. "You haven't been going off alone to the woods and coves all the time, have you?"

Rose felt the color rising in her face. "Don't be silly," she told her sister-in-law weakly. Rose swallowed and went on, "Sometimes there are so many people in that house. I want quiet time to read, so I take myself to the garden or the cove. I am always within calling distance and the children are always around."

Emily shrugged, "Sam Gardner is a nuisance. Just be careful and make sure he doesn't follow you on one of your walks."

Rose, horrified at the thought, thanked her sister in law for her words. It was something that she had not thought about before. While she and Marcus were very careful, there was always the possibility of discovery. Had Sam Gardner been following them?

Speaking of Marcus, Rose looked up and saw Marcus watching her from across the square. Even from a distance she could see the light of desire in his eyes. Marcus nodded to Rose slightly and disappeared down a shady path in the park. Emily, watching her sister-in-law, was surprised at the light that suddenly appeared on Rose's face. Frowning, Emily turned to see where Rose was staring. She saw only Peregrine Fitch standing close to Christopher in conversation.

A shocking thought went through Emily's head. She was not surprised a moment later when Rose excused herself and began to walk across the square. Peregrine moved on and could not be seen anywhere. Emily watched as Rose, with a glance over her shoulder, casually entered a shaded path. Emily sank back into her chair. Could Rose and Peregrine be starting a summer romance? After all these years? Emily decided that she would need to think some more about this.

Rose strolled down the shady paths of the park, nodding at people she met and trying unobtrusively to peer into dark corners. She neared the area where she caught Collin and Lavinia kissing on that fateful night in June. As she passed by she heard a faint "Pssst." Not quite sure what she heard, she paused and heard the noise again.

She stepped into the leafy bower and felt Marcus' arms wrap around her. "Are you insane?" she asked against his lips, giggling a little. "We are going to be discovered."

"Shhh," Marcus hushed her. "You are such a toothsome dish I could not pass this opportunity. Collin sometimes has the best ideas..." His kiss deepened and she returned it with enthusiasm, Rose slowly opened her eyes and turned cold. Over Marcus' shoulder she felt a shadowy presence.

Rose tore herself away from Marcus and whispered, raggedly, "There was someone there, watching us."

Marcus looked over his shoulder and saw no one. Quickly, he walked up and down the path peering into dark corners. He came back and found Rose shaking. "I don't see anyone," he told her. "I doubt they could see who it was." Marcus reached out and patted Rose's arm. "Oh, my love, it will be fine."

Rose stopped shaking and stared at him, "My love?" she asked, trying to be light.

"My love," he repeated. "This is not the time or place to say such things, a place where we could be discovered. There are things I want to say to you." Rose continued to stare at him. Marcus said urgently, "I want you to go back now and meet me later in the garden. Do you think you can manage?"

Rose nodded. She gave Marcus one last quick kiss and, peering in every dark corner, she walked to the entrance of the park.

Emily was certain she was on to something when Rose emerged from the path a few minutes later looking slightly flushed. Not three minutes later Peregrine, too, stepped from the same path. He went up to Rose and started a conversation with her like he had not seen her all evening. Rose looked slightly distracted and her cheeks blazed vividly pink. Emily, watching, raised her eyebrows and a small smile of speculation crossed her lips.

Rose sat in her dark bedroom, still dressed. She waited for the house to go to sleep so she could slip out to meet Marcus in the garden. Rose thought about their stolen minutes in the park, and her blood ran cold every time she remembered that shadowy presence. Someone had been there. Someone had watched her and Marcus in an embrace. But who?

Rose knew that she and Marcus were taking more and more chances. What if they were discovered? Rose pulled herself up and began to pace the floor. She and Marcus were adults. Would it be so bad if it were known? Rose felt sure that Marcus was accepted by Eaton Pond families, and those families made up some of the cream of Boston society. Rose knew that not only a man's wealth made him acceptable in Boston society, but also his manners. And there in lay the rub. Marcus and Collin slowly built a reputation as gentlemen, regardless of their Western background; but if rumors circulated that the older Mr. Underhill was carrying on with the

Widow Brewster, their reputations could suffer, including the reputations of their children. Rose and Marcus did not want that to happen.

Still, like a bright flame draws a moth, Rose could not resist Marcus. She knew he awaited her in the garden. Amelia would return tomorrow and time to slip away would be limited, if not impossible. What was one more night? Cautiously, Rose slipped off her shoes and, carrying them, began to quietly open her door. Rose listened intently to the silence of the house. Faint snuffling noises could be heard from the Great Aunts' bedroom, along with the ticking of the grandfather clock in the drawing room. The hallway was very dark as Rose cautiously groped her way towards the back servants' stairs.

Suddenly, from the nursery, she heard wailing. Rose paused and listened as Abigail's sobs shook the house. In a moment, Sarah's screams joined her sister. Rose, listening, realized that a full on drama was taking place on the third floor. With a sigh she firmly opened the servants' stairs and climbed to the third floor instead of the kitchen.

Two hours later Rose finished in the nursery. After indulging in too many sweets at the concert, Abigail had been sick in her bed. Her twin sister, shortly joined her sister in the vomiting and Rose and Phoebe spent time cleaning up the mess. Kitty, awakened by the noise, began to feel queasy herself. Eventually, Rose and Phoebe bedded the older children into the dormitory with Edmund, cleaned up the little girls and soothed them back to sleep.

When Rose had entered the nursery fully dressed, Phoebe raised an eyebrow, but said nothing. Later, Rose wearily retraced her steps to the second floor. She went to her bedroom and looked at the star filled sky. Down in the woods, the first birds started their sleepy dawn chorus. She wondered if Marcus still waited for her, but was sure that he had come and gone. He may have been able to hear the noises in the nursery from the walled garden.

Sighing, Rose changed into her nightgown and climbed into bed exhausted. As she thought of Marcus, tears slowly slid down her face.

Torie was having a bad morning. No one in the nursery had a restful night's sleep. Torie and Kitty began the day with cross words when Kitty could not find a particular hair ribbon and discovered it under the window seat crumpled and torn. Torie maintained her innocence; after all it could have been one of those wretched little girls. But Phoebe, exhausted from the midnight nursery turmoil, took Kitty's side and scolded Torie. Alice had not had the opportunity to hire a new nanny and the care of the extra children began to wear on Phoebe.

Phoebe felt bereft. She had not been able to count on Miss Rose to help her with the children as Rose always seemed to be going off by herself. Phoebe, at times, felt run off of her feet. Miss Rose's appearance in the middle of the night, fully dressed, led Phoebe to wonder what was going on. Her employer divulged nothing.

Torie abandoned the nursery and descended to breakfast. Entering the smaller dining room, she found her grandfather seated alone reading the paper and eating his breakfast.

The Colonel thumped the paper and shook his head. He barked, "Women wanting to vote. That is ridiculous. They would simply vote the way their men told them to vote." He said, "It just gives men a chance to vote more than once."

"Grandpapa," Torie said earnestly, "did you know that women can vote in New Zealand?"

The Colonel frowned at Torie and said, "Well, if the good people of New Zealand have any politics that are important, I hope their government doesn't run to ruin because they have let the silly things vote."

Torie munched a piece of bacon and thought about this. She said to her grandfather, "I wouldn't let my husband tell me how to vote. I read newspapers; I know how to make decisions."

"Victoria," her grandfather's coffee cup rattled and he scowled, "you should stop reading newspapers. It does you no good."

"But how else do I know what is going on in the world?" Torie asked surprised.

"You could not worry about the world so much and concentrate on what your grandmother and mother feel is important, like your French and your schooling." He continued to glare at her. The Colonel still felt annoyed over his argument with

Rose and was not interested in listening to any more notions from Rose or her children.

Torie shrugged, missing his lowering brow and said, "Why can't women in America vote?"

"Too hard on their brains," the Colonel retorted, as if that answered her question. The Colonel opened his newspaper with a snap and pointedly ignored Torie.

Torie mulled over his comment as she continued to eat her breakfast. "It is almost 1900," she argued. "I think the world is changing. I think women should be involved in news of the world." Her grandfather did not comment but continued to read his paper. "Grandpapa?" Torie asked.

"What, Victoria?" the Colonel grumbled, very annoyed.

Torie missed his frown as she followed her thoughts, and said, "But Grandpapa, Grandmother doesn't always agree with you. What would you do if she wanted to vote for someone else?"

"Your grandmother would never want to vote," the Colonel told her succinctly. "She is a lady and does not involve herself in dirty politics."

Torie spread fresh raspberry jam on a slice of toast as she thought about this. She asked, "Where can women vote in America?"

Her grandfather dropped his paper and glared at her with his brow lowered. "Wyoming has allowed women to vote for almost 40 years," he told Torie. "Much good it has done that state. Of course, I understand there aren't that many women in Wyoming. Don't tell me, young lady," he said glaring at her, "that you are thinking about becoming one of those blasted suffragettes."

Torie finished her breakfast, came around the table and gave her grandfather a kiss. With a twinkle in her eye, she teased, "I think I will move to Wyoming when I grow up."

At that, her grandfather's fist banged on the table and he glared at her. "A Brewster in Wyoming?" he expostulated.

The Colonel missed Amelia and he was tired of his attempts to conform Rose and William's children to the proper Brewster way. "Victoria," he barked, his ire raised, "no Brewster woman is ever going to vote. To vote you have to go to those dirty polling places and subject yourself to all kinds of men from different stations of life. No granddaughter of mine would ever want to be caught in one of those places, or Wyoming!"

Torie, unfazed by his tone, walked to the door of the dining room. She turned, blew him a kiss and skipped from the room. The Colonel, his breakfast interrupted, picked up his paper and stalked from the room.

Torie and Edmund worked in comfortable companionship as they sailed the small boat. Edmund guided the rudder and Torie crewed by pulling in the sheet and adjusting the lines. Twenty minutes later with the fresh breeze blowing in her face and the feel of the boat skidding across the waves, Torie breathed a deep sigh of contentment. Edmund kept silent during the sail, except for the occasional order to adjust the sail. Torie looked across Eaton Pond to Eastwood. She gazed at the quiet house settled among the trees with its bursting blooms and wide lawn. It looked peaceful and Torie lovingly admired the tall stately house with the fluttering curtains and the neatly manicured flower beds. To Torie, Eastwood was summer. The sail boat bumped up to a small island and Edmund and Torie expertly landed it. Edmund jumped out and pulled the boat up on the sandy beach.

Companionably, Edmund and Torie walked into the forest and finding a shady log, sat down and rested. Torie told Edmund about the conversation she had over breakfast with their grandfather.

Torie reached down and picked up a pine cone off the ground. She said, "Maybe he just needs to realize that it is time for a change. That he and Grandmother need to stop telling everyone what to do and to allow our parents to make decisions for us."

Edmund listened in silence. He grabbed a stick and began drawing little characters in the sand. Finally, he raised his head and said, "You are right."

Torie's bright eyes met his and she frowned, waiting for him to go on. "The only reason," Edmund said slowly, "the only reason I am at Slater is because Grandfather wants me there. I heard Mother and Father talking one night; they don't want me there." He hesitated a minute and then admitted, "I hate it."

Torie, her own small woes forgotten, asked Edmund in astonishment, "Edmund! You don't want to be a great soldier?"

Edmund looked at the ground, and slowly shook his head. "No, Torie, I don't."

"But," Torie said, shocked, "you have always liked playing war with me."

"That was when we were little," Edmund protested. He then said feverishly, "Torie, Slater is awful. The big boys pick on the little ones all the time. They make their lives hell. It's supposed to toughen us up and make us soldiers. I hate the hazing and in another year I am going to be one of those big boys and be expected to torture the little ones."

Torie was truly shocked. "But both of our fathers and Uncle Christopher went to Slater. My father became a great soldier," Torie protested.

Edmund raised his head and looked at Torie, a slightly pitying expression in his eyes that she did not understand. "I don't think," he said slowly, "that your father liked it."

"Why, whatever do you mean?" Torie asked, shocked.

"It was a conversation I heard between Mother and Father. Something about Slater almost ruining Uncle William, and the Indian Wars finished him off. Papa said your father wrote in his will that Henry would not have to go to Slater."

Torie surged to her feet. "That just isn't true," she exclaimed. "Edmund, my father became a great soldier. He went to war for his country. And as for Henry, Mama just thinks he is delicate; that is why he isn't going to Slater."

Edmund pulled her back down on the log. "Sshhh," he soothed her. "I know your father was a great soldier. But Torie," Edmund struggled to find the words, "one of the things a soldier is taught to do is always to obey orders. Maybe your father was a great soldier because he obeyed. Maybe his heart was not in it." They sat in silence digesting this for a minute. Then Edmund said, his shoulders hunched, "But, being a soldier isn't what I want to do."

Torie stared at Edmund with astonishment. This would take some thinking. All Brewster men were soldiers. She had been raised on that principle. Mother was reluctant to allow Henry to attend Slater, but that was only because he was so little. All Brewster boys graduated from Slater; anything else was unthinkable. Torie was aware of the arguments surrounding Henry and Slater. She also knew no one ever successfully brooked grandfather about anything, including schooling for the boys. Torie always assumed that Henry would sooner or later be admitted to Slater and become a soldier.

But, Torie argued with herself, wasn't this the same argument that she had just had with her grandfather? That she wanted to be allowed to become the person she wanted to be, not what grandmother felt she should be?

Torie turned and really looked at Edmund. Her dark eyes peered into his set face and took in the hunched shoulders. This was the boy who stood up for her in battles, laughed with her over jokes, and ran across the wide lawns of Eastwood when they were little. They had been punished together as children and had wiped each other's tears. Together, they coasted on steep snowy hills and raced across the ice. Edmund always defended her when she ran afoul of her grandmother. Torie thought back over their conversation and the argument she had with her grandfather. Was it not the same argument? Was it not true that she wanted to act not like Brewster women had for generations, but as she wanted to be? Not just what someone else wanted for her, not what she must do?

Torie dropped the remnants of the pine cone. She wiped her hands on her dress and said to Edmund, laying her hand on his arm gently, "What is it you want to do?"

Edmund looked at his favorite cousin and knew she understood. "I want to be a doctor," he admitted. "I don't want to kill anyone. I want to heal people."

Torie cast her mind back to the family genealogy and could not remember there ever being a Brewster who was a doctor. Doctors worked very long hours and had to be out and about all hours of the day and night. But, then, so did soldiers. Torie mulled this over in her mind. Being a doctor might not be so different from being a soldier.

"Edmund," she said, her little chin jutting out, "if you want to be a doctor, you need to tell your parents and then Grandpapa." Torie stood up and looked down at Edmund. "Like I said to Grandfather this morning, we are almost to a new century and America and Boston and Brewsters all need to change to a new day, commit to new things in their lives. I will stand by you and help you become a doctor." She looked at him with determination and said, "If need be, I shall tell them for you."

Edmund looked at Torie with pure love and appreciation. Torie was always the rebel, the brave soldier, ready to stand up for anything she believed in. "Torie," he said with a smile of gratitude, "you are the bravest person I have ever met."

Torie shrugged nonchalantly, sitting down beside Edmund. "I take after my father. I want to be just like him, a very brave soldier."

They sat in silence for a while, reflecting upon Edmund's secret. Finally he said slowly, "You know, Torie? I think I will tell my parents and the grandparents, but I don't want to put stress on Mother and Father just now. With Susanna's wedding and the senator and his wife, I don't want to cause problems right now."

Torie opened her mouth to argue, but he interrupted her, "It wouldn't be fair to them and I can go to Slater at least until Christmas. By then, Mother will have recovered from the wedding and we can talk over Christmas break. I can survive one more term at Slater."

Torie wondered privately if Edmund would come to appreciate military school now that he was not in the beginning class, but she kept the thought to herself.

"And you," Edmund asked her, "what are you going to do?"

"I promised Mama that I would not cause any problems this summer," Torie told him. "I already broke that promise with my argument with Grandfather and I have been tormenting Kitty," she admitted, making a clean breast. "You know, I am not going back to Miss Mable's. It is kind of a secret. Mama was really upset with me, but Miss Mable has asked me not to return."

Edmund looked at Torie for a minute and then burst out laughing. "What did you do to get kicked out of that prissy school?"

Torie shrugged and said, "Oh it was just a lot of little things. Not sewing a fine seam, talking back, arguing with my teachers. I used a bad word in a French essay. I thought 'Merde' meant 'murder', but I guess it is a bad word in French. Miss Mable told Mama that she did not think I was a good fit." Torie laughed ruefully, "Miss Mable told Mama that I would never be a lady."

Edmund could not help himself. He started laughing so hard he fell backwards off the log. "Torie Brewster," he told her, "I don't think there will ever be another Torie. You are the bravest woman I know. But, I can just imagine Grandmother's face when she heard that you were deemed a total failure by Miss Mable."

Edmund stood up and looked down at his favorite cousin, pulling her to her feet. "We should get you back," Edmund told her, "before you get into any more trouble." The two of them laughed together and moved toward the boat.

Edmund and Torie sailed some more and as they headed back to the landing at Eastwood, Edmund raised his hand to shade his eyes from the sun. "It looks like we have company," Edmund said.

Torie shaded her eyes with her hands and squinted at the Easwood verandah. Catching sight of a certain gray haired woman, she sat back down in the boat with a gasp. "Grandmother has returned," she said flatly. She looked down at her dress which had grass stains on it and a muddy hem. Her shoes were sandy and putting a hand to her hair she realized that her braids had come undone and her hair was flying around. Torie looked at Edmund, "Grandmother is going to have a fit if she sees me looking like this," she said, a small glimmer of trepidation in her eyes.

Edmund turned the boat and sailed past the landing, past the small harbor wall, Edging the boat into the smaller cove past an outcropping of bushes. "I am going to drop you here," he told her. "Then you can skip up and go up the backstairs. Give me ten minutes to land the boat and I will go up and distract Grandmother. That way you can get clean and tidy before she sees you."

Torie gave Edmund a deep look of gratitude. Torie reached over and gave her cousin a small kiss on the cheek. Torie slipped out of the boat with a laugh and sinking into the wet mud gave him a wave as she danced up the small beach. She sat down on a small boulder and removed her shoes to pour the water out of them when she heard a small "ahem."

In alarm, Torie jumped and looking around found Marcus Underwood, sitting on a blanket under a tree with a book, a small picnic basket beside him. "Oh, Mr. Underwood," she exclaimed. "I thought you were Grandmother."

Marcus laughed and said, "I get that all the time." Marcus took in Torie's appearance from head to toe, her wind blown hair, her grass stained skirt and muddy shoes. Marcus raised a questioning eyebrow.

Torie explained, "I was out sailing with Edmund and we saw that Grandmother returned while we were gone. Grandmother thinks ladies should be able to sail without ever messing a curl. So, Edmund dropped me here so that I can go up the backstairs and be tidy before I greet her."

Marcus smiled at her explanation, but asked, "Your grandmother has returned?"

Torie nodded, "Yes, they must have come back early. And if she sees me like this, I will be in trouble." Torie looked at Marcus with a small frown, "What are you doing here?"

Marcus smiled at her and said, "Torie, I shall keep your secret if you keep mine. I like this little cove. It is a nice place to sit and read a book. Very quiet and private."

Torie thought this was strange, as Eaton Pond had many little coves and inlets, and she knew from her exploring with Edmund that Summerfield boasted several little coves that matched this one. Torie shrugged as her continued absence became more pressing. Torie finished emptying her shoes of water, jumped up and with a wave, disappeared up the path.

Marcus sat back on the blanket. Torie's appearance had given him quite a start. He had been waiting to meet Rose and spend a quiet hour or two with her. Having her daughter come out as if from the sea had proved startling. It gave him pause for thought. Rose continued to insist that their romance stay secret between them and to realize how easily they could be discovered was unsettling. And by her young daughter! Their romance was quickly becoming beyond decorous and more and more they were taking chances. Eaton Pond and Eaton's Grove were too small for this to continue if they did not want to be discovered.

Up at Eastwood, Rose had her own startling discovery when she walked out on the verandah on her way to the cove and heard the crunch of wheels on the gravel drive and discovered her returning family. Lavinia threw herself into her mother's arms and covered her in kisses. Alice and Susanna alighted from the carriage, also excited to see her, and although very dignified and stately, Amelia warmly kissed and greeted her daughter-in-law.

Among the throng of Brewsters coming to greet each other, Amelia's sharp eyes lingered on Rose. Something was different, a gentle glow surrounding her. Noticing that Rose had a hat on and stout walking shoes, Amelia inquired where she had been headed.

Rose blushed a little and laughed. "Oh," she stammered, "I have been keeping an eye on some of your gardening. Without you, the vases have not been filled quite so often."

Amelia's eyes went past Rose to the large round table in the foyer and looked at the gorgeous, if slightly overfilled vase of roses arranged there and frowned.

"Oh, Mama," Lavinia said, with her arm around her mother's waist as they started up the steps, "Washington was divine. We got to see so many lovely monuments. Alexander's father had us as his special guests for a meeting in Congress. And Mama, you will never guess, we got to meet the Vice President."

Rose smiled at Lavinia's excitement and pinched her cheek, "I am so happy that you had a wonderful time. Why don't you get refreshed and I shall make sure that Mrs. Pratt has luncheon under control."

Twenty minutes later, Amelia, changed out of her traveling clothes, sat on the verandah listening to Kitty as Kitty showed her the doll's wedding wardrobe she had been sewing. Torie made her entrance. Torie's wind tangled curls were smooth and pulled back by a crimson ribbon, and her frock was fresh and uncreased. Amelia looked pleased at her wayward granddaughter and smiled a warm welcome. "Torie," she said as Torie came across the verandah to embrace her, "you look like such a young lady. I thought I saw you out sailing with Edmund, but you look very tidy."

By this time, Edmund had berthed the boat and joined the party on the verandah. Behind Amelia, Edmund made a funny face at Torie. Torie ignored him and returned her grandmother's hug. "Welcome home, Grandmother," she said formally, but with a happy smile on her face.

CHAPTER 10

Alice, Amelia and Susanna returned from Washington, D.C. ready to plunge into wedding plans. Lavinia followed her mother from room to room discussing the details of her fall wardrobe and her eventual departure for college. It was rare that Rose had time to herself.

Only late at night when Rose sat at her window seat in her bedroom, looking over the tree tops at the lights at Summerfield, did she find time to think about Marcus. Rose missed him dreadfully, not just his kisses, warm strong arms and their long comfortable talks, but his beautiful brown eyes that lit up when he looked at her. Now that the house and gardens filled with people again, it was too risky for Rose to sneak out. She and Marcus were becoming more and more careless with their meetings.

The late July days rolled into the early days of August and the social season around Eaton's Pond continued. Mrs. Pratt was busy in the kitchen putting up jars of fruits and vegetables for the winter. The walls of the cool pump house were lined with shelves that were filling up with jars of dark red Bing cherries, golden peaches, green beans and tomatoes, and Mrs. Pratt's specialty: Piccalilli. Young Tilly's back ached from the hours spent blanching and peeling peaches and tomatoes.

Matilda and the twins triumphantly returned with husband and father, Captain Jasper Bingham. Jovial, light hearted Jasper was a favorite and every afternoon friends and neighbors dropped by to catch up with Jasper's exotic adventures. The house was once more filled with young ladies and men, as the girls were back in residence along with Myles and Cooper. The thwacking sound of the tennis court rang out and laughter and shouts could be heard from every corner of Eastwood. At night, the verandah was always filled with groups playing games and singing songs accompanied by Warner Covington's banjo.

Rose immersed herself in the wedding plans. There was wedding sewing to be done and in the afternoons, she, Alice and Emily often talked on the verandah, their hands full of delicate fabrics. Alice had so much to tell them about Washington, D.C., the Peabodys and the parties and teas they had attended. Rose and

Emily would sit and sew and quietly listen, but with their thoughts on other things.

Since the band concert, Emily watched Rose. There was a light in Rose's face that Emily had never seen. Rose would be sewing, but a small smile on her lips betrayed the fact that her thoughts were far away. Sometimes Peregrine Fitch, accompanied by the owner of Summerfield, would pay a call in the afternoons to talk business with the Colonel.

At these times, Emily would see Rose's face brighten with a flush of pleasure, but she was equally warm and gracious to both men. Emily watched in vain to see if Rose would favor Peregrine and she thought at times Rose might squeeze Peregrine's arm when talking to him.

Amelia, too, noticed the change in Rose since her return and asked her husband about it. Gruffly he answered her, "There is nothing new with Rose, unless it is pure obstinance." He snapped, "We had a discussion over Henry and she was quite rude about it." The Colonel was still put out with Rose. He shared with Amelia the argument with Rose and ended it with, "I don't know what to expect of her children, a rebel everyone of them, barely to be considered a Brewster. No soldiering for Henry, Torie determined to be a suffragette, God knows when Lavinia will ever accept a man and marry one. The rate she is going she will have to become Mormon and marry them all."

Amelia looked at her husband with some surprise. "George," she protested. "you knew that Rose was not going to give in on Henry this year. You and I talked about it, and agreed that next summer would be when we start discussions with her. And Lavinia was a perfect dear the entire time we were in Washington. I think there is great hope for Vinnie and possibly Senator Stone's boy."

The Colonel snorted, but Amelia smiled at him, her thoughts on Lavinia. Amelia said, "Lavinia and Thomas Stone spent time together at every party, and often walked in the park in the afternoons. Thomas Stone will be attending Harvard next year and she will be next door at Radcliffe." Amelia turned her thoughts to Torie. She continued on, "And since we have returned, Torie has been on very good behavior. I think she has turned the corner. She is tidy and her manners have been everything a grandmother would want. She and Kitty seem to be getting along very well, too."

"I am a little puzzled over Rose, though, if the two of you had such a falling out," Amelia said with a frown. "Rose just seems to be bursting with happiness. I have never seen her look like this. It is almost as if," her voice trailed away.

The Colonel looked at her and said, "As if what?" The Colonel frowned at his wife.

"Oh, I don't know," Amelia did not finish, deciding to not rile the Colonel any more. "She just seems very happy," she shrugged.

"I told you she is happy because the stubborn woman is getting her way with my grandson," the Colonel huffed at her.

Amelia was noncommittal. "George, dear," she soothed, "watch your blood pressure. All will be worked out in time. Let's not worry about it just now. I know Rose Brewster. She is a very tractable daughter-in-law, and in the end she will realize that you are correct."

The Brewsters were dining out at Briar Hill, the Brown family's summer residence, on a warm summer evening. Briar Hill stood across the pond from Eastwood and was designed in the Greek Revival style. Cordelia Brown was proud of the enormous white columns and wide piazza fronting her house and this evening she held her party al fresco. As Rose and the Brewster clan stood on the lawn greeting their host and hostess, Rose felt someone by her elbow. She knew it would be Marcus before she turned. Rose nodded coolly to Marcus, but his eyes danced as he returned her greeting. Peregrine, standing beside Marcus, leaned down and gave her a small brotherly kiss on the cheek.

A starched white tablecloth covered the large table on Cordelia's verandah. She creatively set her table with her most expensive crystal and china. Small vases of roses dotted the table with bright reds and pinks and soft cream petals. During dinner, talk turned to Susanna's impending wedding and someone called down the table to Rose, "So who has Lavinia set her heart on? I think that you should start planning the next wedding! Next summer?"

Rose laughed along with the rest, but shook her head and said, "Lavinia firmly believes she is a Gibson Girl. She is more interested in who wants to partner her in tennis or go for a bicycle ride or just float around the pond on a summer afternoon. Lavinia is determined to graduate from college, not because of the degree, but because of the fun!"

Amid the general laughter, Rose felt Samuel Gardner, who had been seated beside her, turn and look at her. Samuel, with his round middle, suffered from the heat and a film of sweat beaded his brow. "Girl should get married," he stated. Rose turned to him, as he said flatly, "You are a bad example for the girl; you should get married."

Startled, Rose could only stare and try to laugh off his boorish comment. Although his voice was quiet, Rose glanced around to see if anyone else had heard. Everyone else was involved in their own conversations. Cordelia Brown entered into a story about her own daughter wanting to drive one of those new horseless carriages and her plans to tour Europe the following summer without her parents.

"Mr. Gardner," Rose reminded him softly, "I am a widow. I feel that I am the best example of proper decorum for my daughter." With those words, she turned her back on him and engaged in conversation with Arthur Harlow.

Samuel hissed, "Really, Widow Brewster?" He went on, a menacing tone in his voice. "You never wander in the woods alone with men?" At the shocking words, Rose eyes snapped back to him, a very surprised and wary look on her face. Rose could smell alcohol on Sam Gardner's breath. She realized that his voice had carried and there was a sudden silence on the Brown verandah.

Rose tried to look entirely innocent, but in her mind she cast back over her encounters with Marcus. Could Sam have been following them? It took everything in her to not glance down the table at Marcus. "I don't understand," she stammered, her face flaming red, very aware of listening ears.

Once again, Samuel said, his voice carrying, "Been strolling in the park at night with men, Widow Brewster? As pure as the driven snow? What you need is a husband!"

Marcus seated halfway down the table, started to rise, but Peregrine Finch and Christopher Brewster rose first and each firmly grasped Samuel by the arm, lifting him from his seat. "Samuel, my old friend," Peregrine said gently, "I think you need a little air." Heaving Samuel from his chair, the two men hustled him down the steps and around the house. Rose could not meet anyone's eyes, but felt the entire room staring at her. Her cheeks flooded with color.

In the silence, Cordelia rose and said gently, "Ladies, shall we retire to the drawing room?"

Rose, her eyes downcast, followed the crowd of women into the house. Once in the drawing room, the conversation was awkward and strained. Rose sank into a chair her eyes downcast, until forthright Cordelia took Rose's cold hands in her own and said in her clear voice, "I think Samuel Gardner is a pig!"

At that statement, weak laughter broke out. Cordelia went on, "I don't know what that man is insinuating, but you and Perry Finch have been friends since before you and William were married. I say, if you want to walk with Perry Finch in the park, you should!" Amid the strained laughter, she added, in her strong way, "And if you want to do more, you should do that too!"

Rose allowed herself a small smile and slowly raised her head in the room. Women laughed and the ice had been broken. Tea was sipped and conversation turned to other things. Rose realized that Amelia's sharp eyes were fixed on her and Amelia was not smiling.

Amelia thought back to the change she noticed in Rose since they had returned from Washington. The woman glowed. Was there some truth to Sam Gardner's words?

Emily sat beside Rose and squeezed her hand comfortingly. Emily allowed a small satisfied smile to cross her lips.

The men joined the ladies, but conversation was stilted and the festive atmosphere of the dinner party was broken. Marcus and Peregrine joined the Colonel and kept him talking, neither paying any attention to Rose. As Rose stood in the hall saying her good byes to Cordelia, she heard Marcus murmur something about "walled garden."

Nothing was said by the Brewsters until they were in the carriage. The Colonel was furious with Samuel Gardner, and he defended Rose. "I will say this for you, Rose. Your behavior has always been exemplary. You are a fine example of how a proper widow acts when it comes to men. I don't know what came over Sam Gardner tonight."

Rose's face was paper white. She barely acknowledged the Colonel's words before she turned her face to the window. Alice reached over and squeezed her hand, and Rose returned the pressure.

Eastwood was bulging with young people when they arrived home. Laughter and singing came from the parlor including the sound of many feet pattering in dance. Rose did not pause but went up the stairs and firmly shut her bedroom door.

Inside her bedroom, Rose paced the floor. Her face flamed yet she was icy in the pit of her stomach. Rose had lived her entire life by what other people thought and until she met Marcus Underhill she had never chosen to act in any way but as society dictated. To have Samuel Gardner of all people accuse her of impropriety caused her to scald with embarrassment. To have Samuel Gardner speak to her the way he did tonight proved that he was no gentleman. Rose was worried. Had she and Marcus brought shame on the family and their children?

Simple walks in the woods, a few stolen kisses. People would believe what they wanted to believe and Rose was concerned about what was said behind her back. She knew that she and Marcus had been flirting with danger for some time, but was their attachment that obvious?

Rose continued to pace the floor of her room, her lonely bed very uninviting. Rose knew that Marcus would be waiting in the walled garden, but, it was too risky. The house was full of Lavinia and Susanna's friends and it would be hours before everyone settled down. Rose never wanted to be in Marcus' arms more than she did tonight; she needed him. Rose stopped her pacing in astonishment. She needed Marcus. How had Marcus come to mean so much to her that she needed him? Rose realized she needed Marcus to hold her and make her feel safe. She needed the world to know that this man protected her and that no hurt or harm could come to her as long as he stood by her side.

Pausing by the open window, Rose looked over the treetops towards Summerfield. Rose realized that her need for Marcus proved she loved him. The thought took Rose's breath away. Love? Rose knew in her lonely soul that she had never felt before what she felt for Marcus. Rose loved Marcus Underhill and she wanted the world to know.

Rose longed to go to the walled garden, but could not find the courage to venture out of her room. The tinkling of the piano faintly drifted up the stairs, and from the dark verandah she heard laughter and voices.

Rose finally crept into her lonely bed and, worn out with worry and longing, fell asleep. Sometime later Rose slowly awakened. The house was silent, the revelers had gone. In her deep troubled sleep, Rose never heard Lavinia and Susanna tripping by her bedroom door. The full moon shone through the open window onto her bed, but some sound awakened her. She lay there half drowsy when she became aware someone was in her room. Rose opened her mouth to scream, but Marcus' hand covered her half opened mouth. "Shhhh," he whispered, barely breathing.

From her open window, Rose could hear the sounds of one of the great aunts gently snoring from down the hall and realized in the quiet night how sounds carried. Rose struggled out of bed and, pulling her robe to her breast, stared in the dark at Marcus. He quietly crossed the room and closed her open window. Instantly, Rose's room felt stuffy. Marcus turned back to Rose. She followed him across the room and urgently whispered, "Marcus, what are you doing here? How did you get in here? Marcus, you heard Sam Gardner tonight. You must leave or we will be caught."

Marcus sat down on the window seat and pulled her down beside him. He leaned over and kissed her, silencing her words. Rose returned the kiss deeply and then, as he pulled away, buried her face in his chest. Rose said, "It must have been Sam Gardner that night at the park. He must have been the one who watched us."

Marcus held her tight, and kissed the top of her head. In a low voice he said, "Rose, would it surprise you to know that Sam Gardner is a desperate man?"

"I have known all summer. Everyone knows he is looking for a mother for those children of his," Rose told him. "He has attempted to court me all summer, and he has been after the Colonel and Amelia to encourage me. Thank God, they do not agree with him."

Marcus explained, "I didn't mean that kind of desperate. Sam Gardner is also in financial troubles. Peregrine Fitch and I are working with your brothers-in-law to buy out his business."

Rose raised her head in surprise. "I knew you were all working together, but I did not know anything about that." Quoting the Colonel she said, bitterly, "Women have no business in business."

They sat on the window seat holding each other. Marcus, rubbing his hands up and down Rose's arms, said quietly, "Rose, I have to leave."

With a sigh Rose drew away, "I agree. This is very dangerous. At any moment someone could hear us."

"No," Marcus corrected her, "I need to leave Eaton Pond."

In the moonlight, Rose raised her head and looked at Marcus. "Marcus, why?" Rose breathed.

"Because I can't keep my distance from you," Marcus told Rose. "I want to be with you all the time, and after tonight, even more eyes are going to be on you." Marcus sighed, and he lifted her hand and kissed her fingers. He said, "Unless we are honest with your family and friends, we can't keep going on like this."

"You know we can't do that," she answered, her voice breaking. "You know why."

"I do know why," Marcus said to Rose, caressing her arms. "But, you see, I have fallen in love with you."

Rose, thinking about her own thoughts earlier in the evening, was silent; her breath caught in her throat.

"Yes, my fine little woman," Marcus told Rose with passion. "Love. I have fallen madly in love with you. I want you by my side for the rest of my life and not skulking down by the cove or the walled garden or any of the other damnable places around here that we always risk discovery due to the enormous amount of Brewsters who are forever hanging around you."

Rose said slowly, as she pulled his face to hers, "And I love you, Marcus Underhill. Right now in the dark, I don't care who finds us or what this does to turn my very correct mother-in-law on her ear. I love you."

The loving kiss they shared was filled with longing and the taste of Rose's tears. Gradually the kiss broke and Rose pulled back. "You said something else," she questioned with tears in her voice. "You said you were going away. Forever?"

"No, my darling," Marcus told her, "not forever. You said yourself that Eaton Pond was small and we risk discovery every time we are together. I am going just until the summer is over. I have business to tend to in Boston, and I will leave you to the Brewsters, hopefully under the protection of Charles and Christopher and Peregrine, NOT Sam Gardner."

Rose started to say something and Marcus went on, "In the fall, you will be back in your own establishment and Lavinia and Collin will be in college and Henry will be off to boarding school. Torie will also be in school. We will have time then to make plans."

"Plans?" Rose asked faintly.

"Plans," he answered firmly. "Rose, my darling girl, I want to make you my wife." She started to interrupt, but Marcus went on, "I don't care about the will. I am determined to make the Brewsters realize that they should not try to control your life."

"It isn't my life I am worried about," Rose said sadly.

Marcus kissed her and said, "I know. You are worried about Henry and your girls." Marcus' hand soothed her hair and said, "Rose, I want you to trust me in this. I hope when all is settled, your children will be happy, and even more importantly, that you and I will be together."

Rose shook her head and started to argue, but Marcus went on, "Enough. I did not risk life and limb by scaling up that wall to come up here to discuss the Brewsters or your children."

With a small smile, Rose asked, "Why did you come up?"

"To hold you," he said succinctly with a smile, "to kiss you, to squeeze you." And Marcus did all three.

Rose slowly said, "Marcus, come to bed with me."

Marcus pulled back, peering at her face in the moonlight. "Rose?" he questioned.

Rose reached up and began to unbutton his shirt, "Come to bed with me now." Rose undid Marcus' buttons with trembling fingers and pulled his shirt from his waist band. The cotton of his shirt felt warm and slightly damp. Shyly, Rose ran her fingers over his bare, smooth broad chest, his muscled ribs. Standing, her hands slipped to his hand and she pulled him across the room to her bed. Rose's heart thudded in her chest, her breath caught in her throat. She was thankful for the darkness as it hid her shyness.

Marcus, in wonder, allowed Rose to lead him across the room. As he stood by the bed she perched herself on the side and turned towards him. In the moonlight, he could see her eyes glittering and then as he slowly lowered his mouth to hers, her face fell into shadow. His hot mouth covered hers in a deep passionate kiss, his tongue playing with hers. His mouth trailed searing kisses over her jaw line and down her neck to the high necked collar of her nightgown. Rose's hands assisted him as he undid the buttons on her nightdress, slipping it off of her shoulders and pulling it open for access to her breasts. The breath caught in her throat as Marcus's warm hand gently reached down and cupped her heavy white breast, his thumb brushing over the nipple. Rose gasped at his touch and sat up straighter. As he began to kiss her neck again, she relaxed against him, her neck falling back to give him better access. Marcus slipped her nightgown over her head, running his hands down her bare slim arms. The night air on her bare body caused Rose to shiver a little, not from coolness but from the sensual feeling of air on naked skin. Thankful for the darkness, she reached out and tentatively ran her fingers over his muscled hairy arm.

Marcus continued to massage her breasts as he watched her blurred form. Rose looked up at him, trust and desire in her shining eyes. Slowly she lay down on the bed, her head on the pillow, and held her arms up, looking at him invitingly. Quickly Marcus pulled off his boots and shucked his pants, standing before her nude and erect. Rose's breath caught in her throat and she swallowed as he joined her on the bed. Rose could barely breathe as she felt his warm naked body against hers. She could feel his heart beating strongly in his chest. Marcus lowered his head and began to kiss her again, deeper and with intensity. Rose felt as if she were melting under his fire hot kisses, returning them with abandon. Marcus lowered his head and began to lathe and suckle at her nipples with his open mouth. Rose, never having felt a man's mouth on her breast, panted at these new and unexpected feelings. She entwined her fingers in his dark silky hair and kissed the top of his head. Marcus' hands lightly stroked her slender waist and hips and then, reaching lower, lightly caressed the tangle of soft curls below. Rose's breathing stopped as he softly fondled and ran his finger along her womanly lines. As his fingers explored her silky inner thighs and soft womanliness, his searing mouth returned to hers and she joined him in a hot turgid kiss, deeper and deeper, her arms gripping him. Marcus poised his body over hers, and Rose spread her thighs wide, welcoming his weight. Marcus paused and then thrust his manhood deep in her and Rose gasped at this unexpected feeling of pain and pleasure. Marcus paused briefly, raising himself a little to look at her and with Rose's reassuring nod, Marcus began to move within her gently at first and then with more intensity. Rose met each thrust with her own as she clasped her arms around him tightly, breathing out in short hard pants. Marcus and Rose shared deep searing kisses as their bodies moved in unison and their hearts thudded as one.

As their hips thrust together, the small frisson they shared all summer began to build between them and a new indescribable shattering feeling that grew by leaps and bounds expanded to even greater heights. Rose felt bathed in her own sweat as well as Marcus'. The soft feather bed pillowed them as if they were on a downy cloud, the overwhelmingly stifling heat of the closed room added to their passion. Rose was aware of the new feel of his smooth chest against hers, his hairy legs entwined with hers and his stiff manhood deep within her. Rose felt an excitement build inside her that she had never felt before. Mixed in with these physical feelings was the sound of Marcus' harsh rhythmic breathing in her ear as he thrust rhythmically within her. Rose matched his thrusts, her legs by their own volition coming up and encircling his waist, and when her pleasure burst within her in orgasmic spasms, her eyes flew wide in shock.

"Marcus," she gasped as he joined her in her pleasure, flooding her with his essence.

Rose drowsed in Marcus' arms, her head cradled on his chest. Slowly he sat up and swung his legs over the side of the bed. Rose stirred, her fingers trailing over his back. Marcus turned and taking her hand in his, kissed each of her fingers. "I must go," he whispered. "The house will be stirring soon." Rose slowly sat up, reached down and picked up her wrapper and followed him to the window. Marcus raised the window sash, the fresh early morning air flooded the steamy room with the sweet smell of dawn and a cool dewy moistness. Marcus turned to Rose and pulled her to him. He gave her one last long kiss, then silently slid over the sill and carefully worked his way down the wall. Rose watched him walk away, a curl twined around her finger. Long after the sounds of

Marcus' footsteps faded into the dark, Rose stayed at her window and breathed in the fresh cool air. In the east, the sky lightened and the first birds began to twitter in the walled garden. Rose watched but no light lit up the upstairs window at Summerfield. Marcus must have made his way in the predawn hour to bed without lighting a candle.

Rose felt reborn. Never had she known that a man's hands on her body could make her feel so incredible. Rose never experienced the burst of pleasure she felt at the climax of their love making, totally taking her by surprise. She moaned Marcus' name as her body reacted to his own climax. They spent the dark hours making love and cuddling each other, drowsing from time to time. As they lay in the quiet aftermath of their lovemaking, Rose held Marcus fiercely to her, his head pillowed on her breast, as she smoothed and kissed the top of his head.

Rose felt alive inside and out. The complications of taking a man to bed while unmarried should bother her conscience. The fact that she had acted so wantonly with Marcus Underhill and if the Brewsters ever found out there would be hell to pay -- she did not care. At that moment she felt like dancing. Rose stood up from the window seat and hugged herself, glancing at her bed. The rumpled blankets hung totally askew and one pillow was on the floor. Rose felt fairly certain that she looked as disheveled as her bed. With a small sigh, she made her bed, smoothing the feather bed and sheets, and she retrieved her nightgown from the floor. After removing her wrapper, Rose slipped the long cotton gown over her head and buttoned up the front to her neck. With a sigh of pure satisfied joy, Rose clamboured back into her tidied bed and collapsed against her pillow. Rose breathed in the smell of Marcus on her pillow and she smiled at the memory of Marcus' searing lips on her skin, his strong warm hands on her body. Between her legs remained a joyful ache, something she had never felt in her life. With a smile on her face, Rose's heavy eyelids closed and she slumbered peacefully.

Rose came abruptly awake at a tap at her bedroom door. Frowning, she glanced at the sunshine flooding through the open window and realized that it must be late. Rose sat up with a jolt as she remembered the night. The tapping repeated and hurriedly she snatched up her wrapper and looked around the room to see if there were any telltales signs of Marcus. She opened the door cautiously and Amelia Brewster stepped into the room. Amelia looked at Rose's face and saw the remnants of sleep on her daughter-in-law's face. Rose's hair was a tangle of curls and her eyes were heavy; rarely had her daughter-in-law looked so unkempt.

"My dear," Amelia exclaimed sympathetically, and took Rose's hands. "You have slept late. Did you have a hard time falling asleep last night? Were you worrying about that disastrous dinner party?"

Rose, belting her dressing gown firmly to her waist, was caught off guard. Grasping at her mother-in-law's words, Rose apologized, "Amelia, I am so sorry. I did not fall asleep until almost dawn." This was a true statement, although not in the way Amelia construed it. "Can you give me a few minutes? I will be down in 10 minutes ready to start the day."

"Actually," Amelia crossed the room and seated herself on the window seat, "I wanted a word alone. We need to speak of a very delicate matter." Amelia's words were gentle, but there was a glint of steel in her eyes.

A flush of guilt flooded Rose's face. Did Amelia know Marcus had been in her room last night? A second glance assured her that Amelia would be much more upset if that had been the case.

Amelia watched Rose's face turn bright red and saw the guilty look on her face, Amelia frowned and said, "That nonsense of Sam Gardner's last night. It has made me wonder..."

Rose silently stared at Amelia, a guilty look on her face.

Amelia, choosing her words carefully, said, "I realize that you are still a young woman. It is not hard to have your head turned when a man pays you marked attention. But, do I need to remind you of your station?" While said softly, Amelia's voice was firm.

Rose walked over to the window and stared out without seeing the beautiful day. The men and boys had finished their morning swim and headed towards the back of the house. Even from this distance, Rose saw Henry laughing at something his cousin Myles said.

After a long silence, Amelia continued to Rose's back, "I have noticed a change in you this summer. And since my return I have heard of your solitary wanderings." Rose glanced at her mother-in-law, then returned her eyes to the window. She could no longer see her son.

Amelia watched Rose, the silence lengthening. Finally, Amelia said, "I am not going to say anything more at this time. I expect not to hear any more gossip from the neighbors about you wandering alone. I suggest you find a hobby that keeps you at home."

Rose murmured an agreement, but did not turn as Amelia left the room.

Befuddled, Rose set about getting ready for her day. Amelia's words were delicate, but the threat behind them was clear. Rose could think of nothing except her night with Marcus and she had longed to turn to Amelia and argue. Overlaying this was the sight of her happy little son on the lawn.

Rose set about getting ready for her day, eventually slipping into the morning room slightly late for the French lesson. She opened her book, but found she could not concentrate. The pages could have been blank for all that she saw.

The lesson over, Rose was the last to leave the room. She was aware of men's voices from the Colonel's study, but did not pay attention. As she passed the study, her small body ran into a hard masculine body. Jolted, she felt Marcus' arms go around her to steady her and, in confusion, she snatched herself clear. Rose's body felt on fire where his warm hand briefly rested on her waist. Rose was aware that the Colonel and Peregrine watched her. Breathlessly, she nodded to Marcus' murmured apology.

The Colonel told her, "Underhill and Fitch are moving back to Boston to continue working."

Rose, unable to meet anyone's eyes, mumbled an inarticulate answer and fled down the hall. The men followed Rose to the verandah. Amelia stood on the verandah saying goodbye to M. du Gres.

Reaching out to grasp a railing post, Rose raised her head and snatched a glance at Marcus. Rose flushed bright red as she suddenly remembered this man's hands and mouth on her body the past night, his hoarse cries in her ear as he filled her with his essence. Rose glimpsed a longing in Marcus' eyes that matched her own. Aware that her mother-in-law's eyes could turn from M. du Gres to hers, Rose said formally, "It has been a pleasure to meet you this summer, Mr. Underhill. We hope to see you in Boston in the fall. You and Collin will always be welcome at my home."

Marcus murmured an equally banal reply and shortly afterwards the two men drove away, the carriage wheels crunching on the drive. Rose watched the carriage disappear down the driveway and felt an arm around her waist. She turned and found Aunt Easter with a very sympathetic look on her face. "The month will go fast, my dear," Easter told her.

Puzzled, Rose looked into Easter's face and saw a deeper understanding. Not sure what she actually glimpsed, Rose simply smiled and said with a shake, "I need to see what those children are up to." She moved down the steps and around to the back of the house where the children's voices could be heard. Amelia murmured something to Easter as Rose walked away. Rose was aware that more than one pair of eyes followed her.

CHAPTER 11

The month of August flew by. Susanna and Alexander's wedding was scheduled for mid December, and the preparations became all absorbing since all hands were needed. Seamstresses set up residence due to the multitude of sewing required. Amelia continually walked around with sheafs of papers in her hands as she and Alice discussed a seating chart for the wedding dinner.

Susanna went from seamstress to mantua maker. Rarely was her opinion asked and even more rare was her opinion expressed. Slowly, she and Lavinia became immersed in the details and the time to play seemed to be over. The tennis court was actively in use, but more and more the girls were called away to discuss wedding details and their friends played without them.

Susanna spent hours writing long letters to Alexander and also writing 'Mrs. Alexander Peabody' over and over. She and Lavinia poured over magazines and discussed wedding gown styles. Amelia promised her own grandmother's veil for Susanna to wear, and told Susanna she could try it on as soon as they returned to Boston.

Kitty was in ecstasy over the wedding. Dreamily she would sit in the corner and listen to the million and one details discussed by her grandmother and aunts. Kitty's dress, as well as Sarah and Abigail's, would be a dotted swiss pattern in pale pink. Pale pink lace and a pink satin sash finished off the pretty dresses. The girls would wear circles of flowers on their blond heads and they would carry white roses. Even Torie, Edmund and Henry were caught up in bridal fever and watched the plans with fascinated eyes.

Rose missed Marcus desperately, even though she agreed with Marcus' decision to leave Eastwood. She found the cove very lonely when she slipped away for a rare afternoon of solitude. Rose lay awake at night and remembered his strong masculine hands upon her body. The deep lonely feeling she felt in the summer was replaced with a stronger longing to have him by her side. Rose argued with herself and strongly scolded herself for her thoughts. She knew that if he were still at Summerfield it would have been a matter of time before they were caught. Remembering his last night in her bedroom caused her to go cold to think how easily they could have been discovered with the risks they took. Rose argued with herself: would she give up that one night of passion, even if they had been caught?

The hot days of August lagged. Summer afternoons were quieter as it was too hot to play tennis. The Brewster grandchildren spent late afternoons bobbing around in Eaton Pond, relishing the coolness of the water on hot muggy days. Afternoons were spent on the verandah with fanning and desultory conversations. No wind blew and the sail boats stayed moored in their slips. Even the younger children ran out of games of romp across the yard.

Under the same roof with so many personalities, little arguments started to pop up and even Lavinia and Susanna picked at each other. Amelia, recognizing dissension in the ranks, handed out tin pails and ordered the younger children to go huckleberrying. Rose and Alice, tired of their fractious children, agreed with Amelia and after supplying them with picnic baskets, sent the group off to the upper fields of Eastwood where the huckleberries grew fat and plenty.

Myles and Cooper went along to supervise and fill their own pails. The children trooped down through the small wood onto the dusty trail. Henry regaled them with stories of a gigantic black bear from a book Mr. Underhill loaned him. Myles and Cooper were intrigued with the story, especially as Henry related that after the bear had been shot it continued to charge grown men. Kitty, never comfortable in the country, began to peer into the bushes and jump at every crackle in the underbrush. She lagged behind the group and realized they had disappeared from her sight. She trotted to join them.

Once they reached the golden field, Kitty felt a little safer. In the distance she saw a herd of black and white jersey cows who raised their heads, briefly looked at the children and returned to their grazing.

The ripe huckleberries hung in enormous dark clusters, their juicy sweet smell mixed with the smell of the drying grass and general dustiness. The children picked and popped the plump sweet berries into their mouths. Soon they had berry stained lips and teased each other. Occasionally, a thorn would scratch when they pulled the plump berries from the vines, or a bee would buzz them, but all in all the picking went smoothly.

A babbling brook ran along the edge of the berry patch and the children placed their bottles of milk in the brook to keep them cool until lunch. The quiet of the pasture was broken by the laughter and talk as good humor was restored. Mrs. Pratt promised huckleberry pie for dessert and the jam that she and her kitchen crew made would end up in everyone's larders for the winter.

Torie and Edmund worked together and talked about a cooling dip in the pond when they returned from their labors. Kitty found a thick patch of berries and Cooper placed a log on the ground to hold down the vines and make it easier for Kitty to reach the fruit. The log allowed Kitty to reach deeper into the thicket. She picked neatly and quickly and her pail was almost full when she paused at the sound of an ominous crackling on the other side of the bushes. She glanced around and realized that she could not see any of her cousins or Edmund. Their voices coming from over the high bushes sounded distant to her.

Kitty paused and listened intently and then hearing nothing more, returned to her picking. Once again, she heard an ominous crackling. Kitty decided to find herself a new picking spot, closer to the rest of her cousins, when she glimpsed something large and dark through the tangled vines. Panicked she dropped her bucket and turned to flee, forgetting all about the log that Cooper used to flatten the vines. Kitty screamed as she tripped and went down in a pile of thorns and vines. Through her tears, Kitty shrieked, "A bear! There's a bear on the other side of the bush!"

Kitty's shrieks of terror brought all rushing to her. They found her lying on the ground bleeding from several scratches just as a large black cow ambled around the thicket. Torie and Henry flew at the cow to drive her away using loud cries and smacks on her hind quarters. Myles and Cooper reached in and started to gently extract Kitty; Edmund retrieved her pail. The cow snorted and trotted a few yards away and placidly ruminated as she watched the excitement.

Kitty, finally extracted from the thorns, was pulled to her feet. She shrieked in pain as she tried to put her foot down. "My ankle," she gasped. "My ankle really hurts."

Cooper lifted her into his strong arms and carried her to the brook. Gently he set her down and Torie wetted her handkerchief and wiped Kitty's hot dusty face while Edmund gently removed her boot and examined her swelling ankle. Torie, borrowing the other boy's handkerchiefs, wet these as well and began to wash away the blood from the scratches on Kitty's arms and legs.

After examining the ankle, Edmund looked up at the worried faces and said, "I don't think it is broken, but I think it is a bad sprain. She is not going to be able to walk home." He looked at his older twin cousins, and said, "Can one of you get the farm wagon and let Grandmother know that Dr. Johnson should be sent for?"

After a short discussion, it was decided that both Myles and Cooper would go, so that one could bring the wagon back and the other could retrieve the doctor. The twins turned and soon disappeared into the quiet. Edmund and Torie maneuvered Kitty so she could sit on a flat rock and bathe her foot in the creek. Edmund examined her scratches and wrapped up the worst one on her arm with a clean handkerchief. Torie retrieved the lunch basket and poured Kitty a drink of cool milk and then opened up the basket and handed her cousin some rolls stuffed with ham and tomatoes. Torie sliced and pitted a peach and offered it to her cousin. Henry began to tell his cousin gentle tales of fairies who frolicked in the woods and helped weary travelers.

Kitty, who was in great pain, tried to eat but the throbbing pain in her ankle would not allow more than a nibble. It felt like forever, but soon the hay wagon came across the field driven by Uncle Jasper. The children and pails of berries were quickly loaded in to the wagon. Kitty was carefully placed on the bench with her aching ankle propped up. It was an agonizing ride as each jostle of the wagon brought a fresh spasm of pain. Torie held her cousin's hand and massaged her head. Edmund sat at Kitty's injured foot and did his best to keep it from jostling.

Thanks to the quick action of Myles and Cooper, the wagon and children lurched to a halt, as the doctor's buggy pulled up in front of Eastwood. The Colonel himself carried Kitty into the house and up to the nursery where Phoebe and Alice made Kitty as comfortable as possible.

Dr. Johnson, after examining the ankle, praised Edmund for his care of the foot. The doctor then rewrapped the ankle and ordered the patient to stay off of it for two weeks.

With Kitty injured, Alice decided that it was time to pack up and return to Boston. The nursery on the third floor was terribly inconvenient for someone who was not supposed to walk, and it was time Alice hired a nanny for her little twins. It was much harder to hire a Boston nanny while residing in Eastwood, and in Boston Alice would have easier access to the agencies.

In addition to finishing up Susanna's wedding plans, Alice and Susanna needed to put Susanna's new home in order. Alexander's parents bought the soon-to-be-wedded couple a small brick home not far from Charles and Alice's house. The home needed to be furnished and organized. It was decided that Edmund would stay on at Eastwood with Rose and her children until they returned to town the following week. Edmund was not interested in wedding plans or the other feminine pursuits they would follow in Boston.

Matilda, Jasper, and the twins, Myles and Cooper, were the next to leave. They had plans to spend a week with Jasper's family on the cape before the boys had to report to West Point.

With so many gone, the large dining room table shrunk to a smaller size and the house seemed roomier. Edmund and Torie spent their afternoons sailing on the pond and playing in the yard with Henry, but the echoes of the children were quieter. Lavinia urged her mother to pack up and head back to Boston. Lavinia felt she was missing out on details of Susanna's wedding and she wanted to start preparing for Radcliffe.

Rose knew she needed to start the packing up process, but was awash with emotions over what to do. Rose longed to see Marcus; she missed him desperately. At the same time she was unsure how she would feel when she saw him again. Alone in her bed at night, Rose would relive their summer together and remember a thousand different instances. She would lie in bed and remember the lock of hair that fell over his forehead as he read sonnets to her, or the twinkle in his eyes when he caught her glance from across a crowded dinner table. Rose could still feel Marcus' hands upon her body, his hot kisses that made her melt. Restlessly, she abandoned her tossed bed and sat at the window seat, looking out across the woods to Summerfield. No lights pierced the night sky; the house was closed and quiet.

What would happen in Boston? Rose was unsure how to confront Amelia with her love for Marcus. He is an acceptable husband, Rose would argue with the phantom Amelia. He may not have been born into Boston society, but he has the manners and acceptable wealth that allow him to take a place by her side in Boston society. Amelia argued back at her in her mind: if you marry we will send Henry to Slater. It is what your husband promised us. The Colonel will not be thwarted.

Reluctantly Rose began packing up and made plans to return to Boston. With Lavinia attending college and Henry starting at Ashcroft, there was much to do from purchasing uniforms and sewing in name tapes, to wardrobes ordered and sewn. The goal was to make Lavinia's dorm room feel as cozy as home. Vinnie, in particular, was very excited about her new adventure and encouraged Rose to make the move back to Boston. Lavinia yearned to be involved in details over Susanna's wedding and was eager to return home.

Torie mourned leaving Eastwood. Although she had gotten her way about her schooling for the new year, leaving Eastwood meant leaving behind Edmund and all the fun the two had all summer. No more sailing! No more racing the pony cart! It would be Susanna's wedding in December before Torie saw Edmund again. She felt anxious for him. Torie and Edmund talked further about him leaving Slater, and ever since Torie watched Edmund take care of Kitty the day of her accident, Torie fully supported Edmund's desire to become a doctor. Torie pestered Edmund to talk to his parents, but he stayed firm that he did not want to cause his parents any distress until after the wedding. Torie, not convinced, stopped hectoring him.

At last, everyone left Eastwood. Even the great aunts departed with Christopher and Emily and their children, promising to see them safely home. Staying on until the middle of September were the Colonel and Amelia. They spent the last beautiful golden days of summer enjoying the peace and quiet after the never ending hubbub brought on by three generations under one roof.

Even the majority of the servants departed. Mrs. Musgrave left to spend the month of September with her daughter in Rhode

Island. The Pratts remained to assist the elderly Brewsters in any entertaining they might do, and to oversee the permanent skeletal staff that maintained Eastwood year round until Mrs. Musgrave's return.

Mr. Martini and Amelia spent several mornings putting summer garden beds to sleep for the winter, pruning back shrubs and bushes and overseeing the cleaning of gardening sheds.

The last morning dawned and Amelia and the Colonel walked through the silent rooms, remembering the laughter and excitement of this summer. The Colonel looked down at his little wife and said, "When we return next summer we shall be in a new century."

Amelia looked up at her husband fondly. "A new century. I wonder what it will bring us?" she asked with a smile.

"America is growing and changing," her husband said. "Do you think we need to change?"

Amelia cocked her head to one side and surveyed her husband. She laughed, "I don't think it is possible for you or me to change." Then thinking about her conversations with Torie, she shrugged, "Well, maybe just a little."

The Colonel pinched her cheek. "I think we should start making changes. Maybe even invest in one of those horseless carriages."

Amelia looked at him in surprise. Her eyes twinkled and she said, "George, you would be the envy of every one of your grandsons."

"Torie, too," the Colonel said with a chuckle. "I heard her at the train station trying to convince Brooks Carter to teach her to drive his."

Laughing, they took one last walk onto the porch, looking across the wide green lawn to the pond. "Do you think you and I should try, what did Edmund call it, 'skinny dipping' next summer." he laughed at her.

Amelia gently tapped him on the arm and shook her head. Looking across the lawn at the arbor, she said dreamily, "I wonder if we will have another wedding next summer?"

"If so," her husband said drawing her near, "I don't want you to work so hard. Let someone else be in charge."

Amelia drew herself up and looked at him. She said, "I like being in charge. Besides, those girls (referring to Rose and Alice) would muck things up. I just do not believe they could organize all those details."

The Colonel let the subject go. "You know what I like best about our summers?" he asked her gently. Amelia smiled up at him and waited. "I like," he told her, "when I come out on the verandah and see you sitting there, surrounded by your daughter, your daughters-in-law and your grandchildren and you smiling like a queen holding court."

"I like that too," she admitted. "It is nice to have the family so close." She shivered, "Home is going to be very quiet when it is just us and the great aunts."

"Oh," he disagreed, "you are always at some social do or charity event. I am truly surprised that your charities survived another summer without your involvement."

Back in Boston, Rose was delighted to find herself once more in her pretty brick house. Her small staff welcomed her home. She found her home neat and spotless. Over the summer, Rose's general maid had been hired as an upstairs maid to another family, so Rose brought Tilly, the little scullery maid at Eastwood, with her. Tilly experienced a lot of firsts: she had never been to the city, she had never ridden a train and she had never lived so far away from her family. The biggest change in Tilly's life was that for the first time in her young life, she had an entire bedroom to herself in the attic. Granted, her bedroom was the tiniest of rooms, barely larger than a closet and it looked out over the dank gray alley, but it was all hers.

Hobbs, Rose's butler, and Helen the Cook, occupied larger rooms across the hall from Tilly. Their rooms overlooked the park, but Tilly realized how fortunate she was and fell to learning how to maid for Mrs. William with great industry, if not always success.

Hobbs, as Tilly's superior and Rose's right hand man, instructed the tiny maid in how to dust and clean properly.

Rose and her children settled back into 23 Hampshire Place and immersed themselves in preparing Lavinia and Henry for being away at school and Torie's new day school. Rose spent one long afternoon with Henry dragging him from store to store as he was outfitted in the regulatory uniform of Ashcroft. Rose, exhausted, truly felt outfitting Henry for military school could not be quicker or shorter. She signed for the purchases and was promised they would all be delivered later that day to her home. She knew that she and Phoebe had hours ahead of them sewing name tapes in all of his clothing.

Rose spent several days with Lavinia helping her prepare for college. Vinnie had definite ideas over what a young lady needed to bring to college and did not always agree with her mother on choices. Rose was surprised that her usual tractable daughter was slightly obstinate about this, but the two of them worked out the details and soon Vinnie's trunks, lately emptied of her summer wardrobe, were once again filled with fall and winter needs.

Torie was a bit easier. She would be a day student and, while still required to wear a uniform, her list was not nearly as long as her brother and sister. Torie was excited about her new school. She and Henry reacquainted themselves with the neighborhood children. Kitty hobbled around and she and Edmund, as well as Damarus and Dorcas came to play in the park, their joyous shrieks once more filled the neighborhood.

Rose found that her preparation for her children and rejoining her charitable works and societies, caused her to be away from home almost every afternoon and evening. She spent hours devoted to children and social expectations, but Rose found her mind on Marcus constantly. Rose awoke every morning and fixed her hair specially, hoping to hear from Marcus. Rose hurried home from shopping with the children or volunteering at the hospital or her Literary Guild Society meetings hoping he had called. But, there was no word from Marcus.

Certainly Marcus' name seemed to be on everyone's lips. Under the wing of Cordelia Brown, Marcus was included in many events. Rose was speechless one evening when she came into Mary Sparrow's parlor for Literary Guild meeting and found Marcus sitting across the room with his hostess. Rose felt herself flush as he looked across the room and smiled at her. In confusion, Rose dropped her book. The entire meeting passed in a fog as Rose could not focus on anything.

After the meeting, they all stood in the front hall while Stephen Brown asked Marcus how he enjoyed the meeting. With a glance at Rose, Marcus said that he enjoyed the meeting very much, but was not sure how often he could attend as he was currently spending time in Baltimore on business.

Still he did not call on her. After a few days, Rose began to feel bereft and full of doubt. Had Marcus been trifling with her? Had he come back to town and found some other younger and more suitable woman on which to focus his attentions? Rose thought about her wanton behavior the night Marcus came to her room, and she burned with the thought that it meant anything to him. May be he had simply been biding his time at Eaton Pond and found the Widow Brewster had been an easy target. From glowing and excited, Rose crashed down into silence and an occasional short temper with her children.

Rose came home one sunny afternoon from her DAR meeting and Hobbs told her she had a gentleman caller in her small drawing room. Rose eagerly pushed her packages into the butler's hands and dashed into the drawing room. At the sight of Peregrine Fitch, the light in her eyes died. Peregrine, startled at her expression, asked, "Are you not happy to see me?"

"Oh Perry," Rose came across the room and greeted him by pressing his hand and kissing him lightly on the cheek. "It isn't that I am not glad to see you. I just had something else on my mind."

Peregrine took both of her hands in his and returned her kiss. Peregrine said, "I have come to take Torie and Henry for ice cream in my horseless carriage."

At that moment Torie and Henry burst in. "Uncle Peregrine!" they shouted in glee as they pounced on him.

Peregrine talked with them and heard about their activities since their return, including their plans for school and Susanna's wedding.

Torie turned to her mother, "Uncle Peregrine is going to stay for dinner, right?"

It was Peregrine's turn to answer. "Oh, chicken, I would love to, but not tonight," he told her, as he reached out and gently pulled one of Torie's ringlets. "But, I will take you for ice cream right now," he said to her. Turning to Henry he asked, "When do you leave for school, Henry?"

"Monday," Henry told him with a glitter of excitement in his eyes. "I am packed and I have already corresponded with Dr. Nicholson. He is the professor of Archeology at Ashcroft."

Torie and Henry bustled out of the house and climbed in the car. Rose walked Peregrine to the door. He stood with his hat in his hand. Peregrine turned to her and said, "Rose there is something we need to talk about. When are you free?"

Rose shook her head with a sigh, "Until I get everyone settled in school, I really do not seem to have any free time. Possibly later next week."

On the following Monday, Rose, Torie and Lavinia escorted Henry to Ashcroft. Once Henry was established in his room, the three women left him with gentle good byes and hugs. Henry stood in front of his dormitory and watched them drive away, his steel spectacles glinting in the late afternoon sun. As the wheels of the carriage turned from Ashcroft, Rose sat and watched the small slight figure of her son disappear from view. It was silent in the carriage as the three females in Henry's life held hands and shed a few tears.

A few days later, Lavinia stood in her new dorm room at Radcliffe, surveying with great satisfaction the comings and goings in the hall outside her room. The hall was filled with shrieks of welcome as old friends greeted each other and trunks were hauled into various rooms. Susanna came to see her cousin off to college, and while she glimpsed the possibilities of the fun her cousin would have, she dreamily thought of her impending wedding. Rose and Lavinia clung to each other when it was time to leave, and Rose once again sobbed on the carriage ride home.

Rose's little house was very quiet with only Torie at home. On evenings when Rose had no social commitments, Phoebe would join Rose and the two women would sit with a much diminished mending basket and talk over Henry's latest letter or how Torie was doing in her new school. Rose saw very little of Alice Brewster, who was busy with her own organizing of Edmund back to Slater and Kitty to Miss Mable's, and the million details of Susanna's wedding. Alice had at last hired a new nanny, an experienced Irish woman named Mary Margaret. Mary Margaret was a well built girl with strong arms and a no nonsense attitude. Mary Margaret had firm control of the nursery and of all Alice's children. Edmund told Torie that she had even invaded his bath to make sure that he had washed behind his ears.

Rose came in one afternoon from the first meeting of the DAR. Rose stopped to look through the mail and found a letter from Henry. Rose missed Henry and Lavinia terribly. Henry dutifully wrote once a week and his letters were filled with his excitement over his classes and the library at Ashcroft. Henry settled at Ashcroft better than Rose would have ever hoped, and she knew Henry corresponded with the Colonel, as well. Rose and Torie resumed Sunday dinners with the elder Brewsters and occasionally the Colonel would bark an observation about Henry to her. Rose was certain that the matter of Henry's schooling was not finished, just temporarily shelved, that more arguments would follow. But, as yet the Colonel found little to complain about Ashcroft.

Rose received fewer letters from Lavinia. Lavinia found that college was everything that she imagined. Her classes were interesting, but Lavinia never expected some of her professors to be so attractive. A constant stream of young men asked her if they could escort her to the many college dances, debate teams or to watch football matches. Lavinia had little time to write home unless she needed her mother to send something she forgot. Rose, amused and delighted at her daughter's escapades, cheerfully packed up the requests and sent notes reminding her daughter to study.

Rose felt a sudden lightness of responsibility. With only Torie home, the house was quiet most days. In the evenings that she was home, Rose ate an early dinner with Torie and Phoebe. Torie, excited to be sitting at the dining room table with her mother, rather than a nursery supper with Phoebe, behaved beautifully. Torie came downstairs every night with her curls smooth and tidy and her dress impeccably clean. Torie enjoyed her conversations with her mother. Rose opened up a little and talked about her upbringing by her aunt and uncle after her parents died. Rose told Torie about what it was like in the years after the war when so many of her friends were fatherless.

One evening, Peregrine joined them for dinner. Peregrine made Torie laugh as he regaled her with stories of his childhood days at Eastwood with her father, William. "Even then," Peregrine told Torie, "the Colonel had all the boys up early doing calisthenics and swimming in the pond first thing in the morning." Remembering how cold the pond was at dawn, Peregrine shivered at the memory. "Your father hated it," he added.

Torie looked at Peregrine indignantly. "The boys complain about it, but they don't hate it, not even Henry," she protested. "Uncle Peregrine, my father was a great military man. Why would he hate grandfather's morning routine? It was what you did every morning at Slater, minus the swim in Eaton's Pond."

Peregrine studied Torie over his glass. "How old are you, young lady?" he asked with a quizzical look in his eyes.

"Thirteen, almost fourteen," she told him. "Why?"

"I think it is time you knew the truth," he said, suddenly very serious. A firm look came over Peregrine's normally easy going face.

Rose made a noise and put out a detaining hand, but Peregrine covered her hand with his own and said flatly, "Torie, the truth is that your father hated military school and he hated fighting in any war."

Torie, totally shocked, shook her head and insisted, "Uncle Peregrine, my father was a great soldier. He won medals of honor for bravery. He loved riding with the calvary."

Peregrine nodded, and went on more gently, "Victoria, your father was a great soldier because he followed orders. Your father was awarded medals because he fought as he was ordered to do. And your father did love his beloved horses. But," he paused and looked at her, "he hated every minute of it, every day."

"NO!" Torie protested, her voice rising. "Uncle Peregrine, you are wrong. Grandfather says Brewsters are always great soldiers. Brewsters love war; they love to fight for the glory of their country." Torie was adamant in her words. "War is what makes Brewsters great businessmen, great statesmen. It prepares Brewster men for a great life." Tears filled Torie's eyes as she stared at Peregrine's face; she saw the look of pity in his eyes.

"Torie," Peregrine said, his tone very gentle. He reached out a hand for her but she snatched it back; her staring accusing eyes never left his face. He continued, "There was no glory in the Indian Wars. It was a horrible hard war and your father was not proud of his role in it." She started to interrupt, but his words covered hers, "Torie, William, your father, followed every order. He did exactly what was required of him. He cleared the land of Indians, but they weren't all savages. He had to kill innocent..." Peregrine, looking into Torie's anguished young face, could not finish his sentence.

As she listened, tears poured down Torie's face. Her sobs shook her entire small body. "Uncle Peregrine, you have it wrong," she pleaded, her eyes fastened on Peregrine's set face.

Rose, who had been silent through this exchange, reached over and patted the sobbing girl. "Torie, look at me," Rose said quietly, her own eyes full of tears.

Torie turned her tear-streaked face to her mother. Rose tried to speak, swallowed and started again, "Your grandfather was a great soldier and he fought for his country. He fought to keep our country together and strong. Your great-great-grandfather fought for the liberty of our country. Your grandfather, like his father, wanted all of his sons to be great soldiers. Your father was a great soldier, but he did not like it." As Torie started to protest, her mother said gently, "Your father told me so. He did not believe in the cause he was fighting for. But, like a good soldier, he obeyed orders."

Torie looked from her mother to Peregrine. They had the same sober looks on their faces. Torie shook her head wildly, then shrieked, "You are wrong. My father wanted to grow up to be a soldier. That is all he ever wanted to be. He was a Brewster. Brewster men always want to be soldiers!" Torie then stood, her chair falling backwards as she raced from the room sobbing.

Torie's sobs and stamping feet could be heard as she ran up the stairs to the nursery. A moment later the sound of her bedroom door slamming shut was heard. Rose winced and, in the echoing silence of the dining room, she looked at Peregrine bleakly. Peregrine wore the saddest look imaginable on his face. Rose sighed and said consolingly, "Perry, you said what was needed to be said for a very long time to Torie."

"She is still just a child." Peregrine fiddled with his fork and drummed a beat on the table. "I am sorry, Rose," he apologized.

Rose had tears in her eyes. She shook her head and said, "Please don't feel that way. Torie has built her father up into some grand soldier who came riding in on a white stead and vanquished the Indians. What she does not understand was how horrible the treatment of the Indians was, how much innocent blood was shed. And how much her father hated every minute of his time in the military."

Rose played with her food, her appetite gone. She pushed her plate away. There was a small silence and then Peregrine said, "William only talked to me once after he came back about the war. We were riding in the country and stopped on a hill. As we looked out over the valley we talked a little about it. To William's dying day he relived in his mind the slaughter of Indian women and children. William hated everything about the military. From the first day at Slater."

Rose looked at Peregrine. "You were a good friend to William," she said inadequately. "When we were first married, William used to tell me a little about Slater. It sounded like hell."

Peregrine looking back, agreed with vehemence, "Slater was hell." The lines on his face deepened as he grimaced. Peregrine shook his head and told Rose, "I don't know why, but from the first day at Slater, William was picked on the most. He was singled out by the instructors and taunted by the other boys. William could not hide how much it bothered him and it just drove the hazing more deeply. He was never left alone."

Peregrine raised his head and Rose saw that he had tears in his eyes as he went on, "We were best friends since we were very young. Both of our fathers were away fighting in the War between the States and our mothers were close friends. William and I always spent a lot of time together. My mother and I went with Amelia and William to Eastwood for the summers during the war years and when the time came, William and I were sent away to school together. I don't think I would have made it through Slater without William." Peregrine's hands trembled as he reached out and took Rose's hand.

Rose squeezed Peregrine's hand and looked at him. She said passionately, "William loved you, Peregrine. You were his best friend and he always spoke of you fondly." Peregrine raised his head and looked at Rose. In his eyes was sorrow and something else she could not understand. She thought back to what the young William must have been like, sensitive and not overly robust, forced to be in a place in his life that he had no understanding. No one to back him up. If he had written complaints home they would have fallen on deaf ears. But, William always had Peregrine.

Peregrine looked at Rose. "Do you think I have damaged Torie?" he asked bleakly.

Rose removed her hand from his grasp and folded her napkin. She shook her head, "Torie has so much Colonel George Brewster in her that she is going to believe as she wishes. I will go check on her. She might be willing to listen to reason by now."

They both stood up and Rose waited until Peregrine's hat and coat had been fetched. Quietly, Peregrine took her hand and looked down at her wordlessly.

Rose smiled gently and reaching up, she lay her hand on his cheek and said softly, "Peregrine, thank you for saying what you said to Torie. I can not thank you enough for all that you have done for my children and me over the years. You have filled the spot of William very adequately. We all truly love you."

Peregrine smiled faintly and leaning down kissed her gently on the cheek. The door closed behind him and Rose stood for a moment. Then drawing a deep breath, she climbed the stairs to the nursery.

Rose knocked gently and walked into the nursery. Softly she came to the bed where Torie lay with her face to the wall, her shoulders hunched, pretending to be asleep. Rose looked down at her daughter's tossed curls and then leaned over and gave her daughter a gentle kiss on the head before she turned down the light and closed the door quietly behind her.

After her mother left the room, Torie broke into a fresh torrent of tears. How could Uncle Peregrine be so mean and say that her father did not want to be a soldier? Brewsters always wanted to be soldiers. If Brewster men did not want to be soldiers there had to be something wrong with them. Torie longed for Edmund to be here so she could talk to him about it, to back her up. Torie paused and frowned, thinking back to her conversation at Eastwood with Edmund. Edmund did not want to be a soldier either. Edmund wanted to leave Slater.

Could her grandfather be wrong? Torie thought about Myles and Cooper. They wanted to be soldiers; they loved being at Slater and looked forward to attending West Point this year. Torie knew to the core of her being that Myles and Cooper were going to become great soldiers. They carried the mantle of greatness upon their broad soldiers. There was no question that each would become an officer and bring glory to the Brewster name.

Truly Torie never understood why her mother was so adamant about Henry not going to military school. Torie adored her younger brother but sometimes puzzled over his bookish ways. Henry talked forever about digging up ancient ruins. Torie allowed a small smile as she remembered Kitty falling into the hole that Henry dug when they played "discovering ancient Alexandra." Henry did not seem upset that his mother did not want him at Slater. While Henry never expressed his feelings one way or the other about his schooling, the halls of Ashcroft felt like a better fit for bookish Henry.

It was a big step for a little girl to take. Could Brewster men grow up to be other things besides soldiers and still be successful? Torie fell into a troubled sleep.

The next morning, a subdued Torie stood before the mirror. She dressed for school and stood, for once, docile as Phoebe brushed and fixed her hair. Torie's face had been thoroughly washed with cooling clothes and her swollen eyes looked a little more normal although still a little bleak.

Phoebe finished braiding Torie's dark long hair into a fat braid and tied a wide blue bow at the nape of her neck. Phoebe reached out and gave Torie a small pat and asked, "Do you want to talk about it?"

Torie glanced around at Phoebe and saw understanding in her eyes. "Did Mother," she began furiously, "tell you what Uncle Peregrine said about my father?" Torie felt once again the tears welling to the surface.

Phoebe was all business. "Torie," she said with emphasis, "Mr. Fitch did not tell you what he thought because he is mean. Mr. Fitch was your father's best friend and he probably knew your father better than anyone except your mother. He would not tell you these things unless he thought you were old enough to understand."

Torie looked at Phoebe in astonishment. Phoebe went on, "Your grandfather is always so sure of his decisions. Now, as a soldier that is a good thing. An officer needs to know when he gives a command, it is best for his regiment. If he second guesses himself, well, it could cost many lives. But, families are different."

Torie looked a little puzzled and her stony face turned to stare out the window, avoiding Phoebe's eyes.

Phoebe continued, "Men generally join the army because they want to be there. Along with that decision, they follow orders from their commanding officer. You don't join a family; you are born into a family. It is high time your grandparents realized that." Phoebe spoke with such emphasis that Torie turned her head and looked at Phoebe, her eyes wide.

"I have said too much," Phoebe said abruptly. It was her turn to avoid Torie's eyes as Phoebe stooped and picked up Torie's nightgown. "Torie, you are a smart young lady and you are forever talking about change because America is moving into a new century. Maybe it is time you realized that change begins at home. Your mother let Mr. Fitch talk to you because you are growing up. Remember, Mr. Fitch was at Slater with your father and he was his best friend." Phoebe carefully folded Torie's nightgown and turned to give Torie a kiss. "Go to school, Miss Torie. You will feel better."

Torie slowly descended the stairs thinking about Phoebe's words. She entered the dining room and slipped into her chair and began to nibble bacon. Her mother looked at her searchingly, but Torie simply smiled at her mother and said, "Mama, we have a spelling bee today at school. I hope I do well."

Rose set down her coffee cup and stared at her daughter. Torie smiled back, finished with her breakfast. Torie wiped her mouth delicately with her napkin, stood up and gave her mother a small kiss before she departed for school. Rose sat for a long time staring after her daughter.

CHAPTER 12

A few days later as Rose shuffled through the post on the hall table, she came across a package. The handwriting looked familiar, although there was no return address. Rose carried it to her bedroom, shut the door and using her pen knife, slit the wrapper. Out fell a book of Shakespeare's sonnets. Opening the book she found a single page written in Marcus' handwriting.

"Do not despair, my love," it read, "business has called me out of town and I am biding my time until I can spend the time I desire with you. Please understand that you are in my constant thoughts. Do not believe the gossip you hear. I am creating a distraction to salve your name and to draw the Brewsters off of our track. M."

As a love note, it left much to be desired. Rose held it against her heart and knew that Marcus' hands had held it too. Rose reread the note and frowned over the mention of gossip. Had gossip followed her from Eastwood to Boston? Rose sincerely hoped no gossip would reach Amelia Brewster's ears or she would be in for more scoldings and accusations.

Rose sat by the fire hemming an apron when the door bell rang and Peregrine was announced. Perry came in, formally dressed for the evening in a black suit and crisp white shirt. From his shining black shoes to his expertly tied bow tie, Peregrine epitomized the picture of perfection.

Peregrine glanced down at Rose, worry in his eyes, and explained, "I am off to the Van Schwitzels, but I wanted to check on Torie. How is she? Do you think she has forgiven my words about her father?"

Rose smiled in appreciation. "Dear Perry" she said as she reached up and squeezed his hand, "Torie seems to be doing very well. She has been a little quieter than usual, but I think she is growing up. She has been corresponding with Edmund, and who knows what he is advising her."

Peregrine smiled at Rose and said "That makes me feel relieved. I adore that scrappy little sprite of yours and hated to make her cry." Rose smiled at his words, but a puzzled frown crossed her face as Peregrine restlessly prowled the room. Peregrine looked down at Rose with a small smile.

At Rose's return smile, Peregrine said, "You were one of the most beautiful brides I ever saw. On your wedding day I remember watching you walk down the aisle on your uncle's arm. I was so happy for you and William."

Rose, slightly puzzled, blushed, "Thank you, Perry. You were always a good friend to William."

"He was my best friend." Peregrine looked into the fire, even now anguish in his eyes. "After he died," he went on, "I watched over you, for William's sake. I wanted to make sure that you would always be taken care of. It has not been easy on your own, even with all the Brewsters help."

There was no answer for this and Rose waited in silence.

Peregrine continued to look at her, mulling something over in his mind. Slowly he said, "I have gotten to know Marcus Underhill very well."

Rose returned to her sewing and drew a stitch. His words caused her hands to still. Although she continued to stare at the fabric, her thoughts raced and she felt her face flushing. Had Marcus confided to Peregrine his feelings for her? Surely not. Rose darted Peregrine a look. When their eyes met she dropped them again but she said nothing.

"Marcus Underhill," Peregrine repeated, "the best thing that ever happened to you."

This time Rose's head came up and she looked at Peregrine longer, a small question in her eyes.

Peregrine nodded and smiled gently at Rose. "All summer, at Eastwood," Perry went on, "I watched you light up and glow. You have always been a beautiful woman; you were a beautiful girl. As a widow, you always looked so reserved, no sparkle even when you laughed." Rose's green eyes glittered and her cheeks bloomed with color. Peregrine went on, "I have watched you this summer, Rose. You have blossomed and look happier than I have ever known you to be. At times, you look as young as Lavinia." Rose started to stammer something, but Peregrine went on, "Rose, I have known you almost 20 years. I have watched you endure everything the Brewsters have demanded of you and you have done it graciously and without complaint. I saw you put William's children ahead of anything else you might need to make you happy."

Rose interrupted Peregrine. "They are my children too," she said quietly.

Peregrine paused and nodded his head, accepting her comment, then continued, "This summer, you had an inner joy about you. It did not take me long to figure out what caused your joy and I was so happy for you."

Rose now looked at Peregrine with intensity, listening to his every word. Perry continued, "I was afraid for you, afraid you would get hurt. Either you would get caught by the Brewsters or Underhill was trifling with you. So, to protect you, I had a conversation with Marcus."

Peregrine went on, "I have the utmost respect for Marcus Underhill as a business partner and a gentleman. But you already face an uphill battle with the Brewsters over the possibilities of educating Henry. To be honest, I buttonholed Marcus while we were in Baltimore; we had a fairly frank conversation."

Rose, barely breathing, listened to Peregrine intently. Her breath caught in her throat and her face flamed.

Peregrine stared at her silently for a minute and she dropped her eyes. "Rose, I am not in any way chiding you. I entered into a business partnership with Underhill and I have come to realize that he is a worthy man for you. I want you to know that if the two of you pursue your relationship, there will be some very tough times ahead for you. I want you to know that I will stand by you if you choose to confront the Brewsters."

Suddenly Peregrine impatiently said, "Rose, you deserve to be happy. I want you to marry, Rose, and be happy."

Peregrine looked at her earnestly, "Rose, this may not be my place, but I think you have fallen in love with Marcus Underhill this summer."

Rose gazed at Peregrine, eyes shining with emotion and stated, "I do love him, Perry. We never intended for this to happen. I mean, we just started talking..." Rose's voice trailed off. She looked at Peregrine and admitted, "I don't know what to do about it. The Colonel and Amelia will fight me to the death over this. You already know the gossip about us."

Listening to the bitterness of her voice, Peregrine continued, "Marcus Underhill is something new to gossip about. And when the pretty Widow Brewster seems to be paying attention to him, there is whispered speculation. I wanted to make sure that he was not going to hurt you," Peregrine explained. Abruptly he changed the subject, "I have watched over you for years, Rose. William would want you to be happy."

Rose raised her eyes and stared at Peregrine. Her eyes were shining with tears. "Oh, Perry," she sighed, "I love you."

Peregrine laughed, "That is not quite the correct answer when we are speaking of your love for someone else."

Peregrine stood up and paced the room, choosing his words, "It isn't really my place to tell you, but Marcus admitted he cares for you very much."

Rose blushed with happiness and her eyes took on a brighter shine.

Peregrine sat down on the ottoman by Rose and took her hand. He paused and then said, "In business the easiest way to overcome your business adversary sometimes is to create a diversion. Make them think they are getting what they want and then, with smoke and mirrors, pull the rug right out from under their feet."

Rose looked at Peregrine with a puzzled frown, as he smiled reassuringly.

Peregrine went on, "Rumors are swirling a bit and Marcus and I don't want Amelia censuring you. We two men put our heads together and created a diversion. Marcus will be seen escorting young ladies around town. In particular, Annabelle Morris." He said this last with a flourish, but Rose looked at him in bewilderment.

Rose frowned, "Why Annabelle?"

"Because," Peregrine explained, "Annabelle and her parents are set on Annabelle becoming a duchess and plan on sailing for London right after the first of the year. Annabelle, who has visions of tiaras and castles, frankly explained to me that she is not interested in any American. The Morris' have plenty of money but a very slim social standing. Annabelle plans on following in the footsteps of Consuela Vanderbilt and become a dollar princess."

Rose still looked befuddled. "Rose," Peregrine patiently explained, "this will silence any gossip and speculation generated by Sam Gardner. You know that Samuel Gardner is on his last legs financially and Marcus and I are in the process of taking over his business. It is only a matter of time before Sam Gardner faces financial ruin, which will lead him to social ruin. He is a very dangerous man, and you need to be protected from him."

"Sam wouldn't hurt me," Rose protested. "Sam Gardner is all bluff and bluster. He is harmless. Everyone knows he is just a big puff of hot air."

Peregrine went on, "This business with Sam Gardner started long before he made you the object of his gossip. After we finish with the Gardner buyout, you and Marcus will be in a stronger position to tackle the Brewsters. Your don't want your children to be affected by the gossip. We hope this helps all be well."

Rose continued to look puzzled. Peregrine patiently explained, "A cornered dog is always the most dangerous, Rose. Sam Gardner is going to lash out against anything that is connected with the Brewsters, Fitches or Underhills. He is dangerous and needs to be respected. Sam is also upset that you rejected him and he is out to score against the Brewsters. You, in his eyes, are the weakest link."

Rose shivered as she thought about Peregrine's words. In her head, she turned over the plot that Marcus and Peregrine created. Rose shrugged and said, "I have barely seen Marcus since I returned to town. There is little to gossip about. I think you all are making mountains out of molehills."

Rose sighed and rubbed her forehead. Another thought crossed her mind. She looked up at Peregrine and said, "What if Marcus falls for Annabelle? She is a very pretty girl."

"Marcus only has eyes for you," Peregrine assured her with a small laugh. "And Felicity Morris is set on launching herself into society. The only way that will happen is if her daughter marries at the very least a duke. Morris told me himself that Marcus would never be considered for his darling daughter. In their eyes not only is he new money, but he was born on the wrong side of the Rockies."

Peregrine took her hand, leaned over and kissed Rose gently on the cheek. "I need to leave for my dinner. I am already late. I came here to reassure you and let you know that I have your back."

Rose gave him a faint smile, but continued to sit and stare at the fire after he left, mulling over the conversation.

Lavinia arrived home for the weekend. Rose did not exactly kill the fatted calf, but her dinner table groaned with Lavinia's favorite dishes. Peregrine joined them for dinner on this Friday evening. Surprisingly, so did Collin Underhill. Lavinia caught a ride home with Collin in his horseless carriage and later he would collect his father from the train at 11:30. So, Lavinia invited Collin to join them for dinner.

Rose watched Collin from across the table and saw a strong resemblance to Marcus in his amber brown eyes and engaging smile. Collin had a boyish charm that set both Lavinia and Torie into gales of giggles as the conversation was filled with stories from both Lavinia and Collin and their college escapades.

Peregrine and Collin fell into a discussion over the differences between their two horseless carriages. After dinner the three Brewster women stood on the front step and watched as both Peregrine and Collin wheeled down the street in their individual automobiles.

Later, as Lavinia was snuggled in her own bed, there was a tap on the door and her mother poked her head around the corner.

Lavinia moved over a little so that her mother could perch on the edge of her bed. Lavinia looked very happy as she told her mother story after story about the fun she was having in college. Rose wondered to herself what Lavinia's marks would show when it came to the end of the term. She promised herself a talk with Lavinia before she returned to Radcliffe on Sunday night, as well as a reminder that Lavinia behave herself. But tonight Rose's thoughts dwelled on something else.

"Collin seems to be settling into college," Rose ventured as an opening gambit to Lavinia.

Lavinia yawned luxuriously and stretched, "It was so nice to be brought home in his horseless carriage. It goes so fast! And Collin is an excellent driver."

Rose paused, unsure of how to couch her next question, "Does he spend a lot of time with you?" she asked hesitantly.

Lavinia opened her green eyes wide and sat up, "Mama, I know where you are going with this. You are still harking back to last summer! It was just a kiss!"

Rose, surprised at Lavinia's words, shook her head in denial. "I have nothing against Collin Underhill," she argued with her daughter. "I am just trying to understand where your heart is."

Lavinia rolled her eyes, "Well, for your information, even if I did have a tendre for Collin, it wouldn't matter. Since the first week of college, Collin has had eyes for only Amy Snow."

Rose looked at Lavinia in surprise. "Amy Snow?" Rose asked.

Lavinia nodded her head. "And I know what you are thinking. Mrs. Snow will have a fit when she finds out. She has her sights on Amy marrying Brooks Carter. But, the feeling is mutual and Amy really likes Collin."

"Well," Rose said lightly, "they are young and who knows how they will feel in six months."

Rose and Lavinia chatted a little longer until Lavinia's eyes began to droop. Rose kissed her oldest daughter tenderly and turned down the lamp.

The next morning Lavinia woke early and fixed her hair. She and Susanna planned to spend the day together. First they would visit the home where Alexander and Susanna would live, and then the girls planned a shopping expedition.

Lavinia looked with interest at the future Peabody honeymoon cottage. It was a small brick house filled with tiny rooms and furnished from the Peabody and Brewster attics. All appeared neat and tidy and it reminded Lavinia of an oversized doll's house. Lavinia could not imagine her cousin living there with Alexander. It seemed so grown up.

"And," Susanna was explaining to Lavinia, "Alexander's mother unearthed this cousin of her cook's who will be in charge of the kitchen. She will have the room in the basement. So far she has been really cranky with me. I will also have a girl come in to help with daily chores and to serve on calling days. Otherwise, it will be just Alexander and I."

Lavinia, bored with admiring crockery and teaspoons, said with a smile, without a trace of envy, "I can just see you living here and being Mrs. Alexander Peabody." She changed the subject, "The clam bake tonight is going to be so fun! I am glad you and Alexander are coming. I am riding out to the cape with Collin and Amy Snow."

Susanna shrugged, and said with a scowl, "I don't know if Alexander is coming. He might decide to have dinner with Papa and talk politics."

Lavinia frowned and asked, "What does that mean?"

Susanna turned and looked out on her scrap of a back garden. For a moment tears dimmed her vision; she took a big breath. "Alexander and I have had a quarrel," she admitted to her cousin.

Lavinia looked at her cousin's back in surprise. Susanna inherited her mother's good nature and she never quarreled with anyone. "What was it about?" Lavinia asked.

Susanna shrugged and said, "Alexander came over for dinner the other night and he and Papa spent the entire evening talking politics. It was so unutterably boring that I could barely keep from yawning. He didn't want to hear one word about the flowers I am planning for our wedding."

Lavinia did not know how to respond to this. "Oh Susanna," Lavinia said inadequately.

Susanna kept her back to her cousin, and did not admit to the details of the quarrel. Alexander, after spending the entire evening droning on and on with her father, eventually turned to her when her parents retired. Susanna, feeling quite ignored, had not appreciated Alexander's amorous pursuits and rejected him. Alexander, shocked at his sweet Susanna's coldness, left in a huff.

Susanna turned from the window and wiped a tear from her eye. She and Lavinia hugged each other and Lavinia said comfortingly, "I am sure Alexander was only trying to be nice to Uncle Charles. I know you will kiss and make up."

The two young women left the house and walked to the shopping district. Lavinia lingered at the glove counter being fitted for a new pair of gloves. While Susanna chose a hair ribbon, she felt a presence beside her. Glancing up, she came face to face with Warner Covington. Warner had been at Princeton and Susanna had not seen Warner since leaving Eastwood. Warner's blue eyes had a warm appreciative light as he smiled down at Susanna. They talked of inconsequential topics until Lavinia finished with her glove fitting. Warner then offered to stand the two young women an ice cream.

Sitting at a small cafe, Lavinia sat back and watched her cousin and Warner. Lavinia knew that Warner had always been sweet on Susanna. There was no question that today Susanna encouraged his attention. Lavinia's attention wandered as she thought about her own secret. Lavinia had developed a crush on her English professor. Professor Barnard had dark soulful eyes and his jet black tangled curls always fell across his forehead. Lavinia was sure that Professor Barnard looked exactly like Heathcliff from Wuthering Heights. Lavinia found every reason to stay after class and ask questions, and Professor Barnard seemed to appreciate her interest in literature. Professor Barnard made every boy who escorted her to dances and parties seem immature and slightly boring.

Susanna laughed at something Warner said and placed her hand on his arm when a shadow fell across the three of them. Susanna looked up in surprise to see Alexander Peabody's hurt eyes observing her and Warner. Alexander spun on his heel and marched out of the cafe. Susanna went ashen, jumped up and rushed after Alexander. Lavinia and Warner exchanged guilty and shocked looks.

Alexander strode furiously down the sidewalk. Susanna following, gasped his name and plucked at his sleeve. "Alexander, please," she pleaded.

Alexander did not reply and turned to a path that ran by the river. Susanna followed as she fought back tears. "Alexander," Susanna sobbed, "I can't keep up. Please stop."

Alexander turned and glared at Susanna. She shrank from his look and dabbed at the tears on her cheeks. Alexander at last spoke, "Do you want to marry Warner?"

Susanna shook her head vigorously, "I want to marry you."

Alexander snorted and stalked down the path, Susanna following.

Alexander turned abruptly back to Susanna, "Then why do you flirt with Warner every chance you get?" Alexander asked. "I have watched you, Susanna Brewster. If you would rather have Warner, go have him."

"But I want to marry you," Susanna protested.

"You rejected me last night," Alexander pointed out.

"But, Alexander," Susanna objected, petulant, "you spent all evening talking boring old politics with Papa and then when he left, you just wanted to kiss me. You did not want to hear about the flowers I have chosen for the wedding."

Alexander frowned at Susanna, "Susanna, my father is a senator. I want to be a senator some day and politics is always going to be a part of my life. As my wife, you will need to hostess many men who want to talk about politics. Besides, the only thing you ever talk about any more is the wedding."

Susanna looked at Alexander in astonishment. "But, Alexander," Susanna said, "it is our wedding."

"Really?" Alexander asked, still annoyed. He went on, "Susanna, a wedding is one day. I want to talk about our life together."

Susanna looked up into his eyes and her own cornflower blue eyes suddenly shone. "Our life?" she asked breathlessly.

"Our life," Alexander echoed. The anger dimmed from Alexander's eyes and he said, "Susanna, the wedding will be beautiful. But you and I are going to have a life together. I want you by my side when I become a senator. I want to come home at night to our home and find you waiting for me. I want to sit at the breakfast table and smile at you. And I want to have children with you."

"Oh," Susanna breathed as Alexander pulled her close and kissed her.

Later that evening, at the clam bake, Lavinia sat next to Warner Covington and the two of them watched Susanna and Alexander sitting on a log side by side. Susanna laughed as she looked up into Alexander's eyes; then she snuggled her head on his shoulder, his head rested against her blonde curls.

The look on Warner's face displayed petulance. The smile on Lavinia's face was pure satisfaction.

CHAPTER 13

One evening Charles and Alice swung by to collect Rose and Peregrine. They were on their way to the Literary Society Meeting at Christopher and Emily Brewster's house. The society was discussing <u>The Mill On The Floss</u>, and Rose had been disturbed when she read the book. The description of Maggie Tulliver and her woodsy ramblings with Philip Wakem caused her to think of her own strolls with Marcus at Eastwood. Poor Maggie struggled all of her life with her family and social acceptance, torn between her attraction to Stephen and duty to Philip. The book had riveted Rose.

In conversation with a group of ladies about the Brewster's summer, Rose watched Marcus stroll into the drawing room. Rose missed him dreadfully, since that hot August night when they had lain in each other's arms. Her heart began to pound in her chest as she stared at him; her breath seemed to choke in her throat. Rose realized where she was standing and turned to hear Mary Sparrow ask something about the "magical summer at Eastwood."

The word "magical" hit Rose hard. The most magical summer of her life flashed in front of her. Suddenly, she felt Marcus' warm hands upon her body and she flushed. Blushing, she stuttered, "It was a wonderful summer. The usual with everyone at Eastwood, plus all the wedding plans."

The conversation veered around to the wedding and Rose stepped away only to come face to face with the person who had made her summer magical. Marcus smiled at Rose, and she trembled in confusion. Suddenly, there was a strong arm around her and Peregrine's voice, "How do you do, Underwood? Miss Morris, it is a pleasure to see you again."

Rose had stared only at Marcus, but now her eyes moved on to greet Annabelle Morris. Annabelle was a buxom dark haired sultry beauty. Some deep emotion shone from Annabelle that always made every woman in the room slightly uncomfortable, and every man react to her hidden sexuality. Twenty years old and very pretty, Annabelle held a proprietary hold on Marcus' arm as she smiled a greeting at Rose and Peregrine. The two men shook hands and after a short conversation, moved on. Rose, flushed and shaking, attempted to compose herself; she took a deep breath. Mary Sparrow called the meeting to order and Rose sank down on a sofa with Peregrine at her side. Marcus and Annabelle sat across the room. Rose remained silent during the meeting, very aware that she was sitting in the same room as Marcus.

When the book discussion finished, they moved into Emily's dining room where small sandwiches, scones and tea were served. Rose helped herself to a cup of tea when she looked up and saw Marcus staring at her. There was the light of desire in his eyes and a small smile on his face. Rose paused in the act of pouring her tea and was lost in his gaze. Startled, she was bumped gently by Fanny Snow, a well known gossip.

"Rose Brewster," Fanny exclaimed, "you are just blooming. Whatever have you been up to?"

Rose flushed at Fanny's words and turned her face away from Marcus. She shrugged and attempted a weak laugh, "I think it was all the country air over the summer."

Fanny gave her a small piercing look and said, "I think I want some of that country air myself."

Rose looked back at Fanny with a small puzzled look. Was there more to that statement? Fanny Snow was a notorious gossip and would pounce on any small tidbit of information and worry it like a dog with a rat until she could find every last detail.

Rose turned from the table, but Fanny followed her, whispering in her ear, "Marcus Underhill is a very attractive man."

The breath caught in Rose's throat as she tried to say nonchalantly, "I guess. I hadn't really noticed. His son was certainly at Eastwood a lot this summer. He and Lavinia are great friends."

Fanny smirked, "Well, gossip has it that Marcus Underhill is out to set himself up in Boston society." Fanny spoke in a tone of someone who enjoyed a good gossip. "It seems his wife was from Maryland, a Morgan, from Baltimore."

"I have heard that," Rose said with a small smile, remembering Marcus' conversations about Collin's mother.

"Well, watch out there, Rose," Fanny said. "He is out for himself or his son to marry a 'daughter of Boston.'"

Rose annoyed with the conversation, looked at Fanny with distaste, 'Daughter of Boston' indeed! Rose spoke with a bite to her voice, "Lavinia is not ready to settle down. She wants to attend college before she even thinks of marriage. And Collin Underhill is a gentleman. Cordelia Brown just adores that boy." The last was said as Cordelia's acceptance of someone in Boston was never questioned.

Fanny shrugged and repeated herself, "I just thought I would give you a warning." Then Fanny said, with a curious tone to her voice, "It must be nice to have all the children off to school and out of the house."

"Well, Fanny," Rose said in cool tones, "I would not know. As you recall, Torie is still at home."

Rose had enough of Fanny's spiteful words. Setting her tea cup down, she stepped out of the house for a fresh breath of air. The mid September evening was cool. It had rained earlier in the day and the air smelled clean. At the sound of the door opening, she turned and found herself face to face with Sam Gardner.

During the book discussion, Sam had been silent, but Rose felt him staring at her with a baleful look on his face. Now Sam reached out and took Rose's hand in his own. Sam Gardner's hands were wet with perspiration. Rose tried to pull away, but Sam held onto her firmly and started to talk. "Want to ask you something," he told her.

Rose looked from his hand on her arm to his face. She raised a delicate eyebrow in question and he continued, with an ugly glint in his eye. "Do you think you could get your man friend to call off the hounds?"

Startled, Rose stared at Sam and again tried to pull away, but he held onto her tighter. "Your man friend, that everybody thinks I was lying about last summer. I know what I saw then, and I know what I saw tonight."

"Mr. Gardner, please," Rose said, quietly. "I don't know what you are talking about," she protested.

"Sure you don't," he said somewhat viciously. "I saw you with him last summer and now he is setting out to ruin me. He and Fitch and those brothers-in-law of yours," he spat at her. "Fitch is always looking after you. But I know all about him, too."

Sam pulled her close with a hurtful grip and whispered in her ear in a threatening voice, "I know all about Fitch and your husband, William. Yeah, I do."

Rose with a twist wrenched herself from his hand and without a backward glance stepped back into the house. She stood in the hall, breathing hard. Sam followed and looked as if he would continue the conversation.

Charles and Peregrine stood just inside the drawing room. They gave Sam a look which caused him to move away, and both moved towards Rose. Charles asked, "Rose, are you alright?"

Rose was as white as a sheet and was shaking. "I have a bit of a headache," she whispered. "I want to go home."

With a short discussion, Peregrine went to retrieve Alice and Charles escorted Rose to his carriage.

Once settled in the corner of the carriage, Charles asked quietly, "What did he say?"

Rose shook her head, a look of confusion in her eyes. "It isn't important, Charles. He was talking rubbish. I detest the man."

Charles began to rub and chaff her hands. "You don't hide your emotions very well and most of the summer you have been blooming and glowing. I know Gardner's been saying things, but I find it hard to believe that he spoke to you directly. Rose, I need to know what Gardner said. I don't know what just happened, except that Sam Gardner is a very dangerous man."

"Sam Gardner says you and Marcus and Peregrine are out to ruin him," she said in a strangled voice.

"We are," Charles said flatly. Rose raised her eyes and looked at him. "Not because of you," he promised. "This is something that has been going on for some time. We have been corresponding and working on this business for close to two years. We have put together several business deals and Gardner has been on our list of take overs for some time."

Business was something that Rose had little interest in, but she asked, "Are you ruining Sam?"

"No," Charles promised her. He said shortly, "We are not. Gardner ruined himself."

"Is everyone watching me?" Rose asked in anguished tones. "Does everyone suspect that Marcus and I are carrying on?"

Charles shook his head. He said truthfully, "I don't know. But, Matilda and my mother are watching you like a hawk."

Peregrine appeared and told Charles that he could not locate Alice. Charles left the carriage to look for his wife and

Peregrine sat down next to Rose. Peregrine looked at Rose, a very serious expression on his face, and said, "I want to ask you a question. Was that all Gardner said?"

Rose looked at him. At his words, a troubled light came into her eyes. "I think there is something very wrong with Sam," she told him. "He was making threatening noises that I did not understand. Something about you and William."

Rose looked at Peregrine and saw a frozen look overtake his face. Alarmed, she reached out a hand to touch him, but he pulled back. At that moment, Alice climbed into the carriage. "There you are," she said, her eyes alight with sympathy. "Charles said you have a headache."

Rose nodded at Alice and turned back to Peregrine, surprised by the sad look on his face. He took Rose's hand and kissed it, then said quietly, "Good night, Miss Rose, Miss Alice. I think I would like to walk home." Then he stepped out of the carriage.

Alice and Rose watched him with puzzled frowns on their faces. Alice turned to Rose and asked, "What is wrong with Peregrine?"

Rose continued to stare after him. "I don't know," she told Alice honestly.

Marcus and Rose began meeting each other very casually in the park in the afternoons. Rose found that after her round of charitable and society duties, she would walk home and spy his broad shoulders in the distance. She chose a side street that was filled with leafy trees and suddenly Marcus would be beside her. They spent time talking and laughing. Not every day did Marcus find the opportunity to stretch his legs. His business ventures grew and he was needed often. Rose, too, found that on days when she made calls with Amelia that it was impossible to walk home. Amelia would insist that she drop her off at home in the carriage. On these days, Rose returned to her little home and lonely fireplace. After an early dinner with Torie, Rose sat and stared into the fire, her mending forgotten on her lap. Rose remembered meeting Marcus at the cove on Eaton Pond, listening to him read poetry or the essays of Emerson. He even read from Walden Pond. "Simplify, simplify..."

Rose would look around her pretty little room and long for it all to be gone. To be a simple wife, with a man to love her. A man to share meals, to create a home, to share laughter and quiet evenings by the fire.

The fall day dawned bright and clear. There was a definite tinge of coolness to the air, although the sun shone brightly. In the park, the leaves turned red and gold and began to drift to the ground.

Shortly after lunch, Rose prepared to meet Marcus in the park. She wore a new hat and her moss green jacket brought out the red in her hair. Coming down the stairs, she pulled on her gloves and gave instructions to Hobbs when there was a knock at the door. Hobbs opened it and on Rose's doorstep stood her mother-in-law and Matilda.

"Amelia, Matilda," she said in surprise. "Come in."

Amelia took in Rose's outdoor clothing and asked, "Were you going out?"

"Just for a walk in the park. It is such a beautiful day," Rose told them. She gestured to Hobbs, "Please take Mrs. Brewster and Mrs. Bingham's coats. Show them into the drawing room. I shan't be five minutes."

Rose hurried upstairs and took off her hat and coat. She went to the window and looked across the street at the park. The trees were changing color, but too many leaves remained on the trees and she could not see if Marcus waited for her in the park.

Resigned to staying in, Rose sighed with resignation, descended the stairs and walked into the drawing room to join her in laws. Hobbs brought the tea and Rose busied herself handing around tea and small sandwiches and joined in the idle chatter with Amelia and Matilda.

Once Hobbs left the room, Matilda stood and crossed the room to shut the door firmly. Alarmed, Rose looked from Amelia to Matilda. "What is it?" Rose asked. "This seems serious."

Amelia sipped from her tea cup and looked at her daughter-in-law with steely determination. "It seems," she began, "that you have become an object of gossip."

Rose looked at her mother-in-law and then at Matilda. Matilda had been playing tattle tale. Rose gazed at Amelia directly and said, trying to keep her color from rising, "What gossip?"

"About you and Mr. Underhill," Amelia said in icy tones. "It seems that the gossip last summer at Eastwood was true about you and Marcus Underhill. Rose Brewster," Amelia asked in an accusing tone, "what have you been doing?"

Rose looked at her mother-in-law in shock and could feel the color drain from her face. "What have I been doing?" she asked, her mouth dry. "You spent the summer with me, Amelia. What could I possibly have been doing?"

"Rose," Amelia said, not unkindly, "you have been a widow for a very long time, and it would be understandable for you to be lonely and long for a husband. You and I discussed that at Eastwood, but my dear, not Marcus Underhill. And not carrying on in a way that causes gossip."

Before Rose could say anything, Matilda chimed in, "Rose Brewster, you need to be reminded of your station. Of your position in Boston. Brewsters do not chase after men or new money."

Rose turned to Matilda, her face flaming, but she managed to say evenly, "Matilda, I am very aware of the Brewsters' position in this town. Furthermore," she choked out, "I am not chasing after any one."

Amelia shushed her daughter and turned to Rose, "Now Rose, Matilda means well. She is only thinking of your children and how any scandal could hurt their chances for good marriages."

"I would never allow scandal to hurt my children," Rose struggled to keep her tone even. "I have done nothing wrong," she enunciated each word clearly.

The argument could have continued if at that moment Hobbs had not knocked softly at the door. At Rose's call for entrance, Hobbs opened the door and said formally, "Mr. Underhill, madam."

Matilda glared accusingly at Rose as Marcus walked into the room. Marcus took in Rose's guilty look and Amelia and Matilda's accusing stares. "Ladies," he cordially said, bowing to the group, "I was in the neighborhood and thought I would take the opportunity to stop and thank Mrs. Brewster for her hospitality towards Collin last summer. I expect I should be thanking all of you."

Matilda continued to glare accusingly from Rose to Marcus, but Amelia drew herself up to her full tiny height and commanded coldly, "Please sit down, Mr. Underhill."

Marcus, his eyebrows raised, sat in a chair as Amelia poured him a cup of tea. Passing it to him, she said quietly, "Mr. Underhill, I know that you are new to Boston and to Boston society." She nodded her head as if to excuse him for his ignorance. "It has come to my knowledge that you are paying marked attention to my daughter-in-law."

Rose opened her mouth, but at a look from her mother-in-law, settled back in her chair.

Amelia went on, "As a widow and a kindhearted individual, I can understand my daughter in law's attitude toward you. But, Mr. Underhill, I will not allow gossip to be attached to the Brewster name."

Marcus looked at Amelia's cold haughty eyes and slowly said, "Mrs. Brewster, I understand what you are implying, but I promise you that I hold Mrs. Rose in nothing but the highest regard. I enjoyed discussing literature with her last summer and we loaned books to each other from time to time. Miss Lavinia and Miss Susanna were kind to Collin and included him in many of their activities, for which I was grateful."

Marcus, took a sip of tea and said, "Since coming back to Boston, I assure you that I have not marked Mrs. Brewster out for attention. Truly, with the exception of a few parties, I have not had any conversation with her. Harmful gossip is quite often brought about by unhappy people. I strongly urge you to look from whom the gossip is spread and that is where you might start your accusations."

As a reprimand, it was gentle, but Amelia's eyes became colder. "Mr. Underhill, I will thank you to not chastise me," she spoke crisply. "Whatever your attentions are towards my daughter-in-law, it has become a matter of idle gossip in this town. I will not be embarrassed by the two of you. Mr. Underhill, I am going to ask, no insist, that you not be seen with Rose. That you cease visiting her at her house."

"Amelia," Rose gasped, "this is the first time Mr. Underhill has been to my home."

Matilda's look said it all. Before anyone could say anything, Marcus stood and crossed to Rose. He took her hand and said gently, "Mrs. Brewster, I apologize if my presence has caused any harm to come to you or your children. I won't be calling on you again." Bowing to Amelia and Matilda, Marcus strode from the room. Rose, unsure what his words meant, stared after his broad back. A stricken look crossed her face.

A moment of silence followed his departure and then Matilda began, "Rose Brewster, how dare you bring shame on this family!"

Amelia snapped, "Hush Matilda." Amelia turned to Rose, and said severely, "This is exactly what I am speaking about. Peregrine visited you for years and I allowed it because I know he was William's friend. But to open your doors to a single man, an outsider. Rose Brewster, what could you be thinking? Do you have no care for your children?"

Amelia would have continued on, but Rose stood and turned to her in-laws. "I am a grown woman," she said with some vehemence. "I have allowed you to dictate my life for some years now, Amelia. I would think that you would know that I would never do anything to damage my children's reputation. I always put my children first." With those choked words, Rose rushed from the room and her footsteps could be heard hurrying up the stairs. A moment later, her bedroom door shut firmly, but not slammed.

Amelia and Matilda exchanged glances and departed.

In her room, Rose was shaken by Amelia's words. Had she and Marcus become the object of speculation and gossip? Even while Marcus danced attendance on Annabelle Morris, did Boston still watch avidly every time he stood up with Rose? What had Sam Gardner said? Rose had no doubt that Sam gossiped in smoke-filled rooms to other husbands, and those same husbands went home and whispered stories to their wives at night. Rose burned with the thought of the conjecture and lies that Sam spread.

Rose became extremely watchful of eyes on her when she walked into parties or meetings. Any words said to her she evaluated for hidden meanings. The Brewsters closed ranks and someone, quite often Alice or Amelia, stood by Rose's side.

Amelia did not bring the matter up again, but Rose felt constant scrutiny under her mother-in-law's protective but censuring eye. She longed to meet Marcus in the park, but was frightened of whose eyes were watching.

Rose buried herself in her volunteer activities and Torie. Torie excelled in her new school and seemed to be the model of deportment. Rose received no written messages from teachers complaining about her behavior. Torie rapidly made friends and Rose quite often found the nursery full of young girls she did not recognize. They all dressed neatly, but the quality of their clothes were not as fine. They were polite little girls who enjoyed Torie's ideas for games and filled the house with laughter and chat.

Rose, afraid that total avoidance of Marcus would bring even more gossip, would coolly nod to Marcus at parties. He never asked her to dance and she avoided watching him dance with other women. Marcus for his part, did his duty faithfully at every party. He continued to escort the dashing Annabelle to many parties, and he spent most of his evenings dancing with dowagers and matrons. Marcus could also be found in studies sharing cigars and talking man talk, but he avoided the billiard and card rooms where Sam Gardner tended to be.

Rose walked home one beautiful late October afternoon when in the distance, she spied Marcus. They locked eyes and he immediately turned and walked down a quiet side street. Rose, nonchalantly looking around to see if anyone else in the park watched, turned and slowly ambled down the quiet street. Half way down, a hand came out of a darkened doorway and Marcus pulled her into the shadows.

Rose, after an initial gasp, threw herself into his arms and kissed him fiercely. As they drew apart, tears streamed down her face as she struggled to control her breathing. Marcus whispered, "Oh, Rose, I have missed you so much."

"Marcus," Rose said, "I have missed you. All of Boston is watching us. It must be Sam Gardner."

Marcus, who knew more about what was being said than Rose, promised, "It is just gossip, Rose. It will die down."

"You don't know Boston," Rose said bitterly. "Even today, we could be followed. We shouldn't be doing this."

"Rose, I have missed you," Marcus said, his lips against hers. "Come away with me."

"Come away?" Rose protested with a laugh. "I can't run away with you."

Marcus kissed her fingers and looked into her shocked eyes, his own warm, brown and reassuring. "Not forever," he said, "just for a week. Can't you make an excuse and leave the gossip behind and take a small break? We could go away, just the two of us. No one needs to know."

Rose thought about this. To step away from speculative glances, whispers behind fans and the feeling that people constantly stared. Rose looked up at Marcus, her hands clenching his sleeve. To spend a week alone with this man. Suddenly, Rose remembered with clarity the night at Eastwood. The hot stifled room, two bodies coming together with passion.

Rose was silent for so long that Marcus started to say, "Never mind, it was just an idea."

She interrupted him, "I could decide to visit my cousin Dorothy." Rose said slowly, "She lives in New London and is elderly. I don't visit her very often, but I could say I received a note that she is poorly."

Rose thought more about this, shook her head and said, "No, not New London. Marcus, my mother was born in New London. I know too many people there. We couldn't meet in New London. Where could we go where no one would see us?"

"Summerfield," Marcus said decisively.

Rose looked at him in astonishment. "Summerfield?" she echoed, "But Marcus, that is Eaton's Grove and everyone in the town knows the Brewsters."

Marcus began to think clearly. "Listen, Rose," he told her, "you could take the train south as if you were going to New London. At Greenfield Crossing, you could change trains and go north to Jefferson's Hollow. I would have someone meet you there and take you to Summerfield."

"Your house staff at Summerfield must know me or be related to Eastwood staff," Rose protested.

"No," Marcus argued. "At the end of the summer I closed up Summerfield. There will be no one there, and as long as we don't venture into the town, we won't risk seeing anyone."

All of a sudden, it sounded wonderful. Rose looked up at Marcus and knew that nothing would give her greater pleasure than to spend a week in this man's arms. And to leave the constant censure and speculation behind!

Arrangements turned out to be relatively simple. Amelia, who knew Rose was under stress from the gossip, accepted Rose's explanation without comment. Amelia, involved in planning Susanna's wedding, frankly felt having Rose out of town for a couple of weeks would help calm talk and speculation. Certainly, it was understood that Marcus Underhill left town the Thursday before on business in Maryland. Having both of them out of town would cause gossip to hopefully stop. The strained look that Rose wore on her face when she told her mother-in-law her plans caused Amelia to speak sympathetically as she kissed Rose on the cheek and told her by all means she should visit her cousin Dorothy and not hurry her return. If Phoebe could not take care of Torie, Torie was always welcome to come stay at her grandparents. Rose, cold with nerves and from telling lies, choked out that she thought Torie would be fine under Phoebe's supervision.

Rose took Phoebe into her confidence. Someone needed to know where she was in case of emergency, and Phoebe would never tell. Long true friends, Phoebe energetically began to help Rose pack and gave her encouragement.

As Rose packed, she opened her bureau drawer to pull out crisp white linen nightgowns. Pretty and lacy, the nightgowns buttoned up to the top of the neck and the sleeves were tight at the wrist. Rose looked down in the drawer and something blue and filmy caught her eye. Wrapped in tissue and buried at the bottom of her nightgown drawer, lay the negligee Rose wore on her wedding night with William. Rose tried to remember back to her wedding night. Her friends and attendants helped dress her in the filmy blue gown; it was low necked with tiny puffed sleeves. A darker satin ribbon held the gown closed under her breasts and the lightness of the fabric had left nothing to the imagination. It was a gown designed to entice a man.

Rose, 17 years old, had been helped into her negligee by her attendants. Her hair had been brushed before she was escorted to the big wide bed. Rose sat with her hair hanging in curls to her waist. The blankets had been folded back so Rose lay there feeling very exposed and nervous, waiting for her groom. After some time, William emerged from his dressing room, a robe belted tightly around his waist. Rose remembered William's set face as he silently gazed down at her for a few minutes. No words, no smiles. William with a resigned sigh blew out the lamp and climbed into bed with her.

Rose vaguely remembered the embarrassment, the pain. Long after William ceased, the two of them laid there in the darkness, both awake but no words spoken.

Rose realized that she clenched the tissue paper around her wedding negligee. Angrily, she smoothed the paper and shoved it back to the bottom and firmly closed the drawer.

CHAPTER 14

Rose stepped down onto the unfamiliar station at Jefferson's Hollow. A small pretty figure, Rose stood on the platform on a dreary wet early November day, anxiously looking for Marcus. It had been a long day of traveling south and then north; she had been on the train for hours. Rose realized the station master was frowning at her, so she picked up her valise, moved through the station and out on the boardwalk of the small hamlet. As she emerged, a strange man approached her. "Mrs. Brewster?" he asked very quietly.

Slightly alarmed, Rose looked at him suspiciously, but nodded her head.

"Your party is waiting around the corner for you; he apologizes for the delay." The man spoke with a Western twang as he held out his hand for her luggage tag. "If you walk around the corner, he will be waiting for you. I will collect your trunk."

The man escorted her as far as the corner and nodded towards a small carriage with covered windows. Rose looked back to see him head into the station. Rose glanced around to see if anyone watched as she approached the wagon. Suddenly, the door swung open and Marcus peeked out without departing from the interior. At the sight of his dear face, Rose put her foot on the step, reaching up to grasp his warm hand, and was pulled into the carriage. Marcus enveloped Rose in a warm welcoming kiss and embrace. Suddenly shy, Rose pulled herself from his embrace and in some confusion, dropped her eyes.

Marcus, looking at the top of her hat with a profusion of flowers, feather and netting, said with a smile, "My darling girl, you wear the most enchanting little hat, but I think the face beneath it is much prettier."

Rose glanced up and smiled nervously, but continued her silence. Marcus, realizing what might be amiss, leaned back in his seat, although he captured her gloved hand and kissed the fingers. His man returned with Rose's trunk, strapping it on securely, then clamboured on top and a short time later the carriage moved off.

After a drive through the wooded countryside, the carriage passed through Eaton's Grove and the bridge of Eaton Pond. Rose knew every bit of the road between Eaton's Grove and Eastwood and as the carriage rattled over the bridge, she reached out and lifted the curtain aside to look at the pond and countryside. The pond, on this cool November afternoon, was slate grey and empty. The fields looked barren and brown; the trees, with glorious orange and red leaves still abundant, dripped in the cold rain. As they passed the driveway to Eastwood, Rose sat forward and looked out curiously. The house appeared shuttered and cold. No lights shown in any windows, although smoke curled from one chimney toward the back of the house. The landing was bereft of boats which had been stored in the barn for the winter; the lawn was unadorned of chairs, tables or tennis nets. A large dose of guilt and nerves swamped Rose and she dropped the curtain and slumped back in her seat, staring forward. Marcus, sensing her trepidation, began to talk gently of fall in the Pacific Northwest.

As the wheels crunched on the gravel and drew to a halt, Rose cast a darting glance at Marcus and then down at her hands. Her face appeared very white and her hands felt cold. Marcus reached past her and opened the carriage door. He stepped down and turned to help her alight. Rose looked at his outstretched hand and then up at his face. Marcus' eyes were warm and his smile was reassuring. Rose managed a weak smile, took his hand with shaking fingers, and stepped down from the carriage. Rose looked at the small stone cottage that stood in front of them and then back at Marcus with a questioning look.

Marcus explained, "This is the caretaker's cottage behind Summerfield. I felt it would be more private."

Rose looked from the cottage to the view through the trees of the larger building of Summerfield. She took in the shrubs and trees that crowded close to the small front porch. She nodded in understanding, but continued to be silent. The man who met her at the station carried her trunk to the porch and set it down. He spoke to Marcus, then climbed up onto the front of the carriage, and drove away. Rose watched him leave and turned to Marcus, suddenly very frightened.

Marcus looked at Rose's set face and said in an uncertain voice, "Shall we go in?" Marcus went up the two steps onto the small stone porch. He unlocked the door and lifted her small trunk.

He pushed the door open and gestured to Rose. She stood hesitantly and then followed Marcus into the house.

The door opened onto a small hall that ran the length of the cottage. To the right was a small living room floored in oak with a large stone fireplace flanked by windows framed with chintz curtains. The simple wooden furniture was set off with deep cushions of green and blue plaid. Shelves lined one wall with a few books standing on the empty shelves. A painting, which upon closer inspection turned out to be an older watercolor of Summerfield, hung on the opposite wall. Across the hall from the living room was a small dining room furnished with a dark walnut round table, chairs and a side board. Rose followed Marcus down the hall and saw that two more rooms opened off of the hall. Behind the dining room was a simple kitchen where a small stove simmered warmly. Marcus carried Rose's trunk into the last room on the right, a bedroom. Rose stood in the hall staring in the bedroom. A bureau stood on one wall; a tall wardrobe and a small washstand with pitcher and bowl stood in the corner. Most of the space held a wide bed, covered in a red and white checked counterpane. White pillows were piled at the head of the bed, and a window was covered in white lace curtains.

Rose took one look at the bed and turned and fled down the hall to the living room. Marcus set the trunk down and listened in the silence to her hurried footsteps. Marcus went into the kitchen, boiled a kettle of water and made a pot of tea. He placed the tea and a plate of scones on a tray and carried them into the living room. He found Rose slumped in a chair staring at the fire. Marcus spent a few minutes arranging the tea things on a small table and brought Rose a cup of tea. Rose's nervous hands grasped the cup, shaking so fiercely that she hastily set it down.

"Rose," Marcus said softly. She glanced at him confusedly and then looked down at her hands. "Rose," he said again in a reassuring tone, "it is going to be all right."

Rose looked at him and then at the fire. In a strangled voice she said, "This was a mistake."

"Mistake?" Marcus asked.

Before he could say anything else, Rose looked at him with tears in her eyes. Shaking her head she said, "Coming here was a mistake. Lying to my family, all of this," she gestured at the room. "We have made a mistake."

Marcus knelt down by Rose's feet, taking her cold hands in his warm ones and gently rubbing them, before dropping a small kiss. "Rose," he said gently, "I want you to know I am not going to ask you to do anything that you aren't ready for. Remember we talked about this in Boston. We need to get to know each other without anyone watching. We need to spend time together without worrying about censure or spies."

Rose looked at Marcus, then down at his hands holding hers. She gently squeezed his hands and whispered, "Thank you. Thank you for understanding."

Marcus looked out the window and saw that the rain had stopped and a wan sun shone through the window. Marcus said to Rose, "Let's go for a walk."

Rose stood and, as she had not even removed her jacket, followed Marcus with relief from the house. Outside, the air felt cool and smelled musky, of wet leaves and bushes, of greenery dying in the cool autumn air. As Marcus and Rose walked down the driveway to the big house of Summerfield, they heard the constant dripping of leaves. Marcus reached out and took Rose's hand in a firm grip. She smiled shyly at him, and hand in hand they walked around the big white house to the front door. Compared to Eastwood, Summerfield was much smaller, more of an oversized farmhouse. Summerfield did not present the grand edifice that Eastwood did, but the wide porch, smothered in dying vines was welcoming in the summer. Rose stood on the porch while Marcus unlocked the front door. She turned and looked down the sloping lawn to Eaton's Pond. Summerfield was perched on a small hill at the top of Eaton's Pond. From the house, the pond, with all of its grand residences and fields, spread out majestically. The white bridge shown in the distance with Eaton's Grove shrunk by distance into tiny tidiness, the church's gleaming white steeple piercing the sky. From the porch, Rose glimpsed the bandstand and beyond that the shadowy park.

As Marcus wrestled the door open, she turned as he opened it with a flourish. Formally, he said, "Mrs. Brewster, welcome to Summerfield."

For the first time a small smile crossed Rose's set face and she entered Marcus' summer home. Inside, all had been settled for the winter. Rose looked in the drawing room where furniture was hidden by dust covers and in the dining room beyond. A crystal chandelier also swathed in a sheet tinkled gently in a stray breeze. As they moved from room to room exploring, Marcus explained, "I did not want to have to undo my housekeeper's hard work of closing the house for the winter, so I thought we would be comfortable in the caretaker's cottage. As I don't have a caretaker at the moment, I had it cleaned and made ready for you."

Rose smiled at his thoughtfulness and assured him, "Marcus, I am fine in the smaller cottage. It is very cozy, but this house is marvelous. It feels very much like a home. It was so sad to see Summerfield stand empty for so many years, but you have restored it beautifully. It still has the feel of an older home, but beautifully updated."

The house felt chilly and Rose shivered. They ventured outside and continued their exploration of the woods. Rose found she could talk with Marcus about inconsequential things, and she began to relax a little. Marcus made a witty remark and Rose laughed. Marcus turned to her and seeing the sparkle in Rose's green eyes leaned down and kissed her swiftly. He raised his head and Rose looked up at him and reaching up she pulled his head down for a longer kiss. The weeks of stress and being apart broke and Rose leaned into Marcus and her lips trembled as she wrapped her arms around him and felt him pull her tightly against him.

The kiss broken, Marcus continued to hold her and look down at her. "I love you," he said simply.

Rose smiled back at him and said, "And I love you, Marcus Underhill. For this one week, for the first time in my life, I am not going to worry about what is correct, or what someone might say or if I am causing problems for anyone else. You are the only one I am going to think about. I. Love. You." The last three words were accentuated with a kiss for each word.

Marcus bundled her closely and the kiss would have continued, except the rain returned with a vengeance. Rose, with rain drops on her face, looked up into Marcus' face and laughed, before they turned and dashed down the path to the cottage.

Both were soaked by the time they returned to the cottage and Marcus escorted Rose to the bedroom door and left her. Rose moved to the wash stand and retrieved a towel. She began to dry off her face and hair when she turned and faced the wide double bed and was filled with doubts once again. Memories of sleeping with William filled her mind: the uncomfortableness, the awkwardness, the used feelings of her body after he would leave her. Against this memory was the indescribable night of passion with Marcus on that hot summer night. "Get a hold of yourself," Rose sternly admonished herself. "This is Marcus, not William, you will be sleeping with tonight. Marcus loves you." This thought brought Rose up sharply. Had William loved her? Trying to remember, Rose could not recall a time her husband had used those words with her. Rose turned her back to the bed and changed her clothes and shoes.

Once tidy, Rose returned to the living room and Marcus excused himself to change into dry clothes. Once he finished, he did not return to her but went into the small kitchen. Rose followed him into the room as he pulled a raw chicken out of the larder and began peeling potatoes. Marcus looked at Rose with a grin, "I am going to be your chef tonight, my lady."

Rose's eyebrows went up in surprise. "You can cook?" she asked in astonishment.

Marcus laughed at her expression. "Living in the woods when you fell trees, causes you to either learn to cook or to starve. I am not a fancy cook, but I don't think we will starve."

Rose admitted, "I have never even tried to cook." It was Marcus' turn to look surprised. Rose shrugged. "I mean, I can make tea, but," she thought about this and finished, "that is just about it." Suddenly, Rose felt horribly inadequate.

"Hmmm," Marcus smiled at her embarrassed expression, "how about setting the table then? You will find plates in that cupboard and silverware and napkins in the sideboard in the dining room."

Glad to be of some assistance, Rose went to explore the dining room sideboard. She found a blue checked table cloth and spread it over the rough table and set out plates and silverware. Inside the cupboard, she found a small red glass vase and Rose slipped outside where she had seen late yellow Chrysanthemums growing on the side of the house. She filled the red vase with the bright yellow heads and set the arrangement in the middle of the table. By now, the house smelled heavenly of frying chicken and baking biscuits. Rose went into the living room and closed the curtains against the dying day. She turned and surveyed the room. Small and spare, the room felt very cozy with the warm fire and the drawn curtains.

"Dinner is served," Marcus said behind her.

Rose turned and smiled. Over a dinner of fried chicken, flaky rolls, mashed potatoes and brussel sprouts, Rose's nervousness returned once again and she toyed with her food, and was unable to eat very much. Marcus filled in the silence with idle chat about his youth in San Francisco. How the mouth to the harbor had not been discovered for many years because of the fogginess of the area.

After dinner, Rose helped Marcus clean the kitchen, another first for her. Rose found it rather enchanting to fill the small tub with soapy warm water and wash, while Marcus rinsed and dried. There was a very domestic feel as they moved around the kitchen bumping gently into each other from time to time, and Rose began to relax in this domestic chore.

Afterwards, they retired to the living room and Marcus read the poem "Evangeline" to her while Rose sat and did needlework. The poem finished, Marcus stood and pulled Rose to her feet. "Would you like to get ready for bed while I close up the house?" Marcus asked her gently.

Rose nodded, her stomach fluttering, as she retired to the bedroom. Once there, she lit the lamp with shaking fingers and tried to breathe. To calm her nerves, she began her nightly routine of getting ready for bed. Rose undressed and shivered in the unheated bedroom. She buttoned her nightdress to the top of her throat and pulled a woolen wrapper around her, tightening the sash firmly. She pulled the pins from her hair and began to brush her thick curls, thinking about the day she had spent with Marcus and trying not to think about the night she would spend with him.

A quiet knock on the door caused Rose to drop her brush and as the door swung open, Marcus stood there looking at her as she stooped over to retrieve her brush. Rose straightened, her face ashen, her eyes bright with emotion. Marcus took in the frightened look, but also her beautiful hair flowing and tumbling down her back in curls, the red highlights glinting in the lamplight. Rose stood small and straight, clasping the brush to her breast. She opened her mouth to say something, but words escaped her.

Marcus closed the door quietly and walked slowly across the room, took the brush from her nerveless fingers. Setting the brush down, he cupped her small face in his large warm hands and slowly lowered his mouth. "You are so very beautiful," he whispered against her lips. Rose's lips trembled as she returned the kiss. Marcus enveloped her in his strong arms and as the kiss deepened, his hand reached up and cupped her breast through her nightgown. Rose's breath caught in her throat and she opened her eyes to look wide eyed at Marcus. He smiled reassuringly at her and continued to kiss her deeply, his warm hand gently fondling her breast.

On her own volition, Rose reached up and undid the top buttons on Marcus' shirt. She pulled his shirt open and slipped her hands inside against his smooth warm skin. Gently she explored his well muscled chest; her thumbs curiously felt his hard little nipples. They stopped kissing and stared at each other for a long moment. Rose leaned forward and kissed Marcus' chest with her warm open mouth. With a growl, Marcus opened the sash on her robe and she shrugged and the robe fell to her feet. Marcus stooped and lifted Rose into his strong arms. With two strides he crossed the room and pulled the quilt back, kissing Rose deeply as he laid her down on the crisp white sheets without breaking their embrace.

Rose felt her bones turn to water under the onslaught of searing kisses that Marcus covered her face and neck. At some point he undid the buttons on her nightgown and impatiently pulled it over her head. Marcus stood up and began toeing off his slippers as Rose sat up and leaned on one elbow to watch as Marcus tore off his clothes, dumping them in a careless heap on the floor. Her breath caught in her throat at her first glimpse of his naked body in the golden lamplight. Marcus stood before Rose, his broad shoulders tapered from a smooth well-muscled chest to a flat tummy and small hips. Rose ran her eyes over his body and skipped a glance over the most private part of him. She closed her eyes, her breath caught in her throat, afraid to look.

Rose collapsed back into the pillows, her breathing ragged, her eyes half open as Marcus joined her on the bed. Marcus looked at her full ripe breasts, partially hidden by a thick curtain of curly hair that fell over her shoulder. Her tiny waist flared out to rounded hips and slender legs. Marcus snuggled his bare, smooth body to Rose's warm curves and consumed Rose with a deep hot kiss. His mouth trailed over her jaw line and neck as he began to lathe and nibble on her breasts. Rose could not breathe. She felt fluttering in her tummy and a curious ache in the apex between her thighs. Rose's heart thudded deeply in her chest as she began to feel intense warmth emanating from deep inside of her. She burrowed back into the downy pillows, attempting to take in so many new and unexpected feelings. Her slender arms clasped Marcus and as he lowered his mouth to her breast, she ran her fingers through his hair and over his broad muscled back. Marcus' mouth breathed hot breath across her creamy skin and Rose felt her nipples puckering into sharp points. He continued to bathe her breasts with his tongue. Rose lay helpless with emotions and a deep ache that needed to be salved. A low moan escaped from her lips as she shifted her body and opened her thighs. Marcus settled his weight between her thighs and drove home with a sharp urgent push. Rose gasped at the heated weight that entered her and her eyes flew open. Marcus paused and looked at her for assurance and she panted as she nodded her head in encouragement.

Marcus continued to kiss Rose passionately and heavily as their bodies found a matching rhythm. Their two bodies entwined closely as the combined heat built to an unendurable point. Rose was vaguely aware that her hoarse cries mingled with Marcus' ragged breathing, their hearts beat as one as they thrust heavier and deeper. Rose's small scream as they exploded together was smothered by Marcus' mouth as they once again kissed. The explosion went on and on into a rainbow haze.

Quietly, in the aftermath, they lay together, holding onto each other tightly. Rose, her head buried into Marcus' neck, felt tears on her cheeks and could not stifle a small sob. Marcus adjusted his weight, and without withdrawing from her, looked at her in question. At her tears, he made to move but she gripped him tightly, holding him to her. "Are you in pain?" he asked anxiously.

Rose shook her head and a half laugh, half sob escaped her. She looked up at him, her eyes swimming with tears. "I have never been so happy in my life," she told him, her voice choked.

Marcus kissed her tears, and rolled to his side, taking her with him. They adjusted their heads on the pillow and pulled the quilt up against the coolness of the room. "That was pretty special," Marcus told Rose with a small smile.

Rose looked up at him innocently. "I don't know much about these matters," she admitted. She went on, gesturing, unsure of how to describe everything. "Does that always happen?"

Marcus laughed and pulled her head to his chest and kissed the top of her silky head. "My darling girl," he told her, "no, not always. I think when you have as much passion as you have hidden under that prim exterior of yours, it could happen often."

Rose joined him in his laughter a little uncertainly, and nestled into him. "I had no idea," she admitted. With Marcus's well muscular body solidly against hers, she felt a small flutter of excitement begin to grow again. She looked up at him and reaching up kissed him deeply. "Can we do it again?" she asked as she thrust against his hip.

Marcus looked at her in surprise and laughed. "Oh my God," he swore, "you are going to wear me out. I do need a little time to gather my strength."

Rose smiled mischievously and shyly reached out and curiously circled his nipple with her tongue. Marcus' breath caught in his throat at the feeling of her small mouth sucking on his nipple. With a growl, Marcus rolled Rose onto her back and began to kiss her. "You are insatiable," he murmured against her neck.

Rose laughed in return, but their smiles faded as they stared deeply into each other's eyes. As Marcus bent his head slowly to once again kiss her, Rose's tummy let out a small gurgle. Marcus raised his head and looked at her. A small grin crossed his face as Rose covered the offending stomach with her hand. "A small symphony?" Marcus asked planting a kiss on her tummy.

"Beast," Rose answered with a smile. "I was so nervous I could not eat much dinner."

"Hungry?" Marcus asked.

Rose nodded her head and admitted, "Starving, but I can wait for breakfast."

"Unnecessary," Marcus told Rose and rolled out of bed. Rose frowned at Marcus as he tucked the blankets around her and gave her a quick kiss. "I will be right back," he told her as he scuttled naked out of the room.

Rose, the sheets tucked under her arms, with her head nestled on fluffy pillows, lay listening to vague noises coming from the kitchen. She never knew anyone to walk around naked before and it embarrassed her. She decided that it might be something she might have to get used to.

Marcus returned with a small platter of cold chicken left over from dinner. He paused briefly looking at the charming picture Rose made, propped up on pillows, with the quilt tucked primly over her naked breasts and her shining hair a tangle of curls and swirls. Marcus set the platter down on the bedside table and ordered Rose, "Scoot over, it is freezing out there." His cold naked body slid under the covers and sidled up next to her. Rose shrank briefly from his coldness and then cuddled next to him as he offered her the platter.

Rose raised her eyebrows delicately as he obviously expected her to eat with her fingers. Rose took a drumstick and began to nibble, but looked askance at Marcus as he gave her a small kiss and helped himself to a piece of chicken.

Rose gave a small smile and realizing how hungry she truly was, began to relish her food. They munched in companionable silence. Rose was quiet while they ate, a little overwhelmed by their recent lovemaking and Marcus' naked body against the length of her own equally naked body.

Finished, Rose leaned over Marcus to place the chicken bone on the platter, her heavy breast brushing against his bare arm. At the unexpected spark, they both paused. Marcus looked at Rose, her mouth slightly open, shiny with grease from the chicken and he could not resist kissing her deeply, licking the grease from her lips. Rose returned the kiss, resting her wrists on his shoulders, her greasy fingers splayed.

Marcus raised his head and looked down at her, the light of passion once again ignited. Marcus took Rose's greasy fingers, kissed, suckled and licked them clean. Rose, her breath caught in her throat, could not believe the amazingly sensual feeling this caused. Marcus, no longer hungry, cast aside his own piece of chicken and reached for Rose. Rose, with a daring, but shy look in her eyes, took Marcus' own hand in both of her hands, looked down at his greasy fingers, then back at Marcus. Rose's green eyes intently stared into Marcus' brown eyes and she pulled his index finger into her mouth. Her tongue circled his finger and she closed her pink lips and sucked on his finger, her eyes never leaving his. She continued to do the same to each of his greasy fingers, around and around went her tongue, while her mouth created a deep moist suction.

Marcus, his mouth dry, asked in a strained tone, "Where did you learn to do that?"

Rose looked at him with a small wanton smile. "I'm a quick learner," she told him. "Isn't this what you just did to me?" She returned his fingers to her pink pouting mouth and sucked as she stared invitingly at Marcus.

Marcus again attempted to swallow and pushed her back against the pillows, pulling the sheet away from her body. "You know," he breathed as he lowered himself to her mouth, "there are other things that can be sucked on."

Rose moaned as he began to nibble on her neck and breasts. When his mouth descended to her smooth flat stomach, she gasped over the hot and cold sensations that raced up and down her spine. Marcus' fingers reached down and fluffed her curls, then began to stroke Rose's womanliness. As he pushed his finger deep into her she cried out in shock as a sudden shudder shook her pelvis. Rose felt overwhelmed with the sensations his fingers caused inside her body, her head tossing back and forth on the pillow. She reached down and grasped Marcus' free hand and began to suck and lick on his finger in rhythm with his strokes on her body. Marcus, shocked at her passion, could feel himself harden and close to explosion. He pulled his fingers from her body, and grabbed her hips to position her. Rose, her thighs already wide, pulled on his shoulders as he pushed deep within her with his manhood and they were once again, caught up in a world of hot, searing heights, the center of each other's world.

They fell asleep in each other's arms, for the moment sated and satisfied. Sometime during the night, Marcus awoke to feel Rose's silken thighs nestled close to his hip and his tumescence grew. Turning, Marcus found Rose's eyes glittering in the moonlight shining through the lace curtained window. As he shifted, he reached for her and once more they were lost in each other's passion.

Afterwards, as they lay cuddling, Marcus asked softly, "Have you slept at all?"

Rose whispered, as she held Marcus close, "A little." She sighed and admitted, "I have never felt so happy in my life and I don't want to miss a minute of it."

Marcus ran his fingers through her hair. "I promise you I won't let you miss a minute of anything," he said with a smile. "But, you need to get some rest."

"I'm just afraid," Rose said, as she clutched him, "that I will awake and it will all have been a dream."

"It is a dream," Marcus assured her, "but a waking dream. One that will never go away. Go to sleep and I will be here when you awake." As Marcus drifted off, he whispered, "I love you."

Rose, encircled in Marcus' strong arms, his heart beating strongly under her ear, sighed and drifted off to a replete sleep.

Morning came and Rose woke to find herself alone in her bed. She stretched and realized she felt incredibly happy and satisfied. She looked quickly and saw the indentation of where Marcus' head had lain upon the pillow and she also became aware of the smell of crisp bacon and strong coffee.

Rose pushed back the covers and shivering, found her crumpled dressing gown on the floor, where they had left it the night before. She crossed to the window and saw sodden grey skies and dripping leaves. She could hear the pounding of raindrops on the roof and turned her head from such an ugly view and began to dress.

Marcus and Rose spent the day talking and reading to each other. The weather never lightened, so they stayed inside. An afternoon nap turned into an afternoon romp, and Rose was introduced to the delights of passion under the light of day, although a rather dreary light.

Over a dinner of roast beef, they talked of inconsequential things and Rose admitted to Marcus that she had never felt so indolent.

"At home in Boston," she explained, "there are always committees to advise, or fundraisers to organize, visitors to host or call on and a household to run. Even on those evenings when I stay home, I have a mending basket always waiting for me."

Marcus said to Rose, a trifle wistfully, "I have often longed for a woman to do my mending for me. Mrs. Cartwright, my housekeeper, takes care of those things, but she always looks so sad that I don't take better care of my socks, that I feel bad about asking her to do my darning. It is one of the things I did not learn living in the woods."

"But your socks must have developed holes," Rose said with a frown.

"Ah, but socks you wear in the woods are heavy and woolen; they stand up to a lot of abuse." Marcus explained, "These fine silk socks that we wear in the city, give up after one night of dancing."

"You shouldn't do so much dancing," Rose said unsympathetically, but with a smile. "I would be happy to darn your socks for you," she promised him.

That evening, they sat by the fire, a bundle of Marcus' socks in Rose's lap. Marcus sat in the chair across from the fire and read to her. Rose, as she turned a sock inside out for darning, sighed with pure bliss. She felt contented and very domestic, from time to time raising her eyes from her needle to gaze adoringly at Marcus. The thought of what Amelia Brewster would say if she knew what was going on passed through her mind, but Rose firmly shut out those thoughts.

The story ended and Marcus shut the book, his hands on the leather binding. He smiled at the very domestic picture of Rose mending his socks. Marcus stood and pulled Rose to her feet, giving her a warm kiss and said huskily, "The best part of the day. Time for bed for you, my darling."

Rose, smiled in anticipation, and echoed, "The best part of the day."

In bed, Marcus and Rose cuddled together as Marcus began to kiss Rose's neck and breasts. Slowly as he worked his searing mouth down her body his hot breath tickled her ribs and Rose moaned and gasped softly. Marcus, his tongue leaving a trail of fire across Rose's smooth stomach, gripped her round bottom and kneaded it gently. His hand dipped lower to stroke her womanliness, followed by his hot mouth.

Rose reveled in new found feelings and she gasped and writhed at the feel of his mouth on her tummy. When Marcus' mouth went lower and he breathed on her curls, it was like cold water on Rose; her eyes flew open and she reached down and covered her womanliness. "Marcus," she gasped in shocked tones, "what are you doing?"

Marcus, wild with passion, his mouth open and ready to taste her sweetness, struggled to contain himself. Part of him urged himself to carry on, sure that Rose would enjoy it; the other part of him realized that it was her innocence and ignorance that brought about this shock.

Marcus, with a frustrated sigh, hauled himself up next to Rose and pulled up the covers, firmly covering her naked breasts. Silently, Rose with her chest heaving, continued to look at him as if he were deranged. Marcus swallowed a couple times and blew out a few gusty sighs. He ran his fingers through his hair and struggled to find the words to explain.

"Rose," he began, reaching for her clenched fingers, "there are many forms of making love, of expressing your desire for each other." Rose looked at Marcus as if he were crazed, but did not say anything. Marcus continued on, "Rose, as long as both parties agree to the rules of making love, it is acceptable to make love in any position that both find agreeable." Marcus struggled to find the words under her accusing stare. He kissed her fingers and gripped them tightly.

"But Marcus," Rose protested, "that couldn't be decent. I mean you were going to put your mouth where, where," her voice trailed away, unable to meet his eyes, unable to express her shock and embarrassment.

Marcus said in his deep voice, "Rose, look at me." Rose glanced at him and then away, all of a sudden thinking about the fact that she was alone, naked in a strange cottage with a man she was not married to. All of her doubts and concerns once again were in her mind.

Marcus said again, this time in a more commanding tone, "Rose, I said look at me."

Rose turned her head and looked at him, her eyes full of questions. Marcus said to Rose, "Man and woman have had relations since the dawn of time, and over time many different positions have been tried. It is all right to touch, to kiss, to lick, any part of each other."

"Husbands and wives," she corrected him coldly, her face red. He looked at her puzzled and she repeated, "Husbands and wives have relations. You said all kinds of men and women."

"No Rose," Marcus argued, "men and women. That is how we have populated the earth, all the way back to Adam and Eve." She looked at him as if she would argue, but he went on, "My darling innocent, I only want to make love to you in ways that pleasure you. I want to introduce you to the many joys of expressing love for someone. I am only doing something that any other couple in love might do."

Rose thought about this and said, "But that, what you were doing; it doesn't seem clean. Why would you want to do that?"

Marcus could not help it and he burst out laughing, "My darling girl, I assure you that many many men and women do that every night and it brings intense pleasure to both."

Rose thought about this for a minute. "I am sure," she said firmly, "that none of my friends would ever consider doing it. I mean, I would have heard about it." Marcus silently disagreed, but did not say anything. Rose shook her head with assurance, "No decent woman would ever..." her voice trailed away. She thought for a moment and then said slowly, "I know William would never have..."

Marcus, a small noise of irritation in his throat, said, "No, Rose, I cannot imagine William ever doing that to you. Can we agree to not," he said a little shortly, "discuss your dead husband in this bed?"

Rose jumped at the tone in his voice and continued with her thoughts. "You wouldn't expect me to do that to you?" she asked in shocked tones, "I mean put my mouth," again she could not put the thoughts into words.

Marcus who privately would have loved for her to do such a thing, decided not to answer. He reached out and ran his hands up and down her cool arms. "Rose," he said, with a sigh, "it is only a symbol of passion. I promised you that I would not do anything that made you uncomfortable. Now I think I have upset you enough that we should go to sleep."

Marcus got out of bed and turned down the lamp. He crawled back in and pulled Rose to him, gave her a small kiss and leaned back into the pillows, silently. Rose, her head pillowed on his chest, lay there, feeling a small frustration emanating from him. Rose snuggled up to Marcus, listening as his heart beat strongly under her ear. She could not sleep, and was fairly certain Marcus lay awake as well. Some strange desire had been awakened in her and she tried to think about it. Did decent women? Did Charles and Alice? Rose thought back to her many friends; some seemed so in love with their husbands. Behind closed doors?

Many positions? Rose thought over Marcus' words. Rose thought how Marcus' hands and mouth roamed over her body. Every inch of her body that he touched felt on fire. Would he enjoy her touching? Rose thought about his reaction to her suckling his fingers and his nipples. She was sure she could never put her mouth... she could not even think the words. Her curiosity aroused, what about touching? Seeing Marcus naked, she had had a hard time not looking away from his manhood. What would it feel like to touch?

Marcus' breathing deepened and Rose, wide awake, felt a need to have Marcus deep inside of her.

Suddenly, Rose wanted Marcus awake. Rose kissed his neck and nudged Marcus gently, but he continued to sleep. Rose kissed his bare shoulder and neck, but there was still no response. Rose tentatively stroked her hand down his shoulder and across his stomach. Beyond his belly button a soft furring led to the apex of his manhood. Rose, her hands shaking, reached and tentatively touched his penis. It felt soft and pliable. Under her touch it began to grow and harden. It felt velvety, but also hard as steel.

Marcus came out of a dream with a shock, feeling amazing sensations caused by Rose Brewster's hand. He rolled over and reached for Rose and she whispered, "Mr. Underhill, I was thinking about what you said and how as long as two people want something, they should do it."

Marcus, with a smile in his voice, said, "What is it you want, little one?"

Rose whispered, as she placed a silken thigh on top of his, "For you to make love to me."

As the days and nights flowed together, Rose began to know the man Marcus. As they spoke of their pasts, she began to understand what a happy marriage he had with his wife, Maggie, and how the two of them created an empire in the Pacific Northwest through hard work and partnership.

Marcus understood a little better about the lack of love that Rose experienced in her marriage. Married to a total stranger and giving up her body at age seventeen was understood as a woman's duty. Marcus had a much clearer understanding of what being married into the Brewster family entailed. Amelia and Colonel Brewster forever made decisions for the young couple, all dramas discussed among all family members.

For Rose, the days flew past as in a dream. Rose spent her days longing for night when she could once again hold Marcus in her arms. She lay awake at night holding him close, longing for daylight when she could gaze upon his dear face.

When the rain stopped, they wandered through the woods, taking in the fresh air and talking companionably. The fields and woods were deserted for the season, and never did they see another soul. One afternoon, as Marcus and Rose wandered through the woods, they came out into the clearing at the edge of Eastwood. They faced the outer edge of the greenhouses and beyond towered the west wall of Eastwood. Rose stopped and looked up the wall to her bedroom window. The windows were curtained and shuttered and the house had an abandoned feel to it.

Rose stood and stared at the window for some time, thinking about all the lonely years she had spent within those walls. She thought she had been happy. She had certainly done her duty, and she had loved her time with her children. She suddenly realized how stifled all those years had been. She looked from the house to Marcus, and suddenly threw herself into his arms, exclaiming, "I love you."

Marcus watched the play of emotions on her face and returned her embrace warmly. Rose pulled herself from his arms and firmly turned her back on Eastwood, and marched down the path towards Summerfield.

One afternoon, they had been out and the rain returned with a vengeance. Rose and Marcus took shelter in the Summerfield barn. Summerfield was a summer enterprise, so this time of year the barn stood empty of animals, but still full of hay. They stood side by side looking out at the downpour, deciding whether to dash for the cottage or wait out the storm.

Rose turned from the dismal rain and walked around the barn, shivering and looking at the farm implements tidily stored for the winter. Marcus' canoe lay upside down across two saw horses, ready for calking in the spring.

Rose turned to find Marcus watching her. "Shall we stay or go?" she asked, shivering, "We are going to get plenty soaked if we go for it, but I am cold."

Marcus walked over to her and wrapped her in his strong arms, warming her. They began to kiss, and he whispered huskily, "There are other things we can do while we are waiting out the storm."

Rose, her eyes alight with passion, but a little surprised, said, "Here? In the barn?"

Marcus laughed as he pulled her down with him, "The hay is soft, and I will keep you warm."

Returning to the cottage late in the afternoon, Rose went directly to the bedroom and began to brush straw from her hair. Rose stopped as she gazed at herself in the mirror. Her eyes were dreamy with sated passion; her skin was blooming a soft pink. She could see bits and pieces of straw still clinging to her tangled curls that fell from her head and down her back. Rose realized that she was looking at a woman in love.

The last evening, the rain stopped and a weak sun shone in the cottage as Marcus and Rose ate a quiet dinner. That afternoon, Marcus' man stopped by briefly to clarify that he would pick up Rose early the next morning and escort her to the train depot. Rose would then take the train south, change trains and go north again to Boston. That way, if anyone saw her at the Boston train station, they would think she had spent the week with her cousin Dorothy.

Quietly Marcus and Rose ate dinner, occasionally glancing at each other, both silent. Companionably, they cleaned the kitchen and retired to the living room. Rose darned the last of Marcus' socks as he read <u>Romeo and Juliet</u> to her. Rose had been drawn to the story the previous summer, but hearing the love story now that she understood passion, read in Marcus' deep voice, brought out nuances that Rose had never guessed.

Finished, Marcus sat on the floor, one knee drawn up and his arm resting on it as he gazed into the fire silently. Rose set her mending basket aside and reached out and trailed her fingers over Marcus' broad shoulders. He turned his face and she was shocked to see tears in his eyes. "Marcus?" Rose queried.

Marcus swallowed and wiped his eyes impatiently. "I just don't know what is going to happen," he told her with a break in his voice. Before she could say anything, he went on, "You are going back to Boston tomorrow and resume your life and I don't know how I will be able to look at you at parties and not want to carry you off with me. I want to spend the rest of my life with you."

Rose heard his words and sighed, "I don't know, Marcus." She struggled to find words, "I love you so much, but we have to think of the children." Marcus turned and glared at Rose and she went on doggedly, "I believe the Colonel would have Henry at Slater before we drew our next breath. And you know how scandal hurts children. If it came out that we were lovers, not only would it damage Lavinia and my other two, but Collin, as well."

"What about as my wife?" Marcus asked, looking at her intently.

"Your wife?" Rose choked. Rose slid out of her chair and knelt beside Marcus, taking his face in her two hands. "Marcus, it would be my pleasure to be your wife, to be Mrs. Marcus Underhill." Marcus slid his arms around her waist, "But," she finished gently, "you forget Henry."

Marcus growled, "I can reason with Colonel Brewster."

Rose shook her head decisively, "No one reasons with the Colonel."

"What if I threatened the Colonel with scandal?" Marcus countered. "Tell him that you and I would live in sin if he doesn't allow you and me to be married and I take full responsibility of Henry."

"Scandal?" Rose gasped. "Marcus, that takes us back to our children. We could not do that to our children and you know it. And if you and I flouted that many conventions, the Colonel would try and take my children away."

"On what grounds?" Marcus asked.

Rose said, "Marcus, he could claim indecency. We seemed to have gotten away with this week, but we don't know. If the Colonel ever knew about this week," Rose's voice trailed away.

"What if we went far away?" Marcus asked, quietly looking at Rose. "If I took you and your children and we went away to San Francisco, Chicago, Europe."

"Away," Rose felt she was echoing everything Marcus was saying. She shook her head and said, "Marcus, I would follow you to the ends of the earth." She took his fingers and kissed them, sitting back on her haunches. Rose looked intently at Marcus and said, "I can't do that to my children. I mean, they are all settled in their schools and are happy. If you can just wait until Henry gains his majority."

Marcus looked at her like she was crazed. "Rose," he demanded, "are you suggesting that we wait until Henry is 21 before we marry? That doesn't make sense. I love you. I want to be with you now."

Rose dropped her face, but continued to idly pat Marcus' arm. "Marcus, what I am very good at doing in this life is putting my children first." Her bosom heaved and she said, "That is how I lived through the years of my marriage and widowhood. I put my children first. That is how I live with myself now."

"Children first," it was Marcus' turn to echo Rose. "And, Rose, what if you are pregnant?" Rose stared at him and he went on, "Rose, we did not do anything this week to stop that from happening."

"Pregnant?" Rose said in shocked tones, shaking her head. "I am too old to become pregnant."

"My dear," Marcus said gently, "you are not too old. You still have your monthly cycles?"

Rose blushed. As much time as they had spent getting to know each other this past week, it was still a delicate and embarrassing subject that ladies did not discuss with men.

Marcus took her hands in his and kissed them. "Rose, if you were pregnant and had a child out of wedlock, well, that would create a scandal that our unborn child would never live down."

Rose pulled her hands from Marcus and looked at him shocked. "I am not pregnant," she insisted. "Marcus, this has been the most wonderful week of my life, but I can not go back to

Boston and face Amelia and the Colonel and tell them we are getting married. I have had enough arguments with them over Henry's education. I can not go through it all again." A single tear slipped from her eye and slid down her cheek.

Marcus, frustrated, reached out and wiped the tear away with his thumb. "And how do you propose we act in Boston?" he asked her sharply. "Do we just pretend that this week never happened?"

Rose raised her head. "This week happened, Marcus," she said as a tear trickled down her cheek. "This week was a stolen week, a dream, something to live on." He continued to look at her and she fluttered her hands, "I don't know what to say about Boston."

"Would you marry me?" he asked her, his tone short.

"Oh Marcus," Rose cried, looking at him. "I would marry you if it weren't for Henry. I want to spend the rest of my life with you, but," she paused, "I just can't do it right now."

"Let me understand you." Marcus asked with a frown, "Do you propose we go back to Boston and occasionally I sneak into your bedroom window and spend the night with you and then we go back to our separate lives?"

Rose shook her head. "I said," she said, petulantly, "I don't know how it will work. Nothing can be settled tonight." She thought about Boston. "Can we just leave it alone until after Susanna's wedding? There is too much going on until Susanna marries the senator's son." The last was said bitterly.

Marcus stood and looked down at Rose. "Heaven forbid that we upset Senator Peabody's son," he said sarcastically. Marcus looked down at the tears on Rose's cheeks. Marcus reached down and pulled her to her feet. "Rose," he whispered, "don't cry. I just want to be able to tell the world that I love you. I don't care about senators' sons, Brewsters and all of Boston."

Rose said brokenly, "Marcus, I love you. I don't have a solution. This week was something that I never thought I would do in this life, and now you are asking me to flaunt conventions that would hurt my children. I need time to think."

Marcus gave in, although reluctantly.

Early the next morning, Marcus woke Rose with a cup of hot coffee. They had held each other tightly late into the night. All had been said at the fireside, and it was a time to clasp each other and long for more. Rose stirred, her eyes heavy with little rest and found Marcus dressed, encouraging her to drink the coffee. Rose had packed the afternoon before. She quickly dressed in the shivering cold and put the last few items in her trunk.

Her trunk loaded on the carriage, Marcus and Rose stood in the pre-dawn light. They stared at each other for a long minute before he enfolded her in his arms. Rose was wordless as she gazed at his beloved face. Marcus looked long and hard in her eyes and spoke softly, "Stop worrying. It will all work out. I promise I won't do anything or say anything until after the wedding."

The trip home was long and tiring for Rose. She barely slept the night before as she lay clasped in Marcus' arms, listening to the ticking of the clock, staring into the darkness. Rose came to no solution of their predicament.

CHAPTER 15

Rose spent a quiet week at home. After her time with Marcus, she felt she could not face Amelia or other society matrons so she sent a note pleading a cold. On this cool mid November afternoon, she excused herself from the DAR meeting, insisting that she continued to feel sickly.

Rose sat in her drawing room, staring into the fire with her forgotten needlework in her lap. She thought back to her week with Marcus and remembered the feel of his hands on her body. Since her return to Boston, she had no word from him. From Summerfield, Marcus travelled directly to Providence on business and would not return to Boston for some time. Rose was roused from her reverie by the sound of the door knocker and heard Hobbs' muffled voice answering her door. Indistinguishable female voices could be heard, and a moment later Hobbs appeared with her silver salver. Rose looked at the calling cards of Alice Brewster and Cordelia Brown. She attempted to decide how to turn them away, when Alice appeared behind Hobbs. "There you are," Alice said with a smile. "We heard you had been under the weather, but decided to see how your visit went with your cousin Dorothy."

Rose smiled faintly and struggled to her feet, greeting warmly two of her oldest friends. Cordelia reached to give her a hug, then paused." Rose," she said with a friendly smile, but staring intently at her friend, "what have you been doing with yourself?"

Rose flushed, looking slightly guilty, and asked, "What do you mean?"

Before Cordelia could answer, Hobbs appeared with the tea tray, and Rose bent to pour tea for her friends, offering them small refreshments. She looked up to see both Alice and Cordelia looking at her speculatively.

Rose shrugged and said breathlessly to Alice, "Cousin Dorothy was just fine."

Alice glanced at the funny look on Rose's face to Cordelia's speculative stare and asked lightly, "Did you visit Anastasia Snow while you were there?"

"Um, no," Rose stumbled over the words. Trying to change the subject, she asked, "So what has been going on here in Boston?"

Cordelia continued to look at Rose searchingly. Alice said, "Oh the usual. The DAR has decided on the date for the Bazaar for the Widows and Orphans. I think Matilda signed you up to be in charge of refreshments."

"Wonderful," Rose responded. The conversation lagged,

"Rose Brewster," Cordelia Brown exclaimed, "I don't know what you have been doing, but you have never looked lovelier. If I didn't know better, I would say you were in love!"

Rose, sipping her tea, choked on the words. Her teacup rattled in her saucer as she gasped, "In love?" Rose swallowed again and said weakly, "Don't be silly."

Alice moved across the room in two strides. She stood over Rose and pounced, "That is what is so different about you, Rose. You look truly happy. Rose, what is going on?"

Rose's eyes regarded first Alice's face and then Cordelia's. She shook her head in denial, but she could feel a telltale blush stealing on her cheeks. "I don't know what you are talking about," she protested, her voice faint.

Cordelia grabbed Rose's hand and gave it a small squeeze. "Rose," she said, in a most confidential manner, "we all heard the gossip this fall about you and," she paused delicately, "Marcus Underhill."

Before Cordelia could continue, Rose exclaimed, "Marcus? So, you too heard that gossip?"

Cordelia shrugged, silently noting the familiar use of Marcus' first name only. "Oh, Stephen told me, of course." Referring to her husband, she said, "You know how men gossip. He didn't tell me everything, but Sam Gardner talked about you and Mr. Underhill at their club one day."

"What did he say?" Rose asked, bitterly. Rose looked at Alice, "Charles, too?"

Alice knelt down beside Rose. "Rose, you are closer to me than my own sisters," Alice told Rose. "We all know that there has been gossip. Charles doesn't tell me everything, and I tend to discount what has been said. But, my dear," Alice rushed on, "at Eastwood last summer you looked happier than I have ever seen you. And if you are in love with Marcus Underhill, well, Rose, that is just marvelous!"

Rose stared at her sister-in-law. Cordelia stepped in as Rose stuttered, "Rose Brewster, you deserve a handsome man in your life, and Marcus Underhill is one very attractive man. What would be wrong with you having some happiness in your life?"

Rose looked from one woman to the other and all of a sudden the three of them laughed and hugged each other. Rose admitted that she had fallen in love with Marcus, but swore her friends to secrecy.

"Why on earth," Cordelia began in her forthright manner.

"Because of Susanna's wedding," Rose said gently, looking at Alice. "The Colonel and Amelia will not be happy about this, and I don't want to cause speculation or emotional arguments before the wedding."

Alice reached out and gave Rose a squeeze. She looked at Rose knowingly, and nodded slightly. "Thank you, Rose," she said softly, "but, after the wedding I want to help you with this. Together we will tackle Amelia and the Colonel."

Cordelia started to argue, then sighed. Cordelia knew how close the Brewsters could be when they chose to be; no amount of scolding would change that. Instead, she sighed and said, "Tell us all the details. I want to know more about this handsome man of yours."

"Well, I think we will leave the details to your imagination," Rose said with a twinkle. The three laughed hilariously and once again hugged each other. Torie, home from school, peeked in at her mother and her guests and shaking her head, tiptoed away.

Rose spent an afternoon at her mother-in-law's assisting Amelia in receiving callers. It had been a cold rainy November afternoon, a dismal damp day; a threat of sleet was in the air. Upon arriving home Hobbs took Rose's jacket and dripping umbrella. Rose walked upstairs to change for dinner. Her feet hurt and she wanted to remove her new shoes and relax. She felt full of tea and small edibles and did not want to think about supper. Her dress for dinner was laid out and Rose only had to ring the bell for Phoebe to help her change. With a sigh, Rose tucked her feet into her slippers and wearily sank down on her chaise lounge, looking out the window at the dull weather. The leaves had mostly fallen from the trees in the park and the black barren branches stood out bleakly against the damp twilight.

This foul weather precluded walks in the park. Since Rose returned from her trip with Marcus, she had not heard from him. Peregrine let her know that Marcus remained in Providence, tied up with business. Rose sighed. She missed Marcus dreadfully, feeling an aching loneliness. Was it not time to stand up to the world? Rose thought back to the letter she had received from Henry's professor that morning. Henry was excelling at Ashcroft and Professor Ward hoped that Rose would come to Ashcroft on the 22nd of November to see Henry receive a special award.

While delighted with the news of his success and the knowledge that she was right to stand up for Henry, the loneliness Rose experienced at times was overwhelming. Before she met Marcus, Rose had not known that she was lonely. She never knew what she had been missing before Marcus Underhill awakened a part of her that she did not know existed. Rose continued to sit and brood, staring out at the bleak cold afternoon.

Rose came out of her reverie, shook her head and gave a deep sigh. This would not do. Rose stood up to make sure that Torie would join her for dinner. She needed her bright funny daughter for conversation tonight. Since her talk with Peregrine some weeks ago, Torie remained quieter with her mother, keeping some thoughts to herself. Rose felt intuitively that her daughter had come to realize some inner understanding of her father's memory and was making peace with the truth. Rose witnessed Torie's maturation as the promise of the beautiful woman she would become shone on her blooming cheeks and bright eyes. Torie had grown tall over the summer and her stockinged legs seemed to stretch forever under her short skirts.

Rose strained to hear any voices in the house. Faintly from the kitchen came the sounds and smells of delicious cooking; across the hall in the nursery all seemed to be silent. Still outfitted in her calling dress, Rose crossed the hall to the nursery. She opened the door as Torie hastily shut her wardrobe door and looked at her mother, a mixture of excitement and guilt on her face. There also was a look of fear. Rose frowned slightly as she gazed at her daughter's face searchingly, then at the shut wardrobe door. Shep stood near the wardrobe, whining and scratching at it. He gave a small yip. Rose took in the look on her daughter's face and the little dog's interest and she came directly to the point, "All right, Torie, what do you have hidden in the wardrobe?"

Torie turned her wide eyes to her mother, but shook her head vigorously. "The wardrobe? What do you mean, Mama?"

"Is it a puppy?" her mother asked sternly, as this had happened before.

"No, not a puppy. I don't know what is wrong with Shep," Torie turned to walk across the room. Brightly, she said, "I'm famished, Mama. Shall we go down and eat?"

Rose looked from her daughter to the busy small terrier and, without a word, crossed the room and opened the door to the wardrobe. To her immense surprise and amazement, Edmund Brewster stood there in his military uniform, his coat torn at the shoulder and exceedingly dirty. Edmund sported a large bruise on the side of his face; his left eye was closed and his lip was swollen and scabbed over. His large blue eyes looked suspiciously tearful. Edmund shivered and he held his arm in a funny position against his body.

"Edmund," Rose gasped.

Torie stepped between her mother and Edmund. "Please, Mama," she begged, fiercely, "don't tell Uncle Charles and Aunt Alice. They will send him back to Slater."

Rose looked at her nephew in bewilderment, "Edmund, what are you doing here? How did you get here?"

Edmund stepped gingerly from the closet. At that moment he looked very young as he stared at Rose with a hunted expression in his eyes and said simply, "I have run away from school." Then he dropped his head and began to sob, loud gulping sobs wrenching from deep inside of him.

Rose reached out and gathered Edmund to her, stroking his head. His blonde curls had been shorn before he returned to school and his scrubby short hair felt rough under her soothing hands. Rose felt Edmund wince as she put her arms around him, as if he were in pain.

Rose held Edmund and murmured soothing words when Phoebe came into the room with a fresh pile of ironed linens in her arms. Phoebe stopped in shock. "Edmund?" Phoebe echoed Rose's

words of a few minutes earlier. Rose looked over her shoulder at
Phoebe, a worried look in her eyes.

Taking charge, Phoebe bustled across the room and extracted
Edmund from Rose's arms. Torie hovered around the group.
Phoebe handed Edmund a fresh hankie and examined the bruises
on his face with gentle fingers. "Miss Torie," Phoebe ordered in a
calm voice, "run down and ask Cook for a bit of cold raw
beefsteak. Also, ask her for a basin of hot water." As Torie turned
to run from the room, Phoebe stated, "Miss Torie, don't tell them
in the kitchen what is going on. Just tell them I said I needed it.
And Miss Torie, don't spill the water; walk carefully."

Torie raced from the room on her errand, her swift footsteps
clattering down the stairs. Phoebe and Rose sat Edmund down on
the side of Henry's bed and carefully removed his coat. As they
pulled the coat away, Edmund moaned in pain. They found
evidence of other bruises, blood stains and welts on his body. After
seeing the brutal body damage, they exchanged horrified looks and
exclamations of shock, but to Edmund they made soothing noises.
Rose heard Torie coming down the hall. She did not want her
daughter to see her cousin in his bloodied and bruised state. Rising
swiftly, Rose opened the door and stepped out into the hall,
reaching for the bowl of water Torie carried. Torie was furious.
"Cook wouldn't give me the beefsteak. She said unless you or
Phoebe asked her directly, she would not hand it over. She said she
thought I wanted it for Shep." Torie started to push past her mother
but was stopped by her mother's firm hand on her shoulder.

"Darling, give me the water and stay here," her mother
ordered. "I, we, I don't want you in there right now. Let Phoebe
and I take care of Edmund." Torie ignored her mother and tried to
push past, but her mother firmly took her by the arm. "Torie,"
Rose said, urgency in her voice. "Phoebe and I need to get Edmund
to bed. Stay out."

"But, Mama, it's Edmund," Torie argued, trying to push past
her mother into the room. Gentle Rose gave her daughter a very
ungentle shove and, stepping into the room, firmly turned the lock.
Torie, astonished, slumped to the floor outside the door and started
crying from fear and concern for her cousin. Inside the room, she
could hear exclamations from her mother and Phoebe and an
occasional moan or cry from Edmund.

Phoebe and Rose cleaned Edmund's wounds and examined him thoroughly. Together the two women looked at each other. Edmund tried to bear their ministrations, but pleaded with his aunt, "Please don't tell my parents; they will send me back."

Rose, soothing his head said, "Edmund, I have to tell your parents. When the school tells them you are missing, they will be worried sick. They may already know." He shook his head and thrashed but stopped, gasping in pain. "Darling," Rose said, "I am sending for Dr. Edwards. I think your ribs are broken and I don't know what else. You need medical help."

Torie huddled against the wall opposite the nursery door when Rose came out. She jumped to her feet, but Rose closed the door and, sweeping past Torie, hurried downstairs. Torie could hear her mother in the back hall on the phone calling Dr. Edwards, her voice urgent. Rose hung up and after a moment of silence she lifted the receiver and rang for Charles and Alice, praying they would be at home for the evening. Rose's voice was quieter, hushed and gentle as she spoke to Charles.

In the next hour, the house became alive with people. Edmund's parents and the doctor converged on the house at the same time. Alice's cries of shock when she saw her son's damages were echoed more quietly by her husband's own horrified tones. Edmund gasped, "Mama, don't cry," and then began to cry himself. It had taken Edmund more than 24 hours to reach Boston from his school on the coast, and he was in very bad shape from sleeping outside in the cold and rain one night. Hot water bottles were packed around him to relieve his shivering.

Dr. Edwards, assessing the damage, administered a sleeping draught. Aside from two broken ribs, and broken bones in his right hand, the majority of the wounds were bruises and small cuts. While Edmund would be in severe pain for some time, none of the damage appeared permanent.

Torie, still not admitted to the nursery, sat in the hall and sobbed. The tears ran down her face unabated as her small hands lay clenched in her skirt balling up the fabric. Charles and Alice pushed past her and into the nursery without a glance. At a particularly loud cry of pain from Edmund, Torie jumped up and ran downstairs. She snatched up her jacket and raced from the house. It was three miles to her grandparents' house and quite dark by this time. There was a pouring icy rain. Bareheaded, Torie raced through the streets heedless of people's looks, or the cold wet showering down on her. Once she was almost knocked down by a horse and carriage as she dashed across the street. She paused briefly, her wide staring eyes taking in the rearing horse's hooves inches from her, then ran on; the driver's shout did not slow her down.

Out of breath and panting, Torie saw her grandparents' house. With a final effort she raced up the steps and pounded on the door. Pratt appeared and saw a gasping Torie leaning against the porch post, bareheaded and sopping wet, her cloak barely hanging on around her shoulders. "Miss Victoria!" he gasped in amazement.

Torie pulled herself up and pushed past him into the hall, her cloak trailing water in her wake. She paused and hearing voices in the dining room, ran in that direction. The Colonel and Amelia were just sitting down to dinner along with the great aunts and their daughter Matilda.

As Torie burst into the dining room unannounced, the sight of her dishevelled appearance and tear streaked face froze the room's inhabitants. Torie gasped for breath but could not find her voice. Her grandmother was the first to move at the same moment that Pratt reached her and put his hands on her shoulders in an attempt to turn her from the room. Torie jerked away from Pratt. She had eyes only for the Colonel. She rounded the table and grabbed his arm. "You must come at once to my house," she panted. "Something awful has happened to Edmund. Come." she commanded, her face pinched and her voice high pitched with terror. She tugged at his arm.

At her words, the Colonel went cold. He could barely utter one word, "Dead?" A gasp could be heard from Aunt Easter.

Torie shook her head and the story came out incoherently through her sobs, "Not yet. He has run away from school because he was beaten. The doctor is there now and I heard uncle say it was bad. They beat him. They beat him," she repeated over and over, her voice rising louder and louder until the last words were a scream. She burst out, accusingly, "If Edmund dies it will be all your fault. He did not want to go to Slater, but you made him!"

Her grandparents and aunts stared at Torie for a moment, taking in her shocking words. The Colonel and Amelia exchanged glances and the Colonel sprang into action, throwing his napkin down as he rushed out into the hall. He ordered Pratt to have the carriage brought around immediately.

Torie would have followed him, but her grandmother wrapped her arms around her granddaughter. Amelia smoothed Torie's hot forehead, pulled off her sodden cloak and pushed her into a chair. A towel was fetched and wrapped turban style around Torie's sopping wet hair. At a nod from Amelia, Matilda brought a snifter of brandy and they forced Torie to drink it. Torie coughed and sputtered, but the warmth that spread through was calming. Amelia turned to Torie, attempting to soothe her, "I think you are being a little over dramatic. I am sure it is nothing to be concerned about. The Colonel will deal with it."

Torie looked at her grandmother in amazement. "Nothing?" Torie burst out. "Nothing, Grandmother? Edmund might die and you think it is nothing?"

Matilda, her arms around Torie, attempted to shush her, but Amelia took a long look at Torie and said, "Victoria, enough of this. You are hysterical. I need to get you home and into warm clothes."

The sound of the carriage's arrrival could be heard and the Colonel, wrapped in a cloak was going out the door when Amelia came out of the dining room. "George," Amelia called, "please wait for one minute. Torie and I will be coming with you."

Matilda, behind her mother, pulled cloaks off the hooks and placed one around her mother's shoulders, another dry one around Torie. Taking Torie by the hand, Matilda and Amelia headed for the carriage with the Colonel following.

Amelia and Torie sat side by side in the carriage, the Colonel and Matilda sat opposite. Amelia held Torie's hands and from time to time would lean over and kiss the top of Torie's head. "Victoria," she said quietly, "when we get to your mother's you must run up and get into something dry and warm. We can't have you sick as well." Amelia continued to talk, almost as if to calm herself. She went on, "Edmund is going to be fine, my dear. Dr. Edwards will take beautiful care of him. You know," she went on into the silence, "I am sure this is just a quarrel between boys. I remember when your father was at Slater,"

"Father hated Slater," Torie said flatly, interrupting her grandmother.

The Colonel, who had been silent until now stirred, "Torie," he remonstrated.

Torie turned an accusing face from Amelia to the Colonel. "Uncle Peregrine told me so," she spat. "He said you made Father go to Slater and they picked on him. He hated it."

"Torie," her grandmother said quietly, "you are too young to understand."

Torie shook her head and turned to look with flashing eyes at her grandmother. "I think I understand perfectly."

As the carriage stopped in front of Rose's house, Torie surged upstairs ahead of her grandparents and aunt, leaving Hobbs to take their hats and coats. She pushed her way into the nursery and saw Edmund asleep from the draught the doctor had given him. Torie's first sight of Edmund was horrifying. When she found him in the bushes at the end of the driveway, she thought he was just tired and dirty from his long tramp home. At the sight of her cousin's white bandages and bruised face and arms, Torie could hardly breathe. Slowly she approached the bed and stared down at her cousin and then up at her grandfather as he approached the bed.

"This is all your fault," Torie spat at her grandfather, fear and anger causing her voice to shake. "You made Uncle Charles send him to Slater and look what happened!"

The Colonel, shocked over the sight of Edmund, turned to Torie, looking aged and weary. The Colonel stared at Torie for a long moment, an anguished look in his eyes, then back at Edmund. Wordlessly, he walked around the bed, kissed his granddaughter and walked out of the room. Amelia and Matilda paused at the aged look in the Colonel's eyes and then back at Edmund. Their shocked questions were answered briefly by Charles and Rose. Alice, slumped in a chair close to the bed, held Edmund's hand and stared at him, tears falling unheeded down her cheeks. Rose and Phoebe hovered in the background, tidying Edmund's discarded clothes and removing bloody bowls of water.

"What happened?" Amelia's voice faltered as she continued to stare at Edmund. Charles raised his shocked eyes from his son's face and looked at his mother. "I think," he said slowly, "this is not the place to discuss this. Shall we all go downstairs?"

Matilda, who was holding her mother's arm, said softly, "Come Mama. Charles is right. Let us go down and join Papa in the drawing room." All but Alice and Torie, who refused to leave Edmund's bedside, exited the nursery. Rose's drawing room was crowded with Brewsters as Amelia sank into a soft chair by the fire, for once her ramrod straight back slumped against the cushions.

Rose busied herself ordering tea and Hobbs reminded her that she had not eaten dinner. She shook her head at him ruefully. Hobbs also burst into an apology that Cook had not given Torie the beefsteak. Seeing the sorrowed look on Hobbs' face, Rose reached out and patted his arm. "Mr. Edmund will be fine. Please let Cook know that we hold nothing against her."

In the grimly silent drawing room, Hobbs and Tilly brought in the tea service. No one spoke until Hobbs and Tilly withdrew, shutting the drawing room door softly behind them. The shock of the brutal beating that Edmund endured caused all of them to sit in silence. From the back hallway Charles had called Western Union and a telegram had been dispatched to the military school advising them that Edmund had been found. Charles terse words on the telephone were the only words that had been spoken aloud.

The Colonel paced and regained some of his equilibrium. Suddenly, he stopped and stared into the fire, and in his best commander's voice, he said forcefully, "I am sure it is some grubby boys' brawl; patch him together and send him back. It is the best way."

Charles, his hand on the mantle, white as a ghost, also stared into the fire. "Edmund will not return to Slater," Charles said quietly and firmly.

"Don't mollycoddle him. This will make him a better soldier." Even as the Colonel said the words, he hesitated, his thoughts on the battered boy upstairs.

Charles repeated quietly, "Edmund will not be returning to Slater, Father."

"Nonsense," his father barked. "A little brawling never hurt anyone. Makes a better soldier out of him. Teaches him to control his temper. All Brewsters make great soldiers. Besides," he continued, attempting to say something positive, "Edmund showed great bravery coming all this way with injuries. Sign of a good soldier."

Charles raised his head and stared at his Father. "No father," he said very steadily. "not all Brewsters make great soldiers. Edmund will not return to Slater." Charles looked at his father fiercely, but he swallowed twice before he said, "Edmund is my son and I shall decide where he will be schooled." Charles' words were quiet but very firm.

Matilda spoke up, supporting her father. "You are speaking nonsense, Charles. Raised around all those girls made Edmund soft. My boys were fine at Slater. Send Edmund back to Slater. He will face punishment for leaving, but that is what makes a man."

Charles turned and stared at his sister, brief hatred filling his eyes. Amelia made a small sound as Charles faced his father. "It is time to stop. Generations of Brewsters have been military men because the older generation insisted that it be a necessity of life. It is time to stop."

Charles walked over to the sideboard, poured himself a brandy and tossed it back. "My brother, and your son, William, hated the military and you forced him into it. William hated it so much that he wrote that damnable will that has ruined Rose's life." Rose, sitting white and limp in the window seat, raised her hand at this, but Charles went on to his father, "I have allowed myself to follow in your footsteps because you demanded it. I even have allowed you to dictate my son's life, but that ends tonight. My son hates military school so much that he somehow walked for two days with broken bones and numerous injuries to escape. Edmund will not return to Slater or any other military establishment."

He crossed the room and faced his father. Even in his anger, Charles swallowed before he said, "Father, you are wrong. The military was the correct life for you. I believe it is the correct life for Matilda's twins, but it is not for everyone. And," he paused, "it is not for my son." At that Charles broke into a sob, "My son. What if I lose my only son?"

The silence of the room was broken by soft weeping from Rose and Amelia. Amelia stood and went to her own son. She looked at the Colonel and she looked at her son. The bitterness and pain from losing William, and the fear of losing Edmund shown on her face. Facing Charles, she said brokenly, "I have lost a son. I have known the pain of watching my own son die. I don't want that to happen to you." She turned to the Colonel. "George," she said softly, "I have supported you in every decision you have made with the boys and our children and grandchildren. But, it is time to lay it down and stand 'at ease.'"

The Colonel stared at his wife. He started to expostulate, but she interrupted him, "I am not saying you are wrong, but it is time for you and I to allow this generation to make decisions for their own children. Let it go." Her husband started to say more, and she laid a hand gently on his arm, "George, let it go."

The Colonel and Amelia stared at each other for a long moment, then the Colonel turned to Charles and Rose and glared at each of them. "Do what you want with your sons," he spat and stalked from the room.

Amelia watched her husband go and with a sigh she gestured to Matilda. As Amelia kissed Charles, her face showed signs of organization. She said, "I am sure Kitty and the little girls are wondering what has happened. Matilda and I shall go to your house and collect them. We will take them to Emily's house for the night. I would gather up Torie as well, but I seriously doubt even heaven could budge her from Edmund's bedside, and I am not up for any more dramatics tonight. We will make more plans in the morning." Amelia reached out and pulled Charles' face down and kissed his cheek; his hand came up and lingered over his mother's own small hand. Amelia swept out of the room, Matilda in her wake. There was murmuring in the hall, and then the front door closed behind them quietly.

While the adults were in discussion downstairs, Alice and Torie sat by Edmund's bed watching him sleep. Even with a sleeping draught, from time to time a shadow of pain passed over his face. A moan occasionally emanated from Edmund and he would move his head restlessly on the pillow. Torie cuddled next to Alice in the big nursery rocker and they both shed tears as they watched the sleeping boy. "He didn't want to go back to Slater," Torie whispered. "He told me so last summer."

Another tear slipped down Torie's face, "It's all my fault."

Alice turned and looked down at Torie's stricken face. Alice smoothed Torie's damp curls. "No, Torie," she said, "I knew that he was troubled, and I did nothing about it. I did not ask him what was bothering him because I did not want your father or I to have to argue with the Colonel. I allowed the Colonel to insist that Edmund return for a second year, even though I knew he did not want to go back."

Torie shook her head. "I should have listened to him, Auntie Alice. Edmund has always listened to me and helped me. Edmund has always been my best friend. I wanted to be a soldier so bad, so I wanted him to be the soldier I could never be, and Edmund told me he hated it." she said with a sob.

Alice gathered up Torie and held her closely while Torie sobbed against her aunt's pillowy bosom. When Torie finally finished, she lay exhausted and looked out from her aunt's comforting arms to the sleeping boy.

As Torie watched Edmund, he stirred a little. The draught began to wear off. Torie slid from Alice's lap and they both went on either side of Edmund's bed. Edmund moved his head while his one good eye flickered open. Torie reached out and touched Edmund's uninjured hand. "I am so sorry," she whispered as a tear slid down her face.

Edmund gripped her fingers gently and his head moved restlessly on the pillow. "Torie," he whispered, "not your fault." Edmund rolled his eyes and realized his mother stood by his bed and a look of alarm passed over his face. "Mama?" he asked.

Tearily Alice soothed Edmund and answered, "I am here, my darling. You need to just sleep now, and not worry about anything. Papa will take care of everything." Alice passed her hand over his head, her words were choked, "I should have listened to you, too, Edmund. Last summer. I should have stood up to the Colonel for you."

Edmund stirred. "Nobody's fault." he repeated. He grimaced in pain, and a tear trickled out of his eye. "Nobody's fault. Thank you."

Phoebe rose quietly from the corner of the room and mixed a fresh sleeping draught. She looked at Torie over the rim, and told her, "Edmund has been through a lot and not making sense. The best thing for him right now is sleep. Help me lift him so I can give him his fresh medicine. Sleeping is what he needs." Even with the gentle hands of his mother and cousin, Edmund groaned in pain as they lifted him. He sipped the drink and fell back wearily onto the pillow. Exhausted and in pain, Edmund moved his head a little on the pillow and then went back to sleep.

Torie refused to move from Edmund's side. Clutching his fingers, she put her head down on the mattress and fell asleep. Sometime later Torie drowsily half woke to find Uncle Charles lifting her up gently and carrying her across the room to her own bed. Torie was aware of Phoebe and her mother removing her shoes and pulling her nightdress over her head. As she felt the covers drawn up under her chin, Torie drowsily said, "Uncle Charles, please don't send Edmund back to Slater."

Charles bent down and brushed a kiss across Torie's forehead. "No, my darling," he promised, "Edmund won't be going back to military school."

Torie struggled to stay awake, "He told me he wants to be a doctor."

Charles kissed her once again. "Go to sleep, Torie," he said a little more firmly. Charles whispered, "His mother and I will sit up with him tonight."

Rose, too, kissed Torie and then left the room. Torie drifted off, waking once during the night to see her uncle sitting by Edmund's bed. Charles was not sleeping, but staring at his only son. He had the most intense anguished look in his eyes.

Chapter 16

Morning dawned and Torie woke groggily to Phoebe gently shaking her. "Miss Torie," Phoebe said insistently, "wake up. You need to get ready for school."

Torie awoke suddenly remembering Edmund. She sat up and asked, "Edmund?" as she pushed back the bed covers and looked at her cousin. The chair next to Edmund's bed was empty and the boy still lay asleep. Faint light crept through the window onto the small table covered in bottles and half empty glasses. Edmund's military uniform sat neatly folded on the hearth. A small bowl of water and a cloth were tucked underneath the bed.

"Leave him alone," Phoebe told her. "Mr. Edmund is going to rest today. Miss Torie, you must go to school."

Torie argued but Phoebe insisted. Reluctantly, Torie dressed and after lingering briefly by Edmund's side, she allowed Phoebe to lead her downstairs to breakfast. Torie passed the drawing room, and when she glanced in she saw a general air of untidiness. The fire had not been relit and cold ashes still filled the hearth. Half filled tea cups sat on tables and the large tea urn stood in cold reproachful silence. Cushions were dented or pushed haphazardly into corners.

Torie ate very little breakfast, her mother silent beside her. Places were set for Uncle Charles and Aunt Alice, but neither appeared for breakfast. Shortly after finishing the meal, Torie was kissed tenderly by her mother and sent on her way. Torie came out of the house to find a clear, cold morning. The rain from the night had blown through and a soft, weak sun shone through the black limbs of the trees across the street in the park. Torie took a deep breath of fresh air and turned in the direction of her school.

Sometime later Edmund sat up in bed, propped up on pillows. He ate a little breakfast as Charles and Alice watched anxiously. Edmund was silent that morning and every breath proved painful. Manfully, he sipped some broth under his mother's anxious eye. He looked up as Rose escorted his grandfather into the nursery. Alice, after a glance from Charles, kissed Edmund gently and withdrew taking Rose with her. The Colonel settled himself into the soft nursery chair that Alice had abandoned. The Colonel avoided Charles' cold stare from across the bed.

Edmund, eating only to please his mother, dropped his spoon and pushed the tray away. Charles took the tray and set it down by the hearth. Charles had not spoken to his father since last night and he did not speak to his father now.

The Colonel ignored his son and looked at Edmund speculatively. "Edmund," he began. Edmund and Charles both stared at the Colonel, a tense look passing over Edmund's face. The Colonel cleared his throat and began again, "Edmund, I understand that things did not go well at Slater this term. I need you to tell me about it. Your mother will not allow me to be here talking to you very long, so I need to get the facts."

Edmund looked at his grandfather's face and realized that the Colonel did not mean to speak so abruptly. In his grandfather's eyes, Edmund saw a look of intense anguish and, for the first time, a touch of doubt.

Edmund shrugged, and wincing in pain, he said quietly, "It was just a boy's quarrel, sir."

At Edmund's silence, his grandfather tried again. "Better get it out, boy," he said, not unkindly. "Your parents have decided not to send you back to Slater and I am not going to argue with them. They are your parents and they think they know best." There was a tinge of bitterness in the Colonel's voice as he said, " I need to understand what happened."

Edmund looked from his grandfather to his father. Charles, his face set, nodded to his son. For the first time Charles spoke, "Edmund, we need to know what happened. We will decide where your next school will be. But I, your mother and I, need to know what happened."

Edmund looked at his father, a troubled glint in his one good eye. "I don't want Mother to know," he said gruffly.

His grandfather and father exchanged glances. The Colonel said, "All right, Edmund. This will just be between us men."

Edmund thought about what happened and tried to gather the words to speak. The silence stretched out and the Colonel and Charles once again exchanged glances. Charles was just about to say something when Edmund began to talk in a small unemotional voice. "It was Giles Gardner," he said softly.

Charles drew in his breath, but Edmund struggled on, "Giles has always been a bully. Even before Slater he had always picked on little kids, kittens, anything small and weak. He feels more powerful when he can pick on somebody, especially anyone or anything smaller than he is."

Edmund glanced at the Colonel and then down at his bandaged broken hand. "It seemed this year that Giles has been even more brutal. We had barely returned to school when he started to pick on first years, beyond what anyone would call hazing. He kept saying little things in passing to me." Edmund paused and then blurted out, "Sir, you need to know, I did throw the first punch."

The Colonel and Charles exchanged glances. Charles said, "Edmund, why?"

Edmund swallowed and said, "Giles picked on the little kids but he also started saying things." Edmund paused and then said, "Things about Aunt Rose."

Charles started to exclaim, but the Colonel silenced him with a motion. Edmund's grandfather's brow furrowed and he repeated in a suspicious tone, "Your Aunt Rose?"

"Aunt Rose," Edmund repeated, but he faltered. "Giles was saying that she was a bad woman, that she spent last summer...." Edmund's eyes lowered, but he drew a breath and rushed out, "that she was doing things with Mr. Underhill."

The Colonel's indrawn breath was one of anger. His eyes flashing, he exchanged glances with Charles. Edmund went on, "He could say what he wanted about Aunt Rose, and I would have still fought to defend her, but he also said some other things."

Edmund's hands started to shake. He raised his tear-filled eyes. Edmund looked directly at the Colonel, then dropped his eyes. Edmund's face drained of color as he whispered, "He said things about Uncle William... and Peregrine Fitch."

The Colonel, his fury at Rose building inside of him, went cold at the last words. The Colonel struggled out of the chair and stood over Edmund. Sharply he demanded, "What about William and Fitch?"

Charles reached out a hand to protect his son, but the Colonel did not touch Edmund. "Boy," the Colonel thundered in tones that could not be brooked, "I want you to tell me what that Gardner boy said, every word."

Edmund struggled, "Giles is a pig, Grandfather. He can't know what he was talking about."

Charles spoke gently, "Edmund, we need to know what was said. You have been a very brave boy, and it sounds like you defended the Brewster name. Giles may need to be expelled, but we need to know what he said." Unnoticed by Edmund and the men, Rose slipped into the nursery with a pile of fresh bandages, accompanied by Peregrine Fitch. Peregrine stopped by unannounced and Rose told him briefly what had happened. Rose brought Peregrine upstairs to see Edmund, but at the mention of William's name, the two stood frozen, listening to Edmund's words.

With Charles' encouragement, Edmund found the strength to speak the shameful words. "Giles said that Uncle William and Peregrine," again he paused, struggling for words. "He said that when they were at Slater, Uncle William and Peregrine were, were, lovers." The last was whispered so quietly that those in the room could barely hear him. Edmund dropped his head back on his pillow and began to weep childish tears. "I don't understand," he sobbed. "I didn't know what he meant, but it sounded bad and so I hit him. I couldn't help myself; I just kept hitting him. He beat me, but I broke my hand on his nose."

Rose made a small sound and the two Brewster men turned to see Rose standing there ashen, the bandages she had been holding dropped into an pile on the floor. Peregrine stood behind her, a look of shame and horror on his face. Charles looked from the weeping boy to the woman and made as if to take a step towards Rose, just as Peregrine tried to put his arms around her. Rose shook her head and wrenched herself away from Peregrine, staring uncomprehendingly from the boy to Peregrine. A dawning look of enlightenment lit up Rose's eyes before she put her hands behind her back and stepped backwards out of the room. Her footsteps clattered on the stairs and a moment later the front door slammed.

Peregrine, Charles and the Colonel looked at each other helplessly. Edmund continued to sob from the bed.

Rose snatched up her cloak and hat and pulled open the heavy front door, slamming it shut behind her. The carriage with Amelia pulled up in front of her house and Amelia emerged. Amelia took one look at Rose's face, the cloak over her arm, her hat in her hand, her wide staring eyes and ashen face. Amelia grabbed Rose's arm. "My dear, what is it?" Amelia asked urgently.

Rose pulled her arm away from her mother-in-law's hand and shaking her head, hurried down the street without saying a word. Amelia stood on the step and watched Rose's hurrying form with a frown. A cold drop of rain fell on Amelia's cheek and she realized her coachman watched curiously.

Realizing that something dire must have happened, and puzzled where Rose was going, Amelia turned and went into the house, pushing open the heavy front door. She walked into Rose's house as the Colonel came heavily down the stairs. "George," Amelia cried, hurrying to him. "You look ghastly. I just saw Rose leaving. What is it? Has Edmund taken a turn for the worse?"

The Colonel stared at Amelia as if he did not recognize her. Amelia realized that Hobbs was hovering, took her husband's hand gently and led him into the drawing room. The Colonel allowed her to escort him into the room and shut the door firmly behind them.

Amelia set the Colonel down by the fireplace, went to the cupboard and poured him some brandy. As he drank, Amelia looked out at the bleak day, the sleety rain returned and bushes rapped against the panes of glass. The Colonel sat silently for some time as Amelia waited. Finally, she could endure the suspense no longer and asked gently, "George, is Edmund not going to recover? Is the damage permanent?"

The Colonel shook his head and gave a short mirthless laugh. He turned to her and his eyes were full of bitterness and sorrow. "Edmund will recover. Plenty of bumps and bruises, but he was a brave boy. His parents are taking good care of him. Edmund stood up for the family honor against malicious gossip from that Gardner boy."

Amelia looked perplexed. "What kind of gossip, George?" she began, then stopped. "Gossip about Rose?' she asked hesitating, her irritation beginning to grow.

The Colonel drained his glass and stared at the bottom of it; grimly he shook his head. Then nodded, "It started with taunts about Rose," the Colonel said, "and Underhill."

Amelia looked at the Colonel; full blown irritation with her daughter-in-law filled her. "Gossip about Rose and Marcus Underhill?" she asked while shaking her head in fury. "I warned Rose this would happen and she would not listen to me." Amelia flapped her hands, "George, this is just a bunch of boys talking dirty talk. It sounds like Edmund overreacted. It means nothing, George. I am surprised that there has never been gossip about Rose and Peregrine Fitch. As much time as he has spent with her." The last was said bitterly.

At Peregrine's name, the Colonel winced. Amelia saw his expression and she went cold. Amelia asked almost hesitantly, "It was about Rose and Mr. Underhill, wasn't it George?"

The Colonel poured himself another brandy and took another swallow. Finally, he shook his head and said very quietly, "It was about William." The Colonel raised his eyes and looked at Amelia bleakly.

Amelia held her breath, the beginning of horror in her eyes. The Colonel continued, "It was about William and," he hesitated and finally said, "Peregrine Fitch."

Amelia crossed the room to the Colonel and grabbed his sleeve. "There can be no gossip," she said horrified. "That all happened a long time ago and there was never any proof, George. No proof!" She looked at the Colonel with concern, "Where could Giles Gardner have heard anything about that?"

"You will remember that Samuel Gardner attended Slater the same time as William," the Colonel said quietly.

Amelia's face went as white as a sheet. "No," she managed, shaking her head from side to side. She said, "George, this means nothing but scandal and ruin. Has that gossip always been out there and we weren't aware of it?" She thought about this and shook her head. "No. I would have known if something was being said. But why would Samuel Gardner choose now to bring all that up again? And they were just suspicions. And that is all they could be, George. There was never any proof that William and Peregrine..." her voice trailed away. She could not voice the words.

The Colonel turned to her and said, "Gardner is financially ruined. Our sons, as well as Peregrine Fitch and Marcus Underhill joined forces to bring Gardner down. This all had to do with business, not a personal vendetta."

Amelia continued to clutch the Colonel's arm. "Then you must stop it," Amelia said flatly. "Sam Gardner may be financially ruined, but he will tell everyone we know about William. And it won't matter that it happened over 25 years ago. It will be fresh and interesting; people will talk."

The Colonel stared at her and shook his head, "It can't be stopped. Sam Gardner put himself on the road to ruin; we just took advantage of it."

"George," Amelia pleaded, "think of William's children. Think of all of our grandchildren. The gossip will reach their ears and it will hurt them so. The wedding is in just a few weeks. We cannot have this at this time."

"I am afraid," the Colonel said slowly, "that there is nothing we can do. We paid off the school and bore the gossip last time. It was silenced quickly enough with William's marriage to Rose."

The Colonel shook his head bleakly, "Let's wait and see what happens next," he told Amelia. "We need to know what is being said at Slater. I need to think about this and talk it over with Charles when he has settled down over Edmund. Right now we need to make sure the boy is going to recover."

"And Peregrine?" Amelia asked, acid in her voice.

"I cannot look him in the face," the Colonel spat out. "He caused all the trouble the first time and it just never goes away. Why could he have not died alongside of William?"

"George," Amelia exclaimed, shocked. "Don't ever say that. William was our son and I do not pretend to say I understood what happened, but to wish anyone dead.... " She drew a breath and said, "This will do us no good. How did Rose hear? Where was she going?"

The Colonel shrugged his shoulders, "She heard what the boy said, came in to the room at the wrong time. I don't care where she is; this is all her fault." The Colonel's words sounded harsh.

"I don't understand how this could be her fault," Amelia said reasonably. Then seeing his face, she stopped, crossed the room and rang the bell for tea.

Sometime after lunch, the Colonel and Amelia knocked gently on the nursery door. They had talked and talked, but could not come to a solution. Edmund had slept and felt restored from his nap. His grandfather looked haggard and his grandmother's face was set. Charles and Alice turned to look at the elder Brewsters and Alice stood so that Amelia could sit in the comfortable chair.

The Colonel was provided with a chair that he pulled close to his grandson's bedside.

The Colonel looked at Edmund. Edmund anxiously watched his grandfather and father with his one eye. His other eye was swollen shut and bruised and his bandages had been refreshed. The Colonel looked down at his grandson. "Sounds like you were defending the family honor," he said at length.

"Yes sir," Edmund said quietly. There was a suspicion of tears in his eyes.

"Brave boy," his grandfather told him. "Mark of a good soldier, standing up for what you believe." Charles made a sound at his elbow, but the Colonel continued, "I understand you don't like Slater, that you don't want to be a soldier."

Edmund looked from his grandfather to his father, and he shook his head a little. "No, sir," he said softly.

The Colonel gruffly said, "Want to go to medical school, I hear?"

Edmund nodded, "Yes, sir."

The Colonel nodded back. "Then I want you to be the best damn doctor you can be."

Edmund gaped at his grandfather, but did not say anything.

The Colonel eyed Edmund, then dropped his own eyes. "Edmund, a good soldier knows when to keep knowledge that comes to his ears quiet. I am not going to talk any more about what was said at Slater, and neither are you. Boys have a habit of making up nasty stories. Young Gardner has a great imagination, sounds like he is making up stories. I want you to forget what was said."

Edmund looked at his grandfather and dropped his eyes, picking at a loose thread on the blanket. Edmund did not say anything.

As the Colonel stood up, he leaned down and gently patted his grandson. "Proud of you, my boy, proud of you." He turned and walked to the door followed by Amelia. He looked back, and said, "Makings of a good soldier. What a waste." He walked out the door.

Alice took the vacated chair and looked down at her son. Charles perched on the bed. "You have stirred things up a bit, my boy," he told Edmund. "I am taking the train down to the school tomorrow and have a word with the headmaster. I think that you shall be home recovering until Christmas and then we shall see where you shall be placed."

Edmund moved, his body ached. "School?" he asked.

Charles answered, "We will figure it out. You might join Henry at Ashcroft. For now, I just want you to rest."

"Father," Edmund asked, moving restlessly, "what about Giles? I don't think he will stop with his talk."

Charles patted Edmund gently. "Don't worry about that, son. It shall be handled. We just want you to rest now and get well. The doctor doesn't really want you moved for a few days, so you will be staying here at Aunt Rose's house. I am sure Torie will help keep you entertained."

With school finished for the day, Torie arrived home. It did not feel quite like home. Uncle Charles' and Aunt Alice's things hung in the front hall. Peering around the corner, Torie spied both Aunt Alice and Grandmother sitting in her mother's drawing room, with no sign of her mother. Torie listened for a minute to the two women talk. Torie was pleased to hear them talking about enrolling Edmund in Ashcroft. Torie smiled in satisfaction. Uncle Charles must have convinced Grandfather somehow. She also heard Amelia say in firm tones that Edmund showed much bravery and something about family honor.

Backing up, Torie took a quick look at her crumpled dress. Her hand touched her damp hair and felt the untidiness from her brisk walk home in the rain. She eyed the open doorway and the stairs beyond it. She would never make it across the foyer without her grandmother's commenting on her untidiness.

Quietly Torie stepped out the front door and slipped around the house to the kitchen. Once inside, Torie found Cook and Tilly working on what looked like a feast. Phoebe sat with a basket of mending in her lap.

At Torie's appearance, Phoebe held open her arms and Torie nestled for a minute against her nanny's bosom. "Master Edmund is on the mend," Phoebe assured Torie. "He has been resting, but I think he would welcome your company."

Torie gave Phoebe a kiss on the cheek and turned as Cook offered her a fresh baked crueller. Torie took two, one for her and one for Edmund, and skipped up the servants' stairs to the upper hall. Torie moved along the hall to the nursery and quietly slipped into the room.

Edmund was awake in the dim late afternoon light, staring at nothing. A cheerful fire burned in the fireplace as he looked out the window solemnly. Torie quietly approached the bed. "Feeling better?" she asked.

Edmund turned to her and gave her a wan smile. "A little" he grimaced. The bruises on his face were turning interesting shades of maroon and purple. His eye was not quite as swollen as the day before. His split lip was shiny with salve, and his neatly bandaged hand lay against the covers.

Torie offered Edmund a crueller. Edmund smiled at her and nibbled on it without much interest. Torie, hungry after a long day at school, devoured her own crueller in companionable silence. Finished, she delicately licked her fingers and said, "I heard Grandmother talking to your mother. She said you were a very brave soldier to fight Giles. Something about you standing up for family honor."

Edmund looked at her in some alarm, "Did she say what the fight was about?"

Torie shook her head, "Not really. I didn't really hear that much, but they are thinking you will join Henry at Ashcroft after Christmas."

Edmund smiled, but grimaced at the pain. He told Torie, "I think Father stood up to Grandfather. Anyway, Grandfather has told me that I can become a doctor if I want to be one."

Torie looked wide eyed at her cousin, "I can't believe Grandfather giving in to anyone over anything. I mean, I was sure that eventually he would wear Mother down, and force Henry to enroll at Slater. He must be so impressed with you fighting for family honor that he gave in. What was the fight about?"

Edmund did not answer, he put the crueller down and said, "Torie, I am really tired. I think I don't want to talk anymore."

Torie looked at Edmund and reached out and gave him a gentle understanding pat. Her mind raced ahead to Edmund studying to become a doctor. Irrepressibly, she asked, "How soon do you think you will learn medicine? I heard it said that when you study to be a doctor you work on dead bodies." Torie looked at Edmund and shivered a delicious little thrill. "Can I work on the body with you?"

Edmund had to laugh, which caused him pain, but he shook his head at his favorite cousin. A small grin passed over his face along with a mischievous look. "Let's tell Grandfather that you want to become a doctor. Or better yet, let's tell Grandmother."

They both laughed and then Edmund yawned. "I think I need to rest now, Torie," he told her. "Thanks for the crueller."

Torie left him and went across the room to her own wardrobe. Torie tidily brushed her hair, changed into a freshly ironed pinafore and went downstairs. It was going to be a new century soon and it was time to meet her grandmother on her own terms. Cheerfully she went downstairs with the knowledge that she was as tidy as her grandmother would wish. Crossing the drawing room, she approached her grandmother and gave her a kiss and then turned to her aunt Alice. "Good afternoon," she greeted them.

Chapter 17

Rose snatched her cloak and hat from the hall and fled from the house. She had blindly walked for miles through residential streets until she found a small park. Through the shrub lined paths, she paced up and down, her thoughts and mind in total turmoil. Scandal. All that would be left of the Brewster name when word escaped. Scandal of the worst order. She spent the last few months barely avoiding scandal and now she faced so much more. Whispers of her and Marcus obviously had been bandied about, and to know that covert eyes had watched as Rose went about her life here in Boston was disturbing.

Edmund's second statement seemed the most horrifying and mysterious, making the idea of her carrying on with Marcus Brewster small in comparison. Rose did not quite understand what Edmund referred to. In her 35 years she had never heard of men being lovers. Affectionate, of course, that was friendship. But lovers? Her mind could not fathom Edmund's meaning. The embarrassed and anguished look on Peregrine's face told her the statement was not a lie.

The day wore on and the skies darkened in the late afternoon light. Rose continued to walk for miles in the icy rain, unaware of where her feet took her. People stopped and watched after the dripping figure as she silently passed them, her face ashen, her green eyes glittering with unshed tears. But Rose had eyes for no one. As she walked, she tried to quietly parse her life with William. She thought back to his shyness, his diffident nature, and his continued awkwardness with her. In comparison, Rose remembered glimpses of Charles and Alice together, of other married couples, of her time with Marcus.

One night at Eastwood, she returned to the house after sitting on the dock and came upon Charles and Alice on the darkened porch in a deep embrace. Charles said something softly in his deep voice as his hand gently cupped Alice's breast. Alice laughed in reply and taking his hand, pulled him into the house. Embarrassed, Rose gave them a few minutes and entered.

Rose feverishly thought of the aching desire that Marcus had aroused every time he touched her. An aching unknown to her with

William. William's fumblings in the dark always seemed an embarrassment to both of them, but Rose performed her wifely duty. After William left her alone in the dark, she would lie awake wondering why men and women participated in such embarrassing and painful rituals to create children.

Over the years, Rose caught conversations when clustered with other matrons of occurrences she could not relate to. Charles and Alice raised nine children and buried four and their affection for each other remained always in evidence. Their children grew up with parents who clearly were in love with each other, with parents who touched and spoke words of endearment.

Rose remembered her week with Marcus, his hands on her body, his lips on her skin. He excited her and brought out emotions and feelings she was unaware that she had. She knew that while she laid under William and had bore him three children, she never felt passion, never felt excitement when he touched her. Now she was certain that William never reacted strongly to the touch of her body.

But did men, grown men, do what a man and woman did? The mechanics and thoughts remained beyond Rose's imagination and she shrank from the thought of men even kissing each other on the lips. And beyond that...

And Peregrine Fitch? Perry had always supported her. Perry was William's best friend since childhood. Since William's death, Perry had been as close a friend to Rose as she would have wished and was wonderful to William's children. Perry told her he wanted to take care of her for William's sake.

Over the years, Perry never held her with desire or kissed more than her hand or her cheek. Escorting Rose to social events, Perry seemed about as devoted as an aged uncle. Rose thought back over the years of knowing Peregrine. She could not remember a time when he courted any female, although his name had been attached to one beautiful woman after another. Certainly, he had escorted many women over the years to social events, and danced with every beautiful woman in Boston, although Rose could never remember seeing the fire of desire light up Perry's eyes.

The hours passed and Rose's mind churned in circles that made no sense and gave no relief. Had the Colonel and Amelia known about William and Peregrine? Rose reasoned they must have since they were so quick to choose innocent 17-year-old Rose for their son's bride. Rose realized that everything drummed into her was that William symbolized a good match, and it was a woman's duty to marry well. Rose tried to recall William's proposal, but all she could remember was his soft sweet smile when she said yes. Rose thought about the fact that she and William created three children together. Had the Colonel demanded that William marry Rose to produce children? The recurring thought that Rose shrank from as her weary feet trod over the miles remained that William never loved her. She could not remember him pronouncing the words; there had never been the affectionate touching in passing. Had William created children because he followed orders like a good soldier, but had always wanted...

Rose would arrive at a conclusion and then shrink away from finishing her thoughts. She was confused and sad; her eyes burned from unshed tears; her head ached.

The sun made a brief appearance and began to set in the late afternoon sky as Rose realized she was soaking wet, icy cold and extremely weary. Her toes felt numb in her boots and her fingers fumbled as they reached in her pocket for her hanky. Rose shivered and longed for her warm bed, to crawl into the softness and pull the covers up and face no one. She shrank from the idea of returning to her house and facing the Brewsters. What could she say to Amelia? To the Colonel? Rose shuddered thinking about any of them. Unfortunately, she had left the house with no money and could not even sit in a cafe and buy a cup of coffee. Shivering, Rose decided to hail a cab and pay once she returned home. Wearily, she started towards a busy street.

As she walked, a figure approached her, Peregrine Fitch. Both Rose and Peregrine stopped and stared at each other. Rose dropped her eyes from Peregrine's and shaking, held up a hand. Peregrine paused and then came to her, but did not embrace her. "We have been combing the streets for you," he told Rose. "We have been worried sick."

Rose refused to meet his eyes. All she said was, "We?"

"Christopher Brewster, Marcus and I," Peregrine said. He reached for her ungloved hand, but she crossed her arms. Peregrine dropped his eyes and pressed his lips together.

"Marcus?" she asked.

Peregrine understood her slight, and paused for a long moment, a look of sadness crossing his face. "I sent for Marcus as soon as I heard. He returned to Boston early this afternoon. We were all very concerned about you. We searched the city trying to find you. Rose, you are frozen to the bone. My carriage is over here."

Rose stood rigidly, her arms tightly folded, her head downcast.

Peregrine said fervently, "Rose, for God's sake, you are soaked to the bone. We need to get you warm and dry."

Rose refused to look at Peregrine as she shook her head, "I can not go back to my house. I can not face the Brewsters," her voice was quiet, but ragged.

"I will take you to my apartment," Peregrine said. Rose continued to stand there, shaking her head, "Rose, please for God's sake, you can not just stand here."

At his pleading. Rose relinquished and followed him limply to his carriage, refusing to allow him to touch her. Rose climbed up in the carriage unassisted and slumped in the corner, continuing to shiver as she closed her eyes. Rose was barely aware of the carriage stopping a short time later and Peregrine alighted. Christopher's voice could be heard and she raised her head as the two men briefly conversed. Peregrine clambered back in alone and shut the door.

"Christopher will let the Brewsters know that you have been found. You and I," Peregrine told Rose briefly, "are going to my apartment to talk." She prepared to interrupt but he continued on, "You and I need to have a serious conversation, Rose. The Brewsters know you are safe; the search has been called off. Underhill is going to come a little later and take you home."

"Home," Rose softly echoed the word. It sounded so safe and yet, at this moment so alien. Home was invaded at the moment by Brewsters who were taking over her life once again. Brewsters who would want to have discussions and arguments and make plans. Rose's eyes burned with unshed tears that refused to fall. Exhausted and chilled, she dully nodded her head.

Once at his apartment, Peregrine stopped to give directions to his man for a bath to be run as he led Rose into the study and removed her dripping cloak and hat. He poured her a small glass of brandy and insisted that she drink. The beverage burned in her empty stomach, but the warmth began fingering its way through her body. Peregrine took Rose to his own bedroom; the bathroom beyond was lit and the sound of water could be heard running. With firm orders to disrobe and to take a warm bath, Rose with her head down nodded quietly. She felt too exhausted and too uncomfortable to disagree. She peeled off her sodden clothes and dropped them on the floor of the bedroom in a heap. Rose sunk into the steaming hot bath and lay back with her head against the rim. She was so tired, so very tired, but every time she closed her eyes she could hear Edmund's words ringing in her mind. When Rose was warmer, her skin pink, she tiredly dried herself off with a large thirsty towel and slipped into the heavy silk bathrobe she found hanging on the back of the door. The robe hung on her, too large and very masculine. Rose rolled up the sleeves and gathered it up to walk. Reluctantly she left the bathroom. In the bedroom her clothes were spread before the fire to dry out.

Hesitantly, Rose abandoned the bedroom and walked, barefooted, down the hall to Peregrine's drawing room. Peregrine had ordered tea, brandy and a hot meal and built the fire. Rose stood clutching the robe to her neck. Peregrine barely glanced at her. A table was set up with steaming hot soup and a plate with boiled potatoes and sizzling steak. Peregrine reached out and once again Rose shrank from him. With a set look on his face, Peregrine pointed towards the chair and Rose settled herself there. Peregrine gave strict instructions to his butler that he was to be home to no one except Marcus Underhill, and when Marcus arrived to show him into the smaller study, but to not disturb Peregrine.

Rose raised her head briefly. "Marcus?"she asked. Vaguely she remembered Peregrine saying something about Marcus out on the street.

"I sent for him this morning after you left your house," Peregrine told her gently. "He arrived early this afternoon and helped look for you."

The closing of the door sounded very loud in the silence. Rose huddled in her chair and stared at the fire. Peregrine poured her a second brandy and insisted she drink it. Having nothing else in her stomach, the brandy burned and immediately took a little of the pain away. At Peregrine's insistence, Rose began to sip the soup. Between the brandy and the hot soup, Rose began to feel her bones revive. Rose was surprised to find that the sizzling steak went down easily as the combination of warm fire and alcohol kindled her hunger. The entire time that Rose ate, she did not look at or speak to Peregrine.

Peregrine thought that as long as Rose had been in his world, he had always felt protective of her. She had taken such beautiful care of William, and for that he was forever grateful.

As Rose finished her dinner, Peregrine poured her some coffee and liberally laced it with brandy. He removed her tray and pulled a small ottoman over in front of Rose, sitting on it. He reached for her fingers and squeezed. Rose, revived somewhat by bath, meal and brandy, kept her head averted and stared at the fire, but did not resist his touch.

"Rose," Peregrine said softly, "I want to talk to you."

"I don't want to talk, Perry," Rose said softly. She had yet to look him in the eye. She fluttered her hands as if to ward off his words. She spent the afternoon trying to determine what she couldn't imagine; if he put the thoughts into words she was sure she would run screaming from the room. Rose made a small noise and tried to pull her hands away, but Peregrine held onto them. "I need," he said in a tortured voice, "to make you understand about William and," Peregrine paused, "and me."

For the first time Rose turned her head and could only stare at him with glittering green eyes. She looked deeply into his eyes and saw a mixture of shame, agony and love, begging for acceptance, and a longing for forgiveness. Rose set her coffee cup down and looked at Peregrine. This was the same Peregrine who had always been there for her. Rose swallowed, folded her hands together and then gently nodded her head, encouraging him to begin.

"William and I had known each other forever," Peregrine said. "As small boys, our families were together often and I spent my summers at Eastwood along with the rest of the crowd. From our earliest days, William and I were best friends. We were inseparable and supportive of each other. Fishing, swimming, boating, playing tag on the lawn and catching fireflies in the dark... just like your children."

Rose and Peregrine shared a faint smile at the memories.

"When it came time for school, our parents sent us to the same military academy. The Colonel, home briefly from the war, was unhappy with how soft William seemed, so William was sent away at a young age. The war killed so many fine young men, that it was not unusual for younger boys to start their military educations earlier. My parents were slightly reluctant, but William and I were such fast friends they thought it would be easier if we started at Slater together." There was a moment of long silence, then Peregrine said, "From the first, William was an outcast." Perry paused as he stared into the fire and then he continued, "I always tried to stand up for him, but the other boys hazed him and picked on him. William was very sensitive and tried to do his father's bidding, but he absolutely hated it."

Rose thought of dear sweet William treated so horribly at school, but no where to go, no one to talk to. Rose thought of her battles over Henry, and reassured herself that every fight she had with the Colonel was worth it.

Peregrine went on, "Back at home, the Colonel was proud of his boy and sure that the military would toughen up his oldest son. William told no one at home the horrors he experienced. He endured it, but he turned inwards. William always had me, and when we were together we could fight off the bullies together."

Peregrine paused and took a drink of his own brandy. He set down his drink very carefully on the table beside Rose. Peregrine smoothed his moustache and opened and closed his mouth hesitating over his next words. Peregrine said in a very quiet voice, "Around age 14 William and I discovered we were more than friends." At this change of subject, Rose moved and held up a splayed hand, and Perry told her, "I am not going to go into any detail, my darling Rose. I need your forgiveness and I need you to understand that William and I loved each other very much. We did not want to feel what we did, but we did."

There was a long silence as Rose raised her head and looked into Peregrine's eyes for the first time. She could see the warm love for William reflected there, as well as pain, but for once no shame or regret.

Peregrine reached out and gripped her fingers and turned to stare into the fire. He went on, "I did not know what these feelings were. I just knew that I had always felt differently. I don't think it took William by surprise. I think he had recognized earlier that he felt about..." Hoarsely, Peregrine paused and then said, "William felt like a failure. He hated the future his father laid out for him; at school William was exhausted fighting off the ridicule and torture. When we discovered what we felt for each other, William was horrified. He knew that if they found out at home, his life would be worse for him. He would be an even bigger disappointment to his father." Peregrine's voice trailed away and he stared into the fire.

Peregrine told Rose, "We cautiously began to talk about our feelings." Rose hunched her shoulders at his words and shook her head. Peregrine said, "Rose, look at me."

Reluctantly, she raised her eyes briefly then lowered them again.

Peregrine again said, "Rose, look at me."

This time she did. As her green eyes met his brown eyes, Rose realized she looked at someone who had deeply loved and lost. Peregrine had carried a burden of sorrow for many years.

Peregrine stared into her eyes for a long time and then said, "William and I were very careful. We were ashamed of our feelings and tried to ignore them. As time went on, we realized that we could not ignore our feelings and we took a few chances."

Rose sipped her brandy laced coffee; her hands were shaking as she raised the cup to her lips. She had enough alcohol to begin to feel woozy, as if her head and body were no longer connected. Her heart continued to ache dreadfully, and at Peregrine's words she placed her small hand over her hurting heart.

"There was a scandal at school, a small one. I am not going to go into it," Peregrine's voice was strained. He choked, "Just before graduation. So my father paid a lot of money to ensure my graduation and sent me to Harvard. Eventually, he took me into the family business, away from the Brewsters and William. The Colonel and Amelia also paid out money to silence the school and to avoid scandal. William was sent away to Officer's Training school. After he became an officer, a bride was found for him."

Rose closed her eyes. She could see how it had been. The Colonel and Amelia, horrified over the possibility of a scandal, took precipitous action to send the offender away and then cover any hint of a scandal by finding a bride to hide behind. Rose, wealthy, young and an orphan, represented the perfect girl to bring in to bury the whispers. And poor William?

"You were so good to William, Rose," Peregrine said, his words echoing her thoughts. "You were so young and gentle and you did not fuss at William as so many woman would have done. The Brewsters encouraged your aunt and uncle to make the match and your aunt and uncle were excited to see your fortune joined with the Brewsters. I am sure the gossip had never reached your aunt and uncle's ears or yours." He said the last as not a question but a statement.

"I was very happy for William," Peregrine promised Rose. "I realized that in our society there was no place for him and me. I wanted him to have a happy life and children. You were such a beautiful bride. I watched you and William on your wedding day and knew I could never be by William's side, so I was happy for him." Peregrine said simply, "I hoped desperately that the two of you would enjoy a happy marriage, that William would forget these feelings for me. The Colonel continued to worry about gossip and he had his heart set on his son being a great soldier, so after Lavinia was born, the Colonel arranged for William to go West and fight the Indians."

There was a long pause. Rose did not know what to say. Peregrine went on gently, "I think, with you, William did find a kind of peace. All the acceptance he could find in this life he found with you. And certainly your children brought great joy to him."

Peregrine, wanting to make Rose understand everything, said, "My parents would have liked me to take the same path, to find a woman and settle down, but I could not." He shook his head, and repeated, "I could not. After William's death, I looked after you because William would have wanted me to. Before he went to the Indian Wars he made me promise that if something ever happened to him, I would take care of you."

Rose raised her head and looked at Peregrine. "You have done your duty well," she said drily.

"No, no," he protested. "It was not a duty. It was my honor to take care of you, for all that you did for William. That damnable will. I argued with William over it, that it wasn't fair to deny you the right to marry again. But, he was so afraid that his parents would somehow wrest control away from you and the most important thing for William remained that any of his sons NOT be subjected to the same torture he had experienced. That history would not repeat itself."

Rose felt numb and exhausted. The last twenty four hours had been hideous and her life turned upside down. She wanted to crawl into her bed, pull up the blankets and hide. It was too much. First Edmund's horrible beating and the reason behind it, followed by ideas that she had no understanding of. She knew at some point she had to face the Brewsters but she wondered if she could find the strength.

This very long day would never end.

"Peregrine," she asked very softly, breaking a long silence, asking the question that had tortured her all day, "did William ever love me?"

Peregrine struggled with the answer. "I think," he said slowly and honestly, "that William loved you as much as he could love any woman. I think he knew you would never hurt him. I am not sure he even trusted me not to hurt him. I think the Colonel suspected early on from something he saw in William's childhood and was tougher on him than any of his other sons. The Colonel was afraid."

Peregrine squeezed her fingers again, and this time a small pressure was returned. Peregrine told Rose, "William hated his feelings for me. He loved me, but he hated being different. Deep in William was the longing to be accepted, to be liked. He wanted so desperately for his father's approval but he always felt that he was a failure. The one desire he had in this world he could not attain: his father's love. With you, he at last found someone to accept him without asking for more than he could give."

There were questions that Rose could not ask. If she lived to be one hundred she did not want to know the details of William and Peregrine's relationship. Her mind could not imagine men touching each other as she and Marcus... A sad part of Rose wondered if William and Peregrine continued as lovers after her marriage, but she shrank from the thought.

Rose put her head back on the chair and rested her head wearily, the alcohol and the day spent in the elements taking a toll on her. She thought over William's life and her own. She gripped the leather chair she was nestled in and finally, slow tears began to ooze from under her closed eyelids. The tears flowed slowly and became full gulping sobs. Peregrine stood and murmured helplessly, "Oh, my dear, my dear."

Vaguely, Rose became aware of someone else in the room. She could not open her eyes or stop her weeping. She was lifted from the chair and found herself in Marcus' strong safe arms as he swung her around and sat down in the chair and pulled her into his lap. Rose realized she felt safer in Marcus' arms than anywhere else in this world. Rose sobbed against his chest as she clung to him. Rose cried for the sad life that had been William Brewster's and she cried for Peregrine and lost love and she sobbed for all the years she had spent being used by the Brewsters. Some time passed before the flood slowed and she was left with hiccoughs. Her head pounded from her weeping and her throat was sore from her wails. Rose did not feel she had the strength to wipe away her tears.

Marcus spoke little as he held her tightly and stroked her head. When the tears finally slowed, he said in his deep even voice, "Rose, my darling, we will go away. I want to take you far away from all of this and I will take care of you. That is what I have always wanted to do, from the first day I met you. First, I need you to know some things."

Rose did not answer, but he could feel her listening. "After what the Brewsters have done to you, they will never say a word against you or your actions or I will bring a scandal down on them. You also need to know, as of this day, Gardner is finished in this town. What Fitch and the Brewsters and I started last summer, finished today. At this moment, Sam Gardner has pulled his son from Slater and is, under my man's watchful eye, standing on the train platform ready to leave town. Right now, I feel like taking the Gardner mansion, which I now own, and pull it apart brick by brick and throw it in the street. For now we have stopped Sam Gardner and his vicious tongue." The last was said with some force.

Rose sat up and looked at Marcus. She took his handkerchief and wiped her tears and blew her nose. Rose said wearily, "It wasn't Sam, but his son who caused the damage."

Marcus nodded and continued on, "I know, but as much as I hated to do it, I have given Gardner a small path to a fresh start. He will take those miserable children and settle in Colorado and I shall stake him a small purse to begin a new business as long as he never shows his face or contacts anyone in this town again. Otherwise, he is on his own."

Rose moved restively. "Marcus, the gossip is out there. There will always be someone who will believe the gossip." Thinking about all the things that have been said, Rose said bitterly, "All of the gossip."

"Then," Marcus said, "we shall have to get married."

Rose stared at him with swollen eyes. "Married? Marcus, we have been over this. The Brewsters..."

Marcus shook his head and interrupted her, "Damn the Brewsters. If they don't want their name associated with a hell of a scandal, they will not stand in our way. I would marry you tomorrow because I love you, regardless of scandal. Rose Brewster, I have loved you ever since last summer when I caught you sobbing over <u>Romeo and Juliet</u>."

Rose looked into his brown eyes. She shook her head, and glanced at Peregrine and then looked away. "There is worse gossip," she said, her voice teary again.

Marcus looked at her bent head and then steeled himself to look at Peregrine. Even for him it was not comfortable to meet Peregrine's eyes. Peregrine and Marcus had a long talk as they combed the streets earlier in the day. Peregrine told Marcus the truth. Marcus shrank from Peregrine, but as the long day stretched on with the search of Rose, Marcus tried to understand.

Peregrine retreated to the hearth as Rose cried, leaning his head against the marble mantle. Marcus swallowed and said gruffly, "Let the gossips say what they want. I find Peregrine Fitch to be an admirable business partner and I would trust him with any business ventures I should choose to be involved in. He has always taken care of the woman I love and I am honored to be his friend."

At Marcus' words, Peregrine raised his head and his sad eyes met Marcus' look unflinchingly. Peregrine nodded his head in acknowledgment and tears shone in his eyes. Marcus gently pushed Rose from his lap and stood. Crossing the room he extended his hand to Peregrine. Peregrine looked from the hand to Marcus' open look and then reached out to shake it. "Thank you," Peregrine said, softly.

"No," Marcus rejoined, "thank you for taking such beautiful care of the woman I am going to marry."

Rose looked at Peregrine for a very long minute. She realized that she was looking at the man who had loved her husband without reservations. Because of that love, he had always looked out for her and her children. Rose realized that this was a man who had known love and loss. Hesitatingly, Rose reached up and wrapped her arms around Peregrine and kissed his cheek. "Thank you for telling me," she whispered in his ear.

Peregrine reached out and clenched her fingers. "I am so sorry, Rose," he whispered. "I never wanted you to be hurt." A tear trickled down Peregrine's cheek. Rose reached up and wiped the tear away as she looked deeply into Peregrine's eyes. Beyond the intense sorrow she saw there, the love for William shown brightly. Rose still felt slightly repelled, as she tried to understand. What Rose did know was Peregrine remained Peregrine, the man who had watched over her always.

Peregrine released Rose and said, his voice husky, "I am going to excuse myself now. I will check on Rose's clothes to see if they are dry and, Marcus, I trust that you shall see her home safely."

Rose looked up at Peregrine and shook her head, "Peregrine, I want you and Marcus to both come home with me. It has been a hellish day, but I am going to have it out with the Brewsters tonight. If I am ever going to rest again, I need you beside me when I confront the Brewsters."

Peregrine paused and looked at Rose. "The Brewsters will not want to see me," he told her with assurance.

Marcus came up behind her and put his hands on her shoulders. "Yes, Peregrine," Marcus agreed, "come with us. We, Rose and I, need you."

Peregrine stood and looked from Marcus to Rose. Slowly he nodded his head, and left the room.

As the door shut, Rose became aware that she was in Peregrine's robe and her feet were bare. She pulled the sash tighter and turned from Marcus, suddenly shy at her dishabille.

Marcus turned Rose to face him, wrapped his arms around her and held her tightly against his chest. Rose breathed deeply. Marcus smelled of tobacco and whiskey; good strong manly smells. Marcus' broad warm chest felt so safe and Rose knew that in his arms she would never be alone or afraid again. Together they would face down society gossip and the Brewsters. She and Marcus and all of their children would become a family. Marcus would give nothing but love and support to Vinnie, Torie and

Henry and Rose would in turn give Collin the help and love that only a mother could offer.

Chapter 18

Peregrine's coach pulled up in front of her house and Rose, with a hard swallow and a tentative glance at both men, alighted from the carriage and looked up at her little brick house. Warm inviting lights shown from the downstairs windows and her bedroom. Rose wanted nothing more than to ascend those stairs and sleep in her own bed, but she sighed as she steeled herself for what lay ahead.

Rose wearily entered the house followed by the two men. Amelia, Charles and the Colonel came out of the drawing room and looked at the group with mixed emotions. Amelia rushed to her daughter-in-law and hugged Rose. "My dear, we have been so worried about you, " Amelia told her.

Rose gratefully returned the embrace and asked, "How is Edmund?"

"Much better," Alice reassured her with a smile. "He ate a good dinner and Torie is upstairs reading to him right now with Alice sitting close by."

Amelia pointedly ignored Marcus and Peregrine.

Rose looked to Charles and said, "I am glad to hear that Edmund is going to recover. You must be very proud of your son."

Charles gave Rose a small kiss and answered, "We are. But, how are you?"

Rose shrugged, feeling tears spring up from the kind words. She nodded her head, unable to speak. Amelia took charge. "I think," she said, "that you should go upstairs and have a hot bath and dinner in bed."

Rose squared her shoulders and answered, "I have already had a bath and dinner at Peregrine's." At Amelia's raised eyebrow, Rose said, "We have come to talk."

"My dear," Amelia argued. "there have been already too many dramas today. I think we should save this for tomorrow."

"No Amelia," Rose said quietly, but firmly, "it must be tonight."

Charles murmured something about checking on Edmund and left the small group in the foyer. Amelia and Rose, followed by

Marcus, Peregrine and the Colonel, went into the drawing room and shut the door.

Inside, Amelia turned and looked at the three of them. The Colonel settled himself in the chair he recently abandoned and silently glared at the small group. Amelia drew herself to her full height, chin resolute. "We are going to have to work hard to avoid a scandal on the Brewster name," she began in her hardest tone of voice. Rose stared at her mother-in-law. Knowing all that had been said, Rose was not surprised that Amelia's first concern was with scandal.

The Colonel finally spoke up, looking at Rose, "You think you know so much. You won't ever listen to anyone and look what has happened. It is all your fault that boy got beaten."

Rose, shocked, stayed silent but stared at her father-in-law. Marcus placed his hands protectively on Rose's shoulders and started to speak, but she shook her head slightly. Rose drew a deep breath and looked the Colonel in the eye. "No, Colonel Brewster, this is not my fault. This begins and ends with William and you. And your ineptitude of being a father."

The Colonel turned bright red and his words came out with a roar, "Who do you think you are to accuse me of not being a good father to William?"

Rose quivered slightly from the force of his wrath, but struggled on. The amount of brandy she previously consumed helped her with her courage as she continued, "All William ever wanted was for you to love him. He wanted it so much that he endured torture and pain hoping that would finally buy your love. He never complained about military school or marrying me or even those horrific Indian Wars. All William ever wanted from you was for you to be proud of him and to love him."

"You don't know what you are talking about," the Colonel barked. "Who are you to say these things?"

Rose, white as a sheet, continued in a strained voice, "You once accused me of not being a good wife to William. That it was my fault he was so unhappy. That I did not do enough in our marriage." Rose crossed the room and glared at the Colonel, her voice choked with emotion. She said, "You are wrong. You see, I did love William and I tried to let him know that who he was was enough."

The Colonel glared at Rose, his mouth opening and shutting. Tiny Amelia stepped between them and said quietly, "Rose, you owe the Colonel an apology. William was our pride and joy. How can you say those things?"

Rose looked from Amelia to the Colonel. The Colonel continued to glare at her, fury in his eyes. Rose said, balling up her hands in fists as she spoke, "I will not apologize. When I married William, I knew he was unhappy and I always thought if I tried a little harder, he would become happy. If I only could discover the magic potion, William would love me." Rose's voice grew thick as she glanced at Peregrine and continued, "I realize now that no matter what I did I never could have made William fall in love with me. I know William felt great guilt for not being able to love me. Just as he felt pain for you not loving him."

The Colonel spit out, "What do you know of love? Sneaking around with Underhill here -- you are no better than a strumpet. And you always defy me and raise your children in opposition to my way."

Amelia drew herself up and said to Rose, "You accuse us of not loving William. What do you know about having a child continually turn from you. Do you know how as a mother that made me feel? Sometimes, Rose, no matter how much you love someone you fail them."

Amelia looked at Marcus' hands on Rose's shoulders. "I don't know what Sam Gardner saw last summer," Amelia said, "but it was enough to raise suspicion. If the two of you," and she glared at Rose and Marcus, "would have acted above reproach, there would be no gossip. We would not be in such a mess now. Even after I warned you, you have continued to sneak around and meet in parks and God knows where else."

Rose was surprised at the change of topic. Amelia went on, "It has come to my ears and the ears of my daughter that the two of you have been seen together in the park, slipping out of balls and in dark doorways at the opera." Rose's mouth gaped at her mother-in-law. "Nothing but conversation has been reported to me. Rose, I have no doubt something is going on here."

In the silence, Rose looked sideways at Marcus.

Before Rose could speak, Amelia spoke in a different tone of voice, "While the gossip about that is bad enough, I think we could curb it. But, there is a second part to this story."

Rose raised her hand to stop her mother-in-law, shaking her head. Amelia ignored her, "I am not going to go into the details. There are enough people who know that William's name has been besmirched. I will not have it."

Amelia looked directly at Peregrine with loathing. "I will not have it."

Peregrine moved his head side to side. "Mrs. Brewster," he protested, "we are talking about something that happened more than 20 years ago."

"Mr. Fitch," the Colonel spoke up, correcting Peregrine, "nothing ever happened. It was gossip then and your father and I paid a fair amount of money to silence that gossip. Edmund's beating shows the gossip remains and shame on you for bringing this scandal on the Brewster name. Look how it has affected my grandson."

Peregrine, white as a sheet, said, "Colonel Brewster, you chose to send William to that hell hole and you chose to send your grandsons to the same place. You have never taken responsibility for what you did to William and it is time that you did."

"I will not ever discuss what went on between William and me with you, Fitch." The Colonel was incensed and said, "It is no one's business, but this time I blame you and Rose for that boy's beating."

Peregrine flinched over the Colonel's words. Peregrine and the Colonel glared at each other wordlessly.

Amelia stood up and said, "Stop this, both of you. This is pointless. The important thing tonight is to figure out how to salvage the Brewster name. I have spent the afternoon pondering this and this is how we are going to handle the mess you have landed us in."

Amelia looked at the three of them as if they were small children. "Mr. Underhill, you are going to leave town," Amelia informed Marcus. "I truly do not know where you came from or where you go, but I want you to never speak to my daughter-in-law again. There are many other cities that you can practice your business, and I suggest that you find somewhere else to live."

Before Marcus could say a word, Amelia turned to Rose. "You have brought so much of this shame down on us. If you care for your children at all, you will listen to my plans and follow them accordingly."

"I blame you for so much of this." Amelia spoke to Peregrine with loathing. "You shamed us once and we allowed you to stay friends with our family only to silence gossip. The way we will stop this is you will marry Rose. Any gossip will be silenced by the fact that she is now Mrs. Peregrine Fitch. There will never be any talk of William and Peregrine again."

Rose stared at her mother-in-law in disbelief. Disengaging herself from Marcus, she stepped forward. "No. I am not going to marry Perry," she gently told Amelia. "You and your social standing," she said with similar loathing. "Amelia, it is time to move forward. It is time to stop running everyone's lives." Rose took a breath and tears caught in her throat. "You convinced my aunt and uncle to encourage me into that loveless marriage with William to stop the gossip. The two of you caused so much unhappiness for William. You never thought about my life, what it might mean to me to have a husband who did not love me. Now you want me to marry Perry? Amelia, history is NOT going to repeat itself."

Rose turned to Peregrine. "Perry," she said softly, "you have always been so good to me. You have always stood by me and I thank you for all you did today. If this scandal breaks, I will assist you and stand by you in any way you need. It is my turn to stand up for you."

Peregrine bowed to Rose. He reached forward and took Rose's hand and kissed her cheek. He said, "Dear Rose. I thank you for your understanding and support."

Peregrine looked over Rose's head to Marcus. "I leave her in your care," Peregrine told Marcus as he shook his hand. "I know the two of you will be very happy."

Peregrine bowed to Amelia and the Colonel and left the room. Peregrine shut the drawing room door behind him and crossed the foyer when he heard his name. Turning, Peregrine saw Torie coming down the stairs. "I didn't know you were here," Torie exclaimed as she gave him a hug. "Are you leaving?"

Peregrine took Torie by the hand and they sat side by side on the stairs. "Chicken," Peregrine said slowly, "I am thinking about taking a trip to Europe."

"Europe? Why, Uncle Peregrine?" Torie asked looking at him surprised.

Peregrine looked at her and said, "Well, I have always wanted to take the grand tour and I was kind of waiting for you and Henry and Vinnie to grow up before I went. You seem to be growing up, so I have decided it is time to travel."

Torie looked at Peregrine and saw a sadness in his eyes. Her eyes glanced over to the closed drawing room door and the murmur of voices. Torie leaned against his shoulder. "How long will you be gone, Uncle Peregrine?" she asked.

Peregrine shrugged. "Oh, I will probably be gone for a couple of years," he said with a sigh.

"But," Torie told him in protest, "I always thought you would stand up with me for my Father/Daughter when I come out."

Peregrine looked at Torie in some surprise. "You mean," he said with a small smile, "you want to become a debutant instead of a soldier?"

Torie shrugged, "Being a soldier doesn't sound as fun as it used to. Uncle Peregrine, I shall miss you!" Impulsively, she reached up and kissed his cheek.

"I will tell you what," Peregrine told Torie, cuddling her to him. "In a couple of years, when you are a grown up young lady, I will send for you and we can explore Europe together."

Torie thought about this, a gleam of excitement beginning to burn in her eyes. "Uncle Peregrine, that sounds like so much fun. Maybe by then Henry will be an archeologist and he will be on some dig and we can help him dig for mummies!"

"That sounds good, Torie," Peregrine said, a small smile crossing his worn face. Peregrine stood up and held her close and kissed her.

For a long moment, Torie snuggled into him. They stood up and Torie stepped back and looked up at tall Peregrine. Peregrine looked down at Torie, reached for her fingers and for the first time in her life, he kissed the back of her hand. Peregrine then turned and went softly out the front door. Torie, holding her hand to her heart, watched him go.

After Peregrine shut the drawing room door, Rose stood silently staring at the Brewsters. Marcus, putting his arm around Rose, for the first time spoke to Amelia, "It is time to stop all of the nonsense and untruths. What gossip comes up, comes up; we will all weather it. You should have faced the truth 20 years ago instead of finding a scapegoat to marry your son. Shame on you, shame on you."

Amelia was furious. "Don't you start lecturing us, you upstart," she began, drawing herself up to her full height.

The Colonel started to remonstrate, but Marcus cut across the words, "I am going to marry Rose. Rose deserves happiness in this life. She was not just some pawn you chose to hide scandal behind. Does her life not mean anything to you? Does Rose not deserve happiness? I am going to marry Rose. You try and stop us or take her children away from her and I will smear your name over every paper in the country."

The Colonel started to argue, but Amelia laid her hand on his arm. "Shush, George," she said. Amelia turned to Rose, a sad look on her face. Amelia reached out and patted Rose's face. "Rose, I am so sorry that we caused you sorrow," Amelia said. "I do believe that William was happy with you and I tried to show you over the years how much I appreciated all of your attention to William. He was my first born and I always felt that I failed him," Amelia admitted the last softly, a strained look on her face.

Amelia turned to Marcus, "Young man, I expect you to take beautiful care of her. If you choose to stay in Boston, my home will always be open to you. I know you will take care of my grandchildren, and I will always be there for them."

The Colonel looked from Marcus to Rose to Amelia. "I don't like this," the Colonel said quietly. "I don't like the idea of my grandson raised by some outsider."

Amelia turned and quelled the Colonel with a look. Wearily, she reached out and kissed Rose on the cheek. "Be happy," Amelia said with a small stiff smile.

Amelia, then took the Colonel's arm and led him out, closing the door behind them.

Rose turned to Marcus. Rose, who had felt so exhausted from everything that had gone on that day, suddenly felt rejuvenated. Marcus turned Rose to him and slipped his arms around her, pulling her close. "I think," he said with his lips against her, "that Amelia just gave us her blessing."

Smiling back at Marcus, Rose returned his kiss with warm satisfaction. "Marcus Underhill," Rose said with a smile, "I have lived a thousand lives in the past 24 hours. I have experienced every emotion possible, and here in your arms I feel as if I have come home."

"Home," Marcus echoed against her lips. "We have come home."

THE END

ACKNOWLEDGEMENTS

This book started as a Nanowrimo project (November is <u>National Write a Novel Month</u> and the goal is to write 50,000 words in November. The website is nanowrimo.org) and in the month of November, 2011, I wrote 52,000 words. At the end of November all the key elements of Eastwood were written and I knew that Rose and Marcus would live happily ever after. But, I could not have accomplished this book without the love and support of so many people.

First I have to thank C.C. Truex who created the most beautiful book cover I could have imagined. I started with a simple idea and C.C. absolutely ran with it. Plus it was fun to collaborate and discuss what Eastwood, the house, should look like. We spent hours researching and discussing New England flowers and trees, and of course, Marcus and Rose. C.C. took my dream and made a work of art that I would be proud to display on a wall!

I also want to thank my editor Carol Swihart for her beautiful job of taking my wrinkled and run on sentences and ironing and neatening them. I also appreciate Carol for re-teaching me the rules of grammar and punctuation that I had forgotten.

Thank you to all of my friends who never stopped asking me about the novel and who read earlier versions and gave me valuable feedback. Crystle, Sierra, Irum, Osa and Janice -- thank you for your encouragement and unfailing positive natures!

Thank you to all of my clients and my salon sisters, especially Julie, Yvonne, Christie and Jenny -- their love and interest encouraged me when I sometimes felt overwhelmed with working full time and writing a novel. My associates in my BNI group, the Rose City Romance Writers, and my fellow English Country dancers -- all encouraged and supported me and watched in fascination as I followed through with this obsession and made a life long dream come true.

And lastly and most importantly, my children, Alexa and Austin. You will always have my heart and my love. Over and over I want to be a role model and prove that it is never too late to follow your dreams. I know that the two of you will accomplish many dreams in your life -- I can't wait to see how you grow!

Dorothy Dunbar, "The Heart Asks..."

ALL ABOUT DOROTHY

Dorothy Dunbar, a native Oregonian, has always had a passion for writing. She wrote as a teenager and then for years turned her attention to married life and children. Now that her children are grown up and on to their own pursuits, she has dusted off her dreams and spent the last few years honing her writing skills and turning her talents to the imagination filled world of creative writing.

Dorothy lives in Portland with her two small dogs, Monkey and Dominic. Besides writing, Dorothy enjoys walking, dancing, traveling, reading, cooking, a fine glass of wine, sewing and other craft projects.

You can learn more about Dorothy on her website dorothydunbar.weebly.com.

Made in the USA
San Bernardino, CA
13 May 2013